DEFENDERS OF
A LOST EON

DEFENDERS OF A LOST EON

Book 1 of
The Dark Blade of Clover Series

CRAIG R SMITH

Defenders of a Lost Eon: Book 1 of The Dark Blade of Clover Series

Published through Ingram Spark

ISBN: 979-8-9853363-0-6 (Paperback Edition)
ISBN: 979-8-9853363-1-3 (eBook Edition)

FIRST CELESTIAL WAR:

The Rise of the Darkness

PROLOGUE

Sometime in the distant future:

A flash of bright light fills the air with nothing else coexisting. The incandescent illumination was so bright it could blind instantly. Then that blinding light transformed into a ray of purples, blues, bright red and silver lighting, spinning like a pinwheel. The swirling colors begin to blend together, as the vortex of light spun faster until it became impossible to tell one color from another. Suddenly blackness consumes the spinning array until it dissolved into nothingness. That's when the portal opened.

Through the blackness of the portal, a lanky figure appeared, stumbling as if this figure had just come from a wild party and could barely stay on his feet. Travel through portal voids was common in the distant future.

The figure's normally light bronze and olive skin tone seemed to possess a more grayish tone and an ailing look, these days. The visitor had lost all his color, a diseased and dying man that no longer possessed his own soul. This humanoid's features expressed the man's ailing condition and displayed how ill prepared humans were at traveling in this manner. The man threw up right where he had landed but hadn't noticed at all, he was too busy trying to catch his own breath. The black leather cladded figure was bent over with both hands flat on the ground and panting heavily. The newcomer was in a dreadful condition, but it wasn't from his condition or that he was ill. It was the torment traveling through portals did to the human body. Some species had perfected interdimensional travel, but not terrains, yet. To be truthful dimensional traveling was quite new and it showed.

The figure wore his former rank on his tattered military leather jacket. The insignia on his breast told he had been part of the Delta Force squadron, an elite fighting force that had been charged to battle with the Darkness ever evolving invading armies. The coronal had recently retired and hadn't quite settled into his civilian place, before being summoned.

The Delta Force squadron had taken over where the immortals had left off, but had failed miserably. Where the immortals had kept the multitude of militia of shadow at bay, and in some areas, had pushed the invaders back; the human forces had lost that ground and more. But again, they weren't manufactured solders designed for one purpose, warfare. They were merely well-trained mortals.

The figure shook off his wooziness and attempted to fight off the sickness from his interdimensional trip. He stood up and his head spun out of control, so the human stood there with his eyes closed. He took in several deep breaths before taking a few steps into the alien space. Col. Kambiz Nguyen had a nasty scar that enveloped the right half of his face, making the war veteran appear as a Halloween character, disfigured and unpleasant to look at. It was a sore spot for the Delta Force squadron veteran and he tended to stay in the shadows or behind the scenes now-a-days and his trip into the nether realm was no different. Luckily for him the entire place was full of places to hide.

The colonel was slowly gaining the color back to his face, and the nauseating sensation slowly dissipating. Interdimensional travel was never easy on the body and Colonel Nguyen was experiencing this first hand. The colonel still had his stomach in knots. It felt like he had gone seven rounds with a Fargal Zolphane, a massive bear-like beast covered in matted silver hair and razor-shard teeth. But even this upsetting effect was wearing off, much like his dizziness.

The place appeared translucent to the colonel, like it was just all a dream. The walls, floor, even Nguyen's own skin seemed transparent to him. In fact, the whole place he now occupied seemed dream-like except that Col. Nguyen was struggling through the shadowy corners. His labored breathing told him not many living creatures had ventured to this place. But his condition slowly got better unbeknown to Nguyen why.

Have I died and this is what heaven is like? The colonel wondered. The Delta Force commando could only shake his head. He knew better than that. Nguyen decided after doing a quick pass with his eyes adjusting to his new environment that this wasn't his final resting place. *I know if I die, this isn't the place I would go. It has too must mystique about this place.* There was something odd about the place, but if he had died, Nguyen felt like he would know it and wouldn't feel like he was standing naked in the middle of Red Square, back at home. That's the sensation he was feeling.

The place had a hazy atmosphere, only adding to the colonel's disillusion. It also provided a mystical feeling about it, almost like he was in a surreal time and place. That's when a feeling that he wasn't alone in this place hit the special forces commando. Something was drawing him towards it. Into the mist, like a fly to the spider web. A dreamy sensation struck Colonel Nguyen and made him feel groggy and not in control of his own wits. No matter how much he fought, whatever had summoned him to this place was no in complete control.

Through the mist-covered atmosphere he glided, deeper into the translucent dream-infested place. A thousand voices began to whisper into his mortal ear, but he couldn't make any of what was said. It was like a million languages being spoken all at once. Then, suddenly the thick mist vanished and he was stand in a spacious room, all bright and luminous. That's when the transparent apparition approached him from what Kambiz thought was the far corner of the room.

The figure was a gargantuan, phantom-like being with nothing but calm and serenity emanating from its form. The colonel felt he should feel threatened and be on defensive tactics, but he felt calm and at peace and he understood these emotions were coming from the being approaching him.

The apparition didn't speak with its mouth, but through telepathy ability. When it spoke, it had the same calm demeanor emitting from its translucent form. "Welcome Colonel Nguyen. I have been anticipating this meeting for some time. I hope you feel at home."

Nguyen took a step back. Even though the apparition's voice was calm, it still rang loud in his head. He blinked a few times, as if he had been blindsided by a nasty right hook. He awaited the ringing sensation to subside before responding. "Are you the one that summand me to this…" Nguyen scanned the room briskly. "Place?"

The apparition kept a calm and inviting look, even though its form consistently changed shape, like a changeling. "You have been cordially invited here, Col. Nguyen."

"Kambiz. My friends call me Kambiz, but I guess we haven't gotten to that point, have we? I don't even know what to call you?"

The apparition floated downwards towards its guest and placed Kambiz Nguyen on the defensive again. He had never trusted anything he could see, nor half what he heard. But the was probably from his extensive military career experience.

The apparition stopped merely feet in front of the colonel and reached out to motion what Kambiz had to assume was an offer of friendship, but the delta force colonel still wasn't buying it. "Mr. Nguyen," echoed the apparition's monotone voice. "I am called Torrach and I am the representative of a race of entities known as the celestials."

Nguyen had heard of the god-like beings, but only in folklore.

"Your only real in stories."

"Oh, we are quite real colonel. In fact, we are the ones that placed the Darkness in its prison."

A lump washed down Nguyen's throat. His body tensed up and his muscles began to contract. That name sent chills up the most seasoned solder's spine. "That is one entity I can believe in. We have fought its…"

"I'm quite aware of your struggles against the armies of shadow." Echoed Torrach. "In fact, that is the reason you are here."

"What, your intrigued about Delta Force's monumental failures?" Returned Col. Nguyen. His speech is slightly slurred and still unsure of himself.

"You can't blame yourself, Mr. Nguyen. No mortal could ever hope to defeat the armies of the Shadow Empire, they are drenched in dark energy. No one has been able to defeat the Darkness' armies since the time of the immortals."

Kambiz Nguyen let a small laugh escape his lips that seemed a little forced and a bit crazy.

"You mean those that abandon the fight, right before they were about to deliver a crippling blow to the armies of shadow? It's difficult to tell if their heroism was greater than their monumental stupidly. I one admired their courage in battle, but as I grew older, I wonder if that was a myth as well?"

The apparition nodded its transparent head.

"Yes, my friend. The immortals were all living species best hope to defeat the Darkness and its malcontent armies, but it wasn't their failure that allowed all living creature's greatest nemesis to flourish. Humans forgot what it was like to fight for the very existence of all living things and now the Darkness is on the brink of escaping its imposed prison."

"Then we are all doomed." Barked Col. Nguyen.

"No. In fact I have invited you to offer you one last assignment. I want you to command a small group of exceptional beings. Ones the descend from the immortal's bloodline. Once they have learned to work as a team, I will send you to aid the one that will destroy the Darkness once and for all. But only when this collection of young warriors is ready."

"Where would I find these unique individuals?" Questioned Kambiz.

The celestial being motioned with its translucent hand and a blue crystal appeared, floating in air. It slowly drifted towards Nguyen and landed in his open palm. It was cool to the touch and ridged on all sides. The colonel ran his thumb over the crystal's uneven edges. He was quite amazed. Despite its uneven surface, it was still smooth to the touch. He looked up at Torrach waiting for the being to elaborate.

"On this crystal, you will find the location of the individual's you are to recruit. You are to travel through interdimensional gateways, where your small team of renegades will be found. But before you can convince this group of unique warriors to place their own lives at risk, you must understand what you're up against. Your military experience will aid you, but you can never understand how to defeat the armies of darkness, inside its home realm until you understand the complete history."

Torrach waved its celestial hand and an image appeared directly in front of the commando. Kambiz Nguyen stood there staring at the moving images as if he was in a deep trance, which in fact he was. The Delta Force commando could feel the extreme emotions filling up inside him. Death, disappear and darkness tried to overtake the colonel, but he was a resilient solder and fought those emotions back.

That's when the history of the entire celestial wars flooded into him like a raging river rushing down an embankment.

CHAPTER 1

The vision before Col. Kambiz Nguyen cleared up, but it was still difficult to see. At first, there was nothing but darkness, and the commando thought something had gone terribly wrong. Suddenly tiny stars began to appear before him as if someone had turned on a light. At first, only a few stars started to appear, like at the earliest point in time, when very few things existed. Slowly larger, more luminesce stars began to emerge, creating a brighter picture. But by the colonel's estimation, there were far too few stars in this version of the cosmos. From his recollection as a young stargazer, there should be a sky full of stars filling the sky, but this wasn't his own time.

That's when Torrach's voice echoed in the commando's head, like a narration at the beginning of an epic tale.

About two-hundred and fifty million years ago:

In the early cosmos, during the Eon of the Celestial beings, when peace was at its heightened throughout the Cosmos, a race of omniscient beings immerged known as the Celestials. These omniscient beings were the most powerful and enlightened beings that ever have existed, and they sought enlightenment over anything else. These omniscient beings refused to judge those that might not have their insight or omniscient morals; but chose to be guides to lesser species. It's uncertain if these superior beings discovered these inter-dimensional passages through their exceptional intellect or if employing their demiurge (god-like) abilities created these cosmic passages themselves.

The Celestials possessed abilities such as cosmic creation (star systems, planets, galactic structure), astronomical manipulation, telepathy, cosmic illusion, destruction, and many other deity abilities. Very rarely did these celestial beings use their innate abilities on each other or for darker purposes. If they had, the other celestial beings would have intervened and stopped the heinous act. These beings would tolerate no erroneous or ill intent to their kind or anything lesser, or the other celestials would intervene and neutralize the rogue entity.

Originally there were fifteen celestials, but one of the god-like beings started an assault against other celestials, which forced the others to intervene. Torrach's transparent body only stood there without an ounce of emotions. This seemed odd to the commando.

Kambiz Nguyen barked out, "Why didn't you stop this renegade celestial? Why did you allow this being to kill your kind?"

Torrach merely shook his transparent head.

"By then, it was too late, my good colonel."

Even though celestials could be in multiple places at once, each reined over its kingdom throughout the cosmos. Each celestial reined over territorial star systems, planets, and other celestial bodies in its sector, but could also affect another celestial's area. But this rarely happened because of the rage it would inspire, and war wasn't something that the celestials thrived on. Little did they realize this rouge celestial had been waiting to strike at all the celestials.

This rouge entity had already blasted two of the celestials into oblivion with its celestial gifts. Its brothers were taken by surprise and didn't know what hit them when their demise occurred. Since the celestials were the only beings alive and immensely gifted, it was easy to figure out which of them was responsible. The reasonable entity utilized the darkness to shield its movements and actions that the superior beings struggled to track and then capture this celestial.

Its celestial brothers knew this being as the Shadow Entity, but later it would be called the Darkness to those that served it and dreaded its presence. All its malice and all its hatred for its celestial brethren fueled its shadow ops and gave its deviant celestial abilities more power than the rest.

Torrach floated towards the mortal.

"Our kind had never confirmed it, colonel, but our kind believed this dark entity could absorb the omniscient abilities of those it conquered. We believed that in some ways this it could shield its motivations and movements from us all." Torrach only gave a sad look to the mortal.

The Darkness's main goal was to become the most powerful entity in the cosmos. That was the one thing the remaining celestials were sure. Torrach told the commando that all could feel its hatred of all the living. "But that was something we didn't know until we were nearly obliterated. The Darkness had become addicted to an ancient power lingering inside dark energy. Later, it would be referred to as Dark Magic or its ancient name. Dark Omniscience."

This dark magic could absorb any form of energy, transform it into dark energy, and utilize it in magical form. The Darkness consumed so much of this dark energy/dark magic; it drove it insane. With dark omniscience, combined with the Darkness's celestial abilities, it's easy to understand how it deceived the other celestials until the annihilation of other celestials began.

All the celestial beings knew the wickedness and the dark energy that emanated within their kin and did their best to soothe it from wreaking havoc. But nothing would subside this being's rage, and it worked in the shadows where none of the other Celestials could see it at work. They all understood that the Darkness had to be destroyed or contained to limit The Darkness' reach.

In retaliation to the celestial's forming plan, it formed its servants to carry out its devious plans if somehow The Darkness fell to the other celestial beings.

～

Somewhere within a portal in between the ancient cosmos and an undiscovered dimension

A lone celestial being, known only as Youterai, followed an echo the rouge had sensed for some thousands of light-years away. An echo is a vibration or disturbance in space-time, a ripple effect that the celestial being noticed instantly. With Youterai's omnificent abilities, including the ability to sense things from very long distances away, the disturbance drew the celestial to it.

Despite Youterai's senses warning him of potential dangers lurking, the celestial's curiosity won out, and the rouge omniscient being ventured deeper into the portal void. At first, the portal's interior was encased in total darkness but wasn't about to deter the omniscient being. Youterai reached out with his senses and made his way through the maze of cylinder-shaped pathways. The pathway walls were smooth, but the vortex neither had shape or substance. The celestial understood it was all an illusion.

That's when the walls began to transform into magnificent purple, blues, and yellow colors. Youterai glanced back in the direction he had come. It seemed the void of darkness had vanished altogether as if it had never existed at all. The celestial could only shake his head. His thinking was too clouded to make any sense of it all. The celestial was at the point-of-no-return. Even with his cosmic manipulation abilities, he couldn't decipher whether he was in the hallway or lost in his subterranean consciousness.

The array of vortex colors had Youterai in a trance. The celestial was like a fish on an inescapable hook line, and he was at the mercy of whatever was drawing him deeper into the void. The swirling cylinder wall kept Youterai subdued and prevented the celestial from utilizing his other deity powers. Somehow the void prohibited the celestial from breaking its stranglehold on him as if the celestial was in the clutches of an unannounced predator.

Usually, Youterai had complete control of his senses, and since most celestials showed no emotions, the anxiety he was now experiencing aided his immobility. Youterai was helpless to prevent what might happen, and the numbness he felt made the celestial not care at all.

Little did Youterai realize, with the euphoric sensations filling his body, that his life-blood was slowly drained, along with his celestial abilities. Somewhere an invisible thief was lurking, stealing every ounce of life from its victim. Gradually the celestial's momentum slowed to a standstill, and the most intense lamination was shining directly into his eyes. The swirling array of light was now rotating directly in front of Youterai. One large mass of colors as if a massive black hole had swallowed all the cosmos' light, leaving only the void's illumination.

Youterai knew in the back of his mind that nothing had such a power, not even his celestial abilities could condense so much energy into one place. Not even if all the celestials could converge all their power into a confined space such as this could it ever happen? Then, despite the euphoria consuming his celestial form, Youterai fought back enough to recollect something all the celestials had once decided.

Whoever has drawn me into this prison must have opened a dark portal filled with even darker energy. That's the only way something like this could ever happen. It has to be so sinister to draw so much light into one spot. Youterai fought the growing euphoric sensation but with zero headway.

Suddenly, a mass amount of energy was pulled from Youterai's body, like his soul was extracted. A silhouette of energy had been removed from the celestial and disappeared into the swirling vortex. Youterai felt his energy level drop. That's when he understood his body was currently being drained. It was useless to fight. He had no way of escaping, with the evacuation of strength fleeing him and no possible escape routes available.

A sinister laugh began to echo within his mind. "I have you now, Youterai. Soon your celestial energy will be mine, and you will no longer exist." The voice's owner seemed to take in the anxiety Youterai was feeling, like filling its lungs with the celestial's energy wave.

Through telepathy, since this was how the celestials communicated, Youterai cursed the thief. "How dare you attack me! I'm a celestial, and you cannot expect to consume my energy. It will overpower and destroy you from within."

The laugh emerged again, but this time it was slow and more concentrated. As if its owner wanted Youterai to be frightened. Or maybe the thief was toying with the celestial. "Oh, my little celestial. You must understand, I am no longer restricted by the laws of the cosmos. I have transcended anything beyond your wildest dreams. Well, if you dreamed, that is. I have become the most powerful being ever to live, and your idle threats don't phase me."

Youterai fought his euphoric-laden body to curse the voice. "Who are you, thief? Show yourself to me!"

"Thief!" Cried the sinister voice. "I'm no thief. I am the tool of assentation. The next step in the celestial evolution. The deity of generations to come. I am the alpha and the omega, all combined into one!"

Youterai laughed halfhearted laughter, but couldn't exhort too much energy. He was beginning to run out of breath, but the celestial was resilient, and if he could transform into his celestial form, he wouldn't need air to breathe. Suddenly, another silhouette of energy ripped from the celestial. This time the sensation was like someone ripping a vital organ, if the celestial had any, right out of his body. Youterai grimaced once again, but his merger reaction didn't tell how much pain each time the parasite extracted his celestial energy away felt. The celestial was becoming weaker by the moment; his vision blurred, he couldn't transform into his celestial form; the vortex wouldn't allow that to happen. Whether that was the portal restricting this or his capture, Youterai was unsure.

The celestial gathered up what strength remained and called out. "Your nothing but a nuisance! You're not a supreme being, nothing like a celestial. Just a soar eye on time itself."

Suddenly silence filled the void, and chills ran down the dying celestial's entire body.

From the pinwheel of colors, a black mist emerged. At first, it was more like a spilled ink stain seeping into the air. A foreign substance that didn't belong. Then the black mist began to proliferate as if it were a parasite about to invade a host.

Rapidly the blackness grew until it began to take shape. A shadowy, featureless figure stood before the entrapped celestial. The dark spectral figure wasn't much different than the other celestials, except it wasn't transparent. It was solid blackness, much like a shadow. It was almost like looking into a mirror, except for the emptiness that filled the image and without any physical features at all. Then the dark figure transformed into a solid shape, and where pitch darkness was only moments ago, a pair of demonic eyes appeared and stared back at Youterai.

The celestial felt the dark figure, floating before him, was checking Youterai out, like a shopper looking over a potential purchase. But something seemed wrong about the shadow figure—something sinister in its blood-red eyes. Death resonated in its smoky fingertips. Deceit ran around the figure like a decrypted halo.

Youterai took in a deep breath.

"You don't seem so confident now that we are face-to-face." Boomed the dark parasite. "Now can you see the power within? What will the future bring the rest of your omniscient brothers and the rest of the cosmos? Everything dies in the end. Where there is a beginning, there is an end." The shadow figure's sinister voice echoed its ominous message.

Youterai could sense the poison energy emitting from the dark figure's fingertips.

He fought back his fear and snapped back at his tormentor. "No matter what you do to me. The other celestials will be in your path to stop your deceitful rampage. You will be stopped."

The dark figure pulled away from Youterai.

"Your confidence and loyalty in your comrades are touching, but foolish. They will wither and die. Nothing, not even your omniscient comrades, can stop the unstoppable force that is my wrath. I was once like you, but know I have discovered a source that has expanded the horizon to me. My knowledge is limitless. My power is superior to even the most powerful objects in the cosmos. I will be the victor, and no idealistic being such as the celestials can stop me."

Youterai's face squinted up like he had swallowed a lime. His face was in permanent anguish, and it just dawned on the celestial who the shadow figure once had been—a celestial himself.

"Your fantasy plan is childish and overzealous. You're not the overlord of this powerful substance. You are merely a puppet in this play. The substance you have ingested is the real puppet master."

Youterai's taunt sent the shadowy figure in a rage. It howled out a piercing cry that made the celestial prisoner cringe. Then another silhouette of energy was ripped from the celestial. The shard of power burns into the pinwheel as if the spinning whirlpool of colors whereas hot as a star and the ethereal energy mass had suddenly vaporized instantly.

The shadowy figure floated back towards its captive until the two of them were only inches apart. Both beings mirrored each other, despite Youterai having substance, despite his translucent qualities, and the dark silhouette was nothing but a shadow. The celestial was no longer afraid of looking deep into the creature's blood-red eyes. But Youterai understood his time had come. Sands of life had run out, and the being before him was ready to annihilate him from existence.

"Your time has come, Youterai. But I sense you know that. Don't be afraid. Death is merely the beginning of a new journey. One where you will become a part of something greater than your selfish self."

Youterai tried to spit in the dark figure's red eyes but didn't have the energy to do that much.

"You fool! You're not worth the time or effort to spend killing you. But I will be glad to take your celestial abilities anyways."

The dark figure rammed its dark hand into Youterai's chest and sucked what remained of the celestial's life, leaving nothing but darkness. Youterai was gone and now part of the madness of the growing darkness.

Simultaneously, Youterai screams of pain vibrated throughout the cosmos, as a blazar ignited, sending massive amounts of energy in every direction. Luckily enough, not many things were nearby, since it was still early in the cosmos. But a few bits of ionized matter were instantly vaporized.

The celestial echo, as it was known as, had awakened the remaining celestials. Their leader Torrach understood that he would have to bring the rest of the omniscient beings together to deal with this new threat. But it would be far from easy to do it. The Darkness wouldn't be able to shield itself for much longer.

CHAPTER 2

Deep within The Merciless Reach

The Merciless Reach, the adopted home of the Darkness, was a dark and foreboding place. None of the celestial intruders could see very far, with shadows continually creeping upon them. The sky loomed gray overhead, and the air was dense and stale as if something acid-based and corrosive lingered. If the celestials had been anything else but omniscient beings, they all might have suffocated under the realm's extreme pressure. With the dense fog-like atmosphere of the Merciless Reach, the celestials are forced into forming into physical beings, substantial in shape and volume, unlike their usual translucent conditions. If they hadn't, the denseness of the air would have engulfed their phantom-like auras and would drift into the dark abyss that was the homeland of the Darkness.

One of the celestials turned to their leader.

"I have a bad feeling about this, Torrach. This is the Darkness's home, and we have no idea what sorcery the master of shadows has spun on this land. It's so bleak and desolate in this realm. Are there inauspicious traps awaiting our arrival?"

"Calm yourself Vladiveer. We have to spring our trap in the Darkness' home realm to keep it in an eternal prison."

Torrach was an immensely powerful celestial that could command most of the celestial powers, including having absolute knowledge of the universe, cosmic manipulation, omnipresence, and reality-warping, a few. But Torrach wasn't the celestial leader for any of those abilities. Torrach was open to the other celestial's inputs and valued all creation, unlike the Darkness and its malicious vise.

"Why not annihilate the scoundrel? Give it the same treatment it gave the others?" The celestial's form flared out its grayish gills, and its amphibious skin began to pulsate as if the air in The Merciless Reach was making it sick.

Torrach, could only shake his celestial head.

I can sense the other's anxiety and the celestial being needed to corral the rest of them in. We can't afford a division once we face the Darkness. The celestial leader took in a deep breath to chase away his anxiety. "It's not who we are Dunbar, and you know that. We only destroy as the last defense."

Dunbar had been known as an instigator and a skeptic of Torrach's leadership, though Dunbar was afraid to admit it. Dunbar's cynical mannerism was starting to place doubt in the rest. The celestial's purplish, translucent form floated just above the decrypted ground, like a mist rolling in off the ocean.

"Well," continued Vladiveer. "It seems this is a pretty dire need. If we don't react now and obliterate this demon and its essence, our ancestors will likely pay the price for our reluctance."

Vladaveer raised his barrel chest as its primal features flared in anger.

"No!" Torrach returned. "I refuse to stoop to the Darkness' level. I will not play games that force us all down a dark and inescapable path. You talk about preventing retribution on our ancestors. If we annihilate the dark entity now, we will only be condemning them to the same fate as the Darkness has chosen. Is that what you want?"

While the celestials argue among themselves, something moved within the shadows of the Merciless Reach. A dark and undefined figure passed by without drawing any unwanted attention, like a predator using the shadows. Then a loud growl penetrated the gray, thick fog that surrounded the celestials. Something was stalking them.

Suddenly, Torrach sensed the Darkness' presence. The Darkness' aura is tainted with malice and deceit, giving the celestial leader issues in his concentration and telepathic communication with the others. Torrach began to experience some nauseous emotions that he would never have to deal with in his normal celestial form. While the others fought among themselves, the celestial beings' leader was having trouble tracking their foe. *The electrifying atmosphere was toying with my celestial abilities.* Like the Darkness, it was using the gray atmosphere surrounding them like a cloak, blocking Torrach's ability to connect with their former brother.

Even before the celestial leader could see the Darkness, in whatever manifestation it chose to appear as, Torrach began to feel its malice, its deceitfulness, and its hatred of those that had once been its kin. The Darkness had tossed away its decrypt cloak and offered Torrach a chance to see its approach. The master of shadows was taunting the celestials, daring them to stop it, as the Darkness moved into a killing position. But I could feel the Darkness' overconfidence radiating through the gray mist, exposing itself, thought Torrach.

Even though the celestial leader could feel their adversary's approach, he couldn't track their foe's precise movements. Unlike the eleven celestials, the Darkness was refusing to conform to one physical shape. Since the Merciless Reach was its home, the dark celestial didn't have to submit to the restraints that limited the other celestials. Instead, the Darkness chose to utilize its omniscient and infernal form.

The Darkness bounced in and out of its multitude of forms, acting as if the master of shadows couldn't decide whether it wanted to be part of the living or the shadows. That's when Torrach understood that must have been the way his adversary had murdered its previous victims, using uncertainty as to its cloak. *The Darkness would appear in my mind as a venomous figure, with razor-sharp fangs and needle-like claws.* But as soon as the celestial leader grasped a hold of the Darkness's position, our foe would slip away, just as swiftly.

The shrill of death echoed all around the uninvited invaders of the Merciless Reach and sent chills up the celestial's backs. They all understood what was coming for them but not sure where or in what shape or form. Would the Darkness attack them in physical form, or would the master of deceit engage in its dark magic and conceal their deaths from one another?

"Where are you?" Yelled Vladaveer. The celestial's physical form had veins protruding from the celestial's neck. His shout reverberated throughout the seemliness dead realm. "I'm not afraid of you; none of us are! Not one bit."

Sinister laughter suddenly emerged from the shadows, as if the Merciless Reach was taunting the celestial beings. "It would frighten you into oblivion if you understood the peril that you were in and what is about to happen to you all." An even more hostile voice than the sinister laughter echoed in return.

The baleful voice was bouncing all around and encircling the celestial beings. It was like they had walked into an ambush instead of the other way around. That's when Torrach understood that their adversary had arrived.

The celestials looked from their left to their right, not knowing where the attack might come from. The slowly enclosing shadows moved in like fog and soon encased the ambushed celestials. The shadows were dark and menacing, almost like the fog had transformed from its hazy grayish tint to a more perilous and daunting texture. A black inkblot manifesting in the thin air and impeding the celestial's vision and in their current physical form, their senses were less in tune with the surrounding environment, which made them vulnerable to the Darkness' attack.

Torrach felt the ominous being spreading all around them. Even with its omniscient abilities, the Merciless Reach diminished the celestial's abilities. The retched balefulness reduced all their senses and made them vulnerable. That's why the celestial leader understood why the remaining celestials had to enter the dark realm in the physical forms they now possessed. Any other place in the universe would allow them all to utilize their celestial forms and abilities, but this was the Darkness' home. Its dark place, where it thrived on evilness.

Out of the dark, thick misty cloud a wretched howl emerged. That's when Torrach knew the Darkness was about to attack. The scream followed by a sensation of dread came over them all and paralyzed each one of the celestials. The master of shadows, seemed to have gone entirely insane, emerged through the cloud in a wolf-like form—fangs protruding from its canine snout and beady eyes that bleed with hatred and lusted retribution.

The Darkness launched out at its trapped victims with immense acid saliva dripped from the creature's mouth, as the master of shadows, in wolf-form exposed its razor-sharp teeth. Right at that moment, Torrach peered into the empty voids that were the Darkness' eye sockets. The celestial leader transported through the blackness of their adversary's pitch-black eyes. Torrach rushed through the void of darkness as if had been catapulted into an undiscovered portion of the cosmos.

The celestial passed by distant galaxies in a flash, leaving a residue of blurred light. The magnificent colors blending faster than Torrach could see them. The celestial leader was witnessing future civilizations rise and fall in a flash of an eye, but still, Torrach felt his destination was too far off. Torrach had left his physical body back in the Merciless Reach. His phantom-like existence sped up even more, and he comprehended that he had flown to the deepest and unknown parts of the cosmos. This dark and lifeless existence led to doorways to forbidden realms, even the celestials had dared not ventured.

Suddenly, Torrach's essence halted directly in front of a dark looming body of gas. No light penetrated its dark façade. The only thing radiating from the dark cloud of gas was pain and suffering like something was bound to the darkness forever. Torrach felt the malice this evil place possessed and if it wasn't for his omniscient form, it would have driven him mad. Luckily Torrach could deflect the wickedness trying to reach out and chain him in.

Now I understand where the Darkness discovered the wretchedness that resides within it. I know wholeheartedly what happened to the celestial it once was and why we had no other choice but to imprison it. A monstrous cry shattered Torrach>s connection and thrust him back to his physical body.

Back in the Merciless Reach

"You shall all be devoured as the others have." Cried the Darkness. "I will engulf the entire cosmos in my darkness."

Without a chance to think, the eleven celestial beings engaged their adversary. Torrach, utilized his omniscient power and propelled a beam of energy from the celestial's hands. The beam of energy scorched the decrypted air of the Merciless Reach as it raced at the speed of light towards the attacking creature. The strike seemed to be on target, but Torrach wasn't sure if it was or if it would do any damage to their foe. The energy beam struck their adversary with such force; it nearly took the air right out of the entire region. A bright light flashed, and the anticipation that the Darkness might ignite under the intense heat of the strike left the celestials speechless.

As the light from the beam dissipated, nothing was left but smoke and scorched air. But the Darkness had left a trace of its existence in the form of vaper trails. They had done it, but Torrach still didn't feel like they had won.

"We did it. We vanquished that demon creature back to oblivion." Said Vladaveer in a joyous cry of victory.

"That was a little too easy," retorted Torrach.

Something pitted in Torrach's stomach. He knew it wouldn't be that easy to conquer their adversary. The celestial's triple hearts began to beat in unison. Torrach would be the only one that could sense the Darkness approach them, far sooner than they would see the master of shadows reappear before their mortal form eyes.

A swirling collection of gas and air that seemed to have a purple tint to it emerged before the celestials. The gas structure didn't settle and form a specific shape. The formation couldn't have been any more than fifteen feet from their circle of defense. Just as Torrach predicted, the Darkness had reappeared suddenly, and it took its captives by surprise.

"Brace yourselves!" Shouted Torrach. But his booming voice vanished in the shrieks of The Merciless Reach. None of the other celestials heard their commander, they were too scared, frozen by the sudden reemergence of their enemy.

This time the Darkness emerged as a dark figure cloaked in a dark shoal. Its demonist eyes peered through the concealing veil of the grayish cloud. It was as if the Darkness now embodied the dark magic and energy that consumed it. Torrach was now sure this was its new form, the one that embodied what it had become, no longer one of their kind.

The dark magic now embedded inside of the Darkness warped the master of shadows so much that its abnormal shape was so unrecognizable to the ones the celestials appeared as. Its body was missing chunks of flesh. Its fingers were long and came to a point, much like talon claws with razor pointed tips. The shoal and attached cloak appeared worn and old as if the creature before them had traveled long and far, through the cosmos to reach them. Holes covered the material as if moths had gotten a hold of it and shredded it to tatters.

The Darkness growled an ear-shattering sound towards the celestial invaders, forcing the decrypted ground beneath them to quake. The master of shadows should have known its adversaries felt no fear, no hatred or joy, or at least in their omniscient shapes. They were a race of emotionless beings. Torrach wasn't sure if his comrades felt any emotions in their physical forms, but he understood they all had some hint of foreboding for what their colleague had become.

This only enraged the Darkness, and the dark energy embedded within its malformed shape drove it even more insane. Fire illuminated within the Darkness' eye, that's when Torrach's connection with the Darkness severed. The Darkness called upon the dark magic it now command and unleashed its demonic wrath upon the celestials. Sparks of magnetic electricity surfaced from its claw-like fingertips as if it had complete and utter control. The energy ball now resting within the Darkness' grasp was glowing a bright blue, and the ball of electricity illuminated even the dark shadows of the Infernal Reach.

The Darkness let out another hair-splitting howl and launched the ball of energy towards Torrach. Their adversary anticipated the other celestials would offer themselves up willingly, once their leader wasn't in the way. That was the one thing I could sense from the Darkness as the energy ball bared down on the celestial leader.

But instead of conforming to the madding will of the Darkness, the celestials defended their leader. Vladaveer rushed to Torrach's aid, shoved the celestial leader out of the killing path of the attack. Instead of Torrach dying an excreting death, Vladaveer is incinerated by the sparking energy attack. Torrach was still stunned by Vladaveer's actions and shook his head to snap out of the daze. The celestial leader wasn't sure it had even happened, but he understood he had to react, or they all would meet the same fate.

The Darkness was furious by unexpected sacrifice that the celestial had made and let out an even more torturous wail that shook the air, the decrypted ground, and everything inside of the Merciless Reach. But it attacks still had a desirable effect. The energy particles absorbed Vladaveer's essence and omniscient abilities and returned them to its owner. The Darkness took in Vladaveer, as it breathed in every particle of the celestial's being.

Out of rage, the other celestials began to bombard the Darkness with their bare fists, omniscient weapons, and anything else they could get a hold. But in this demented realm, the other celestials, were like children fighting off a grown man. The Darkness absorbed it all, only making it grow stronger.

The Darkness rose its translucent arms and the black, charred ground began to shake immensely. The uninvited invaders staggered as the shaking continued and struggled to stay upright. Fissures began to appear all around the celestials. The unwelcome guests converged into a circle, and the cracks in the surface began to explode all around them. The fissures began oozing fiery hot magma that shot skyward. Many of the celestials began to fall to the ground and that made the dark entity laugh its decrypted laughter.

"You silly little beings. You thought you could come to my homeland and imprison me. None of you are a match for me any longer. I have transcended beyond any celestial, and now I'm more of a deity than you all will ever become."

The Darkness released horrible dark energy at its foes, one that could have sent all the celestials into a state of oblivion, ending the war before it had even begun. None of the invading celestials would have escaped the entrapped void. A dark, diabolical cloud emerged from the master of shadow, one that seemed to transform with every breath the celestial nemesis took. It was like an extension of its deplorable existence. The dark, menacing cloud resonated dark energy from its outer layers. Tiny explosions appeared close to the apex of the dark magical cloud. Torrach could sense their nemesis was inserting a lot of its energy into it, and his comrades might not survive what their adversary had in store for them.

The cloud grew to monstrous proportions, and an immense wind began to swell all around them. A dark void opened directly behind the Darkness and began to suck anything not tied down towards it. That's when Torrach understood that it would eventually suck them in, making the celestials lost forever. Torrach would have to act and swiftly.

Torrach turned to the other celestials.

"We must join our power. All of us, at the same time, to have any chance! Right now!" The celestials propelled their power against the Darkness' attack. The counter-attack started to reflect the Darkness' attack as if their collective abilities were some sort of protective shield. None of the dark energy was effecting the Darkness' victims. The counter-attack acted like a shield of energy, keeping the dark energy at bay.

"We have to distract it before it overpowers us." Called Torrach. The leader looked at each celestial for volunteers, but no one seemed willing to be the decoy. It was almost a suicide assignment. One of the celestials finally reluctantly agreed to do it. They would only get one shot at this. If they failed, the distraction would fail, and they all would expose them all to their adversary's hellfire.

The lone celestial made a break for it in hopes of drawing the attention of their foe. Usually, this would be a bad thing, but the celestial had faith in his fellow celestials. The decoy celestial ran away from the crowd as fast as he could towards the dark ring of shadows that acted as a barrier and away from the menacing void sucking everything in. If only he could make it, he might survive. But this wasn't his home kingdom, and the physical form he chose had been slow and awkward.

The shadows began to creep around the fleeing celestial. It was like they were an extension of the demonic dark magic the Darkness was utilizing. If the Darkness was the shadow entity, these shadows were its continuous shadow. The Darkness let out a horrid scream, once it discovered the fleeing celestial. It sounded more like a thrawing banshee in its last death throws.

The sound of footsteps followed the fleeing omniscient being. The decoy looked behind him, and right on his heels was the grotesque shape of the Darkness, now forced to transform shape once again, back into its original wolf shape. The celestial could hear the demon huffing as it pursued him, but at a slower pace than he expected. Hellfire blew from the omniscient wolf's nostrils, like a fire-breathing dragon. Was the Darkness baiting him in slowing down, or did the dark magic user sense a trap?

"Come back here, you coward." Growled the Darkness in a primal tone.

Torrach had to gather the celestials together quickly if their plan was to work. It would take a collective effort to entrap the more powerful being. One celestial would have to utilize cosmic manipulation to hold the Darkness from escaping the trap while the other celestials use their power to create a prison for the Darkness. The celestial leader could feel the immense anger of their adversary and knew their fellow celestial didn't have much time.

Closer the Darkness came to the fleeing celestial, step-by-step the decoy came to his death. But their nemesis was struggling in its pursuit like the Darkness was moving in a pool of quicksand. Something was impeding its pursuit, and Torrach hoped his manipulation of the ground would work. Its physical form was exposing it to the celestial's omniscience, but the Darkness had to be in this form to run down the fleeing celestial. It couldn't use its translucent form, and the Merciless Reach didn't only affect the intruding celestial's abilities; it prevented The Darkness from destroying its enemies in its celestial form as well.

Suddenly, the Darkness felt something powerful tugging at its coat of fur, as if a leash had been slung around the wolf-like body and began to pull it back in the opposite direction. A snap electrified the dense air. Torrach was using all he had, keeping the dark entity from killing their comrade. But since they were in the Darkness' home realm, it was by far the superior being and was draining Torrach's strength quicker than he was expending it.

The strand of energy sliced through the air, as the celestial leader held its breath, not sure if the effort would result in success. Torrach had never formed such a weapon. The strand of yellowish-orange energy split the air, as the Darkness' wolf form opened its vicious mouthful of teeth. A moment of anticipation hung in the air. Would the celestial energy lasso reach their adversary before the Darkness could snatch the decoy from existence? Just as the wolf leaped at the bait, its momentum seized, and the wolves' torso something yanked it backward violently.

The energy strand was scorching the wolves matted fur. Dark, gassy tendrils rose from the Darkness, as it let out a great howl of pain. The Darkness glanced back at the thing wrapped around it. The celestial energy lasso was wrapped around the wolves' torso, dragging it back towards the other celestials. The wolf's hind legs drawn away from the fleeing celestial, while the Darkness attempted to grip the decrypted earth with its forelegs with little success. The Darkness had been roused into a gambit. The wolf snapped and growled at its entrapment, whipping its body to and fro.

The Darkness tried its best to transform back into its phantom-like celestial form, but the omniscient energy lasso was preventing that from happening. The dark entity was going to have to dig into its bag of tricks to break the connection. The Darkness clawed at the charred earth as it was pulled closer to the celestials he was trying to destroy.

One by one, the celestials began to strike their adversary with all their celestial power and encase it in an inescapable prison. The Darkness needed to change forms swiftly before it could be imprisoned in its canine form. It had to choose a monumental shape, one that would overpower the celestials for good. The Darkness fought for its very life, attempting to break the stranglehold the celestial's ensnarement had on it. Harder and harder, the dark entity struggled with its predicament and trying to change form without success. This wasn't how it had envisioned the take-down of the celestials to go, but it knew it had no other choice but to break the hold the inferior beings had over it.

Then the Darkness dug deep and broke the unrelenting, transforming into a gigantic version of the figure that first appeared to the celestials.

The mountainous creature wore dark clothing under its elongated cloak, and the hood draped over the Darkness' veiled and deformed face produced immense shadows. It was a momentous version of itself or one it enjoyed projecting. The dark gray armor conceals the Darkness' large muscles it wore. The cloak draped from the dark entity's head down past its monumental waistline and down to the Darkness' mid-calf. It was quite the imposing figure, and Torrach understood it might take more than the celestials had in them to trap the Darkness.

The celestials began to bombard the now-massive Darkness, but their strikes seemed not to affect their adversary. The darkness moaned its irritation and swatted the celestial siege aside like gnats, propelling divine energy into a nearby hillside, sending dried earth everywhere. "We need to try something else." Cried Torrach.

The colossal shadow entity dropped to one knee as if some other unannounced entity had struck it a devastating blow.

"Our time is now. Everyone lend me all your power, just for a moment."

Each celestial looked at one another, all confused. None of the celestials knew what to think. "Trust me. "Continued Torrach. "If I fail, at least I will bear the burden and suffering, not the rest of you."

All eleven celestials agreed and merged their omniscient energy with Torrach.

"When I say, unload all your remaining power to imprison their foe. No hesitation or this will fail.

When he was ready, Torrach concentrated all the energy lent to him at the center of the chest of the Darkness. Then in one swift motion, the celestial unleased all the power entrusted to him. The power surge exploded from Torrach, in a surge of energy and singed the air as it made its way towards its intended target. The energy was so intense that the gray shadows were replaced by bright illumination. The Darkness, not one to fret over anything, waited for the attack to strike it.

Torrach observed the effects on their foe, as he felt all his energy slowly drain from him. The celestial felt himself becoming weaker by the minute. The energy beam struck home with such force that parts of the Darkness' chest plate erupted, and fragments fell to the ground. The collision sent The Darkness' mountainous body flying backward as soil fragments were propelled in every direction.

The Darkness crashed into its skin-layered Bastian, slamming the gargantuan creature into its bed chambers, forcing the top part of the roof lining to collapse in on the dark entity, leaving debris scattered all around. The collision with its great home and the strike that landed it there had made the Darkness semi-unconscious. All the master of darkness could do was lay there while the celestials built its imprisonment.

Before Torrach blacked, out he called out. "Now encase him in our web. Imprison it for eternity, brothers."

The celestials, with all they had left to spare, encased the injured malcontent being in a web of Omni energy, a network so powerful even the dark magic user couldn't break the web they were weaving. Layer by layer, the celestials encase the Darkness into its prison. Each integral beam of energy began to wield itself to the other, creating a might, impregnable force field. The celestial strike singed layer after layer of interconnecting walls of flesh and bone, like invisible construction workers wielding the layers of the energy prison into place.

Finally, to prevent The Darkness from ever escaping, a force field was encased around the prison layers that were so unique and immune to even The Darkness' dark magic and energy that the prison could never brake.

Torrach lay on the ground, dying, unable to manifest back into his celestial existence. He understood that he had given far more than even his physical body could handle. If he had been in his omniscient form, one that could utilize his healing powers, he would have survived the drain of energy his attack had taken on him, but in this form, his essence just couldn't bear. In his last moments, he whispered his final commands to the other celestials then passed.

"Promise me, my celestial brothers. Band together and protect the know realms from The Darkness' decrypted reach. The War isn't over; in fact, it only has begun. The universe is a vast place, and you all will need reinforcements to keep evil at bay." Echoed Torrach's fading voice.

CHAPTER 3

During the time, directly after the First Celestial War, when most living things did not exist in the cosmos. The remaining celestials gather in a secluded void to decide the fate of one of their kind, one that had lost its way.

The small room was drenched in deep shadows, surrounded by sparse illumination that created an aura. The grey stone walls were aged, and cracks followed the wall's contour to the ceiling. The remaining celestials gathered in a circle, mimicking the room's spherical design. It reminded them of similar gathering places they once had built, scattered across the cosmos but rarely used because of their omniscient origination.

The room was hidden in an unknown void that not even the celestial's greatest nemesis could find them. The eleven celestial bodies didn't converse with one another verbally or telepathically; they all had been summoned to this illusionary void but none of them knew why or by whom. They all were all waiting, but wasn't sure what for. All the celestial beings had utilized their indistinct transparent figures coming to this undisclosed place, preventing anything that might be malicious following them. Only the remaining celestials possessed the ability to unlock portal doorways and would give access to the celestials and this secret meeting place.

Their omniscient forms possessed a halo aura about each that made them appear deity-like. Each of the eleven celestials possessed its own translucent color identifying its home region in the cosmos.

The silence would be deafening to any mortal, but since the celestial's transcendent beings and were used to long periods of silence, it didn't faze them at all. There wasn't one glint of emotion on any of them. These omniscient beings were the definition of dispassionate. It was innate in their omniscient race, emotions would be embedded in the species that would come after, but not in those celestials that remained. They just waited, time was insignificant to the celestials, and waiting was something they could do well. They never did anything in a hurry, anyways, or carried about the concept of time itself, that was a mortal trait.

Suddenly, a wisp of air blew into the room and a towering, phantom-like image appeared before them. The apparition suddenly appeared as a necromancer out of nothingness. The phantom of the deceased celestial Torrach appeared before the other celestial, floating across the void's colorless flooring. Their deceased leader dressed in a glowing white rope and a look of serenity on him. Despite the state of being Torrach was in, the empty void stayed silent, but that could have been more in shock than respect for the dead celestial, or none of them knew how to respond. Due to the respect, they all had for their fallen leader, none objected to his apparition's appearance.

Torrach glanced over each member as if a guardian was making sure all his children were present and at attention, but the apparition leader sensed something that was rare in the celestial race, panic and chaos frozen within them all. Just as Torrach had appeared in his life, not that celestials lived like mortals, the celestial had a calm and pedestrian demeanor, and the other celestials felt their leaders pose.

Torrach lifts his translucent arms as if to bless them all.

"My celestial brothers and sisters. We all have come to an impasse in our existence. Before we all fade out to our destinations and leave our descendants to fend for themselves, I would like to propose something to you."

The apparition waited until the other celestials had finished whispering to one another, free of their statuesque fear. There was a frenzy about those gathered like they weren't sure how to react, since the celestial before them had been annihilated by their nemisis. He could sense their confusion and bewilderment, despite being omniscient. The celestials all sounded like a million voices mumbling to one another, but Torrach was used to the whispering. Torrach had lived a long time as an omniscient being, and even in his diminished state, he was patient with his celestial kin. Patience was a virtue for a leader, something the celestial being had learned over his immortal lifespan. All he had to do was set up the celestial decedents with a way to combat tyrants and adversaries that might arise from their heinous act of imprisoning the Darkness.

Once the celestials had all quieted down, Torrach continued.

"With our deed complete, and the Darkness imprisoned, we all desire to disappear to our resting places. But I employ you that our deed is not complete. We must have some deterrent to offer our decedents. A way to combat the evil that most definitely arise in the name of our dark adversary. We won't be doing them any favors unless we offer them a way to defend the cosmos."

"What are you suggesting, Torrach? We have passed down our DNA to the Elementals. Isn't that enough to ask from us? Can you demand we offer even more?" Questioned a lone celestial, in a less than confident and non-threating manner.

Torrach could sense the usually unemotional beings' anxiety spike, so he waited for the commotion to die down. He wanted their undivided attention and speaking while the impulse the usually emotionless celestials possessed were radiating to die down. Once that happened, he motioned with the palm of his transparent hand.

"What I'm proposing is a precaution against the Darkness escape from his celestial prison. Since after we transcend, we will no longer be available to aid the elementals or their descendants against the phenomenal power of the Darkness and its dark magic-wielding capabilities. Not acting now, while we still can, would leave the beings of that epoch to suffer at the will of the lord of shadows."

More chattering began between the eleven celestials, and the apparition knew the beings in front of him were in total disarray. Torrach knew there was mass confusion between them, and without their guidance, they might flee to their hidden realms, leaving the cosmos vulnerable to the return of the Darkness, if that was even possible.

Suddenly the commotion died off as one of the celestials, not heard by yet spoke. "You said it yourself, Torrach. We encased the Darkness in an impenetrable prison. Even with the dark magic and dark energy it possesses, it can't possibly expect to escape. It can't get out and, nothing can manage to release it from the outside."

Torrach knew this wasn't the type of job he could rush or force the other celestials to go along with his idea. He needed to convince them that this was the right course of action. Without every single one of them, this plan would fail.

"Nothing is certain. Walls can crumble, prison bars can rust and corrode. The Darkness' entombed prison could one day falter, and without at least one of us left, we must give those left behind a fighting chance. It's the least we can do for those that come after us. Do you indeed except complete and utter failure in our celestial duties? If this realm falls, the rest will follow."

Torrach made a motion of his transparent hands, and a glowing transparent image appeared before them. Numerous species were battling one another. Blood covered the landscape, corpses lay in the distance, and the clanging of crude weapons engulfed the void they occupied. It felt as if the celestials were there in the middle of the battle. Dark, purple humanoids with pointy ears wiped the blood from their weapons as a few lizard creatures with rust-filled armor scanned the scene.

"As you can see. Each realm is interlinked, including each one of our secret realms. The Darkness would discover where we are hiding and come for us if it should ever escape."

The celestial crowd began to buzz at this new revelation.

Then a tall, lanky celestial, one that had a calm and kind demeanor about himself moved to regain the omniscient being's attention. The nameless crowd monitor motioned for the rest to quiet down and then turned to face Torrach's apparition. He looked familiar to Torrach, but at that moment, the deceased celestial couldn't place his name.

"Please, great one. Describe to us what you have in mind. We owe you that much."

The tall celestial bowed to Torrach.

"Thank you, my celestial brother," bowed the apparition.

Once again, Torrach motioned with his hand, and a transparent image appeared before the celestials. The image rotated in a clockwise motion.

The image was a sword of unique strength and design. From its appearance, it was well crafted and had the presence of elegance and grace, along with power and strength. The symmetry was unique, with a well-balanced blade that was perfectly straight. The sword hilt was thick enough for a fire troll to wield the sword. It's wrapped in exotic leather, and it came to a hooked curve to prevent the wielder from dropping it. The image had a blue-tinted glow to it, like the blade's aura was surrounding it like a protective layer of skin.

"This is the Sword of Eternity. Its sole purpose is as a tool against the Darkness, shall it ever break out of the prison we have spun. Its wielder must be a chosen warrior that only the sword can foreordain. This epic defender will possess the exemplary disposition and command great discipline and combative skill, courage, and fortitude. Its only use is to destroy the Darkness, if it comes down to the need."

"Then let's use it against him now, while we still have a chance." Called out a celestial member. "Why wait until the Darkness escapes?"

Torrach shook his transparent head. "We cannot. It's not in our nature to kill another. Even if one of us were to steal away the sword and were strong enough to penetrate and eventually challenge the Darkness without succumbing to its immense, depraved power, the sword would not work for the master of shadows. We are not meant to annihilate the Darkness, and murder would have a ripple effect throughout every realm. It would serve the Darkness and doom ourselves and our decedents to eternal chaos. Darkness all its own would emerge and spread throughout the cosmos like cancer, infecting everything in its path."

Torrach waved his transparent hand, and the sword's image vanishes.

"The weapons master will instill a little bit of each of our omniscience power, while it is forged. This will bound to the sword 'the weapon of destiny' and its sole purpose."

The same lanky celestial stood up again.

"And where would we forge such a weapon? Who has the skill to build a weapon of destiny, such as this?"

"There is a master blacksmith that resides in the Immortal Nexus. A realm that only phantom beings like myself can enter. It's a doomed place and perfect to construct our weapon of destruction. He is a celestial like ourselves, and his one true gift is forging anatomically perfect weapons, such as our Sword. It will be an enigma. Then it will be whisked away by an unannounced carrier to an unknown site where it will lay dormant until its barrier comes for it, shall the need arise."

All the eleven celestials began to discuss this among themselves, which seemed to take an eternity. No words were exchanged, and none were needed. Torrach had done what he came to do.

~

Deep within The Immortal Nexus:

The place was cold, and darkness enshroud the land like a solid cover, blocking any type of incandescent light. Stone and rock formations littered the landscape without much sign of life. The gray mist surrounded a patch of land as if something invisible prevented it from consuming the entire landscape. One province was clear of the densely-packed fog. But despite the fog, nothing seemed to move within the perimeter of this unsullied landscape.

Bright, intensive predatorily eyes pierce the dark, dense fog and watch with great interest.

A *ping, ping* sound echoed from a small enclosed workshop within its perimeter. The single source of illumination flickered through the small workshop's lone entrance doorway. The pronounced pounding noise was the only thing to disrupt the eerie silence of the place. No crickets chirping, no wolves howling, not even the buzzing sound of flying insects could be heard—just more of the deadening sound of a hammer's head striking a solid object repeatedly.

Ping, ping echoed the sound again, just as rhythmic as it had been for the past week. The high-pitched sound resembled something scorching being cooled rapidly. The lone figure, stood stout with broad shoulders and massive forearms, struck the object repeatedly. The blacksmith hammer, pitted from extreme usage over time, collided with the anvil before the skilled worker.

Sparks flew in every direction, with each strike.

Kurzol, the lone celestial blacksmith; a gargantuan being wore a black blacksmith apron. His gray tone skin, creased forehead, and workman's like hands told the blacksmith's tale. He had spent an eternity forging weapons for the celestial beings.

A shadow appeared in the doorway and slowly increased to consume everything that led to the workbench. The blacksmith didn't stop his incestuous pounding and didn't bother to acknowledge his visitor's presence. It was like it wasn't even worth his time to do so.

The figure was shrouded under the cloak hood that kept the identity concealed beneath it. The figure inched closer but staying out of the blacksmith's reach. Caution rang of a thief come to rob the burly smith of his possessions, which would be a mistake, or an assassin coming to collect on a bounty. It was difficult to tell either way since the figure was approaching with utmost vigilance. Closer, the concealed character crept, the more tension arose in the workshop. Still, the blacksmith continued to hammer away diligently at his charge.

Suddenly the veiled figure stopped. Was the blacksmith ready to acknowledge the visitor's presence? If the veiled visitor's face were visible, it most likely would have disquietude upon it. Little did the approaching figure realize the burly blacksmith had indeed sensed his visitor's arrival immediately. The character took in a deep breath and slowly exhaled. The blacksmith could hear the thumping of his guest's duel heart-beats. He knew the cold-blooded bastard from the stench of the clothes it wore, from the aroma of its unwashed garb. It stank of the Immortal Nexus itself, and the guest wore it like a second skin.

The stench of the Infernal Glades could be smelled from miles away. The hued pig scent aroma of the glades loomed around the figure like it was entrenched in the figure's pores. The blacksmith had lived in the realm too long not to pick up on the stench instantly. Suddenly, the blacksmith stopped hammering on his charge and set the heavy-headed tool on his workbench. He refused to halt his work until now.

The hooded figure took a deep breath and waited.

"Chaos, you're late." Said the burly blacksmith.

Chaos flipped back his mud-filled cloak to revel reptilian shaped eyes with lime green irises. He blinked once, then twice to clear them.

"Forgive me Kurzol. I was," Chaos hesitated before continuing. The dwarf-sized messenger was now shaking all about. He swallowed hard, "Delayed somewhat."

The blacksmith turned to face his visitor at last. This pathetic creature was the lone courier residing within the Immortal Nexus. The smith stared down at the little creature with the blacksmith's intimidating, solid golden eyes. Kurzol breathed deeply through his large nostrils. In and out, the sound of stale air rushed to and fro through the celestial blacksmith's nose. Kurzol didn't speak again for a while. When he did, his tone told of his extreme and full of impatience.

"How many times do I have to instruct you not to trek through the marshland. You reek of its stench! I wouldn't be surprised if some predator were waiting outside my door just this minute because of it, because of your stupidity."

Kurzol snarled at the courier, displaying his needle-like teeth.

"I'm sorry Kurzol, I was being chased by Riccedin wolves. You realize they travel in large packs this time of year?"

"Yes, I know all about their nature. It is their breeding season if you didn't understand?"

"Of course, it is Kurzul; how can I forget?" Chaos looked down at his thigh, where an aging scar lingered.

"Most likely, their agitation and pursuit of you are a result of one of the childish games you enjoy playing all the time. They are most likely seeking a little vengeance on you."

Chaos held his lowered his head in shame. "Possibly."

Kurzol stared at Chaos and his mud-covered cloak and garb with a look that would make any species crawl back into its hole. His crystal-blue eyes gave the messenger a bone-chilling stare. He hated waiting on Chaos's continuous line of excuses.

"I keep reminding myself to get a new currier. But I continue to let your antics slide, why is that, Chaos?" The celestial blacksmith flashed his razor-sharp teeth.

The little creature looked up with a confused and shocked look. Chaos' jawline had dropped, and the muscles on the little creature's face had stretched to their limits.

"Well? I'm waiting." Kurzol tapped his gargantuan finger on the workbench. "Do you have it or not?"

"Have it, Kurzol?" The tiny courier had a perplexed look. His small, reptilian eyes had glazed over and looked lost.

"The item you traveled across the Immortal Nexus for and that I'm still waiting for."

"Oh, I'm so sorry."

The reptilian creature reached into his nap sack and pulled out a cube looking device. It was glowing a bright neon blue color. Chaos shielded his eyes from the item's intense illumination.

Kurzol tossed the little creature a bag full of coins.

The bag of coins clunked on the workbench next to the celestial cube. Chaos hesitated but finally retrieved his payment. He opened the bag, shook the bag full of coins, and the sound of his payment rattled inside the leathery bag. Chaos was ecstatic with joy. The little courier's eyes regained their color, and his short, snout-like nose came up as Chaos flashed his own set of teeth. It was the best the little creature could do for a smile, but Kurzol had known Chaos long enough to know when he was in a joyous mood, not that it meant much to the celestial blacksmith.

"For your troubles." Barked Kurzol. "For all its worth."

The blacksmith reached for the glowing cube of energy. "So, this is all the celestial power they have left behind."

Chaos hesitated once more, then curiosity won him over, and he too leaned in and looked at the glowing cube. Neon illumination reflected off Chaos's snout.

"What the heck are you supposed to do with it?"

Kurzol reached back to the weapon he had been working diligently on. The symmetrical blade, perfectly balanced and feather-light.

The thick steel construction reflected the illumination from the celestial cube. Kurzol had built many weapons over the eons, but this was his most exceptional work ever. He knew what it was for, and he had to make sure no weapon had been constructed with more skill, detail, and craftsmanship than the Sword of Eternity. The celestial blacksmith placed his mountainous hands against the smoothness of the blade. Its touch was cool as glass, but he knew it would resist any power in the cosmos. It had to.

The sword pommel was of exquisite design. The symmetry and flow were nearly perfect, and despite having forged more than the celestial weapons master share of weapons, it was the finest Kurzol had ever forged. Kurzol's massively oversized hand, but for a smaller being it would be the perfect fit.

"What are supposed to do with the cube, Kurzol?"

"I have to immerse the blade with the celestial's omniscient power. That will make it the most unique and dangerous weapon in the cosmos. It will become a weapon that changes the destiny of the entire race of the cosmos. It's meant to be a deity slayer that only the right hands can wield."

Kurzol softly grasped the shoulder of his friend.

"After I am through. You are to whisk away this weapon to an undisclosed place. Where no one will find it until the time is right. The Darkness must never know of its location ever."

Chaos blinks his reptilian eyes. "How will I know where to take it?"

"You won't. It will guide you."

Kurzol began to immerse the sword blade with the celestial energy and transform it from a well-crafted weapon into The Sword of Eternity. Since the celestial energy was of a unique origin, the celestial weapons maker would have to act quickly. He first submerged the sword into a steaming hot bath. As soon as the glowing blade touched the liquid, red-hot sparks began to shoot out of the forge, and the sword material started to scream in protest.

The liquid bathing chamber designed unique properties that could withstand millions of degrees; It was a square shape, allowing the blacksmith to place numerous types of weapons in the bath. Kurzol had built the bathing tank himself and, with his unique abilities, forged it from alien dying stars. That's how he knew the bath could take the sword and the cube of energy into its depths without igniting or vaporizing into stardust.

Kurzol quickly dropped the celestial cube of energy into the bath. The liquid began to turn an array of colors instantly. The bath gurgled, and rays of energy shot out as if it was a firework show, showing off the intense celestial energy. The blacksmith knew that placing both in the forging bath wouldn't be enough. He was going to have to use a bonding agent. Kurzol reached for his Elixir of Endless Time to use as the bonding agent. The potation possessed fragments of dead souls from every realm. The power in it was far beyond anything any living creature before or after, had ever experienced.

Kurzol, felt the energy ignite as soon as the powdery substance hit the constantly changing liquid. The rainbow of colors became transparent, and the heat grew to an insurmountable level. It was like the celestial blacksmith was standing next to a massive star. Just before the radiating heat became too much for Kurzol to bear, the bonding agent brought the talisman and the celestial energy together. It wasn't the first time Kurzol had performed this feat, so he knew that the energy floating in the bath wouldn't ignite. He was the best blacksmith that had ever lived, that's why he had been chosen to forge the sword in the first place.

Somewhere deep within the Infernal Reach, the Darkness sat deep in its decrypted bastian, encased in dark shadows and cased in its celestial prison. The energy prison cell was translucent and nearly invisible to the naked eye. The one thing that could decipher where the Darkness' prison walls ended was a flicker of light like you had just awoken from a dream. The transparent mist, at first glance, appeared to be like clear waves from the ocean or a transparent cloud that might be penetrated with ease.

But the last thing anyone would ever want to attempt was sticking a limb through it. The celestial energy keeping the master of shadows in its prison would incinerate anything instantly. It's what kept the Darkness at bay and reeking its dark injustice on every living thing. It wasn't lost on the Darkness; how mighty his prison walls were. The translucent prison kept the Darkness' power at bay, just as much as it kept its physical body imprisoned.

The Darkness seething madness continued to mount, with each passing moment. It's loathing for all living things also increased, along with those that had entrapped it grew more substantial. The dark power that resonated within was itching to get out. Still, with the celestial energy field imprisoning the dark entity, it couldn't utilize its darkness energy, but that wasn't the only tool in the master of shadow's game plan.

A menacing and foreboding growl escaped the master of shadows.

"You can't expect this miserable excuse of a cell to hold me for eternity? But that's not all you have up your celestial sleeve, is it, Torrach?" The Darkness growled some more. An apparition hovered just outside the Darkness' cell as if taunting the master of shadows. It only seemed to enrage the Darkness even further.

"Your talisman will not stop me," moaned the prisoner. "It won't annihilate me as you so naively believe. It won't even penetrate my skin and make my shadowy blood pour. When I get out of this imprisonment, and I will escape it, I will search you and your kind out and annihilate you one by one. I will promise you that much."

Torrach, in his phantom form, didn't bother to respond; understanding it would only fuel the Darkness' rage. His gray, celestial eyes only gazed sadly at his prisoner. The Darkness, menacing, colossal red eyes penetrated the shadow of its imprisoned chamber as if it was a nocturnal predator on the hunt. The deep and sinister voice bellowed outwards towards the dark realm occupants.

"Hear me, my loyal servants. Come to me and do my bidding. Come from every sector of my dark and demented realm. Come and obey your master."

The Darkness closed its colossal, demonic eyes and began to search for the essence of its greatest servant. The dark deity might be prevented physically from hunting down the Sword of Eternity, but it had servants that weren't bound to the Infernal Reach. The master of darkness searched and searched and sent out a message through its celestial ability to communicate telepathically. Then the Darkness reached something. It opened its infernal eyes and chuckled. "There you are my pet."

Suddenly a dark and translucent being floated across the corrupt and decrypted chamber floor. The naked eye would have never picked up on its presence because there was no light in the place, and the being was so translucent that it had no real physical shape what-so-ever. Not bound by the Darkness shackled imprisonment, the being approached its master until it reached the invisible border prison. Now the phantom-like figure had become more profound. Its shape was easier to see with the illumination of the energy prison. It had a luminous purple essence that surrounded its translucent body. It didn't seem to have a face at all until it spoke, which wasn't that often. It relied on its telepathic abilities to communicate.

"Shadow Lord. My oldest and most loyal servant." Boomed the Darkness.

The Shadow Lord wore a black, translucent robe that hung to the floor. An even darker cloak cover The Shadow Lord's backside, which draped from its shoulders and matched the robe's flowing length. The robe itself was tied snuggly together by a dark leather-like belt. The Shadow Lord's claw-like fingers barely protruded through the sleeves of its translucent robe. The most trusted servant of the master of shadows had an oval face that was much closer to a purplish color than gray and appeared that the Shadow Lord was choking. The Shadow Lord seemed to glide over the decrypted floor as if the lord was suspended in the air.

The shadow agent bowed.

"Master. It's always a pleasure serving you. How may I be of assistance?"

"The celestials have built a weapon. Utilize all assets at your disposal to discover where this talisman is and bring it before me."

"To wield against its makers, master?"

"No. I can't wield this weapon. But something tells me someone will come along that will be able to, and I don't want this creature to gain possession of it."

The shadow lord bowed again.

"Of course, not your most powerful one. I will use all our agents to hunt down and take the weapon from the dead, cold grasp of whoever possesses it."

An invisible smile seems to appear through the shadows.

"Good. Don't fail me. I would hate for my retribution to be unleashed on you."

"I shall not fail you, master."

The Shadow Lord bowed one last time before exiting the dark chambers.

The Darkness waited until The Shadow Lord had left, then it began to speak to the darkness itself.

"Now, since that's completed. Maybe it's time to forge my weapon against the celestials and their descendants.

The Darkness contemplates its options.

"But first, I must find me the right specimen for me to forge. Now that will take some time, but so worth it in the end. The hand of retribution will be mine to commend. If the celestials that betrayed me though I have no way to continue my web of deceitfulness, then they are misinformed.

THE SECOND CELESTIAL WAR:

The Eon of the Dark Insurgency

CHAPTER 4

ol. Kambiz Nguyen and the Torrach apparition moved towards the interior of the phantom realm. The deeper they ventured into the place, the less Nguyen could see where they were going. It was like the shadows were getting deeper, the further they ventured towards the place's interior and it was unnerving the coronal. If it wasn't for his apparitional guide, the mortal would be lost. His guide suddenly stopped and Nguyen couldn't tell the difference between the place they currently are and where they had been fifteen minutes ago.

Torrach's apparition was now floating just above the coronal, at shoulder height. Kambiz felt like a student and Torrach was the looming teacher. The former special ops commander had I childlike giddiness; like he was with a childhood hero. But his training kicked in soon after those childish emotions thrust themselves on him. He knew he didn't know what would come next or if he would be blasted into oblivion if his guide chose. The Asian man wondered if his host was currently reading his mind or if the coronal was becoming delusional.

"What happened to the Darkness, once the celestials imprisoned it? How did it grow so powerful?" Quizzed Kambiz Nguyen.

The apparition looked down upon the human with what seemed to be a sympathetic smile, not that a translucent being could ever smile or at least in the way the coronal could. "The Darkness never lost any of its potency, even in its imprisonment. To tell you the truth, it might have made the master of shadows even stronger than before and that is on my hands. I fear our descendants paid the price of that oversite, but I made the snap decision to imprison it, instead of eradicating the Darkness."

"You're referring to the Elementals?"

Torrach's translucent head nodded. Suddenly the loud humming began and the coronal and his phantom host were standing in the middle of a circular structure imprinted on the stone floor. There were strange symbols etched into the floor that appeared alien, but somehow familiar. The circular object and the alien markings began to glow bright orange, as if someone had set them all ablaze.

The celestial apparition waved its ghost-like hand and as if his host was a magician the floor and the spot on the wall adjacent to them came alive, as if they both had been transported to another place. At first Col. Nguyen didn't recognize anything before him, in fact he was still blinded by the sharp orange light that had come before the room had transported them somewhere else. Then Torrach began to speak again.

"Elementals were our greatest option, after the celestials transcended. They were fearless, dedicated to the defense of all living species and had many other qualities that we had imbedded into them. They had great skill in warfare and could match nearly anything that The Darkness could throw at them."

"You're telling me that the Darkness could still wield its dark power even within the confines of its imprisonment?" Question the coronal.

"Not in a way you might think. The prison kept the Darkness at bay, in a physical sense and prevented it from wielding much of its darkness onto its victims, but the power of manipulation and deceit should never be underestimated."

"Then how did these elementals combat the Darkness and for how long?"

"They were given chosen skills, not omniscient ones like their celestial ancestors, mind you, but that would have placed an unfair burden on them. Each elemental had its own unique skills, but one above them all had the power to unite them and have the elementals fight in a cohesive unit. For the length of service, each elemental fought in this war against the Shadow Empire for a millennium maybe even longer."

Kambiz Nguyen was astonished. He had never heard any of this, not from the legends told, not from the scrolls that were said to be lost. The one thing he couldn't understand was how the elementals had battled the Shadow Empire for so long.

"I see the doubt and aww in your eyes. It has been a quarter of a million of your terrain' years that the elementals had battled with the armies of darkness. Then when it was time, like the celestials they transcended, but unlike us they were bound to their own descendants to return one day to finish what they had started. A select group of warriors were created by the elemental's hand, to take their place against the Darkness."

Suddenly the vision before them brightened and a scene began to unfold before them:

During the Afterglow years: approximately eight-thousand years ago.

It was during the age of the growing darkness, during the height of the Second Celestial Wars when the armies of the Darkness had spread far across the cosmos. The defender's numbers had dwindled since the celestials had imprisoned the Darkness into its celestial cage. But none of that seemed to hamper its power over its subjects.

The struggle between dominance, corruption and free will was at its height.

The elementals were the descendants of the celestials, those that had long vanished from existence. These colossal defenders were mountainous, a good five-times larger, if not more than a standard human. Each elemental created with a specific purpose and individual elemental abilities. No elemental had every omniscient ability that their god-like ancestors had, but a selected few had adopted specific celestial traits.

The elementals created their air, and their massive quad lungs acted as filters for the recycled air, where the more massive pair of lungs worked as the respirators for the defenders and the smaller pair as the filtering devices.

The shape-shifting elementals endured long journeys through interstellar space with nothing but their thick and scaly draconian skin. It might be the reason they're known as Intergalactic Tarragons or their more common designation, space dragons. But that name might also be from a direct association of the shape-shifter's enormous draconian wingspan, which could stretch as large as a medium-sized space frigate. Eventually, humans would adopt this imagery for their tales of dragons that spread fear across their lands.

~

On the small moon of Telvoaria, a band of elementals began their raid against a small regime of the Darkness' forces. The next to deserted craggy landscape was a badlands, where nothing seemed to move on the surface. No surface water existed; it was just a floating rock orbiting its host star. There were no signs of settlements, no fossils laying on the cold, desolate and rocky surface, nor were there signs of cultivation. The planet had been left for dead without the attempt to terraform it—an excellent place to hide.

Telvoaria possessed many crags and caverns, making it harder to uncover the Darkness' servant's hideout. But fortunes were on the marine's side that day. The mortal escourts that aided the elementals had tracked the Darkness' loyal servants to an isolated cannon with a cave embedded into the canon walls.

The raiding captain communicated back and forth to his frontline officers.

"Base command, this is forward command. We are in position and awaiting for the go signal from you."

"Very good captain. Stand by to execute the raid." Returned the base commander.

"Roger, sir." The frontline captain heard a sigh, then his communications officer retorted, "Sir, I'm not attempting to be insubordinate, because I truly am great for this opportunity. But I only have seen a few Blackmour Drowmauders and no more than a dozen or two Dragalyite solders, sir. Are you sure we have the right place? It seems such a small prize for the number of soldiers we are using in the siege."

The captain took in a deep breath. "We only do what we are commanded, first lieutenant. Keep your eye open and your ears sharp."

The Blackmour Drowmauders were a race of violet skinned elves that lived beyond the borders of the known cosmos, that had sworn their allegiance to the Darkness. The master of shadows had chosen them as leaders on the battlefield, among the many followers it had accumulated. The Drowmauders were selected for their high level of intelligence and tactical expertise, but not as combat soldiers.

A selected few were chosen to learn the dark magical craft only the Darkness could provide, and those were the Drowmauders that gave the highly skilled elementals the most significant problems. Thank goodness, they were rarely seen.

The field captain leaned back and pondered the involvement of humans in the war against the armies of darkness. He knew mortals had once been used ever since the elemental's emergence, but the mass losses the marines had suffered forced the captain to wonder if they were equal partners in this war of nutrition or just pawns. The elementals had switched from utilizing mortal allies to breeding genetically enhanced ones that could take the punishment of war and not suffered such losses as the marines had at the same time.

This new generation of interstellar soldiers was faster, more agile, and possessed the ability to see in the night over traditional mortal solders. They stood better serving the elementals and their war against the Darkness than the non-enhanced generations. The captain witnessed first-hand these elite solders recover from a battle quicker than his own men, needing less medical attention and giving their platoon more space to carry ammunition than normal mortal regimens.

"Listen up, marines." He knew it was still early, and his men needed a moment to focus on his voice. "Let's stay sharp on this one. We can't afford those purple bastards escaping us this time."

The Drowmauders, from their last raid had given the marines the slip and escaped. Another failed mission from the platoon would set a chain of reprimand from their elemental leaders. Even though the elementals weren't a violent species, they did command loyalty and competent work from the marines.

First lieutenant Ramiel Tiberius returned, scanning the target and the horizon just beyond—still no signs of the drowmauders or their dragalyite escorts. The surface was dead quiet, and in the lieutenant's estimation, that was always a bad thing, especially before a raid. The lieutenant had seen too many things go wrong when targets operated outside of their norm. Did they know the marines were coming? Did they have something special planned for his squad? Tiberius just didn't like the feeling he was receiving.

Extensive movement begun outside the cavern entrance. It was the only way in or out of the rocky dwelling, so there would be no way their targets escaped the commandos this time, was there? The first lieutenant almost felt it was too small to house anything important, but he wasn't about to misjudge their target or their unit's orders. He had been wrong before, and that nearly had cost the marine his life. The cavern entrance was wide on the outside, much like a *Chaundra Five* brothel dancer's puffy facial lips. The marine smiled at the thought of those juicy lips blowing him kisses as the curvaceous dancer moved her body in the wildest and seductive ways.

But just inside, according to their keen eye sights, assisted by thermal binoculars, the interior of the cave entrance shrunk down dramatically. It would barely allow two drowmauders to stand side by side, let alone the mountainous physique of one of those reptilian dragalyite solders. The first lieutenant could utilize that to his advantage. Creating a bottleneck in the cavern and forcing the reptilian bodyguards to offer themselves one-by-one for target practice would be ideal. The reptilians moved slow, and that would make it just that much easier to eliminate the real threat, the drowmauders, once the siege had begun.

The sudden movement began to appear at the cavern's opening. Then the first lieutenant began to hear other marines barking out commands in his comm. Earpiece. "The lizards are starting to scurry around inside. Some are going for their weapons. Shit, I think we've had our cover blown."

"There goes the element of surprise." Mumbled first lieutenant Ramiel Tiberius.

The captain began to layout commands over the com. "Left flank, move in. Right flank stay back and provide cover. Centruin team make your move towards the mouth of the cavern directly after the left flank moves on the target and don't allow them to become exposed."

The siege had begun!

~

The marines engaged the colossal dragalyites. The first lieutenant had been correct when he said utilizing the bulkiness of the reptilian solders and the narrow cavern entrance as a bottleneck allowed the marine snipers to pick off the much larger targets easier. One by one, the Dragalyite bodies began to pile up in front of the narrow entrance, and before the frontline, commandos knew it was preventing them from getting into the interior of the hideout.

First lieutenant Ramiel Tiberius charged the dragalyite frontline, firing his RX-23 Chaos Flux Laser rifle. The standard issue weapon for their platoon. The marine's heart was racing a mile-a-minute, trying to keep his rifle focused on the target ahead. The marine fired at his target, but even with the weapon's accuracy and the first lieutenant's skill, the reptilian soldier refused to go down. The laser shot seemed to be absorbed by the larger-than-life creature. The marine fired again.

Ramiel got too close to his target by this point to retreat. That's when the marine noticed the scorch marks on the dragalyite's rust armor. It was like the reptilian had gotten to close to a dying star and paid the price. He had never seen, in all the years as a marine commando, armor so beaten down and still functional.

Must be tougher than a drop pod's outer hall, thought the commando.

The tough hide of the dragalyites, combined with their rust-laden armor made them a difficult target to kill, that's what the first lieutenant had discovered first hand. He hadn't been forced to kill anything more difficult that a space pirate pilot, since his enlistment activation. He had been working in the counter-intelligence sector before his sudden transfer into the elite commando unit, which wasn't by his request.

With the lieutenant's momentum taking him right into the range of the substantial dragalyite, the creature whipped its sharp curved bladed weapon at the commando. Luckily the bulk-sized weapon took time for the dragalyite to wield, and the commando slid just beneath the weapon's thrust. Ramiel felt the thrust of the weapon and the power of his opponent, with a burst of air current trailing the archaic blade. It nearly knocked the commando off his feet.

As Tiberius slide past his target, he noticed the enormous reptile off-balanced and unable to pursue him. The weapon took that much effort, even for a creature as stout as the dragalyite. Underneath the rusted, blood-stained, and dented armor, the commando could see the reptilian's massive back muscles bulging as the creature attempts to keep the deity-sized weapon under control.

"I guess it's a good thing that blade missed me, or it would have taken my head clean off." Mumbled the first lieutenant.

A sound in the commando's earpiece communicator rang off, but since the communication was a hit-or-miss on the planet, the voice cut out and leaving the first lieutenant unsure if the muted voice was speaking to him, or if it was meant for another commando. The first lieutenant didn't have time to ponder on it for long. The mountainous creature recovered and spotted the first lieutenant well within its grasp.

The dragalyite hissed at the commando and let a gargantuan growl from its hideous, enlarged snout, exposing its malformed teeth inside a green, fleshy mouth. That forced the first lieutenant to freeze. He couldn't raise his weapon, nor could he flee the enormous creature. The enormous lizard raised its deadly, rustic weapon, which at this point seemed to the commando to be the size of a medium-sized starship. The rusty, curved blade swung back like a sharp pendulum. The weapon could have been twice as long as the commando's own body, but the first lieutenant was too scared to notice. All he could feel was the death throws that filled his own body, preventing the commando from escaping his impairment doom.

The commando's adversary launched at him, with its murderous weapon high in the air. It was like watching his execution from outside the commando's body. Anxiety and fear ran down the mortal's spine like a runaway frigate ship. Despite all that, the first lieutenant still couldn't move a muscle. The massively sharp blade began to drop, like a guillotine blade.

Then a blast scorched through the air before the marine could dive out of its attack path, like a screeching predator was swooping down from above and struck the dragalyite dead in the chest. The heavy energy blast slamming into the mountainous beast with such force, the lizard warrior propelled off its feet and landed face down on the ground. Full of fear, the first-lieutenant didn't even see where the blast had come from. Slowly the commando built up enough nerve to approach his adversary. Yes, it was dead, the commando confirmed. Smoke still billowed from underneath, and the smell of burning flesh filled the commando's nostrils. *What had done this?* He wondered.

A yell from a distance. "Your welcome lieutenant!" Waved a commando on an Oblivion Thermos Cannon.

Commandos called them The Hammer of the Gods. And the lieutenant now knew why. It was one of the few weapons that could penetrate dragalyite armor and its rough hide, all in one shot. The mechanism possessed six metal arachnoid legs that attached to an open cab, where the cannon operator sat. The marine commando sat on the swivel chair attached to the cannon stationed less than thirty-five kilometers from the lieutenant's position. It was a good thing the cannon operates had shot his adversary. He knew he would now be dead if the commando hadn't.

Ramiel glared at the cannon operator, with a hint of contempt. *Little cocky bastard!* But the commando was right. The operator saved his life, so he couldn't be too upset. Still, the cannon operator's arrogance was annoying. Anyways, the operation's commander was approaching, so the first lieutenant stiffened up and was prepared to salute his superior's presence. Fortunately, the operation commander waved the effort off and began to scan the damage.

Dragalyite bodies littered the cavern's entrance, and the stench of burning reptilian flesh irritated the first lieutenant's nose. Some of the commandos from the left flanking unit had taken mortal wounds, while field medics were attending others. Despite all the marine's enhanced abilities, the one thing they couldn't prevent was their deaths. They were still mortal, unlike their elemental leadership.

"Shape-up first lieutenant." Called the regimen captain. "Act like you have seen this before and not embarrass me, and I might introduce you to one of our elemental leaders."

"Yes, sir!" The first lieutenant answered. Attempting to solute his superior officer, forgetting that wasn't done in the field. He stopped in mid salute and set his arm back to his side. "Sorry, sir."

The field captain shook his head. "It's fine first lieutenant. I keep forgetting you're an intelligence spy and not a field commando."

First Lieutenant Ramiel Tiberius watched as a survey team entered the cavern entrance. With the dead dragalyite bodies gone, and the cavern was being combed through, but without his thermos binoculars, the first lieutenant couldn't see that deep into the dwelling. This bothered the commando. His training in intelligence gathering made his curious to what the team had found.

"Sir, I don't suppose you can tell me why we attacked a small camp filled with few drowmauders and dragalyite solders? It seems a waste of human resources to me. Doesn't it seem a little trivial to you?"

The field captain sighed and placed his hand gently on the commando's shoulder. The little time Ramiel had known his superior, he had realized the marine captain encouraged his commando's questioning suspect orders; as long as they did what they were told in the end.

"Son, if I knew the answer to that, we both would be smarter for it. But they don't give me enough intel to know anything beyond our mission objectives. I guess we are nothing but grunts without any need to know."

Suddenly a digital siren went off, and all the personal, military, and others stopped what they were doing. The commando and his commanding officer spotted a small entourage approaching.

A commando rushed to their field captain. "The elemental leaders have come to inspect the contents of the cavern, commander."

"Settle down." The commander looked square into the messenger's eyes. "Tell the others we have company. I want everyone on their past behavior."

The commando ran off.

The first lieutenant saw his commander take a deep breath.

Jetsuenete and his small party of elementals were coming towards the cavern entrance.

"Looks like management has come to see what we've found. Shall we greet them?"

~

Jetsuenete was a mountainous being with luminous golden eyes, a barrel-thick chest that made the elemental appear twice the size of his elemental brothers. All the enigmatic defenders towered over most species, but their leader even dwarfed the most colossal of them all. Jetsuenete's breastplate was wide and broad. It had a mountainous crest on the elemental's chest. A titanous bronze shaded dragon with a horrid wingspan filled most of the chest plate and a solid black border around it that seemed to clash with the gold chest-plate. The dragon stood straight up as if to challenge its opponent into a fearful submission.

The elemental entourage, led by their courageous leader, Jetsuenete; move towards the cavern opening. They are stopped by a few marines who attempt to pass on what they have discovered. The elemental tower over the mortal marines, like adults overlooking a playground of children.

"What have you discovered?" Questioned Jetsuenete.

The elemental displayed a stern, but a congenial expression, as if the elemental leader was patiently awaiting.

"Forgive me for the slowness of the report, your excellency. We had a difficult time removing the dragalyite bodies from the cavern entrance."

One of the elementals the had been accompanying the mountainous leader whispered something to his leader. Jetsuenete nodded as if the elemental leader agreed to what was told to him. "We understand this wasn't a normal raid on our enemy, and your men are ill-equipped for the clean-up. It is expected that it would take some time."

The elemental's abrasive comment hit the marine captain like a slap in the face. A sigh came from the unit commander as if relieved he wouldn't have to give a magnificent performance.

"Having said that, what have we discovered?"

The field commander looked back at the elemental leader, with a hint of surprise in the commando's eyes. It seemed like the life had been drained from them. "Ummm." The marine pulled out his data pad and frantically rumbled through the reports he had. "Well." The commander licked his dry lips.

All four elementals stare down at the commando leader with a hint of impatience. Some even have disdain in their expressions. "Well, commander? We are waiting for an answer." Chimed in another elemental. This one had red armor with a cloak to match. The commander looked up and began to run through the report.

"Their force was larger than the intel reported. The dragalyites were tougher than we anticipated. Maybe a special force of reptile solders."

"The dragalyites don't possess any special forces, commander." Echoed the elemental that had been silent to that point. The elemental wore green armor and possessed a pole-like weapon that the commander couldn't quite comprehend.

"But you got the job done, didn't you?" Barked a silver- colored elemental.

The captain nodded. "That wasn't the issue. We could have cleared the scene quicker if we had known what we were in for."

"So, are you criticizing the intelligence you received captain?" Continued the silver-colored elemental with a hint of sarcasm towards the marine commander.

The marine captain closed his pad and handed it to Ramiel Tiberius. "Your excellency. If I may, I would have to say yes, the intel was insignificant for the assignment. If we had known what we would encounter, my marines could have been equipped with better weapons, making the job a lot easier. In turn, we wouldn't have taken so long clearing the bodies, and you would have had a clear path into the dwelling."

"Typical marine." Called a third elemental draped in red. "Always complaining."

The silent elemental in green spoke up again. "What about the drowmauders, commander?"

The field commander frowned. "Drowmauders? From my recollection of the field report, there were a few killed inside the dwelling. We can go and look if you like."

"Only a few?" Barked the elemental with the silver garb.

"Why would the Darkness utilize so many dragalyite solders to guard only a few dark elves, none were elite dark magic wielders, were they?" Boomed the red elemental.

The field commander could only take a deep breath. "I can't answer those questions, your excellency. I'm not an analysis; I'm a field solder."

"I don't care about any of that." Waved off Jetsuenete. "I want to know if you have collected the artifact?"

"Artifact?"

The field commander was confused and not following what was asked.

"You know, the property of an ancient society." Said the silver elemental, in a sarcastic tone.

"He might know it by the term talisman." The red elemental added.

The commander still gave the elemental's a questionable look.

"I'm only interested in the sword, captain. Nothing else."

The captain looked around frantically as if he was attempting to locate the sword but where they all were standing. "Well, maybe it's still in the cavern. I didn't see it on the analysis's report."

"Then, shouldn't we be inside instead of standing out here?" Questioned the red elemental. "Please lead the way."

Jetsuenete stopped at a burning pile of dragalyite bodies. A reptilian arm was dangling from the refuge pile. A mark, no a brand on the creature's shoulder caught Jetsuenete's attention. A few of the elementals look down towards their leader.

"They're not servants of the Darkness," bellowed Jetsuenete. "They are slaves of shadow."

"Born in servitude?" Questioned the silver elemental.

"Maybe. But either way, it seems it's not by choice that they fight for the master of shadows."

"So, what if they weren't given a choice; they still slaughter the innocent and act as the right arm of our nemesis."

"No, that's the drowmauders that act as the Darkness' right hand." Barked another elemental.

"Whatever." Continued the red elemental.

"No. If the dragalyites choose not to serve, then they are victims, just like the rest of the species, the Darkness has threatened. They need to be liberated, not slaughtered." Returned Jetsuenete.

~

The cavern interior is well lit by the time the elemental entourage entered. Techs and military analysis personal were scattered all around the cavern. A swarm of non-military personal. Some were running back and forth as if collecting samples from each dead body. No more than twelve drowmauders lay on the cavern's rocky floor. This seemed to puzzle the four elementals, and their bewilderment resonated from them all.

A few of the elementals hovered over a few dark elf bodies, but they didn't stay at one specific corpse long. The silver elemental touched one of the drowmauders. Purple blood stained the carven floor around the body. The elemental inspected the dark elves forearm. The elemental motioned for one of his brothers to come to look at the body. "I doubt if he was a dark magic-user. He doesn't have the typical marks of their clan."

"Why would the Darkness assign non-magical wielding drowmauders to guard the talisman? Do you think they were all decoys?"

The other shook his colossal head.

"I hope not. For all our sakes. That won't make Jetsuenete all that happy."

The two elementals looked back towards their leader who was looking at another dead drowmauder.

"What then, do you suppose it means?" Questioned the silver elemental.

The silent elemental moved up towards Jetsuenete and asked, "Have you seen so many dead drowmauders before?"

"No." Grunted their leader.

That's when the shorter elemental moved in front of Jetsuenete. "Have you ever faced a dark drowmauder on the battlefield? I hear they can wield identical power as the Darkness itself."

"No, I have never given that opportunity of facing one, let alone killing one. But I do cherish the opportunity when it arises."

Suddenly, one of the entourage members calls out. They all rush towards the voice—the far southwest corner of the cavern. The entourage came up to a dull object that caught all their attention. No one said a word. Silence dominated the moment. Then the red elemental snagged the object by its thin blade. The elemental ripped it from its sand and held it out for the rest to observe. It seemed that the red-clad elemental would crush the flimsy object right before their eyes.

"Is this what we all came here to obtain? This false talisman. It's so weak I could crush it with my bare hands, with absolutely no effort at all."

The silver elemental turned to his leader. "The original sword was crafted to perfection. You could hold the sword in your bare hands and feel the celestial power within. The sword was so perfect, Jetsuenete, that you could follow its blade contour with your own eyes, and it wouldn't waiver one inch."

The elemental leader agreed.

"This is false, I do concur. The real Sword of Eternity is still elusive to our grasp."

"Does that mean the Darkness has it, Jetsuenete? Or is it still at large?" Questioned the red elemental.

The red-clad elemental crushed the fake sword in his grasp, sending sharps of flimsy metal everywhere and allowing the broken pieces to fall from his death grip. "We must find the weapon of destruction before our adversary can."

"No. I don't sense the Sword of Eternity in the hands of our enemy. I believe it's still out there somewhere, and only the council knows the talisman's true location."

"Then why all the theatrics?" Questioned the silver elemental.

Jetsuenete looked at his hand, with the blood green bloodstain in his hand.

"I'm not certain, but I think it was the Darkness' way of mocking our efforts. It knows how diligently we have been looking for it."

The silver elemental looked into his leader's eyes.

"But hasn't the Darkness looking for it as well?"

"For other reasons, I must assume, but mainly to keep it out of our hands. But our search for it has been the focus of our entire war effort. The Darkness uses it as a distraction. A pawn on a chessboard." Jetsuenete glanced back towards the cavern entrance and the smoking dragalyite pile. "Now we have two goals to complete. Obtain the Sword of Destinty, before the Darkness has a chance to destroy it. And rescue these poor dragalyites from their bondage."

After the marine unit and most of the elementals had left, Jetsuenete returned to the cavern, where the fake Sword of Eternity now laid in pieces. The elemental leader, for some unknown reason, wanted to inspect the false talisman. Something was drawing Jetsuenete to it that even the elemental couldn't explain.

The cavern wasn't as lit up with all the auditing personal gone, taking their lighting devices away. But Jetsuenete was an elemental, and he didn't need the aid of illumination devices, he could use his fine-tuned sense to maneuver through the darkness of the cavern. The other thing was Jetsuenete could smell the broken talisman, even though it was a false one.

As the elemental leader approached the location where they had left the broken sword, he discovered it lay in four different quadrants; the sword hilt was lying next to the stone blade display. It shattered at the base of the flimsy blade. The second broken part was the false blade's chappe, which only had a small piece of metal. The next and longest blade shard was the bulk of the sword blade. It and the sword tip lay at perpendicular angles to one another. Both shattered pieces seemed to be nearly utterly broken, with very little missing from the break. Jetsuenete could see a heat signature that was separate from the cold steel. The most likely elemental residue left over.

The elemental leader reached down to touch each shard, and then some power seemed to attempt to take over him. The four broken quadrants suddenly pulled together, and powerful darkness reached out to snag Jetsuenete. But the elemental's swift reflexes allowed him to pull away from the power, leaving the dark energy snatching empty air. The elemental could sense the diabolical wickedness coming from the sword. Now Jetsuenete felt the anger of the Darkness radiating from the now complete sword.

"It had always been meant as a trap to capture any elemental too naive not to realize it was a fake." Mumbled Jetsuenete.

That's when a malevolent voice began to boom from the reconstructed fake talisman. "I see you Jetsuenete, master of the elementals."

Jetsuenete took a step back, feeling the shadow ascendancy emanating from the sword.

"I feel the desolation radiating from your false talisman." The elemental knew instantly what was reaching out for him. "You're the rogue entity that attempted to slay all the celestials. They call you the Darkness. The elemental foe we have been battling since the beginning of existence."

The sinister laughter boomed out of the sword's hilt, making the leathery handle glow like it was on fire. "I know who you are as well, elemental. You think you can resist the darkness and my diabolical snare, but your mistaken."

"The only thing that is mistaken is you, keeper of dark shadows. We are going to free those you have enslaved and lay waste to your decrypted armies."

More demonic laughter bellowed inside the elemental leader's head.

"Little do you know how far my reach is, elemental."

Suddenly a puff of black smoke emerged and shot straight for Jetsuenete's head. The elemental's swift reflexes made the attack miss him.

"You failed in your attempt to subvert me."

"Did I now?" Chuckled the Darkness.

Suddenly a blackness surfaced on the elemental's skin like a rash. The skin plague began to spread rapidly, and Jetsuenete fought to keep the darkness at bay. The elemental's head began to spin, and he began to feel nauseous and sick. The elemental did the best he could to fight this vicious attack, utilizing his elemental abilities to subvert it. The darkness battled the celestial descendent as the two ancient powers played tug-of-war with Jetsuenete's body.

The elemental leader dug deep to resist the attack, but if Jetsuenete was going to repel the Darkness' siege, it was going to take everything he had. A deadening pain began to throb through Jetsuenete's arm, and he could feel the plague destroying every cell in his body that it could grab. Luckily the elemental utilized the celestial abilities handed down to him by the celestials and isolated the affliction his nemesis had attacked him.

The numbness of the assault was beginning to subside. Jetsuenete's efforts were being rewarded. That's when the elemental's right arm suddenly raised over his head like an invisible restraint had been locked down on him and wouldn't let go. The elemental tugged at the invisible force, first physically, jerking his arm from its current position and then through an array of elemental techniques that acted as counter-measures to the Darkness' dark energy. But even these ancient methods failed to release Jetsuenete from his bondage.

It was like the elemental leader was a rat trapped in a cage.

Then the darkness' baleful laughter bellowed inside Jetsuenete's head. "I have you, elemental. You're mine, and no matter what you do, you will never escape me."

"We'll see that." Mumbled Jetsuenete. The elemental began to jerk on his seized arm even harder.

A subtle calm suddenly came over Jetsuenete. The voice seemed like a fatherly voice there to calm the descendent of the celestial beings. "You're fighting with the wrong tools, Jetsuenete. You need to be using your inner connection to the Darkness to control the grasp it has on you. Twist the connection like a cleaning rag, until the pain ripples back at your adversary. It will release you, once you have accomplished this."

"Who are you, and how did you get into my head?" Barned Jetsuenete.

"We are the collective voice of the celestials, once a great council of beings. You are our descendent."

"I know who you are, but how did you get into my head? And how do I break the Darkness' stranglehold on me?" Questioned the elemental.

"Calm down." said the celestial voice. "You need to be calm inside your head. Then when your mind is at rest, dig deep for your celestial abilities. Stretch your mind, and then you will be able to extract the Darkness from your mind and your body."

Jetsuenete did exactly what the collective voice had told him. He cleared his mind of everything. He became calm and tranquil, and suddenly the pain from the plague in his body dissipated, and the elemental's strength began to return to him. It was like the calmness was extracting the plague with a hypodermic needle. The elemental felt the dark energy leaving his body.

Jetsuenete ripped his arm from the Darkness' invisible restraint. The Darkness screamed out in a murderous scream. The Darkness was being expelled back into the false talisman, back into its imprisonment where it belonged. The elemental's arm was no longer black. He was free once again.

Then the Darkness yelled at Jetsuenete, before finally vanishing altogether. "You can't get rid of me that easily! I will possess you before the end of this war. You will be my marionette and I, the puppet master."

Jetsuenete stared down at the shattered talisman. The Darkness' attack on him was all over. He took in a deep breath and exhaled. "I'm glad that's over." The elemental leader said under his breath. "But I have the feeling this confrontation is far from over."

CHAPTER 5

The Darkness and its unstoppable army were wasting everything in its path. Nothing living is left in the approaching doom's wake. The Darkness' brigade and their allies grew in strength and equally in their arrogance. Once the army of darkness had laid waste to all living things on a planet, the Darkness army moved onto its next target, just like a virus. What remained could be said not to resemble anything close to what had been there before the invasion—nothing but the charred ground and rotting corpses nourishing the decrypted earth.

The security forces on each planet could sustain the battles against this every growing fighting force for a short while, but they needed aid, and that aid usually came way too late. Nothing seemed to deflect or even slow down the invaders, and very few were left behind to tell the tale of anguish and suffering they had endured.

The Darkness sent one of its most trusted assets, Sharradomina, an ancient being that was infested with the Darkness' most treacherous powers. He was to guide the ascendancy of its shadow forces. It could call on many forms of the Darkness' evil, and the only beings that could challenge this celestial being were the elementals.

The Ragloerilia sky had darkened over its most cultural city Kanta. It was a beautiful metropolis, with large buildings possessing an elegantly designed and made of steel, stone, and other organic material. It had epicenters that drew hundreds of thousands to it to watch sporting events, concerts, and festivals. The city had a set of wondrous gardens that housed rare and exotic flowers that travelers came from light-years away to witness. The aged stones that made up the capitol buildings weren't native from throughout the galaxy, and the buildings had stood for more than one thousand years.

The more the citizens of Kanta watched the darkening clouds looming in the distance, the further the vast dark sky seemed to stretch. It was as if someone had turned off the lights and was covering them with a thick global blanket. Dark and darker, the daytime sky became, and heinous shadows began to creep up the steps of the capitol building, centered in the middle of the city. The inhabitants became enthralled, unable to look away from the oncoming menacing cloud of darkness. The wind began to pick up, and a howling whistle soared through every street in Kanta.

A noise bellowed from a distance forcing every citizen in Kanta to look for its source. It was such a strange sound; it seemed to disorientate the people of Kanta. At first, the noise was subtle and low pitched. It came from a distance and indistinguishable to anything the inhabitants of Ragloerilia had ever experienced before. Then the wind began to pick up, and slowly the cloud cover started to separate, like a velvet curtain drawing back. Behind the dark cloud, a much darker and menacing object loomed over the expanse of the open terrain just south of the city. But as the dark blanketed cloud spread apart, the object exposed itself to be a gargantuan warship of doom. The shadow of the warship consumed the entire region, making it seem more substantial than the city itself.

The warship had an expansive wingspan that the citizens of Ragloerilia had ever experienced. One wing of the ship made up the city threefold, while the front shape of the warship curved inward on both sides like giant tusks on an even larger bird of prey. The head of the ship was oval, and with the reflection of the luminous cloud cover made the underbelly of the vessel seem grey and uninviting. Four massive laser torrents protruded from each wing. Red, Yellow and green beacon lights constantly flashed on the rear wing, underbelly and fore wing of the ship, reflecting off the dense clouds.

Suddenly, a loud horn blew as the cities warning system started to echo. The alert sirens bellowed throughout the city, warning the citizens of Kanta to take shelter. Everyone in the city understood not to take this lightly because the city's warning system rarely was set off. Citizens began to panic and rushed towards their homes or alternative shelters. This made rush created an uncontrollable mob.

One of the Ragloeriliains who had been frozen by the luminous clouds screamed out. "Look over there, beyond the alcove."

In the distance, emerging out of the shadows of the Slopes of Rock-sevain, figures moved swiftly across the open fields towards Katna. At first, the approaching silhouettes seemed nothing but pinpricks scattered across the plains. Someone used a high-powered set of sightseers to mag-nify the figures. At first, the profiles were fuzzy and out of focused. It made the entire scene seem like it was one giant blur, the Kantairan couldn't get them in focus, with the distance the figures were. Then all at once, the oncoming blob became focused and clear. The Kantairan saw a figure leading the marching infestation.

Sharradomina wore his dark armor, and red cloak draped over his left shoulder, blowing in the increasing wind as if he could fly away at any time, led a horde of invading soldiers towards Katna. Then the entire army came into focus, and the invading force revealed itself. Dragalyites, rep-tilian soldiers with chaotic weapons slung over their massive shoulders and Blackmour Drowmauders, who had been allies of the Darkness for centuries, and wielded their dark magic religiously.

The invading army swept across the plains like a swarm of locust devouring a crop field. Dust clouds emerged in their wake and sending the dirt debris high into the air. The city's security force was small and had no hope deflecting this invasion, but they positioned themselves in the path of the invaders anyways, trying to protect the city and its people.

Sharradomina led the Darkness' army into the capital city, crushed through the city gates, and began to vandalize everything in sight. The invaders started burning buildings, slaughtering men, women, and chil-dren in inhumane ways. The invading army moved swiftly through the fall-ing city, creating extreme havoc and fear. Sharradomina sauntered up the stone stair leading to the capitol building, still unscaved like he was taking in the majestic aura of the entire scene and trying to capture the iconic structure before it fell to the invading army. Sharradomina brought out his arms from his cloak and spread them towards the heavens.

Elation spread through every inch of Sharradomina's mortal body. The emotion empowered him and made him feel immortal. The devastation only added to the pleasure. He hadn't experienced a euphoric experience or anything else that had sparked any emotion since he had dedicated his life to serving the master of shadows. But he was sure if he could, the brief sensation traveling through his body, at that moment, would what joy would feel.

"Dark Lord." Prayed Sharradomina. "Help us win the day and give me the power to show these people your majestic power. Show them a better way of life and brace them deep within our bosom."

A loud explosion occurred, sending stone debris everywhere, some falling around Sharradomina, but he doesn't miss a beat. "Music to my ears," boasted Sharradomina. The ground quakes in unison with the explosion, like an orchestra section striking keynotes at the precise time. It was like the Darkness answering Sharradomina's dark prayer, with the quakes and undefined explosions throughout the city.

The wind increased and howled as it blew through the cultural square. It blew Sharradomina's cloak upward, giving off the image that he had created the sudden wind gust. Murderous screams come from behind as dragalyites soldiers slaughter the last remaining security personal. At the same time, blackmour drowmauders utilize their dark abilities to transform the cultural epicenter into a wasteland of collapsed buildings, ruined monuments, and decrypted carnage. Corpses hung out of window sills, stone deteriorated from the dark magic of the drowmauders, forcing the mortar to melt away, roofs collapsed inwards from the pressure of the ruined building structures. Bodies litter the streets, fires are burning, and thick smoke fills the air.

Sharradomina looked skywards into the thick cloud-covered sky with a smile planted on his wicked, pale face. "Master, you would love seeing all this happen. It won't take us long to finish up."

The agent of darkness turned his attention towards the city government building with extreme trepidation filling his body. Venomous thoughts flooded him to the point the puppeteer of the siege that he thought he might fall to the ground. Sharradomina nostrils flared, and his vision focused on the icon of Kantairan society. *I think it's time to resolve some unresolved issues.*

Sharradomina made his move towards the government building with purpose. Step by step, he approached the building, while anticipation began to build in Sharradomina's stomach. His movements were stiff and mechanical, but he didn't realize this at all. The servant of darkness possessed by termination and desire to please his master. The only thing that was on his mind was retrieving the Sword of Eternity and exposing the hideout of the Celestial Council. He was certain they were hiding in the building he now approached. Sharradomina's obsession enthralled his mind.

Finally, the agent of darkness reached the buildings duel doors and swung them open and stepped inside.

The interior of the capitol building was dark, and only limited sunlight penetrated cracks in the wall and ceiling. Despite the lack of illumination, Sharradomina could see perfectly. A gift from his master. Sharradomina heard movement coming from the rear of the council room. The agent of darkness picked up a lighting shell and turned it on. It didn't provide a lot of light, but it did expose part of the council room. He was determined to expose the hiding figure in the room. The shadow agent swung the light towards the rear of the spacious room exposed the hidden priest. Sharradomina leaped at the half-startled religious man.

The priest stumbled as he attempted to back away from Sharradomina. The religious man was frail and thin with pasty white skin. The priest wore a grey cassock that was dirty and missing several buttons down the front. The priest had silver locks of hair that were as filthy as his robe. The religious man had a shocked look on his human face. It was like he had seen a phantom from his past and a revelation in his heart.

The elderly priest was shaking like a junky needing a fix. The Katnorian eyes frozen on his tormentor.

Sharradomina was steaming, hate in his face, and rage in his heart. A fire raged in the agent of darkness' glossy dark eyes. The priest's body froze stiff, and Sharradomina noticed it immediately. The agent of shadows smiled a crooked, devious smile at the priest. Then the agent made his move before the priest could flee.

Sharradomina reached with an invisible hand, grabbed the priest by the throat, and lifted the old man into the air, squeezing tightly around the priest's throat. The agent's razor-sharp claw-like hand dug into the thin Katnorian skin. Blood dripped from the puncture wounds.

Sharradomina looked deep into the eyes of the scarred priest. Deep resignation and anxiety were living inside those grayish-blue eyes.

"Where's the council?" Screamed Sharradomina. Veins protruded from his neck, and hatred exploded from the agent's pores.

The priest was unresponsive. He could only stare into Sharradomina's dark and gloomy eyes. It was like the agent of darkness had placed his victim in a trance. Sharradomina clenched his fists like a boxer, and his heart rate quickened. The servant of the Darkness was having difficulty containing his rage. He hadn't felt such an arrangement of emotions before. It felt as if he would burst like a raging volcano. First, his exasperation from the destruction of the city and its people. Now the deceit from this mortal, shielding the Celestial Council's where-a-bouts. Sharradomina pressed harder on the priest's throat, and more blood trickled down his neck.

"Answer me! Where are the council members that are supposed to be in this room?" Sharradomina brought the frail man closer. "I know they operate out of this building."

The priest mumbled something inaudible.

"What is that?"

Sharradomina wanted to squeeze the life out of the priest but realized if he did that, he would receive none of the answers he was seeking, so the agent relaxed the pressure on the priest's throat.

"The council was never here. Your information is wrong." Whispered the old man, in between gasps.

Sharradomina pressed onto the priest's throat again. The wrathful infernal intensified.

"I'm wrong?" Sharradomina begins to shake the holy man again, but harder. "No, you are the one that is wrong! The celestial council is housed in this building; my resources are impeccable. They must be here. Where are they?"

"I hate to be the bearer of bad news," mumbled the struggling priest. "But the celestial council are apparitions, not of this realm or any other. The members don't exist, not in the sense we know."

"No! I refuse to believe this."

Sharradomina shook the priest like a rag doll.

"Sorry, but only their images projected in this room and rooms across the galaxy."

Sharradomina's face became red with anger.

"If the council isn't here, then where's the Sword of Eternity?"

The priest gave his tormentor another bewildered look.

"What?"

Sharradomina tightened his grip once more and shook his victim violently.

"Where… is… the. sword?"

Sharradomina squeezed until the sounds of breaking bones could be heard. The priest's body goes limp.

"I'm seriously going to be punished for this failure." Whispered Sharradomina.

He remembered the last time he had witnessed an agent of his master failed.

Flashback:

There are shadow agents that spy for this darkness that move among the living. A shadow agent known only as Darkcloak, an extremely powerful agent of the Darkness, one that even rivaled The Shadow Lord itself, passed through the grimy stone structure without being seen. There was a strong resentment from both agents, ever since the arrival of Darkcloak to the Darkness' presence.

Darkcloak wore dark pants that had no visible access to them, sturdy field boots that could withstand the coldest environments and the hottest as well. The agent of darkness also wore a black tunic that covered the sturdy body armor underneath. The shadow agent was draped with a secluded cloak that rendered the agent nearly transparent when in seclusion.

This servant, much like the Shadow Lord, was nearly void of light and only a flicker of illumination would eminent from its menacing cloak on occasion. Darkcloak's cloak didn't only protect the agent of darkness but acted as a barrier against most threats to its master as well. The cloak could render its owner invisible to anything that would threaten Darkcloak. It could also surround the agent of darkness with a protective field.

Sharradomina and Darkcloak stood just outside of their master's chambers. The aurora of the Darkness' prison chamber radiated just outside the skin covered chamber walls. The two shadow agents converse with each other, awaiting an audience with their master. This incident is neither agents' first face-to-face visit with their dark master, and each knew better than to interrupt their master when it was scolding them. It was best to take their licks and survive and diminished for eternity.

Occasion screams echoed through the main chamber door. The agents of darkness were like the subject being interrogated was being shredded inside-out, and the shrills made even the darkest agents shiver in fear.

The dark eyes of the shape-shifting Darkcloak glared at the outer chamber walls of their Master's chamber. There seemed to be detestable rage and fear all mixed into one dreadful gaze. Sharradomina could feel the terror that emanated from within the other agent, and he took it Darkcloack wasn't a timid agent of darkness. Sharradomina always could feel the other dark agents fear, it was a gift he had been born with, and that could have been the reason the master of shadows had chosen him. Unlike the other dark agents subjugated to the darkness or created from the Darkness' use of dark magic, Sharradomina had been born into a different life than the one he was living.

Sharradomina understood that Darkcloak had many assets through many different realms, and he was just one of them. He had never seen Darkcloak so stirred up. The shadow agent seemed overtly worried, but Sharradomina could see deep enough inside of Darkcloak to recognize the origin of the agent's agony.

"Are you all right?" Questioned Sharradomina. "You seem a little on edge."

Darkcloak glared back with a look that made the shadow agent aware that he was already on thin ice. It wasn't the look in Darkcloak's eyes; it was the sense that the shadow agent was sending to Sharradomina. It was like touching a hot stove, and the burning sensation put Sharradomina on notice.

"I'm fine!" snapped Darkcloak.

A scream louder than any they had heard previously echoed down the skin-laded hallways of the Darkness' Bastian. The adjacent wall move like it was alive. His eyes could have been deceiving him because the walls seemed to swell outwards and then retract as if the room was breathing heavily. A waterfall of blood began to cascade down from all sides. It was like the two agents of darkness were directly under the flow of blood. That's when Sharradomina began to hear echoing moans surrounding them, followed by screams of pain and agony. These skin laded walls were crying for mercy.

Sharradomina became pale with fright. He had the look of a man who had just seen something his eyes should have never seen, and he would be scarred for life.

Darkcloak shook his head. "That hasn't happened in a while."

"What hasn't?" Trembled Sharradomina.

"Blood hasn't flown down the bastin walls for a long time. I can't even remember in all the centuries I've served the Darkness, the last time that happened."

"What does it mean? Is it the prisoner's blood or something more sinister?"

The wide entrance doors flew open, and a body was carried out by demonic sentries.

A shadowy figure emerged in the doorway. It was the Shadow Lord, the Darkness' most reliable servant. The atrocious servant, dressed in a dark cassock that only exposed The Shadow Lord's disfigured hands. Sharradomina had never seen the likes of the agent's hands, and he had dealt with many of the Darkness' many shadow agents. Claw-like fingers were folded together in a jester that said their master was ready for them.

"His eminence will see you know." The Shadow Lord announced, more in the form of telepathy than announcing it. Sharradomina couldn't see the agents face if the Shadow Lord had one, but he thought the being had a malicious smile on its face.

Darkcloak turned to Sharradomina. "Whatever you do, don't look the master in the face. He will take it as disrespect, and you might end up like that last fool they had to carry out."

Sharradomina looked back in the direction the body had been carried off towards.

"Then what am I supposed to do in there?" Questioned Sharradomina.

Darkcloak took a deep sigh and shook his head.

"The master is constantly irritable. Do me a favor and let me do the talking. The last thing the master needs to be reminded about is my last failure."

"Failure?" Questioned Sharradomina. "What happened?"

Darkcloak only shook his head again.

Sharradomina and Darkcloak walked through the wide doors and entered the Darkness' chambers. The room was mostly dark with a dense smothering sensation. Darkcloak stepped forward, and then Sharradomina followed close behind. The Chamber walls are constructed of skin and bones, like the outer walls they had witnessed bleeding. The walls seemed to be breathing. Sharradomina thought he had seen the walls move in and out as if the entire room was alive.

With each step, they took the pressure seemed to become more intensified. The two agents were forced to feel their way through the darkness.

Suddenly a booming voice broke the eerie silence.

"Well, what do you want?"

The sound of the booming voice was sinister and bone-chilling. It seemed like it was nearby and far away from all in one. Chills ran down Sharradomina's spine. He suddenly stopped moving towards the booming voice, despite not remembering doing so. But that was a good thing because a barrier had stopped him dead in his tracks, not allowing him to proceed forward any further.

A giant set of fiery orbs appeared in front of them, startling the agent of darkness.

The Darkness looked from one agent to the other with less than enthusiastic energy.

"Are you going to answer me or do I have to make an example of you both as well."

Darkcloak hesitated for a moment then began.

"Master." Darkcloak hesitated a second time. He could only shake his head.

The giant orbs gleaned, and the Darkness began to groan a deep and earth-shaking sound. Darkcloak and Sharradomina knew what was coming.

"You failed me again, Darkcloak. I can feel deep within your very existence."

"Wait, my master." Cried Darkcloak.

The Darkness didn't even bother listening to the agent. Sharradomina moved away from Darkcloak, sensing something about to happen.

Suddenly an invisible hand swept Darkcloak up high into the air where Sharradomina couldn't see the agent of darkness. Still, he could hear Darkcloak choking high above the shadow agent's current position.

Then the sinister voice boomed out over the spacious chamber.

"Time and time again, you have failed me Darkcloak. I have been more than patient with you, and you know the consequences for failure better than any of my agents. I feel your usefulness has come to an end."

Sharradomina could hear Darkcloak pleading for his life and remembered what Darkcloak had said before entering The Darkness' chambers. "Do me a favor and let me do the talking. The last thing the master needs to be reminded about is my last failure." Darkcloak's words echoing inside Sharradomina's head. *That's it!*

Sharradomina threw himself down at the mercy of the Darkness, kneeling on both knees and his arms spread wide. His cloak covered most of his body. He had the appearance of a tortious in its shell. He appeared as if he was frightened for their lives. In a way, he was, but he was also manipulating their master. The other agents of darkness were remnants of the dark celestial, but Sharradomina had been born and not created from nothing, so the Darkness didn't have as much ability to see into his heart and see the deception.

"What is this?" Bellowed the Darkness.

"I must confess, it was all Darkcloak's doing, failing to obtain the sword of eternity, but trust in me, and I won't fail you master."

The set of fiery orbs left Darkcloak and started concentrating on Sharradomina.

The Darkness tossed Darkcloak against the wall. The collision with the chamber wall sent Darkcloak up in a cloud of dark smoke, vanishing before Sharradomina. It was like a magic act, and the mortal servant of the Darkness knew Darkcloak had many forms and hadn't died. Before Sharradomina could blink, Darkcloack's body began to regenerate itself instantly.

The darkness focused all its dark and demented attention on Sharradomina.

What makes you think you can succeed where the other agents of darkness have failed? You're just a mortal, flesh and blood where they are created from my celestial being. They are immortal."

"That's just it master. My mortality is my strength. They think abstractly, as in instinctually, not intellectually. That is where I will succeed."

Darkcloak had nearly regenerated completely and was kneeling near Sharradomina and listening to what the agent had to say.

"Go on." Bellowed the sinister voice of The Darkness.

"I have a rigorous plan to rid us of the elementals, once and for all."

Just then, a drowmauder officer busted his way into the semi-dark room with purple blood stained on the dark elves' forehead, and he was panting heavily.

"Sir, we are being attacked. Its led by some elementals."

Sharradomina dropped the dead priest instantly. "An elemental attack?" His face lit up like a Christmas tree. His usually pale face was bright red, and fire lit in agent's eyes. He was furious that he hadn't seen this coming. "This could put a damper on my plans."

Once Sharradomina got outside, it was apparent that anarchy had set in. A new invasion had begun, and his boss, the Darkness didn't organize it. A flood of solders was now battling on the deck of the steps leading to the capitol building. Sharradomina looked aft, then forward, seeing the chaos surrounding him.

"What's going on here, corporal?"

Sharradomina's head was spinning. This didn't happen to him. He had already failed to deliver on his promise a few times, and another failure could end badly for him.

"They showed up fifteen minutes ago, sir."

Blackmour Drowmauder soldiers were engaged with human legionnaires. He knew them anywhere, their uniform, the weapons they wielded, everything about them was rambling through his nearly photographic brain. Sharradomina could imagine their conquest of the dedicated mortal aids to the elementals. He knew from experience that the drowmauders were master strategists, and the mortal legionnaires were no match for the dark magic they wielded, possessing merely mechanical weapons.

"Heck," mumbled Sharradomina. "They aren't even elementals. At least then, my foes would stand a chance."

And where were the legendary warriors anyways? He wondered.

The bodies laid out before him were dead Drowmauder solders, bloodied and battered with Dragalyites scattered among the dead.

"Sir, I believe this is the only the first wave of attackers. Rumor has it there may be another wave of legionnaires awaiting to besiege us."

Sharradomina lets out a massive scream and flips up his battle cloak in anger.

CHAPTER 6

With the end of the first Celestial Wars and the disappearance of the celestial beings emerged their decedents, the elementals. These eminent new defenders had their prestige and illustriousness. Some of these cosmic warriors were shapeshifters and could generate massive space dragons that breathed ionized gas and cosmic energy.

The elementals were led by an honorable and virtuous leader named Jetsuenete. All this mysterious being wanted was to defeat the Darkness' reckless army and defend those affected by the plague-filled invaders.

Jetsuenete was a mountainous being with luminous golden eyes, a barrel-thick chest that made the elemental appear twice the size of his elemental brothers. All the enigmatic defenders towered over most species, but their leader even dwarfed the most colossal of them all. Jetsuenete's breastplate was wide and broad. It had an enormous crest on the elemental's chest. A titanous dragon with a horrid wingspan filled most of the chest plate and a solid black border around it. The dragon stood straight up as if to challenge its opponent.

His demeanor was always calm, and level headed, especially in the heat of battle. The elemental leader never lost his head and never led those under his command into risky situations. That didn't mean he hadn't lost warriors; he had, but he always chose to justify the means by considering what their sacrifice meant. It was the goal of peace that they fought for, and losing troops was a necessary evil, or at least that's how Jetsuenete chose to spin it.

Four elementals stood at Jetsuenete's side, Dirdanth, a black colored elemental with a silver and red wolves' skull on his chest plate and red tented eyes with their silver-filled pupils were one of Jetsuenete's most trust lieutenants. Gaitharrul, the Gifted who had cobalt blue skin and gray eyes. He had an eagle with its wings spread wide on his breastplate. Then there were the two shape-shifters; Erreodan the Powerful, a loyal and tactical genius with blood-red skin tone and deadly accurate vision. Nightzeneth, with his emerald-green skin and pitch-black eyes, was lethal in the air and used silver ion gas to create anarchy on the battlefield.

Jetsuenete heard the whispers from the two shape-shifters, but he blandly ignored them. He would take no counsel on the approaching day's battle, that's discussed the previous night. Now it was time to concentrate on their foe. Jetsuenete never underestimated any of the Darkness' mass siege efforts. Its armies were too vast for that. The one advantage they had was their superior fighting ability and cunning. It might be that the armies of darkness had the numbers, but the elementals always utilized that to their advantage. A mob of warriors would never defeat experienced solders.

The dawn sky was hazy and gray, with a mist rolling over the flat plains like a predator making a slow approach. The conditions made it difficult to see their adversaries approach, but Jetsuenete could utilize his elemental instincts to find their targets. The Blackmour Drowmauders and their reptilian escorts, the Dragalyites moved slowly through the mist. The bulky lizard soldiers made most of the noise as they marched across the battlefield, which made it easy to track them.

Besides, dragalyites had an aroma that was indistinguishable, supposedly from their unusual diet of high protein and gauser leaves they consumed, only found on their homeworld. It didn't take Jetsuenete's elemental high sense of smell to sense them coming. The elemental leader sensed their movements long before they were spotted.

The blackmour drowmauders, on the other hand, were harder to track in the thick haze. Their size, which was about the size of an average mortal human, hid well among the much larger reptilian soldiers. They were light on their feet, and despite being considerably smaller than their dragalyite escorts, you couldn't take them lightly on the battlefield. They were elusive and skilled with their ancient short battle swords, making them not only stealthy through the mist cover, but lightning-quick on the bat-tlefield. A formidable opponent indeed, but it was equally challenging to kill one with the reptilian bodyguards. The drowmauders were also highly intelligent and had a thousand years to perfect their fighting prowess.

Jetsuenete scanned the plains in detail, as if he was floodlight in a light-house, scanning the coastline for endangered ships. It was difficult to see in the dawn light, and the rolling haze provided cover for the approaching army. But the elemental had keen eyesight and would catch any move-ment. Then it happened! A shadowy figure emerged from the haze, not all that distinguishable at first, but Jetsuenete could tell what it was.

"A blackmour drowmauder." The elemental leader mumbled.

But that was unusual, thought the elemental leader. The dark elves always were shielded by several dragalyites. He also knew it was a drow-mauder was the elemental could barely hear anything as the shadowy fig-ure moved, gingerly as if it was walking on eggshells. Jetsuenete tensed up but still refused to leap into action. He wanted to be sure what he was witnessing before committing their army to battle.

That's when another shadowy figure emerged. This one was less diffi-cult to discern. The silhouette had broad shoulders and appeared to be a third taller than the first figure. Even without the ability to see the figure's ashy gray reptilian skin and black splotches immersing the skin surface pronouncing it as a colonel dragalyite, Jetsuenete knew them by smell. These were the original dragalyites from the Geogawa moon, a providence to the dragalyite home world, not the ones that had spread out through the cosmos. Jetsuenete herd the figure's heavy footsteps crushing the bare surface, Jetsuenete knew them by smell.

Another shadowy figure emerged, then a third one. The dragalyite escort had arrived, even though they seemed to be lagging their charge.

"There you are, my lizard friends," Mumbled the elemental. "Feeling a little sluggish this morning? Didn't eat a good breakfast, did we?"

That told Jetsuenete something.

From his understanding, the substantial lizard creatures never missed a chance at a meal, and breakfast was a vital portion of their diet. They consumed a lot first thing in the morning. They had to refuel their mountainous bodies but could go nearly all day without feeding. Maybe that's why the Darkness chose them as soldiers, but Jetsuenete knew that would-be speculation, not fact.

If the dragalyite solders were skipping their morning meal, could that mean they were running low on supplies with no way to recoup their losses? Wondered the elemental.

Just at that moment, the figures emerged from the protection of the haze, and Jetsuenete could see the elemental adversaries clear as day. The blackmour drowmauder, with their purple-tinted skin and dark blue armor, stood out on bright sunlight of the day, with his three dragaly-ite escorts. Their movements were deliberate and hadn't changed since emerging from the sea of haze.

The elemental could see the dragalyite's archaic and ancient weap-ons cutting through the haze. Their species had refused to adapt to the changing technology that most armies used. Their species was an ancient one, and they believed their weapons were a sign of their endurance and paid tribute to their ancient heritage. The first lizard soldier carried a long, bronze handle with an elongated blade that seemed as long as its pom-mel. The blade was thick and serrated on the inner half. Jetsuenete had to assume it was used for slashing and beheading the wielder's enemies.

The middle dragalyite carried a rusty sword blade that was thick in the middle and possessed a similar serrated edge. The dragalyite solder held it in one hand that made it appear as a one-handed sword, but the elemental leader understood the size of the lizard solder and assumed it would have been a two-handed sword for must any other species. The third escort possessed what appeared to be a hunting boy with slots for triple arrows. The boy, itself towered just over the massive creature, making the dragaly-ite dwarfed in comparison.

Gaitharrul, the gifted, approached the elemental leader and stopped just to Jetsuenete's left.

Jetsuenete nodded in acknowledgment and said, "A scouting party."

"Or a decoy," Gaitharrul added. "What are your orders, Jetsuenete?"

"We will stand fast and wait until the rest of the army emerges. That shouldn't take much longer. I sense they are not far behind."

Gaitharrul nodded his understanding.

Behind the two elementals, Erreodan's growl is heard.

"Let's strike them now while we have the haze to keep them blinded and unaware."

Jetsuenete raised his elemental fist, and Erreodan halted in his tracks as if a strange force had hit the elemental. He knew not to cross their leader. "No, Erreodan. I don't want to begin the attack before our enemy exposes their numbers."

Erreodan huffed and stormed back to where he was in their observation party.

Nightzeneth was forced to hold his brother back. He could see Erreodan digging his feet into the dirt.

Gaitharrul, with a stern expression, nodded. "Good call."

Jetsuenete took a deep breath and waited for their adversaries. He didn't have to wait long.

Soon more dragalyite and drowmauder soldiers emerged from the murky cover exposing their massive numbers. It was just what the elemental leader had feared. Inch by inch, their adversaries began to consume the plains, like locus to a field of corn. Their adversaries spread out over the baron field. The Darkness' army was larger than the elementals could count. He now could hear Erreodan's mocking tone. "I told you we should have attacked while we had the haze for cover."

That always ate away at Jetsuenete. Erreodan knew how to get under their leader's skin, but he never allowed his troops to know this. The last thing they needed was turmoil in their ranks. That would doom their efforts, and that would crush any chance anyone would have to survive the army of darkness and their malicious intent.

"Prepare the fliers!" Barked the elemental leader. Jetsuenete to Nightzeneth in a no-frills manner. "Nightzeneth use your ion gas fire to give us cover." Jetsuenete knew that without the haze for cover, their approach could be seen from far off. The silver ion gas from Nightzeneth would provide some protection, at the least, once the haze dissipated.

Nightzeneth leaped into action as the shape-shifting elemental propelled his body off the towering ledge, towards the plains below, disappearing into the fading haze. Jetsuenete heard Dirdanth mumble something inaudible under the elemental's breath. The elemental had always hated Nightzeneth's zeal for adventure and leaping off high peaks to the surface below. It was like the shape-shifters were teenagers, and Jetsuenete, Dirdanth, and Gaitharrul; acted as the parents. But the elemental leader didn't have time to worry about Nightzeneth. They had a battle to wage, and they are seriously outnumbered.

That's when they heard leathery wings snap open and began to flap against the wind. That's when they knew Nightzeneth was officially on the prowl. It always had a daunting sound that could unnerve anyone, even a veteran like Jetsuenete. Erreodan followed his brother over the edge and Jetsuenete followed the shape-shifter's decent. The second space dragon opened his wings before disappearing from their sight. So, it had begun.

Without turning towards Dirdanth, Jetsuenete ordered, "Take your troops and cut our uninvited guests off on the western plain."

Dirdanth moved swiftly to execute their leader's demand.

"What about my men?" Questioned Gaitharrul

"As usual, Gaitharrul. You will take the eastern plain and pinch the raging army into a bottleneck. There my regimen will cut them down. Hopefully, our shape-shifting brothers can cut down some of the masses and even out the numbers."

This is how the elementals had always defeated the Darkness' forces. Jetsuenete didn't see any reason to abandon what had always worked for them.

~

The battlefield quickly became a horrendous mess of dead and mutilated bodies. Blue, green, yellow, and red blood stained the battlefield like a blood stew. Severed arms still held their weapons. Boots stuck in the blood-filled mud without their owners anywhere to be found. Soldiers from both sides must maneuver the slippery ground to avoid falling. Metal weapons clash and filling the air with a sound so deafening; it could be heard throughout the plains and beyond.

The silver ion haze draped the battlefield from Nightzeneth. It lingered low and made it difficult for either side to gauge the other's position. Even with their superior senses, the elementals struggled to see the other side of the slaughter. The only way Jetsuenete knew someone had died was by the skin-curling screams of death that emerged from the artificial haze cover.

The elementals and their allies sliced through the allies of the Darkness like they were target practice, not as a threating adversary. Bodies of dragalyites and blackmour drowmauders lay in Jetsuenete's path. There were always elusive to his blade, and Jetsuenete usually was forced to settle on slaughtering more of the lizard soldiers than blackmour drowmauders. The elemental leader swung his flail high over his massive body, smashing the weapon's spiked ball on a thick chain against dragalyite solders, knocking the bulky, slow adversaries aside with ease.

Jetsuenete's huge two-handed sword utilized in killing significant adversaries, such as high-level dark officers. The sword is forged with a mountainous crest, a titanous dragon with a horrid wingspan, and detailed sketching on each wing phalanx and had a specific elemental saying in an ancient language long abandon. There was a solid black border around it the pommel crest, and the dragon stood straight up as if to challenge any would-be enemies. The sword never left its sheave, which is strapped to the elemental's back.

The elemental leader maneuvered around the liter of bodies in his path, searching for more targets. The cling, cling of combatants dueling lingered in the hazy air. As Jetsuenete moved through the mass of engaged soldiers, the sea of combatants thinned, like the leader was parting the red sea. Then three figures appeared directly in front of the elemental leader.

Two dragalyite solders in their rusted, armor, that appeared two sizes too small, with their bulky size, thick barreled chests begging to be released from their restricted prison. These lizard soldiers held their archaic weapons that seemed to be as much a tie to their ancient culture as anything had, tightly in their reptilian grips. These weapons seemed as rusted and chaotic as their armor. Jetsuenete noticed how each dragalyite was gripping their individual weapon. That told the elemental leader just about everything he needed to know about his adversaries. Their grip was tight, with extreme tension; that's how the elemental knew both solders were anxious and tense. That could be used to his advantage.

But he was reluctant to slaughter them. How could the elemental kill the species he was attempting to liberate from the Darkness' grasp? But these two protectors weren't giving him many options.

Then there was the drowmauder officer that was under the lizard solders protection. The dark elf wore his blue-tinted armor that looked as if it had never been used in battle. Jetsuenete's actual target. The drowmauder had the appearance of being newly instated as a field leader and Jetsuenete assumed his armed escort was working diligently to keep this officer looking pristine. Oh, the elemental leader, through the many expeditions he had lead, knew that the drowmauder officer wasn't unarmed. Most possessed field daggers that could be utilized in close combat and as a last resort to commit suicide.

This is going to be a treat. Thought Jetsuenete. *Killing a drowmauder is a rare thing indeed. But it won't make-up for the two slaves I'm about to send to their graves.* Jetsuenete could feel marginal of sorrow for the enslaved bruits.

His sword blade had only ended the lives of a handful of drowmauders. The only thing that would be more satisfying to the elemental leader would be to get his hands on a dark magic-user. These chosen few held the key to the Darkness' power. *That would be a gift, indeed-* Jetsuenete thought.

The elemental looked from one dragalyite to the other. The lizard soldier had a shoulder-length, battle-ready stance. Well trained indeed. The distance between the two lizard soldiers was just enough that you could fit the drowmauder officer they were protecting, but not much more. He would need to be cunning and swift to take them both out. Dragalyites were tough to expose, but Jetsuenete knew their weaknesses since he had fought thousands of them before.

The elemental took one step towards them, forcing the protector to grip it's weapon tighter than before, but not pushing the soldier to engage. Jetsuenete understood they would wait to see what he had in mind before leaving their charge. Unlike most dragalyites, which would blindness leap into a confrontation without having a plan of action, escort trained to keep their charge protected at all costs until they forced to abandon their duties and engage an attacker.

Jetsuenete knew he had the dragalyite protectors on edge. He felt the drowmauder officer becoming anxious. The dark elf kept hiding behind one of his protectors, then switching to another, as if the officer hoped to confuse the elemental. Jetsuenete began to move, swinging his flail, attempting to get the dragalyites to commit to attack.

This only seemed to agitate the lizard soldiers, and they looked at one another as if to gain confidence from the other. Jetsuenete could sense their hesitation, he could even see it in their eyes. If he were going to draw them from their charge, he would have to make both dragalyites feel threatened at the same time. The elemental leader made his move and swept to the left of their protective line, drawing the far left dragalyite.

The other reptilian solder moved to protect the officer in the face of Jetsuenete's farce attack, leaving gaps in the solder's defense.

The engaging dragalyite solder set his reptilian feet to position for the attack, which forced the protector off-balanced and not nearly prepared as the reptile should have been. Jetsuenete whipped his flail towards his target's head, forcing the dragalyite solder to curl into a ball-like defensive stance. The spiked end of the flail struck the dragalyite square in the chest, sending chards of rusted metal in every direction and throwing the reptilian towards the blood-stained ground.

Jetsuenete's false attack fooled both soldiers, and now one was out of the way. The elemental moved swiftly towards his next target. The second dragalyite now had too much ground to protect, leaving the officer exposed. The elemental's opponent shuffled its feet, trying to cover as much ground against the towering elemental. Jetsuenete saw the dragalyite now backing up, as well as losing an excellent defensive angle. By the time the reptilian could gain any solid footing, it was too late.

Jetsuenete slipped by the dragalyite solder, striking his adversary with the spikey end of his flail and the weapon stuck deep into the reptilian's rusty armored chest. Then the elemental ripped his weapon from his opponent's chest, sending green blood flying everywhere and leaving a fatal wound. The elemental then struck the dragalyite in its scaly throat with his broadsword. The attack ripped the reptilian's head from its shoulders and with the dragalyite's head, still inside its battle helmet, rolled away, still seeping reptilian blood.

Jetsuenete and his target were now face-to-face. The drowmauder had no place to flee to, like a rat trapped in a cage. The elemental leader would relish his victim's last remaining moments. The officer staggered about as if not sure how to respond, Jetsuenete figured his adversary wasn't sure if to attack or flee suddenly. The elemental leader tossed down his flail, and the spiked end stuck into the battle ground. He didn't need the spiked weapon any longer. With the difficult part of his siege complete, the elemental began to grip his two-handed sword in his meaty grasp. Despite the lives taken from its still razor-sharp blade, the sword glistened as if it had never been used.

Jetsuenete rotated the sword from one large hand to the other, taunting his victim. The dark elf backed up a few more steps, gaining more space between the two adversaries. There was fear in the dark elves' eyes; Jetsuenete sensed the drowmauder's agitation. In a sudden move of desperation, the drowmauder pulled out a long knife and shook as the officer held it in both hands. The officer was shaking immensely and made Jetsuenete laugh.

"Come now drowmauder," mocked Jetsuenete. "I know you can do better than that. All that's going to do is irritate me."

Jetsuenete witnessed the dark elf take another step back and tighten the grip on the bladed weapon. The elemental understood the blackmour drowmauder was tensing up; trepidation was taking control. Something the elemental leader could take advantage. *But does the servant of darkness planning on taking me on, the leader of the elementals with a knife?*

Jetsuenete raised his colossal broad sword to a fighting position. The sword pommel was just about level with the elemental's breastplate and gripped the sword firmly. His bulging forearm muscles flexed and nearly exploded from beneath Jetsuenete's armor, making the elemental even larger. Nothing except the elemental leader could wield the gargantuan weapon at such a position and keep it steady. It must have frightened his opponent to death, but none of that mattered to Jetsuenete. All he was thinking about was slicing the drowmauder into millions of particles.

The elemental leader took one step at a time, towards the drowmauder, since was no reason to panic or rush this. He wanted to savor every moment, and the euphoria of the moment was quite intoxicating. Jetsuenete had tunnel vision, and nothing would derail this slaughter, not the intense fighting, the clanging of weapons, nor bloodshed surrounding. Not even the siege of ion fire raining down around them like a baptism or the screams of agony and pain.

The elemental leader slowly reduced the distance between himself and the torrid dark elf. The drowmauder wouldn't be allowed to flee, losing the elemental's chance at spilling the dark elves' blood. Jetsuenete gripped the sword pommel a little tighter, feeling the ancient marital in his bare elemental hands. The exquisite martial of the sword pommel just felt right to him. Nothing meant to be one more than the pommel and Jetsuenete's hands.

Suddenly, while Jetsuenete was preoccupied with his prey, something struck the elemental square in the back and snapped his concentration. The blow wasn't debilitating enough to injure the great warrior, but it did manage to draw Jetsuenete's attention. Anger now resonated from the elemental so fierce that could kill his opponent without thrusting the blade at all and that was rare, since elemental rarely displayed emotions at all.

He thrusted the mammoth sword into the battlefield surface, leaving the great pommel and a third of the sword blade exposed; as if the devastated ground was a place holder. The mountainous elemental spun around to face the dragalyite he hadn't killed. Jetsuenete clenched his fists and held back the massive rage he felt within himself.

The elemental shook his head. How could he have been so naive? Forgetting the guardian as he had. Now Jetsuenete had the reptilian's rust weapon protruding from his back. The elemental reached back and extracted the dragalyite's weapon from his back. The mammoth warrior stared at the rust, curved blade of the crude and ancient weapon. The material's pitted, as if it had been around for over a millennium. The elemental could feel all the lives it had taken, all the blood it had spilled, all the victories it had won.

Jetsuenete ran his finger over the crudely produced blade. The entire dragalyite ancestry flushed from the blade into the elemental. All the reptilian cultures could be seen in one flash. More than a millennium and a half rushed through Jetsuenete in a heartbeat. The elemental finally understood their species—a tear formed in his right eye. Jetsuenete felt the species, pain, their agony, all their loss.

The elemental received a rush of pain so severe that it nearly sent the elemental to his knees. The agony that followed like a train car with no brakes. It wasn't something as simple as if Jetsuenete could separate the dragalyite pain from their suffering. The elemental couldn't even stop the rush of emotions; the blade was filling him. It was like nothing he had ever felt before. It felt like he was a flamed, burning to death with no way to subside the agony filling inside.

The dragalyite's hadn't always been loyal to the Darkness. They hadn't lived for the servitude; like the drowmauder, they had been forced into bondage. They lived in slavery and died on worlds they could care less about. If given a choice, the reptilians would never slaughter those that their crude blades shed.

"You, poor soul." Whispered Jetsuenete. "You never stood a chance, did you? You never wanted to slaughter all those that have died by your blade. You have been forced to kill when killing wasn't in your heart."

The elemental looked past, the hate in the dragalyite, looked past all the misgivings it had performed. The elemental experienced this slave's very torture, calling out for help. Killing the reptilian wouldn't be sorrowful; it would be a gift, a releasing of the dragalyite from its bondage. A halo surrounded Jetsuenete's target.

Then the dragalyite snarled at the elemental, snapping Jetsuenete from his vision.

Jetsuenete tosses down the rusty weapon he had been attacked with and had left a superficial wound on his back, as if it was diseased.

The dragalyite solder ripped its battle helmet from its scaly head. The drowmauder protector's reptilian nostrils were flaring madly, and the solder's crooked teeth were now exposed in a horrific snarl. Jetsuenete could tell that the protector had been in its share of conflicts. A portion of its teeth was now missing. The teeth that remained in the dragalyite's mouth were either partially broken off or crooked or misaligned.

Neither combatant possessed a weapon. The dragalyite weapon was lying near Jetsuenete, and the elemental's flail tossed down. The elemental wasn't about to waste the usage of his broadsword on this beaten-down creature. It was evident enough he had enough damage already. Jetsuenete squeezed his large hands open and shut. He knew the only way to take on this unfortunate, demented foe was to battle the dragalyite in hand-to-hand combat.

The elemental bowed at his opponent.

"I salute you, my foe. I honor your battle-laden skills and your loyal servitude, even if it's a service to a deceitful master."

The dragalyite let out a loud wail. "What do you know, elemental about my servitude?"

"I understand more than you may fathom. Holding your weapon, as I did, I saw not only the lives you have taken with it but your entire species history. It's one of pain and suffering."

The dragalyite didn't bother to hesitate after that. It was like Jetsuenete's words had triggered something within the reptile. His opponent charged the elemental with all the dragalyite's energy. Even though the protector had a limp and wasn't even as balanced and swift as the elemental leader, he wasn't about to take the reptilian lightly. The dragalyite reached out with its jagged claw-like fingers, but the elemental side-stepped his opponent with ease, forcing the solder to stumble and fall to the blood-soaked ground.

Jetsuenete faced his fallen adversary and waited for the dragalyite to recover. The battered reptile slowly got to its feet, snarling at Jetsuenete. It was like the creature's way of cursing at the elemental. The dragalyite's failed attack only enraged it more. Jetsuenete allowed the dragalyite to make its overly-aggressive move once again. That was his style of fighting. Jetsuenete was never slower than his opponent and could easily react to any assault that any opponent might make.

It didn't take very long before the dragalyite made its next move against Jetsuenete.

The protector leaped at Jetsuenete, but the elemental didn't react too hastily. Patience was an inherent trait of the descendants of the celestials. The elemental awaited until the enormous creature was nearly on top of him before he utilized his lighting quick reactions and snagged the dragalyite by the wrists. The elemental could feel the brute strength of his adversary; fierce and savage. The protector wasn't holding back at all. Jetsuenete believed the rush of emotions the reptilian was experiencing might have made his opponent stronger than normal.

The elemental held the reptilian at arm's length, as the two combatants danced around like a duet who had practiced their dance of death, for hours. One gained momentum over the other for a bit, and then the advantage switched to the other. Both combatants struggled against one another, but no matter how much the dragalyite gained on Jetsuenete, it was never going to win. It was like the elemental leader was merely toying with his opponent.

Suddenly, the reptilian solder got close enough to scratch Jetsuenete on his right cheek. Slowly tangerine blood began to trickle from the wound and the dragalyite's jagged claw. The elemental touched the wound and massaged his blood between his forefinger and thumb. The elemental was now done playing around. Jetsuenete snatched the dragalyite by the throat with such swift aggression, before the reptilian could react. The elemental's opponent struggled with his overpowering grip. Time seemed to all but slip past, as Jetsuenete watched as life slowly was going from his opponent's eyes. Then the elemental leader snapped back to reality and struck the protector drowmauder square in the jaw.

The elemental strike sent the combatant tumbling head over heels before the dragalyite landed face-first.

While the elemental leader's attention was averted and his defense torn away, the elemental was struck in the hip. When Jetsuenete turned around, he noticed the drowmauder officer backing away. His original target had snuck upon him. That's when he noticed the drowmauder dagger stuck in his hip. It hadn't penetrated the armor, but the metal surface was pinching his skin. The only thing that had saved Jetsuenete from injury was his impenetrable armor.

Jetsuenete slowly removed the blade. It was like being relieved of a severe ailment, but the marriage of his armor to his elemental skin still rubbed against him, giving the elemental leader some discomfort he was forced to ignore. The elemental leader began to walk towards the dark elf. "You little conniving…" Jetsuenete began. That's when the sound of the dragalyite solder arising from the ground, as the reptilian moaned in agony. The elemental had a choice to make. Which target to engage?

Would it be the officer, which would be an easy kill or the protector? Either way, he was going to have to deal with the protector. The next question was, did he have the desire to fight two adversaries at once or take on the more skilled fighter and risk letting his target escape? But why hadn't the drowmauder fled while Jetsuenete and his protector were squaring off?

The officer faded into the ion mist, now enveloping the entire battlefield.

The two behemoths stood face to face. Jetsuenete clenched his fists, loosening them up, despite having been engaged with the reptilian already. The two adversaries engage each other, the dragalyite attempting to dig its claws into the elemental's skin, but only managing to catch the sturdy armor plating. Jetsuenete clasped his powerful hands onto the rusted amour of his opponent and nearly ripped it clean off the reptile.

Jetsuenete felt the dragalyite forcing down on his upper armor that refused to give an inch; while he ran his hands up to the scaly neck of his opponent. The elemental grabbed the protector's shoulder line and pressed down. He instantly could sense the dragalyite was in agony. The reptilian's grip loosened, and his opponent nearly fell to the ground. Jetsuenete balled a fist up and struck his opponent, almost in the same spot as before. The dragalyite protector spun around and fell flat.

Jetsuenete knew this time he had knocked the dragalyite out cold. He grabbed hold of the solder's back plate armor, and it nearly crumbled under the elemental's massive strength. He ripped the plate off and that when the elemental leader gasped. Slash marks filled the guardian's back.

He had heard rumors of dragalyite abuse and the stories that accompanied them, but this was the first time the elemental saw first-hand the results of this.

Jetsuenete couldn't finish off the creature. It was one of the reasons the elementals were fighting the Darkness armies, to free those enslaved. The drowmauder officer might have been this poor creature's tormentor. But there were rumors of abuse all over. It might be the reason those that survived, always seemed hardened and difficult to defeat. Their perseverance alone was an attribute Jetsuenete, or any other solder could admire.

This was only fueling Jetsuenete's anger towards the drowmauder.

He left the dragalyite where he lay and marched towards the ion mist.

The level of anger towards his target was now at a level that nothing, outside of his demise, would prevent the elemental leader from killing the blackmour drowmauder officer. He danced through the silver haze like a seasoned captain, guiding his starship to an unknown destination. Jetsuenete may not be able to see through the ion haze, but the elemental didn't need his sight to track the drowmauder. He could sense his targets panic and traced the dark elves movements this way.

Jetsuenete watched with his superior mind as the officer stumbled and made his way through the ever-thickening haze. The dark elf had fallen numerous times, which reduced the distance between them, to the point that drew the elemental leader to within striking distance of no more than twenty meters. That's when the blackmour drowmauder's energy signature outline emerged. The officer was lying on the ground as if he had fallen or was resting. *Could he think he was now safe from my pursuit?* Wondered Jetsuenete.

The elemental emerged from the haze and stood before the drowmauder. Suddenly the officer noticed he was being observed and looked Jetsuenete's way. A look of shock came across the dark elves face. The elemental thought his target was experiencing high levels of anxiety be the way the drowmauder was looking in every direction for an escape route. There was none.

Jetsuenete removed his broadsword from its sheath.

The officer stood up and began to beg for his life, but Jetsuenete was having none of it. He refused to listen to the officer's pleas. The elemental took two steps towards his target, which made the drowmauder stumble as the officer tried to back away from his approaching doom. The dark elf fell over again, this time unable to swiftly get his feet. Jetsuenete raised his weapon as if paying hums to some war god in the sky and allowing the flashes of light that could sneak through the ion haze, reflect off the broadsword's blade.

"You don't deserve the life you have been given." Called out Jetsuenete. "You have chosen the path of deceitfulness and inflicting pain. For this, I will end you. It's not the death you deserve. That's far too good of one for the likes of you, but it is the death I will deliver to you."

Jetsuenete brought down the enormous broadsword down on his victim, slicing the blackmour drowmauder in half, ending the officer's life. Purple blood painted onto Jetsuenete breastplate and his exposed face, making the elemental, just for a brief moment one with his victim.

CHAPTER 7

More than a thousand years ago, during the 2ˢᵗ Great Celestial Wars.

The encased darkness consumed everything inside the Merciless Reach. Even in places where light could penetrate, it appeared as a grayish tint in the sky. Horrid sounds echoed from the farthest shadows as darkness continuously beckoned for Sharradomina, sending shivers up his mortal spine. A continuous stench laced across the land like a looming mist cloud. The smell was like raw sewage covering the dark sky and it made Sharradomina cringe every time he came to the Darkness' home. But that wasn't the only thing that would make the agent of darkness take pause in the Merciless Reach.

If Sharradomina thought the stench in the air was unbearable, he definitely hated the one resonating from the ground, it was ten times as worse. The reeking sensation immenating from the decayed top soil, which was as foul as the one looming airborne over the decrypted terrain.

The atrocious scent reminded Sharradomina of rotting meat that had been left out in the sun for much too long. It made the mortal want to vomit the instant he arrived. Put both smells together and you had the sense of what the Merciless Reach was like to outsiders. One large decaying land mass of rotting meat that only beings such as the Darkness and those in its servitude could bear.

The mortal agent of darkness had never been so afraid in his life, despite having been in the land of his dark master a few times. With each visit to the Merciless Reach, his stomach had become queasy, as if he would throw-up and his skin felt like it would shrivel up like a prune and he would die. And it wasn't just the scent of the place that kept Sharradomina uneasy. Something much more powerful was at work and Sharradomina had never been able to place a finger on what it was.

The pain wasn't just in his gut, but that's where Sharradomina focused most of his undivided attention to. Watching species die in front of him didn't make him queasy, nor did blood and guts spilling onto the battle-field. He had become accustom to the sight and smell of death, but this place was a hole other issue onto itself. Once the aroma of the Reach ran up his humanoid nostrils, it began to work on all Sharradomina's senses at once.

While his attention was diverted towards his nausea, the rest of his body was numb. The agent of darkness hadn't realized his skin was decaying and his muscles had been temporarily encapsulated. But all the Merciless Reach's side effects would reverse once he left.

Sharradomina had lived a normal life up to the point he had been captured and forced to serve under the master of shadow's wing. The memory of the place he used to live in had long past him, along with the location, but what he could remember were the set of demonic eyes emerging out of nowhere as if an empty void had opened and his captures had seized him.

Sharradomina had a numbing feeling that felt like the feeling he was feeling inside the Merciless Reach. Somewhere in the back of his mind he had an answer to it all. Maybe the Darkness' energy was imbedded in the creatures that had come for him, or some other mystery of the cosmos that was unexplainable, but the correlation was there deep inside his cerebral cortex. But all of that had been lost once the Darkness made him into Sharradomina, the most efficient mortal spy of darkness.

The two servant guards drug him along the darkened plain and towards the Darkness' home, the towering bastin that loomed over the dark, decayed land like a leviathan stand guard. He could tell there would be no escaping them, their massive strength barred down on his frail arms like clamps of steel. His escorts didn't just have grips of iron-clad restraints; they were substantial talons with sharp claws that penetrated his very skin. The question that rattled around in his racing mind, seemed to be, were his escort's claws made of steel or were they wearing some type of glorified body armor?

The sound of their foot-falls shook the ground continuously, making Sharradomina's escorts seem like dark leviathans crushing the crusted earth beneath them. Decayed shards of ground flew at their prisoner, as they made their way closer to their destination. The constant rubbing of their rustic armor irritated Sharradomina's senses, while the pain of their death-grip on his shoulders kept his focus derailed from any one agonistic element. That was another thing that confused the mortal prisoner about his captures. In his overactive mind that seemed to wonder, Sharradomina felt they had to be wearing body armor. No species had ever had skin what fought against exterior clothing like the armor, or supposal armor, like his escorts did.

It was like the armor, no matter what it was made of, was fighting the creature's own skin, whatever that was made of. The more Sharradomina pondered the idea, the more he became confused and was lost in his own pit of emptiness known as the mortal's own mind.

Sharradomina didn't see the looming tower prison, but he could feel its damaging effects, once they moved into its colossal shadow. The bastin's shadow was darker than the gray tinted landscape, turning the already dismal realm into an even darker existence. But it wasn't just the imposing shadow that inflicted him. It was the Darkness' own dark power resonating like a dark pulsar star awaiting to unleash havoc on local star systems.

The pressure looming in the Darkness' tower was intense, even more intense than he had ever experienced. It was like a magnificent being sitting on top of Sharradomina's frail chest and he couldn't breathe. With every breath he took in, Sharradomina could feel the burning of the decrypted air that occupied the Merciless Reach. The commination only made it tougher for the mortal to concentrate on the essential functions of life.

The Shadow Lord awaited the visitor at the lone entrance into the Darkness' decrypted fortress. Despite the inability for Sharradomina to see its face, he could tell it was gloating at the sight of Sharradomina. That eerie sense and his gargantuan escorts slowing their pace, told the prisoner he had arrived at his destination. For some odd reason, Sharradomina that his pain had only begun and The Shadow Lord's fun was about to begin.

Sharradomina felt the Shadow Lord's gratification in seeing him fail, and the sight of his body being dragged across the darkened plain was immensely pleasurable for the Shadow Lord. The mortal agent of darkness could sense the powerful emotion emanating from it, even though, from his own understanding of the immortal servants of darkness, they felt no emotions at all.

The Shadow Lord chortled as Sharradomina's escorts dragged him reluctantly through the front chamber door. The Shadow Lord's voice sounded like a pack of starved demon hounds battling over a discarded piece of meat, to Sharradomina. The prisoner looked up and Sharradomina thought he sensed the agent of darkness smiling at him, but he couldn't tell; The Shadow Lord had no physical shape to concentrate on. The dark being was like a dark phantom floating in the shadows.

"It's so good to see you again Sharradomina." Barked the Shadow Lord. "So much pain. So much torture to do, heck we can't decide where to begin."

Sharradomina squirmed. There was nowhere he could hide from his master's stare. The Darkness could get to him from anywhere it chose.

"Wait! I can explain everything. You don't have to do this."

Shadow Lord's laughter bellowed down the hall as the agent closed the colossal doors behind them.

Sharradomina's escorts drug him into a dark room deep inside The Darkness' resident. It was one of many that Sharradomina had heard about, but never had a chance to experience first-hand. His escorts had been replaced by even larger, darker figures hovering mountainous over his frail body.

Sharradomina was still dizzy from his lengthy trip across decrypted terrain. The Shadow Lord didn't give the mortal any time to recover. The most trusted agent of the Darkness sieged Sharradomina by the throat and lower jaw, digging its lacerating claws into his skin. The mortal agent could feel the bone-crushing strength of the Shadow Lord and he thought the being might just kill him where he lay. That wouldn't be out of character for it, because rumors had told of the Shadow Lord's occasional rage and taste for death. *There goes another thought of emotion,* Sharradomina echoed inside his own mind. *For a being that was supposed to be void of emotion, The Shadow Lord surely expressed more than its share.* Rage was the translucent creature's greatest ally.

Blood began to drip from the wounds inflicted by the Shadow Lord and the translucent being without a face began to toy with its victim. Sharradomina could see the Shadow Lord clearly now and just as he feared, his tormentor had no face at all. The place where the being's face should have been, was nothing but an empty void so black he thought he might be looking into the depths of a black hole, from its event horizon.

Then the Shadow Lord began to speak to Sharradomina in a wicked tongue, meant to insult and undermine its victim without driving them insane. But since the Shadow Lord had no mouth to speak, it used a form of telepathic communication. As the Shadow Lord spoke it was like a horrid deep pitch voice, one that could only be found in the darkest places ever known.

"Now I have you, scum! A rat in a cage with no place to run. Your substantial failures and mortal antics have forced my hand. Now we both must answer for our sins, to the master of darkness. For this, I will crush your very soul with my own hand."

The Shadow Lord released its death grip on Sharradomina and motioned for him to stand.

"Pick him up." Ordered the Shadow Lord, emotionlessly.

A set of behemoth hands gripped Sharradomina tightly and with very little effort lifted him straight up. Then as easily he was lifted, the owner of the barbaric hands dropped him. Sharradomina landed hard on his knees, sending jolts of pain surging up his thighs and paralyzing his already numb legs.

An agonizing cry penetrated Sharradomina's lips and escaped his mouth. The cry oscillated throughout the darkened room and returned to its owner magnified, leaving Sharradomina temporarily paralyzed. The mortal cringed at the oscillation, only adding to the Shadow Lord's amusement. The mortal agent of darkness was now shaking and he couldn't stand on his own. Sharradomina understood he would have to or fall back to the ground and await more of the Shadow Lord's punishment.

"That's right, cry out in pain. It's something you shall get use to for eternity. Your monumental failure, failure to capture either the Sword of Eternity or the Celestial Council has signed your death warrant."

The Shadow Lord struck Sharradomina across the face and he fell back to the floor. This time the mortal arose on his own, but with a timid abandonment. His legs still were like rubber and his normally intoned senses depleted down to being useless. The place he had been brought to had some type of shackling effect on his born abilities, but he didn't understand why. This whole place, the Merciless Reach itself had a deadening effect on his mortal intuition.

But he didn't have time to dwell on his failing intuition, he needed to focus on the present and what might happen next? Sharradomina was panicking by now. His blood was rushing through his veins and his heart sped up, giving him a rush of energy suddenly. But not enough to fight off his tormentor. Only enough to stand on his own. He needed to stall until he could think of a way out of this mess. He would have to rely on instincts, instead of intellect.

"Please!" Begged Sharradomina. "I can explain."

The Shadow Lord struck Sharradomina higher, this time across the jawbone, nearly taking his head off. The strike from his tormentor left a deep laceration, as blood trickled from the new wound. Now the mortal had lacerations on his face as well as puncture wounds in his throat, but they weren't life-threating. The Shadow Lord was done torturing Sharradomina, yet. But the mortal understood, once the translucent creature was, his life would be over.

"No explanation will stop your torture, fool!" The Shadow Lord barked.

The being raised its hand to strike down Sharradomina again, but halted in mid-air as if it was awaiting confirmation to do so. That caught Sharradomina attention immediately. Was there something else in the darkened room with them. He knew it wasn't his colossal escorts. He had watched them leave before his torture had begun. So, what else could be in the room with them?

That's when his intuition picked up on the other being in the room. It was mountainous and entrenched in great power. One that resonated with darkness, drawing in all forms of dark power and energy. Sharradomina's intuition told him the unannounced figure loomed over them, like a black hole beckoning celestial objects towards it. Sharradomina instantly knew then, where they were. They were inside of the Darkness' throne room, its own prison cell and their dark master was watching them both with interest.

Sharradomina couldn't make a mistake now, he had to draw from his experience and intellect if he was going to survive the day. Their lone audience member could crush them both with just a thought, but then the mortal agent remembered the Darkness' had brought him to this place for a purpose. The Darkness never executed agents itself. It had dark assassins to do that and he wouldn't be alive if their dark master wanted that.

In between breaths, Sharradomina said, "I.. have.. a … plan to dispose of the… ele-ment-als once and for all. Master."

The Shadow Lord laughed. The sound seemed to come from deep within the boles of darkness itself. *That laughter would drive any man insane.* Thought Sharradomina. For the first time ever, Sharradomina noticed the Shadow Lord turn any shade of color. His tormentor had always been a dark cloud hovering over the decimated landscape. Now the Shadow Lord was transforming into translucent shades of purple and red colors, as if the being was blushing or an enraged inferno.

"You fool!" Reverberated the Shadow Lord. "None of our assets or allies have been able to defeat the elementals since they ascended from their Celestial heritage. We have tried for eons to destroy the elementals, but they keep returning time and time again. Nothing a pathetic mortal like yourself can uncover to destroy them."

Just as before, when the Shadow Lord peered into the darkness for validation from their invisible master. "Shall I seize the torture master?" Then another pause and a sinister grin suddenly appeared on the Shadow Lord's nearly dark face. "As I expected, master." Sharradomina's torturer looked down at him. "Our master wishes the torture to continue. You haven't learned what the consequences of failure intel's."

Sharradomina finally received confirmation that their dark master was observing the proceedings, but he really didn't need conformation, his intuition had already told him of the Darkness' presence. But Sharradomina continued to play the charade as if he was clueless. Sharradomina wanted his tormentor to believe he was a helpless individual, when in reality, he could sense the unspoken communication between the Darkness and the Shadow Lord. But he also understood that the Darkness could share with Sharradomina's tormentor that their hapless victim was onto their game.

No matter what happened, Sharradomina would survive the day, even if his life was altered significantly. *But what these fools don't know, won't hurt them.* Sharradomina said to himself.

The Shadow Lord reached out and Sharradomina began to choke on his own vomit. His face turned deathly white. No air was getting down his throat and he was afraid no amount of intervention would save him. Had he been overzealous in his estimations? Had their master decided to eliminate Sharradomina after all?

The Darkness' wretched voice bellowed from its throne.

"That will be quite enough torture from you today."

Through the darkness of the room emerged Darkcloak, The Shadow Lord's most hated rival. The agent of darkness' cloak trailing as Darkcloak walked effortlessly towards the two figures.

In imposing, seething look came across The Shadow Agent's face.

"Why are *you* here?"

The Shadow Lord released its grasp on Sharradomina and he struggled to regain breathing.

"I'm here to save my asset from your decrypted, malcontent grasp." Bellowed Darkcloak.

"Asset? Your nothing but an agent of darkness yourself. I alone direct the assets of our dark master."

"Things are changing around here, but your too caught up with your own narcissistic behavior to realize how distraught and furious our master is with our progress. I have convinced the master to hear what Sharradomina has in mind before condemning him to eternal misery."

The Shadow Lord began to steam with rage and its face began to become transparent, instead of the shadowy darkness it normally was.

"That's all a lie! This is a trap of some kind, what are you up to Cloak?"

"Speak to the Darkness yourself?"

The Darkness silhouette appeared as it was sitting on its cryptic throne. Its evil eyes penetrating the two rivals. Both dark assists kneel in respect to The Darkness.

The Darkness' deep and sinister voice bellowed. "Let the mortal asset speak. I wish to hear what he has to say."

Darkcloak motioned to Sharradomina to proceed.

Sharradomina crawled forward.

"Master. I have a way to rid of the elementals forever. But I need excess to many resources. When I'm done, no one will stand in your way."

CHAPTER 8

In an ancient time before the rise of the sinister and malevolent entity known as the Darkness, a rogue celestial secretly searches for unlimited power that would make it superior in ability and might, even to those that it called its celestial brothers. The celestials were never the type to search out such dangerous and maleficent power, that was the reason this lone being kept its movements concealed. The fear of what its kin might react could get the rogue entity in hot water.

The lone celestial did its best to shroud the omniscient beings' movements from the fifteen other celestials, slowly gathering bits and pieces of artifacts that possessed dark energy and dark magic throughout the cosmos. Even though this celestial being didn't know it at the moment, the entity was manipulated by the very power it sought without possessing the mysterious energy source itself.

The artifacts it had collected at this point, would enhance and eventually bring this maleficent power to overtake the rogue being's thoughts. Without the artifacts, this dark power could only fester, much like a parasite without a host. With each new artifact, the rogue celestial collected, the more invincible it began to feel. There were five artifacts collected:

* Portion of an Elemental Ark: This ancient artifact was from a crashed ark that once brought the original celestials from their home dimension, into our own. The ark's material had absorbing properties, which the original celestials had immersed with the omniscient beings' own abilities. The rogue being would be able to absorb other celestial's abilities with it, making it the most powerful entities within the known realms.

* Amulet of the all-seeing: This artifact would allow the rogue celestial the ability to see not just over the vast cosmos, like all celestials could; it

would give the being the ability to see into other realms that were blocked to the celestial's omniscient abilities.

* Mask of Persecution: This artifact drew from the darkest corners of the cosmos and its parallel reams. Once the mask was absorbed, the being could look at a species, no matter its distance and the dark energy would draw towards that species and cast a dark shadow over them and their descendants. Then the rogue being could cast a cloak over its target and create a vanishing cloud over those targeted.

* The Sentinel Gauntlet: This artifact acted like two artifacts in one. First it acted as an invisible suit of armor for the rogue celestial. No matter what its adversaries did, the rogue being would be protected by this artifact. But if the being was cast into a celestial prison, the gauntlet would become useless. The second portion of the artifact acted as an additional omniscient power for the rogue. It would allow the being to bring an anvil of slaughter to any species with an invisible blade of death and destruction. The drawback would be if the rogue being ever was entrapped into an omniscient prison cell, the gauntlet would fail.

* The Scroll of Oblivion: This final artifact was drenched in omniscient blood. Those that perished on the Celestial Ark and other beings from the beginning of time. The scroll would be the rogue beings ultimate tool. It was encased with dark energy and it was created by dark magic and would only enhance the darkness' own abilities once it came together with what was drawing the rogue to it.

Strange emotions began to overwhelm the being, to the point of madness and single-mindedness. The being didn't do anything but search out these artifacts, collect them for its own keepsake and hunger for the power drawing it near annihilation. Once the rogue celestial was consumed with darkness, it didn't have the desire for discovery, or manipulation of the cosmos like the other celestials. Its only focus was the possession of dark energy and magic and these collections of artifacts would, in the being's mind, give it the satisfaction of doing so.

The dark energy within these artifacts was twisting and poisoning the being's ability to think for itself. Soon a whisper began to manipulate and control the celestial's actions and it no longer knew what it was doing.

Something had originally placed the idea of collecting the dark artifacts in the first place. It didn't help that the rogue celestial was hungry for power it didn't possess.

Then it happened. The darkness called out to the isolated being and drew it towards the dark energy's concealment. It was time that the rogue celestial merge with the poisoning properties of the thing the omniscient being desired the most; ultimate power. The rogue being was drawn to a dark planet, encased in shadow. It may have been closer to a moon, with its miniscule size. Itself was a rogue planet with no host star the small planet was attached to or a star system to call its own.

As the rogue celestial approached, it could sense the immense energy flowing from the planets inner core, like it was seeping out of the planet from pores and crevices on the surface. The closer the celestial became, the stronger the dark energy seemed to draw in its victim. The miscreant being could already feel the dark power overwhelming it. It was like it had its own gravitational field and the rogue was trapped, no longer able to change the celestial's mindset and flee

~

Inside a dark cavern underneath the gloomy dark surface.

The place was cold and void of any illumination, what-so-ever. Darkness possessed the dark, isolated cavern that it made the place seem more eerie than if a predator was waiting within in depths. The cavern was dry and possessed no moisture, so it didn't have the normal damp and wet feeling, nor the musky smell looming in the air. The air was stale and lacked coolness that other cavernous structures had. Despite the inability to see in the rocky structure, the lone figure could tell how the cavern was constructed.

The figure felt the rocky, uneven cavern floor that was filled with loose rocks and pebbles that moved as the figure moved about the cavern. The warm stone wall felt coarse and rough, like running its hand against a grate of sand paper. The stale lingering atmosphere residing within the cavern structure told the figure the cavern ceiling could have been more than ten to twelve feet in total height.

Despite the inability to see anything within the place, something loomed in the air, like a fog blanketing a long stretch of countryside. A sensation hoovered within the cavern like a phantom lingering in the shadows. A dark predator with absolutely no form to it, waiting for its next meal. The approaching figure, the rogue celestial, could feel the others presence, but even when the celestial reached out to feel the other's presence with its own omniscient abilities the looming other was able to negate its attempts. This not only frustrated the rogue celestial, but made it that much more impatient as well.

A pin-prick of light emerged ahead, as if someone had opened a door, leaving it ajar, allowing just enough needle-thin illumination to guide the figure towards it. The purplish light had a dullness to it and it was less ambient than most light.

The visitor emerged through the darkness and into a mist of hazy purple. Slowly the celestial approached the purple, translucent cloud. The cloud seemed in contrast to the darkness of the cavern, an alien body not meant to dwell in this place. It's the only thing that battles the darkness and attempts to survive long enough to find a new, compatible host.

The mysterious figure slowly approaches the translucent cloud, like it was caught in a deep and unbreakable trance. The figure had been searching from one end of the cosmos to the other for this looming cloud, this essence that held all the promises and the abilities to unlock limitless doors to realms not yet discovered. The closer the figure came to the looming cloud, the more it had the figure ensnared in its trap.

This is what the figure had been searching for all this time. The chance to possess something that contained more power and wisdom than even the being had access to. The figure, with its omniscient eyes was reaching out to the purple cloud of unknown particles. If he possessed the entities that made the luminous cloud, the being would be transformed forever.

The purple illumination seemed to thump like it had a heartbeat. The dark luminous cloud seemed to be connecting with the beating of the figure's heart. It sent a tingling throughout the physical form, through the veins and singed the being's blood. Soon the figure's heart and the purple cloud seemed to beat the same rhythm. A few 'thump, thumps' echoed in the chamber and the rogue figure began to feel an aching sensation in his heart. The being and the darkness that assimilated the cavern were slowly becoming one.

The figure began to reach out to the hazy, purple mass suspended in the dark, thin air. It was like the being no longer had control over himself, but the stagnant dense mass had taken control for them both. The being's eyes solidified and became dark, empty voids. The closer the being got to the mist, the deeper the purple color radiated and the faster the pounding became.

It was too late, the alien parasite had control and the figure was at the mass's mercy. Slowly the figure reached out and penetrated the hazy mist. Nothing happened at first, only a feeling of euphoria flowed through the figure's flesh. But that was misjudgment on his part and as quickly as the euphoria emerged, a sharp and daunting pain replaced it.

The pain shot right up the figure's arm and began to fill the interior like a plague consuming everything in its path. It felt like someone had rammed a sharp, elongated needle through the being's flesh and it was still finding its way through his body. The figure couldn't breathe. It was like his own lungs had filled up with the dark, purple mass and was blocking out anything else from coming in. An aching sensation began to fill the being's insides and as the poison flowed through him, it consumed living tissue and leaving him feeling empty and void of anything that resembled a living being any longer.

A black substance, one that might be confused with blood, if anyone could witness what was taking place, but they would be dead wrong, coming from the being's nostrils. The beings skin began to darken to almost a black color at his nails, mouth and lower ear lobes. Shadows formed under his eyes, his lips became pitch black like a dead corpse. The figure doesn't move or respond to the torturous actions being induced on him. The being had become like the dead, silent and docile.

Soon the purple mist had taken control of its host and it had complete control. The figure still didn't breathe in and out like a normal living being.

Slowly the being began to transform into a phantom-like creature, one that could spread throughout the cosmos and utilize its celestial power, but with its own twisted agenda.

Something was living inside of him now. The alien parasite living among the purple mist, the embodiment of the dark energy now consuming the rogue figure, becoming one with darkness. It no longer had anything that resembled a celestial, since absorbing dark energy and dark magic. The being was no longer a celestial either in shape or consciousness was the puppet of the darkness it had sought all along.

Suddenly, a voice emerged. Not from the mist or from the possessed being but from a darker place. A place so dark and foreboding and somewhere that would never be discovered, never found by anyone. It would utilize the naïve form of the former celestial to do its bidding. Inside the possessed echoed the sinister voice that would be used to manipulate all that followed.

"Arise my subject. You and I are now one. You have come to me in search of new power. New ways to transform civilizations at will. You have found such power in me."

The possessed entity known as the rouge celestial, started to mumble an incantation. The words were inaudible and the figure spoke quick and with ferocity, but the figure would never remember the words uttered.

The possessed moved its dark hand into a knapsack at its side and removed three glass balls. At first the balls were clear and reflected the mist's purple tint. But soon the translucent balls filled up and became pitch black, just like the possessed eyes had done. The being cried out as if in pain, but his body was numb and had absolutely no feeling to it. No, this cry was to announce the arrival of the parasite, a mating call to its own kind or a warning to other beings to heed.

Sinister laughter came from the possessed blackened lips.

"I can feel the freedom of this body. I can feel the power that it possesses, even in its weakened state. I'm growing more powerful by the moment and I can feel this being reach, which is way beyond I ever imagined. I can sense the other celestials moving about and I can track their movements without them even knowing. I was correct to surmise this vessel's substantial ability."

The possessed being, formally one of the celestials, looked down at its semi translucent body and observed its texture. It had been a long time since it had been free of its eternal vagueness. Its state of nonexistence. Even in the body's decaying form, the parasite felt free. Like it hadn't experienced anything such as this, a prisoner who was free of its shackles, a newborn to the world.

The possessed placed three black glass balls into the knapsack. The newly freed parasite, which had no name at all or if it did had been long forgotten. It was truly the shadow lingering in the darkness. It was the possessor of dark magic and now had retrieved the lost portion of dark energy that had been scattered throughout the cosmos. The celestial's obsession with the dark energy and dark magic was its own undoing and the parasite knew this.

The possessed gripped the blackened smooth balls in its decrypted grasp. It felt the power, the flow of dark matter, dark energy and its own existence in its grasp. Dark energy began to transfer from the devices into the parasite's new shell of a body. The rush of dark power felt exhilarating, but excruciating at the same time. It had the feeling of having blood being syphoned from the body and the parasite didn't like that experience at all. But the alien had to endure what its new body was experiencing. It was now his and there was no escaping it.

The newly transformed being's eyes had become dark voids of nothingness. The former rogue entity no longer had the ability to see things, but it didn't need to. The darkness it now had become, could sense things from vast distances. Like a blind species with heightened senses, the shadow creature now could connect with all sorts of dark and demented things, including the very shadows that filled the voids of space.

The figure's cloak no longer had substance. It now wisped behind the shadow figure, like it was its very shadow. It had become a phantom moving throughout the dark spaces of the cosmos.

The parasite's hand began to glow a dark purplish color, as the dark energy flowed from the blacken glass balls and into the parasite's adopted body. Both the pain and the exhilaration was great; the feeling of both the celestial power and the dark power blending together drove the parasite into a rage. The figure's muscles tightened, its ligaments began to distort and reshape. Now the celestial couldn't just create the shape it wanted to but restructure its physical body, when it used a physical form, utilizing limbs from different species in the same form. The parasite was becoming a superior being, even to its celestial host.

Muscle fibers contorted and rewound themselves into massive, unrecognizable shapes. The being no longer had the appearance of the rogue being it once was. In fact, it had the look of nothing that had existed before. It had the ability to split skin and muscle fibers to create two heads, multiple appendages and consistently reshape its form. But unlike its former kin, the celestials, it could use its transparent shape and move about like a shadow, undetected; or transform into any shape or size it so desired. Nothing restricted the dark character to any laws in this cosmos or any other realm.

The figure's vein began to pop out from under the decrypted skin. They were dark, a deep purple that made it appear that the body was stricken with a decaying disease. This was evident, even with the dark decaying flesh that now covered the infected host. The parasite was having issues breathing and couldn't even scream out in pain.

The power is so immense. Thought the parasite. *I never anticipated it being this strong. I thought it could be overwhelming for whatever host I chose, but I never expected the celestial's power to intensify the dark matter so much.* The parasite finally was able to let out a horrid scream. The outburst became so intense that it shook the cavern walls and small bits of rock came tumbling down from the walls and ceiling.

The scream was so exhausting that once it finished, the body fell to its knees. The scream had taken its toll on the parasite's new body and it had lost almost all its built-up energy, even though the dark energy still resided within. The bodies lungs flexed in and out as they tried to recover from the blockage of air. The parasite felt the heart beating faster. The body was exhausted, but it still had the fuel of dark energy to feed it.

The body scratched at the rocky surface of the cavern. Through the black eyes, everything looked gray and colorless. Gas and particle dust passed its field of vision. The celestial portion of the parasite was reaching out and it was experiencing it all. Clusters of galaxies passed by at a cosmic pace. The parasite began to see doorways to other dimensions. A flash would emerge from the darkness or through a cluster of stars. The parasite felt the dark energy working inside and understood that it was the darker parts of its new body that were giving it this insight. But the invader couldn't negate the celestial's own power altogether. The celestial also had the ability to see these doors, but with the dark power now resonating within, it had become so much more powerful.

The doors began to multiply, bright spots in the sky. A few turned into several, then into thousands and then millions flashed by. It was beginning to be overwhelming to the parasite. *So many doorways I can take. So many civilizations I have the potential to corrupt, maim and devastate. This is all beyond what I could have hoped for. Beyond any idea I had dreamed of.* The parasite closed its eyes and reached out to every doorway, every civilization that hid behind these celestial pathways, both established and those yet to emerge.

Most of these civilizations and the species that would occupy them hadn't grown into the awe-inspiring societies that they would become one day. Most were still in the dark ages, with little technology or not having formed at all. It would be the ripe time to pluck each one for its taking. Become the sole benefactor of each and maybe even denote itself as their god.

∼

Then one of the bursts of light, a doorway to another place and time emerged and unlike the other dimensional gateways, this one was calling to the possessed, as if attempting to attract her lover's attention. The possessed, in its celestial phantom form rushed for the entranceway like a runaway freight train. The parasite reached out as if it was going to force open the door and burst into this new realm.

In its phantom-like state, the celestial rushed into the portal and emerged into a bright, clean aired place. It was quite the contrast to the enclosed cavern and traveling through the cosmos, in its celestial phantom form. The planet of Duzepheria was a warm, bright place with clean air and a multitude of flying species occupying the space the possessed occupied.

The planet's inhabitants go about with their busy daily lives. The surface wasn't cluttered by machines and other technology, like it would in the distant future. This infant society hadn't yet blossomed into the cutting-edge, innovating culture it was bound to be. The people that inhabited the surface were simple, hard-working individuals that hadn't tasted the effects of innovation. An industrial revolution was just blossoming and structures were beginning to go up everywhere. There was opportunity in this place and the possessed celestial had stumbled onto this place on her people just at the right moment.

The parasite, in its celestial phantom form reached out to sense the people of this place and began to laugh a sinister laughter. "These poor souls haven't been corrupted by technology or the greed of power that comes with it. I have an opportunity here, the thing I have been craving the most, since discovering the dark artifacts. The chance to manipulate a society and twist it to my own will."

The phantom reached out towards the surface and began to manipulate the pavement, forcing it to crack and rupture. The parasite cloaked the construction in a haze and if any of the Duzepheriains looked in the direction of its new construction or overheard something unusual, all they would see was a slight distortion.

Soil, concrete and other useless materials were discarded and was replaced with minerals that could be used to construct the vehicle of destruction, an exceptionally advanced manufacturing plant.

The phantom rose its arms high as steel girders, structure beams and other material began to shape the manufacturing building. It gave the parasite immense pleasure watching the construct go up. It was like a father grasping his newborn child in his arms for the first time.

"Yes, rise, rise my vehicle of destruction. You will be the first of many to ransack this and many other societies throughout the cosmic multiverse."

The decrypted being watched as the final touches finished off the invisible building. The advanced metal structure, with its carbon-based frame, beryllium-based bolts and floating catwalks hovered above the possessed like a steel rainbow. Melting ovens to process raw material and create metal structures. Stamping machinery to press the newly formed steel for instant use. He had created this magnificent facility from absolutely nothingness.

It breathed in the smell of new metal, of the new material that stood as a monument of the being's awesome power.

"I've done it!" The decrypted explained, as its sinister voice bounced off the factory's walls. "I feel like a god." The phantom-like being stood there soaking the atmosphere up. "I am a god. These pathetic creatures will know me as such. I will be The Machine God to them all!" The possessed screamed. "And now I must create a leader for my constructed empire. The one I will use in my place. A god must have his prophet."

The possessed raised his arms and the sound of melting metal began to rise from deep within the baking furnaces below the surface floor. The ground was tearing apart and molten earth was forcing its way to the surface.

The thick, monstrous furnace doors exploded from their equally thick hinges, knocking the doors to one side and hanging loosely. Molten metal and fire launch from the factory's dark looming furnaces. The stream of molten metal and fire are drawn towards the possessed being.

As the blazing stream flies by, it leaves its mark, forever imprinting into the newly constructed metal walls. Closer the flare of molten metal was pulled towards The Darkness. It snaked its way up the stairwell and burst into the factory floor, where its master awaited. The figure didn't flinch or even bother opening its closed eye lids, but it didn't need to. The Darkness could feel the rapidly approaching comet of fire and molten metal. It had complete control.

"Come to me my pet."

From every corner of the manufacturing floor, a stream of the inferno from its four mighty furnaces screamed by, never even threating the motionless figure. Each stream slammed into each other at the center of the production floor. Immediately all four streams of thick molten metal and fire erupted in a supernova, sending loose metal in flames in every direction.

A colossal dark smoke cloud immersed the middle of the production floor. The Darkness could feel the inflamed pieces slamming against each other and slowly beginning to form a ridged, jigsaw construct. It knew this because the dark power resonating within it was forming the molten metal in an image of itself.

Heavy cries of pain vibrated from the collection of firestorms, like whatever was being born was in agony, but that was only fueling the dark power, making The Darkness inject even more power into its construction. Molten metal collided with cooling metal, wrapping around the structure like a thick ridged skin before cooling. Then more molten metal would attach to it, sending an enraged madness vibrating from the dark cloud. Slowly a dark figure began to immerge in the cloud of fire. The Darkness' creation was coming together.

Whatever loomed inside the dark cloud was mountainous in size. The creation's shadow consumed three-quarters of the manufacturing floor. The explosions receded and the dark cloud became quiet. The creation was completed and The Darkness had its first servant.

A pair of digital maroon eyes peered down at the being. Slowly the dark cloud receded and exposed the creation in full. It was like staring up at a giant god of metal. The creation had a head made of metal, like a battle helmet. The digital eyes looked through a mask of metal that was shaped like two inverted capital F's that created eye slits for the beast. The base of the inverted F's ran down to create a seem and the beast's ridged nose line. No mouth or jawline was visible. It all was hidden beneath the metal structure.

The possessed raised its arms in celebration.

"I've done it!"

The beast growled back.

"You are going to be my enforcer, my eyes and ears. You will be the greatest dictator ever created. Your nothing but a shell, but once I have inserted my malice, my dark will inside of you, you will tear down this society and create me the greatest army ever built. Once I design you're A.I. in my likeness and insert that malice I promised you, you will no longer need me to rule this." The Darkness looked around as if searching for someway to express itself. "This hell I attend to create. And these beings will be our slaves."

The possessed with The Darkness inside, began to laugh a sinister laugh.

The metal beast let out a forceful growl.

The possessed looked deep into its creations digital eyes.

"I think I will call you The Industrialist."

CHAPTER 9

On the Shadow Fleet's battlecruiser named The Dark Nemesis patrolling an undocumented shadow region of space.

The room was silent, with just one source of illumination shining in the fifteen by eighteen square hoskiasten steel room. The room was designed to use as a prisoner interrogation room. The cold, dark steel chamber possessed a lonely, isolated feeling that lingered. The maleficent and dark shadows help set an ominous apprehension, as they crept up to the lighted portions of the cage, like an unknown predator slowly circling its prey.

At the far bulkhead, a twisted metal frame, that seemed to make an 'X' shape, resided wielded to the metal hull. This structure seemed to have been mangled, twisted, and forged to maximize displeasure, whoever was unfortunate enough to be placed on its diabolical frame. Mechanical Cranking devices are attached to the top of the bulkhead torture device that seems to draw thick chains through the bulkhead floor. It does seem out of place and crude.

A young humanoid is lying on the twisted metal frame, with energy cuffs on his arms and legs to keep the prisoner in place. The prisoner was spread wide, like a well-prepped morsel prepared for an exquisite feast. What was left of the prisoner's uniform had been cut into shreds, as if he had been mauled by a fantastic creature. His face battered and bruised, and lacerations littered his face and all up and down his arms and legs.

Dried blood caked the side of the human's head and down to one side of his cranium. His skin was cracked and dehydrated. The man breathed slowly, as if in a deep sleep. The sound of footsteps could be heard patrolling the outside perimeter on occasion, but none stopped at the chamber's entrance.

A set of undisclosed footsteps slowly approached and stopped outside the room. That's when two sets of low-toned voices heard. But the unknown owners didn't linger long and swiftly moved away. The figure moved briefly and moaned. But the fit passed by quickly, and the human settled back down.

Suddenly another sound of a set of boots approaching the chamber door could be heard. But much like the first set, they seemed like they were in a faraway place. The approaching figure stopped directly outside, but instead of moving on, as the previous ones, the figure waiting outside and nothing spoken. It was like the figure outside the room was waiting on something. But what wasn't clear.

After what seemed like an eternity, the uninvited guest opened the chamber door and walked in. The humanoid slowly came to and watched as the newcomer, cloaked in all black, entered the room like the wind blowing. His uninvited guest didn't utter a word and alone. The small figure removed the oversized cloak, which made the visitor even more like a dwarf than before. The visitor was human, with greying hair and hard lines on the man's face, as if he had a taxing life. But the newcomer had vigor in his eyes, a spark of life that seemed to fuel the visitor's ambition and drive.

Underneath the cloak, the visitor wore a simple black pair of pants and a perfectly fitted military blouse, well-pressed with no wrinkles visibly. The man seemed like he didn't fit the ship's personal, the invading army that was transported on *The Dark Nemesis* or being a servant of the Darkness. But as the detainee slowly looked up at his unassuming visitor, the sinister smile on the newcomer's face told the prisoner another story.

The man in black didn't make any threatening moves or taunt the prisoner, and that's what seemed even more sinister than the man's smile. There was a sense of confidence radiating from the uninvited guest. The dark cladded figure moved forward, but despite the man's frailness, the black cladded figure moved like a much larger man, a man with a purpose. That threw the prisoner off and left the beaten solder off guard for what was about to happen.

"Hello, captain. I'm enthralled that you're awake. Now we can begin our little game together." Sharradomina gave the marine a big, crooked smile. "I have to confess I really do love playing games."

The prisoner mumbled something inaudible.

"What was that?" Sharradomina asked. The agent of darkness leaned in as if to hear his victim better. "I didn't quite catch that." Sharradomina grabbed the marine by the jaw, squeezing harder than the prisoner might have expected, forcing the captain's mouth open wide. "I can't hear you. Oh, I see your throat is parched."

The agent of shadow looked towards the lone table in the chamber. There was a picture of water sitting next to a few torture tools. Sharradomina grabbed a mug and filled it up with the liquid with his free hand. "Let me help you with that." The agent forced the water down the prisoner's throat, nearly drowning him. The captain spat the excess fluid from his mouth, as if the marine had swallowed too much.

"Now, how do you feel? Better, I hope because I do have a game, I'd like to play with you."

The captain looked up at his adversary with hate and contempt. The marine's lungs we still burning, and his chest heaved in and out rapidly as if he had just swum across the English Channel. But the solder's eyes told it all. He had no love for his torturer. His contempt was only mounting, but still with no clue what would happen.

"I'm not talking, you won't get anything out of me," barked the prisoner.

The frail being smiled back. Sharradomina's hands were folded together behind his back. The agent had a calm demeanor as if insults couldn't throw the agent off his game. "My good captain. I don't want you to sing like a Keaoth perched on a Whiteman tree, swaying in the wind." The shadow agent shook his head. "You misunderstood me when I said I wanted to play a game with you. I truly love games and that all I want. Someone besides these crazed idiots aboard this ship. They have no sense of humor, like you and me."

The captain swallowed hard. The marine squinted his eyes, in hopes it would allow the marine to concentrate better. "Who says I have a sense of humor?"

The agent stepped towards the structure his prisoner strapped on. Sharradomina removed his black gloves and tucked them into his pant pocket. "Oh, for your sake, my dear captain. I sure hope you do have one. Nothing would dishearten me more."

The marine swallowed hard, and he began to perspire. "I've heard rumors of your torture techniques. You're supposed to be a master tormentor with crude ways of making those you capture talk." The marine watched as Sharradomina stopped dead in his tracks.

The sinister smile reappeared on the man's face, but the captive could tell if his nemesis was hearing things that had drawn his attention briefly from the game he was playing or if the frail man had caught in a memory. Sharradomina snapped back as if he had read the marine captain's mind.

"I do apologize. You had just reminded me of all the pleasure my position affords me." The frail man leaned inwards and whispered. "I have utilized water torture techniques, beheaded defectors, even used torture tools, such as these." Sharradomina motioned towards the tools on the table behind them. "But rarely do I get to do the thing I love most." The agent placed his bare hand behind the metal structure. "It's ok to scream, captain. In fact, the louder you scream, the more pleasure I will obtain from your pain."

Sharradomina threw the lever forward, and the sound of chains wounding up began. The marine felt a tightness in his arms. That was right before the pain surged from the marine's arms, shooting down to his spine. The captain let out a horrid cry, one that made the solder's torturer smile. The pain was sudden that it nearly put the solder in instant shock. That would have disappointed Sharradomina, because the game would have ended before it had a chance to begin.

The solder couldn't hold back his screams. His pain and agony was far too great to hold it in. The marine let out a tremendous cry; temporarily released the severe pain from his body. Sharradomina took in his captive's cries. It was like a euphoric drug the agent relished. While the marine cried in pain, Sharradomina cried out in pleasure.

The marine captain could feel his lungs burning. His throat was also aflame with stomach acid that had forced its way up to his throat.

"Yes. Yes, my dear captain. I can tell you enjoy this as much as I do. Feel the power in your lungs. Your cries are fueling the intensity and painful emotions your experiencing."

The captain couldn't respond. His pain was too intense. The marine's teeth were chattering, and it felt like the chains were ripping his arms right from their sockets. The solder held back his screams as long as he could, allowing his shivering body to absorb the punishment as it began to intensify. The captain let out another scream. This one nearly made Sharradomina cry in ecstasy. The agent of darkness soaked in his prisoner's pain like a drug.

The marine could hear the rusted chain winding up as the chaotic gears turned at a snail's pace, stretching the prisoner's limbs further from his body. The pain no longer mattered. The marine had chosen to focus on something worth wild and positive. It's what that had driven home into the recruit boot camp. Now of the marine's most dire need, his superiors wanted all marines to keep a positive mindset. It helped when the end was near.

The sound of the rusted chain-link and the chaotic gears winding continued, but the absence of the mortal's cries was making Sharradomina grabbed the man by the face with even more force than before. The marine felt the hot breath of the shadow agent, with their faces only inches apart. "Why aren't you screaming in pain? Why don't you let loose and give me what I desire? You're not playing by the rules, my friend." Sharradomina had begun to grind his teeth.

Without the ability to curse back at his tormentor, the marine could only swallow the residue of pain. He had lost concentration with the shadow agent's accursed threats. The solder concentrated on his breathing as his lungs expanded and contracted. The sound was soothing and anchored the marine to his fading life, but the mortal refused to give into Sharradomina. If he was to die this night, on this cold and isolating ship; he was going to do it on his terms.

"Think about how others had died." Whispered Sharradomina. "Think of their agony. Their cries and their agony. Can you feel it, captain?"

Suddenly, the sound of the rusty chains running over the chaotic crank came to the forefront of the marine's mind. He heard the cries of

Sharradomina's other victims. They all cried out to the marine all at once. The sound was maddening and gut-wrenching and made the marine cringe. The powerful emotions rushed through the prisoner's body, the snapping of ligaments, the stretching of their minds all hit the mortal at one.

He wasn't like the elementals who could block out the pain and the emotions that followed torture. They could even block out the very thought of their kin killed, even though no mortal could ever do such things to them, the marine knew that for sure. The emotions of all those sounds placed him on the verge of snapping, but the marine still wouldn't scream for Sharradomina.

The shadow agent screamed out in frustration. The agent shook the mortal's head violently. "Why won't you scream? That's all I want, just your screams. Is that so hard to ask for? I can make the pain stop, the stretching of your limbs. It all could end."

A tear formed in the shadow agent's eye.

Then a ringing sound, like a bell being rung echoed in the chamber. Sharradomina looked up from his victim. His breathing labored his vision blurred and a somewhat subdued temper. He tried to ignore the sound, but a second ring came directly after the first one. *These crazy Blackmour Drowmauder crews are going to drive me insane.*

The shadow agent released the marine's face and approached the chamber doorway, which was still closed. Sharradomina clicked on the communicator located directly next to the door, and a young drow-mauder was waiting in holographic form. The image flickered once and then cleared. The young commander of the *Dark Nemesis,* Cmd. Cocmis Vulcoon Drovrobit. Sharradomina understood the commander was of drowmauder pureblood because half breed drowmauders didn't utilize a second full name in their titles, and all the dark naval officers were of pure-blood. Their master wouldn't allow half breeds to command.

The drowmauder officer was a fine specimen as far as he could tell, but it didn't matter, they're up bring nor their superior psyches; as long as the star cruiser could deliver him and his legion of armies onto the battlefield.

"Master Sharradomina. The commodore requests your presence on the bridge."

"Does he now?"

There was an awkward silence between the agent of shadow and the ship's commander. The luminescent tan image stood there without anything to say. Then the drowmauder officer, after too many minutes of unbearable silence broke the deadlock. The commodore would like to invite you into his personal chambers for a special meeting," returned the impatience commander.

With a mad insolent response, Sharradomina moved towards his victim. "I don't have time to indulge you, commodore with his petty complaints." The shadow agent shut down the communication device and rushed back to the marine.

"Now, where were we before the intrusion? Oh yes, I was going to introduce a new type of pain to you, captain."

Sharradomina turned to the lone metal table and retrieved a laser-edged cutter. The agent turned it on, and a purple blade ignited before the mortal prisoner. The agent turned towards the prisoner with a wicked smile. "Now, it's time to introduce you to a new kind of pain."

The laser's edge scrapped across the marine's face, as the smell of burning skin filled the air. Instantly the marine began to cry out, and that made Sharradomina gleeful. The frail agent of darkness chuckled. "That's it, my boy, scream for me. Cry me a river." The elderly man licked his lips with his purplish tongue.

Sharradomina leaned back in, this time with the intent to slicing a piece of the marine captain's flesh when a loud ring interrupted the agent's fun. The agent tossed the cutting tool onto the table and rushed to the communication station for a second time. The captain was relived. He wasn't sure he could take much more torture.

Before Sharradomina reached the doorway, the chamber's door separated. The door sectioned into four unequal quadrants. The door opened in the middle, but it had a swirling motion where the four sections split. The top half section curved towards the right of the door and a slight angle. The door seam slow curvature moved to the top corner of the doorway, making swivel-like design. The bottom half was designed nearly the same, except in the opposite direction.

The door opened, and Commodore Robildren, the *Dark Nemesis's* commanding officer, stood before Sharradomina. The aged drowmauder officer had a scowl on his face. His purplish tinted face had the appearance that made the shadow agent think it might explode at any moment. The commodore›s body was tense, and his alien fists balled up into a pair of fists.

"Sharradomina!" The commodore barked. "I've been trying to gain an audience with you for over an hour."

The shadow agent waved off the rebuttal. "I've been busy if you haven't noticed, commodore."

The commodore peered into the chamber at the marine strapped up. "Playing again, I see." The *Dark Nemesis's* commander snickered at Sharradomina's false proclamation. "It's hardly the time to play."

The shadow agent smiled at the dark elves' anger. "It's always a good time to play."

"It's always a good time to play."

"Not right now, it isn't. I've placed the ship on alert. That's why I wanted to discuss with you."

Sharradomina gave the commodore an unpleasant frown. "You and your crew's problems aren't my own. As long as the dark legion and I arrive on Zaskillion, that is all I worry about."

The ship's hull suddenly shook violently. Alarms began to go off all around them.

"See, that might be a problem. The ship had to slow down; we are being engaged by the elemental fleet."

Sharradomina nearly leaped out of his skin. He rushes back to grab his cloak, stares at the marine one last time, and then rushes out of the chamber. The agent of darkness and Commodore Robildren rush down the ship's hall, towards the bridge.

"Commodore, how close to our targeted planet are we?"

"Close. But if we can't get by their blockade, we might have to jettison you and the legion in siege crafts."

"That's unacceptable, Commodore Robildren. There is a high probability we won't even make it to the service." A cherry red face of despicable rage appeared on the agent's face.

"It's possible. But then again, that might be the elemental's plan from the beginning. Capture you and the legion in route."

"Are you suggesting the elementals led you into an ambush, commodore?"

The ship's commander shrugged his drowmauder shoulders. "They did appear out of nowhere. And there are no elemental bases close by for them to launch a seek and destroy mission from."

Sharradomina grabbed the commodore by the collar. "Your incompetence will draw the wrath of the master. Even if we escape this ambush, commodore, and I'm not sure your crew can do that, we will be marked by the Darkness as unworthy to serve."

The commander brushed Sharradomina off him.

"I suggest you prepare your solders for the worst and stop worrying about the future. We have to survive the present first."

The commodore walked away in the direction of the ship's bridge, with another violent shake from the *Dark Nemesis's* hull.

∾

The *Dark Nemesis* is rocked from all sides, as the dark space cruiser flees from its adversaries. Busted auxiliary hoses and minor damage inflicted to the dark fleet warship. The commodore finally reaches the bridge, noticing that only half the bridge crew is at their stations. It was daunting enough to traverse through the cosmos, conflict with their enemy as they went, only half-manned would make their escape such formidable feet. The commander scanned the bridge, trying to gauge where assistance might be needed. But first, he needed to know where they stood.

"Helm, report."

The drowmauder rattled, "We are off heading by seventeen degrees, sir. Aft shields are failing and are down to less than optimal operational capacity. Forward shields are at forty-two percent and holding."

"What about propulsion? Any issues to this point?"

The ship's XO, commander Khesresen responded, "There is a small reactor leak in engine compartment three, but even if we lose that one, we still have the main engine thruster and the one secondary engine."

"That's if they don't continue to target our propulsion." Barked Commodore Robildren. "Navigator Vunniser, how long can we last if our adversaries continue to bombard as at this pace?"

"Less than fifteen minutes, commodore." Responded the navigator.

"That's not very long," mumbled Robildren. "Helm, swing minty percent of our remaining forward shielding to the aft portion of the ship."

An explosion rocks the bridge.

The helm looks up with a frown on his dark, purplish face. "That will expose the bridge and everyone in the forward compartment, sir. We won't stand a chance."

The commodore calmly responded in an authoritative tone, "We don't stand any chance if our propulsion goes out completely. Then we will be dead in space and exposed to the elemental fleet."

The helmsman nods his understanding and begins to as he's ordered. But before any further work can be completed, three elemental warships emerge from a cluster of dust. The sight is quite overwhelming, even for a crew as experienced as the *Dark Nemesis*. All they could do is watch at their adversary's slow approach. *The ambush worked*, thought the commodore. *We flew right into their trap without even realizing it. Sharradomina was right. We don't deserve to serve under the dark master. The Darkness deserves intelligent leadership to guide its war machine, not incompetent fools like myself.*

The *Dark Nemesis* is rocked from behind, once again. That>s when a major alarm goes off on the bridge, keeping any of the crew from doing their jobs. «Sir,» called the helm. «Aft shields completely are gone. All but one aft engine still operating at normal.»

Suddenly, something gargantuan, about two-thirds the size of the Dark Nemesis itself, flew by the bridge. The bridge crew could feel the vibration as whatever had passed them by possessed a massive wingspan that brought strength and agility to a ship the size of the Dark Nemesis. The enormous thing was such a blur to the ship's crew, no one on the bridge got a good look at what it was.

"What the hell was that?" Questioned the helmsmen.

No one on the bridge responded.

~

From the side of the Dark Nemesis, flapping its substantial wingspan, an elemental space dragon demolished the port side of the ship with its silver-red fire. The celestial oddity ran its raging fire all along the side of the ship, penetrating its hull and compromising the Dark Nemesis's integrity. Flames and explosions rocked the inner portion of the dark fleet cruiser, causing it to shake like a ship about to split apart and sink at sea.

Once the space dragon was satisfied with the devastation it had caused, the magnificent creature flapped its wings three times and flew off, as if telling the rest of its elemental allies her job had been completed. What the elemental dragon left behind was a dark fleet star cruiser that seemed to be dead in space. Fires raging from within and a silenced crew.

The emergency lights were still flashing blue, as the dark hallways of the Dark Nemesis had become like a ghost town. Sharradomina skirted across the deserted hall, which seemed to have tilted to the right some, or was the *Dark Nemesis's* new drift pattern? The agent of shadows couldn't tell. He was the tool of destruction, not a naval aviator. Commodore Robildren would know better than he would, wherever the commander of the Dark Nemesis was. But the whereabouts of the commodore wasn't important at the moment. Now, Sharradomina understood it was time to abandon ship. He would love to take his legion of solders with him, in the ship's life ship, but the antics of the elementals had prevented that.

The space dragon hadn't just damaged the ship's hull and set off the evacuation alarms. The damn beast had also damaged the jettison panel at the escape pod docking pad. He had attempted to begin the life ship, but all the circuits had been so wrecked that only the lights on the panel seemed to work. If that was bad enough to anger Sharradomina. Then while attempting to gain access to the birthing compartment where his dark army soldiers were, the catwalk had been destroyed and informed that the entire starboard side of the ship was no longer accessible from any of its twenty-three decks of the ship.

No, Sharradomina had to think of himself. It was beyond time to save the dark legion. Knowing the starboard escape launching pad was devastated by the elemental attack, the agent of darkness moved towards the portside docking pad. From his current position, it wasn't a very long walk. The Shadow Empire operative should arrive in just a few moments. That's when the Dark Nemesis shook abruptly, nearly knocking Sharradomina to the deck.

He quickly got back to his feet. It was time to hurry if he intended to survive. The agent picked up the pace and began to run towards the port docking pad. He wasn't sure if he would be able to reach Zaskillion's surface. He didn't know how far away they were from his destination, and they were in elemental territory, which was evident from the ambush the *Dark Nemesis* had flown into. All he could do was try. If the elementals intercepted the escape pod, he was about to use, and then the agent would deal with the consequences later. Whether he was punished from those, he had inflicted pain and horror on had to be subtler imprisonment than failing the Darkness and assuming his master>s vengeful wrath.

Sharradomina reached the escape pod launching pad and began to turn on everyone pod he could. Many of the pods were deactivated or out of working order. *How in the hell did the crew expect to jettison from the dying cruiser?* He wondered. Then Sharradomina remembered the rumors about the ship's commander. Commodore Robildren was a 'Go down with his ship' type of officer and he had most likely recruited a crew with the same attitude. A crew hand-picked to sacrifice their own lives for the Darkness and their shipmates. Maybe Sharradomina had been wrong about the commodore. Maybe the drowmauder officer was worthy of serving their dark master after all.

Sharradomina shrugged his shoulders as if brushing off a shiver. The ship's commander's apparent suicide wasn't going to affect him one way or another. Much like losing the legions of solders behind, he could always obtain more troops, along with a new ride to each conquest.

The agent of shadow finally discovered a useable escape pod, opened its access door and began to program its flight pattern. Once he was done, he took a hard look at the empty hallway and entered the tiny vessel. He knew one way or another he would reach the Zaskillion surface. One way or another, no matter the outcome was, he would reach his destination.

The escape pod door hissed as it shut and as the pod jettisoned into space, towards the planet below, Sharradomina watched the *Dark Nemesis* begin to break apart at its seams.

CHAPTER 10

Near the end of The 2nd Celestial Wars approximately one thousand years ago:

Alone figure flees across the deserted plains of Zaskillion, a small desert-like satellite in the Cetheron star system. Sharradomina looked back several times, to see if the legionnaire patrol was still tracking him. Even if Sharradomina couldn't see his pursuers chasing him, because a rising sandstorm had arisen from the western plains and moving their way, it didn't mean that they still weren't tracking his flight. In fact, the agent of darkness was sure his pursuers were still hot on his trail.

Sharradomina could feel his legs beginning to waver, and a sharp pain rushed up his back. He wasn't used to running for miles across a desert plain and fleeing for his life. The blood flow in his body seemed to rush to his head and heart, at the same time, making his head spin faster. A pain inside his chest ignited into a fiery of pain, forcing Sharradomina to slow his pace to a slow, near walking pace. He knew he couldn't go on much longer and stopped to catch his breath.

The agent of darkness was waiting for the tracking posse to emerge from the golden sand cloud like a serpent on its way to a feeding frenzy. Sharradomina understood his running was finally over, and even if he could go any further, it would be futile on his health to continue. The legionnaire raiding party was too enormous, and they had brought along a few elementals with them. Eluding the omniscient protectors of the universe was useless; even the Darkness' elite fighting units had failed to kill even one of them.

After sending his deadly package on its way, Sharradomina had ventured across the Ikrish star system, and his little ship had been tracked down by a local patrol garrison. When he refused to allow them to board, a chase ensued across the star system, and his tiny little craft had been forced to crash on this despicable and inhospitable planet.

A legionnaire transport running on tracks moved out of the sandstorm and right for his location. The armored transport appeared to the agent like a mud-brown tortious slowly moving towards his location. An armed escort was escorting the transport, and even that seemed to be overkill to the agent of darkness. He was merely one man, a mortal and unarmed. What possible harm could he inflict on his pursuers? But Sharradomina couldn't blame them. He had, for as long as his memory would allow, wreaked havoc in the name of the Darkness. The devastation he had lead had forced many species extinctions and hundreds of civilizations spread out through the cosmos to become extinct. He was the one that acted as their exterminator and the focus of their hatred. And his network of connections would open vast network of agents that could take down the Darkness' siege.

Air support soon came out of the west, tracking his location. A group of three tracking nats, as he called them because they had fat bodies with two sets of thin wings protruding from the body, but they were nearly microscopic drones designed to track down targets through inferred scanners. These tracking drones didn't make much sound, and that was what made them right for tracking high in the sky. Each nat hovered over his location, and they weren't going to allow him to move any further, wasting more of their owner's time.

Three of the 'Death Squad' troopers, as Sharradomina liked to call them, cladded in all black armor with environmental suits, approached him. Their all-black uniforms made them look as if they were predators emerging from the wasteland tundra. Even their breathing masks were menacing and made them appear like a reincarnation of the walking dead. The mask's appearance and the deep breathing sounds of the armed soldiers gave him chills up his spine.

One was carrying an energy collar, another carried shackle restraints, while another was armed with a snipper lasrifle with a massive scope attached to the weapon. Sharradomina had been fleeing across the sea of golden sand and the seering heat could play tricks on the mind, but the agent of darkness understood this was no mirage. Nothing he could think of would be this threatening. Had he ever seen something as horrid in the nether realm of his master? Sharradomina couldn't remember off-hand, but an image like his new escorts came to mind appearing out of the depths of the decaying ground, within The Merciless Reach.

The squad member holding the shackles announced.

"Sharradomina, you are hereby a prisoner of the Fifth Legionnaire Platoon. The elemental commander is waiting for your arrival back in Oduton."

The legionnaire placed the restraint collar and the shackles on Sharra-domina without any struggle from the slender mortal. Threw him harshly into the back of the tracked transport and his frail body bounced around the metal inners of the creeper transport. He finally was going to be given a chance to rest, after his extensive flight across the nomadic plains. His feet were tired, he had become famished and his throat dry and parched. Even more, Sharradomina emotionally drained. His entire journey flee-ing his enemies had drained his of all fight and he was ready to surrender, despite what it might cost him.

The former agent of darkness bounced around the backend of the track vehicle as it climbed over obstacles in its path to the trader town of Oduton. One moment Sharradomina was slamming into the starboard bulkhead of the tracker, then his body would be flung into the port bulk-head. Each time he would strike his human head into the metal bulkhead, grimacing each time. as the transport rocked like a sea vessel caught in a torrid hurricane at sea. The agent ignored the bruises he incurred from the trip, because his emotional state was even in worse condition than his mortal body.

Finally, the track vehicle broke through the sand storm and immerged on the outskirts of Oduton. Sharradomina had been thrown too many times against the track vehicle's bulkhead; blood ran from wounds on his face, torso, and upper body. His nose was also bleeding, and bruises littered his entire body. There were even bruises in places that his clothing covered. He thought that he might have numerous broken ribs because every time he tried to breathe or turned the wrong way, pain shot through his entire body.

Sharradomina was escorted from the track vehicle, as he stumbled and dragged along the way, since his legs weren't cooperating. The agent of shadow looked like he had been at war, and in a way, he had. The restraints still restricting his very movements and made walking even more difficult. The agent of darkness' escorts was less than gentle to Sharradomina, only adding to his suffering. His head was spinning, and the daytime sun blaring antagonistic rays only made his vision even fuzzier.

Oduton was a trader town that bordered Zaskillion's wasteland, The Cursed Steppe, as it was called, but it was more like a make-shift community rather than an advanced settlement. Buildings within the city are of poor construction, and many let in the hot storm weather that rained sand and cracked earth. The town's buildings weren't in good shape at all. Roofs had caved in, forcing the towns people to flee to their neighbor's or to municipal buildings.

The main roadway wasn't much more than dirt and sand, and small dunes rose everywhere, especially in the middle of town, making travel quite difficult. Torchlight lamps were used in place of standard electricity since the settlement neither had the resources nor the ability to generate its own power. These lamps were in high demand and since a cargo shipment was long overdue, not everyone had access to light.

The people seemed to be as rough as the trading town itself. The townspeople all wore gear appropriate for the surface's torrid conditions. They all kept their faces and hands covered, not telling anyone's identity. Everyone seemed to look alike, outside of the different colors worn and the apparent size variations. No one seemed to be indigenous to the planet, with it being a desert. People wrapped up in many different types of multipurpose weather gear, but most still wore attire that protected them from the harsh, dry conditions.

"Make way, legionnaire prisoner coming through," yelled one of the Death Squad members.

Sharradomina's escorts led him into a municipal building, then to a near-empty room, where his captors had all his restraints removed, not that did much good considering the physical state his body was. Sharradomina was tossed carelessly into a chair made of a hardened sandstone material and nearly fell off the edge of the stone chair. He hung on for dear life, with the little strength he could muster.

"Stay put." Mumbled the Death Squad member. "The elementals will be here shortly for you."

The legionnaire left the dark and secluded room, locking it from the other side.

Sharradomina could see each legionnaire's stare, as one-by-one, they left his field of vision, leaving the former agent of darkness alone. He slowly got to his feet and brushed himself off. His entire body ached from his joyous ride. What would happen next was anybody's guess.

Sharradomina began to pace back and forth in the dark room. He had exchanged one bad situation, the abandonment of his master on this rock and dropped into a new one, his imprisonment. He knew if the elementals didn't vanquish his body, then the Darkness would find a way to do it for his failure. Sharradomina had witnessed his master's immense power first hand. Just because he was far away didn't mean the Darkness couldn't get to him. He doubted if even the elementals could prevent that from happening.

Then the agent of darkness closed his eyes and drifted to another place.

⁓

Sharradomina traveled across a hilly plain and came across a sea of golden grass that rolled on and on forever. The place he had arrived at was tranquil and serene. The sky was bright and blue, and large puffy clouds danced in the air. Mountains stretched along the skyline in the distance and appeared to be Leviathans guiding along the valley below.

Suddenly, in the distance, a small cabin with smoke billowing from its smokestack came into view.

It seemed surreal and simple all at once. But something familiar struck the agent and it should. It was his childhood home, the place where he grew up before becoming Sharradomina, an agent of darkness. He began to move down the hill and towards his long-lost home. Sharradomina had forgotten how simple his parents had lived. He had forgotten what his home and the faces of his parents looked like. He hadn't realized, despite the Darkness' efforts, how much his own memories had been suppressed this memory from farthest reaches of his mind.

Sharradomina approached the home with caution, not wanting to upset anyone he might encounter. It didn't seem like anyone was around, in fact, the home looked deserted, but he wasn't about to take any chances.

The home was no more than a shack. It was missing window shutters, possessed a clay floor, which seemed to be smooth with no signs of recent life occupying the hut. There was a slight natural aroma loomed inside the shack, which had a mixture of flowery scent with a musky wilderness blended in. When he called out, his voice echoed off the thin wood planks acting as interior walls. The sound of his voice sounded ghastly, like a phantom calling to potential victims.

Sharradomina began to panic. His usual stoic demeanor now filled with dread and anxiety. Why had he been brought here? Sharradomina wondered. Was this some type of ploy by his dark master, or was there something else in play. Or had the elementals attempt to rattle him, or was he under a mind-bending chemical, meant to remember things he had been forced to forget? The mortal wasn't sure, and if that wasn't bad enough, he wasn't sure how to react either. Had he ventured too far from his human origins? Had he lost the ability to feel for those he had left behind?

That's when something happened. The sky turned gloomy and gray. The golden sea of grass transformed into a wasteland of blacked dirt and dense rocks. It appeared as if a constant mist hovered just above the place he now stood.

Sharradomina knew exactly where he was, the decimated plains that led to the Bastain of the Darkness. He had been here before, and once you experience the death, the chaos, and the despair in the air, you never forgot it. The sun never made an appearance in the home realm of the Darkness. Nothing ever grew in this place, and nothing truly ever lived. There was just eternal darkness, damnation, and agony.

The only question was how had he arrived from his childhood home to the Merciless Reach? Had it all been some twisted dream or another form of euphoria meant to drive the agent of darkness insane?

Suddenly, two shadow guards dressed in their usual black garb grabbed Sharradomina by the arms. Their razor-sharp grasp dug deep into his flesh, and blood began to drain from his wounds. They began to drag Sharradomina across the decimated field and towards nothingness. But he knew where they were taking him--it was time to pay the bill for all his past failures.

The further they drug him, the darker it seemed to get, like someone was slowly setting a cover over them. But the darkening sky wasn't deterring Sharradomina's armed escorts. The ground became rockier and the footing even less maneuverable. He nearly fell several times, but the black cladded escorts kept his upright and moving forward.

Sharradomina moaned as pain shot down one side.

Out of the mist, a dark shadow that expanded for miles, in an oval shape that ascended towards the dark gray sky, emerged. It seemed to create an enormous void in the middle of nowhere, but Sharradomina understood what it was, and he began to shiver all over his body. Their destination was the home of the Darkness, encased in a prison of nothingness.

Sharradomina could feel the immense presence of the shadow entity itself, but he also felt that the Darkness sensed his presence as well. Something deep inside of him knew that his dark master had brought Sharradomina home. To this baron place, this pit of doom and destruction, this void of despair. The master of shadow was preparing to hand Sharradomina, his overdue payment for failure.

Suddenly Sharradomina's entire body began to shake without warning.

They moved into the baleful shadow of the dark void. It stretched out as dark insidious fingers pulled them inwards. The pressure battered Sharradomina's body and made it quite difficult to breathe, like something was sitting on his chest. With each step they took, it became more difficult to stay upright for the frail figure. Not so much for his demonic escorts. It was like they were being pulled into the void itself and pushed away all at the same time.

Suddenly, a deep and foreboding voice bellowed from the empty void. Sharradomina couldn't understand the language it was utilizing, but he thought it was some ancient dialect from a time before anything roamed the cosmos. Then he began to feel a tug at his very essence as if the shadowy fingers were attempting to rip it out of his very body. The pain was so excruciating he was just waiting for his body to explode, sending flesh, bone, and muscle everywhere.

Everything began to become distorted, and he fell into a state of disorientation. The pain no longer matters, despite still being there. His human essence was nearly gone, and his physical body was becoming frayed and weathered. Muscles started to lose the battle with the void and became mush. His skin was melting under pressure, and despite the fact he hadn't blacked out, he lost any clue of where he was and what was happening to him.

"You are now mine. The toll of your failure paid to me in full, and now you will be a part of me for eternity."

That's when the rest of Sharradomina's body disintegrated into thin particles and disappeared forever.

Sharradomina awoke, screaming at the top of his lungs. He was panting heavily and covered in sweat. He could feel his heart racing a million miles a minute, and his blood surging through his veins, making his face flush. His neck had become cramped, along with the rest of his muscles from sleeping in the stone chair. He wiped the perspiration from his lips that had fallen from the upper part of his face.

He gave an enormous sigh of relief. It had been nothing short of a nightmare, but he was safe, now. Or as safe as he could be.

Suddenly the only door to the darkened room moved violently, slamming open. The sudden rush of light blinded Sharradomina, and he tumbled over the sandstone chair, landing hard on the floor. His dust-filled cloak flipped over his entire body, acting like a blanket. The agent of darkness could only lay there, not sure how to respond. Was his life in jeopardy, or had he overreacted?

A small light illuminated the doorway, and a figure moved into the room, shining its illumination to unveil emptiness. The light penetrated Sharradomina's thin cloak, blinding the frail prisoner. The figure holding the light stepped forward and there directly in front of Sharradomina was a legionnaire, but this one wore a tan uniform instead of the black garb of the Death Squad. The figure was still intimidating to Sharradomina, to say the least. The look on the newcomer's face was less than pleasant to look at, but not as daunting as the breathing masks of his captors.

The man in the tan uniform had a snarl upon his face and displeasure upon his demeanor.

"Come out and show respect, prisoner! You're in the presence of Jetsuenete and his fellow elementals."

Sharradomina peaked out at the figure standing before him and, for the first time, noticing four gargantuan shadows standing just out of the reach of the light. Jetsuenete stepped forward and that's when the scared little man saw the spectacular armor the elemental wore. It had a high crest on the elemental's chest. A titan-sized dragon with a horrid wing-span filled most of the chest plate and a solid black border around it. The dragon stood straight up as if to challenge Sharradomina and dare the little man to oppose its will. It was indeed a daunting sight to behold.

But the armor's owner had none of those ill effects supplanted on his face. The elemental Jetsuenete wore a soft, gentle, and non-confrontational expression on his face. Something inside of Sharradomina warmed up, and the fear he was feeling shattered and melted away. The agent of darkness came out of his hiding and stood in front of the elemental. Now all four of the elemental beings that had come to Oduton to visit the legionnaire prisoner stood in the light, and none of them had any ill-expressions towards Sharradomina.

"We haven't come to do you any harm." Boomed Jetsuenete. His golden, diamond-shaped eyes glistened as the elemental mournfully gazed upon Sharradomina. Jetsuenete took a few steps forward and softly touched Sharradomina's frail, thin hands. Suddenly a warm feeling surged through Sharradomina's cold, bitter body.

The prisoner looked over at the other three other elementals and saw the same kindness in their eyes and felt the same warmth resonating from their armored bodies. It seemed like to Sharradomina that it was like his three long-lost uncles accompany his long-lost father. He thought that much compassion coming from the four elementals. His knees got weak, and his sadness living inside his heart left him. Tears formed in his eyes, and they began to run down his face.

"You have much pain and agony inside of you. You have endured the poison that has been living inside you for far too long now. It has eroded your very soul, and it needs to be extracted." Jetsuenete said in a soft tone.

Sharradomina fell to both knees, as if he was about to confess sins of a previous life. He closed his eyes and was prepared to accept whatever came next. Good or bad, the time for his servitude to the Darkness was ending. The elemental placed his immortal hand, which consumed Sharradomina's entire head and began to work some of its omniscient abilities on him. The former agent of darkness began to experience the venomous position that had lived in his veins leave him. It was both a pleasant and excruciating experience.

The elemental began to hum a tune that had to be in some ancient tongue, possibly an ancient elemental language Sharradomina had never heard of before. It was soothing and hypnotic all in one. The former agent of darkness relaxed his body, letting the elemental control him entirely.

A surge of energy came from the elemental's hand, one that illuminated the entire room, encasing it in bright light. The energy surge blasted into Sharradomina's body, and the man's body stiffened. The foreign body inside of Sharradomina didn't want to relent its home. The former agent of darkness gave out a roaring howl, one that would make you hold onto your ears. It was high pitched and filled with agony. But as swiftly as the tug-of-war had begun, the battle eneded.

Sharradomina opened his eyes. They had transformed from its darkened state into a bright color as if a pond of water, which was contaminated, had been sanitized. Blue eyes looked back at the mortal's savor in rejoice. Jetsuenete brought the evil of the Darkness to the surface, but it was fighting the elemental every step of the way. An aura of energy surrounded Jetsuenete. The elemental's chest plate was glowing in a fluorescent red glow. The elemental stood firm as the dark omniscient power fought its last battle. It, like its owner, was resilient to the end.

Sharradomina's scream transformed into a cry for mercy as blood began to flow in streams from his mouth and nose. If Jetsuenete weren't careful, he would lose the frail man. The last-ditch effort by the dark power, the parasite living inside of Sharradomina lost the fight, and the elemental extracted it and incinerated it into fine particle dust. The last essence of the Darkness fade into thin air, never to materialize again.

Sharradomina lay on the ground, unconscious with blood still dripping from his nose and mouth. Jetsuenete called for something to wrap the frail old man in, and quickly a thick tan blanket was wrapped around the former agent of darkness. Jetsuenete scooped the nearly dead old man and carried him in his elemental arms out of the darkroom. The other three elementals.

Whispering among guests gathered in the tiny room for and what the surprise was under the cover.

That's when the elemental leader, Jetsuenete, stepped forward, and the crowd got quiet. Despite the elemental's calm and cordial demeanor, his superior, colossal physical appearance made even their closest allies take notice. The elemental gave his audience a soft and gentle smile. Jetsuenete had his humongous hands tucked into his elemental garb, which seemed to mirror his armor. The soft, cloth tunic had the same dragon crest as Jetsuenete's armor had.

"Thank you for coming together my friends." The elemental observed the small crowd with his golden eyes. "We all have fought hard against the Darkness and its dark allies. The elementals and legionnaire forces have worked together in unison to defeat the Darkness and its allies for a very long time. Like the Celestial beings before us, our time is short and new defenders must replace us." Jetsuenete looked down at the mortal formally known as Sharradomina. "It starts with the conversion of this agent of darkness. This servant of our enemy to be the keeper of our ancestry."

Cries came from members of the crowd, while others displayed disbelief and denial on their faces. The friends and allies of the elementals were pleading Jetsuenete and his elementals not to leave them. Jetsuenete motioned with his colossal hands for them to quiet down.

"Please, hear us out. We aren't abandoning you to the struggles against the Darkness and his vengeful armies. Therefore, we created the immortals, our descendants. They will have embedded in them strength and abilities to defeat our adversaries."

Jetsuenete motioned to the elemental holding the covered item. The cover was removed and a cream-colored egg, the size of a medium-sized pet was revealed.

"Our energy forms will be transformed into these egg-like devices until we are needed once again. Each elemental will have its egg and each coded by its unique omniscient abilities, and colored accordingly. Our essence can never be destroyed, merely transformed into another living being."

Then the old man that was once Sharradomina was brought forward. The crowd all gasped. The old man had been cleaned up, his hardened dark eyes were clear and full of life, but also seemed worn down by his service to the Darkness. He no longer wore his Sharradomina cloak that everyone was accustom to, but now wore a gray smock with a dragon's head implanted in the center of it. His skin was cleaned of dirt and debris, he had a noticeable limp, and the old man needed the aid of a walking cane.

The old man turned and whispered to Jetsuenete.

"Do not fear, my friend. They will not harm you. Despite what they think you have done or what their opinion of you."

Jetsuenete turned back to the crowd. "Please do not fret, my friends. The man known as Sharradomina is no longer. I want to introduce you to the keeper of the elementals and their secrets. This man is now High Priest Tefbei Nakht. The high priest will oversee relaying the history of the elementals, the story of our origins, and he will convey our message of peace and prosperity."

"No! He will betray us all to the Darkness. Please don't abandon us." Someone shouted.

"No, the high priest will not betray us. He is no longer the servant to darkness he once was. I have seen it in his mind and know that he will serve our cult with dignity and honor. Trust me; you will be all well taken care of."

High Priest Tefbei Nakht moved forward to address the crowd. He slowly raised his head and tried to put on a brave face.

"I know you all remember the tragic monstrosities that I have committed in the name of darkness. You have no reason not to doubt me, but by my actions, I will prove to you, and I will earn this chance at serving the elementals in their struggle against darkness. I will never let anything happen to the elementals as long as I exist."

He stepped back and became quiet again.

CHAPTER 11

Aboard the Grand Battleship The Guantlet

*T*he *Gauntlet* was a starship of stupendous proportions. Its mass was over one-thousand times greater than any other starship in the fleet and was the flagship of the fleet commander, Grand Admiral Regina York. For a human, the fleet commander was an impressive sight. She was tall, well over six feet with wide blue eyes, flowing auburn hair that touched her solder bars, she had long limbs and pasty white skin.

The fleet commander's uniform was in immaculate condition, but the elemental leader would expect nothing less from Adm. York, from what he understood about her character and leadership skills. She might be a human, but the grand admiral had a reputation of being a wild card when it comes to battle tactics. She understood how to position each ship in her fleet to obtain victory. Adm. York may take chances with the ships under her command, but never took losing personal or a warship lightly. She also ran a tight ship; no personal wasn't any place they weren't supposed to be.

The flagship was five times as wide as a super cruiser, making each ship deck spacious and feel like a metropolis. Each deck hosed a division of ship personnel, which Jetsuenete couldn't begin to memorize. There were that many on each level. The bridge was the largest in the fleet, but that made since knowing the size of *The Gauntlet.* There were over a thousand personal on the bridge during a shift. The pilots were housed on the same level as the ship's dock area, making it swift to launch when the time came. The medical and storage level was just under the command deck, where all ship's officers birthed and hung out when not on duty.

A host of support ships supported the Gauntlet; frigates, super battleships, destroyers, and many others that made commanding much easier. An invading navy would be forced to fight too many of the support ships that surrounded the flagship before they ever got close enough to invade the grand battleship. But the *Gauntlet* didn't just rely on the support ships to protect her. The grand admiral had four squads of advanced fighters at his disposal, with twenty-five hundred in each squad; over one hundred transport shuttles. Adm. York had a platoon of marines at his disposal, along with a slew of support vehicles that could be prepped at a moment notice.

Jetsuenete, Dirdanth, and a few of the elemental fleet commanders gathered in the grand battleship's war room. The room was spacious, and the conference table made of beautiful wood and well varnished. The table could sit up to twenty-five occupants, but there was room for more inside the war room if needed. There was ample lighting, more than was required, in fact.

The elemental leader scanned the room. It had been a while since so many of the elemental allies had gathered in one place. Jetsuenete was hoping for some better news from the fleet than his elemental expeditions had experienced. The war in stellar space was just as crucial as the elemental sieges on the battlefield. The oval table could double as a holographic battle map, and each member could receive files from other members of the war council through the millions of circuits embedded in the table.

Grand Admiral York looked sharp as always in her navy white dress. She was surrounded by several other fleet commanders, which Jetsuenete couldn't remember their names off-hand. A few of the commanders were conversing with the admiral. The atmosphere subdued, but tension was still in the air.

The last few council members had just arrived, followed by a fleet administrator decked in all black. The administrator carried a datapad and a smart, no-frills expression. The ship administrator looked at the grand admiral and nodded. The admiral made a coughing sound that quieted down the room and drew the occupant's attention.

"Do we have everyone in attendance, Lt. Mercer?"

The man in black nodded. "All that is capable, mam."

"Very well." The admiral continued. "Shall we begin?"

Grand Admiral York scanned the attendees swiftly.

The ship administrator stepped towards the table and pulled a wand-like device from his trousers. Then he switched on the device. A hologram of the local sector emerged. The hologram spun slowly, giving each war council member a good look at the map. Jetsuenete didn't recognize the sector that was showing on the hologram. The elemental had been to every corner of the galaxy. The elemental leader sighed. *Well, it is a large galaxy.*

Dirdanth leaned over to his friend and whispered, "Are you ok?"

Jetsuenete made a non-committal nod, then looked back to the grand admiral.

Grand Admiral York was pointing towards a section of the holographic map, but from where the elemental leader sat, he couldn't see what. It was like the grand admiral and subordinates were in a different dimension than the elementals seated across the table. All Jetsuenete could see for sure was the orange tint reflecting off the admiral's immaculate uniform.

"We have had several attacks from sector X-39Delta over the last few months." Barked the administrator.

"And what are the nature of those attacks?" Questioned Dirdanth.

The administrator gave the elemental a shocked look.

The other commanders could only stare at the two elementals in attendance. But none dared to lash out, because the grand admiral would certainly reprimand them. Despite being aliens on the ship, they were still elementals. They commanded respect, if nothing else. Besides, most fleet commanders knew the grand accomplishments of the elementals, from stories told by the Marines that served under them.

Neither the looks or the whispers bothered Jetsuenete. He had heard it all, and all he desired was a solution to the problems the fleet was experiencing. The elemental leader waited patiently for the fleet commanders response.

"We were hit in Sigma-None-Delta-Zero-Five." The administrator responded. The officer points to the lower right portion of the hologram. "There were three sieges there in two days."

"Three sieges in two days?" Jetsuenete looked hard at the spot the officer in black had pointed. "It seems that's a quite large quadrant; it possesses three sieges seems perfectly normal for its size."

All the fleet commanders looked to the grand admiral as if they had nothing to say.

The grand admiral looked down at the data flowing in front of her. Then she looked back at the two elementals in her professional manner. "Nothing about these sieges are normal, Jetsuenete. According to my aids," she glanced at the lieutenant before continuing. "…it's a sector that had previously never been struck. Now I have supply ships and less armed patrol scouts being attacked. We have been forced to bring in heavier armed ships to protect them."

"All that proves is they are getting ballsy." Returned Dirdanth.

Jetsuenete noticed that made the lieutenant's head snap back, like something had bitten him.

"That's just in that sector." The administrator glanced at his commander for approval before continuing. "The attacks have increased in the normally attacked areas, which also have seen increased activity." The administrator pointed towards the multitude of dots lining the upper sector of the map. It made the hologram look as if it had contracted the measles. "The red and orange dots are the normal attack areas, while the purple and blue dots are new portions of each sector that have been under siege."

Jetsuenete and Dirdanth study the infected sections of the transparent map as if something had just become apparent to them. Dirdanth leaned over and whispered something to his leader. Jetsuenete nodded in return.

"Anything you care to share?" One of the fleet commanders asked.

"Just discussing the situation with my leader," boomed Dirdanth.

"Do you think these attacks are ambushes that the drowmauder commanders have planned, or is it a coincidence that many of the dark fleet can move around without our fleet's knowledge?" Questioned Jetsuenete.

"What are you insinuating?" Barked a fleet commander that hadn't spoken up yet.

"What I think the elemental leader is suggesting, if I might." Cut in Colonel Maliki Benoit. "Is that you have a traitor in your ranks, gentlemen."

Col. Benoit was the acting commanding officer of the human marines. Their Brigadier General had been killed in a recent battle and hadn't been replaced. Maliki Benoit was the only high ranking officer available to replace the general. What Jetsuenete understood about the colonel was he was strict on his men and always had them prepared, not a lot different from the elemental leader.

"You mean a spy?" Returned Grand Admiral York.

The colonel could only shrug his broad human shoulders. "You know it happens grand admiral, even to the best of us.

The fleet commander was scowling at the marine coronal. Even on best of terms, the navy and marine platoons never saw eye-to-eye, especially among the upper brass. Having the marine colonel excuse the fleet of having disloyalty wasn't helping that relationship.

"That's preposterous?" Screamed another fleet commander.

Col. Beniot's aid whispered something in his ear, and Jetsuenete noticed it didn't make the acting marine CO flinch one bit. Maliki looked back towards the grand admiral and her commanders. He gave them a sly mocking smile. "Is it so shocking? We have had issues of late, from every division. Intel disappearing, surprise ambushes when the dark fleet shouldn't know our operation schedule. Cargo ships being hijacked. Tell me what else could be feeding the Darkness' forces?

Suddenly the grand admiral's administrator stepped in to cool the hotheads in the room.

"We have one of the fleet commanders live. She will tell us firsthand what these new raids have been like."

The holo map dissolved, and the profile of Commander Kimberly Swansen of the *Nightstorm* appeared. The holo image was unclear and flickered off and on like the signal was being disrupted. The commander looked tired, but her facial features didn't necessarily come through clearly. The commander looked around at the assuming faces in the room.

"Can you hear us, commander?" Quizzed the grand admiral.

The connection cut in and out as Cmd. Swansen responded. "Yes, mam. I can hear you, but you're cutting out badly. I'm afraid, between the solar storms the dark fleet has created and the natural radiation in the sector, we can't get much better of reception without abandoning our position. We have even extended our towed array antenna to boost our signal."

"Commander, this is Grand Admiral York."

"Hello, grand admiral." Answered the *Nightstorm's* commander.

"Tell us about the attacks you and the other ships in the sector have been experiencing."

Cmd. Swansen looked around the room as if she was making sure all eyes were on her. "The ambush attacks tend to come out of nowhere."

"Nowhere? That seems highly unlikely commander." Bellowed the grand admiral's aid.

"If you will let me explain, council. I may be able to explain a theory my crew, and I have come up with."

"Go ahead." Ordered Grand Admiral York.

"I think the dark fleet utilizes either dark energy to hide their ships or may I suggest, dark magic. It's like the ships they use come out of the darkness of space and start bombard our ships. But only enough to drain out shields."

"Only?" Questioned Col. Benoit. "What is the point in that?"

"After the dark fleet rushes off, we usually do a preliminary damage report. At least one ship ends up taking on excessive damage, propulsion failure, leaking O2 canisters or even exterior hull damage. It's like they are wounding us just enough so we can't follow them. Then when most of the crew is asleep and ships running a skeleton crew, the dark fleet returns suddenly without warning and snatches the worst damaged ships, usually one per attack."

The marine aid whispers to Col. Benoit, and he nods.

The grand admiral notices this and addresses him. "You seem like you have seen this type of tactic before, colonel."

"This sounds like a drowmauder scheme. The marines have seen drag-alyite soldiers attacking marine camps and stealing away the injured, when they encounter squads too big for their patrols to overtake. But the drag-alyites would never do this on their own. The reptilians have more honor than this, it's the drowmauders who use schemes such as this."

"And it sounds like they have adopted this tactic for their dark fleet." Boomed Dirdanth.

Many of the council started to agree.

"There are a small number of dark magic drowmauders that have learned the dark craft from the Darkness." Jetsuenete added. "Commander Swansen, you said the ships come out of nowhere, correct."

Cmd. Swansen's profile flickers.

"Correct."

"I've never seen them use dark magic before on such a large object such as an attack vessel, but it's possible." Returned the elemental leader.

"And you are think they might employ these dark magic wielders in their fleets?" Questioned the grand admiral.

"It is a remote possibility," returned the elemental. "Risky, because the Darkness only trains the most loyal and intelligent drowmauders to learn the craft, and it takes a long time to master, from my understanding."

"Well, whether they do or not, it sounds like these new tactics are being employed throughout the sector, maybe even the entire galaxy." Boasted Col. Benoit.

"Yes, temporarily." Returned Jetsuenete.

The grand admiral looked around the room. "So, what do we do about this?"

Jetsuenete stood up.

"Have your commanders look for distortions in the sectors they patrol. Rely on their sensors, the dark magic will expose the ambush parties."

"I would recommend adding more escort ships to the patrols as well until we can confirm and formulate a strategic counterattack plan." Boasted the marine colonel.

"That's fine, but what of the spy issue?" Questioned one of the fleet commanders.

Col. Benoit shrugged his shoulders. "That's on you and your ship's crew. I have no issues with traitors in the marines. All my platoons understand how we deal with traitors."

The marine commander gave the council a sly, but cold smile.

"This council meeting is adjourned. Thank you Cmd. Swansen for your report. I will be in touch." Grand Admiral York said.

Outside the war council conference room, a small, two-foot-long machine, appearing like a centipede, stopped recording. It was attached to the other side of the wall, with tentacles buried into the surface of the wall itself. The red illumination lights turned from bright red, which ran down the length of its metal body, to its normal metallic shade. Then a small antenna dish emerged from the creature and began to broadcast it's signal and data package out into deep space.

CHAPTER 12

On the planet Nanzeawei

In a secluded location, in the northern sector in a dark constellation, known as the Dendrobranchiata constellation, a small uninhabited planet resides. The lair was embedded underground. Only the bare minimum supplied to its occupants, the infamous dark assassins, the Derun Dehugezrur. These select few not only were well trained in the art of assassination and becoming invisible to their victims but also trained in dark magic.

The dehugezrur's built their sanctuary under the mountain terrain to give them clandestineness. The rocky walls were cold and uninviting, the perfect place for the dark assassins to make their hive of destruction. The iron foundation acted as a shield, bouncing any search scans right back to their source and preventing anyone from exposing what lived underneath.

There were a few pieces of advanced technology, but even that was limited, reducing the hideout's electronic footprint. These dark elves were an ancient race, and they didn't require high tech gadgets for their work. The dark magic flowing through their veins was more than enough for their use. Liquid lighting illuminated the main forye where a stone workbench occupied the center and surrounded by a small round table and chairs to the right, a small kitchenette, and to the right two synthetic lounge chairs and nothing else.

The only figure in the room was an older dehugezrur named Khroun-zorn Chirelroth, the patriarch of their clan. He had darker skin than a normal drowmauder; his intense purple skin seemed to glow under the luminescent lights. He was of average height for his species and somewhat muscular, in lanky sort-of-way. The younger dehugezrur assassins were of varied sizes and shapes but always seemed to romp around the lair, as if they didn't know what to do with themselves. Chirelroth, in his advanced age, understood to conserve his energy, especially before an assignment.

Usually, Blackmour Drowmauders lived for a few hundred years, inherited into their genes, but with the dark magic infested into the dehugezrur blood, which made it difficult to determine their actual age or how long they could live. Some dark magic wielders were known to live for a millennium or more. The Chirelroth clan had served the darkness for over ten millenniums, and they were loyal to the Darkness. They had commanded more successful assassins than any other clan, during their length of service. It was a pride for Khrounzorn to continue the family business. He had reached the highest rank given to a drowmauder of High Dark Mage.

Khrounzorn couldn't just utilize elements of dark magic, such as chemical reconstruction, dark illusion, and invisibility; he could change shapes, manipulate subject minds for interrogation, the dark mage also tap into dark elemental magic. All of these dark abilities made him the most powerful dark magic user, outside of the Darkness itself. With such a powerful mage in the service of the Shadow Empire, the Darkness forced to keep an eye on Khrounzorn at all times. But that didn't mean the master of shadows never utilized the drowmauder as an extension of its hand. The dark elf could wield magic that even the elementals had never experienced.

Khrounzorn is standing in a lose-fitting clan kamono that was a two-piece attire. He wore an undefined and straightforward undergarment with a robe-like outer with the clan icon on his left breast. The clan symbol is circular with the ends not quite touching, making it appear as a throwing weapon with sharp edges that could shred flesh. The clan icon is colored purple, with a black border. There is a thick bridge area that connects the upper and lower half of the weapon icon. Two thorn-shaped protrusions stick out of the circular center, pointing towards both blade-like edges. The icon mirrors the weapon of choice for the assassins.

The rest of the clan members dressed similarly, but no badging is visible to tell leaders and soldier-assassins apart, either on their causal or field attire.

Khrounzorn is working with a science beaker, mixing some magical cocktail. White smoke billows from the baker's sides, as if a bock of dry ice was inside. The dark magic user says a few incantations under his breath and returns, mixing whatever was inside the glass beaker. None of the other members disturb his work, they know better. The clan leader has an infuriating temper and has shown a vengeful wraith for those that interrupting his work with dark magic.

Once finished, Khrounzorn stairs at the magical cocktail, as a whirlpool of foam surfaces as the contents merge. The High Dark Mage smiles at his new creation. The Alchemy mixture was the dark magic user's finest he had ever produced. Only the master of shadow's training could allow the drowmauder to create it. "Finally," Khrounzorn said under his breath. "I have done it; after years of trial and error. The elemental fleet will feel the terror and retribution of our dark lord."

Something dawns on Khrounzorn. A vision from the past, an event he hadn't thought of in ages. He had just graduated from his mage apprenticeship, which placed Khrounzorn in action making the drowmauder a greenhorn disciple. He was on his own and stronger than he had ever been in dark magic. He was teamed up with another mage fresh from his apprenticeship, Sulyd Yaimaemdra. In training, they hadn't been that close, which made for a miserable relationship. This was the first time either mage didn't have their mentor at their side.

They had been sent, as part of a cadre of mages to convince a village of drowmauders to join the war effort. They mainly wanted the villager's grain crops, but the village was becoming less than corporative. The town is centered between the rolling plains of Rockingmer Pastures and the Valham mountains. The terrain was hilly, creating a barrier around the village and the plains.

The cadre came upon the village with the first adobe homes creating the outskirts of the village. It was early, and not many of the villagers were roaming about. Homes were still dark, and nothing would discover their arrival until it was too late. The multi-layered home structures were built right into the hilly land. It wasn't until the cadre got through the village itself; they would reach the plains where the villagers grew their golden-brown crops of grain. The connecting buildings were staggered, and the mage cadre had to weave through narrow stairways to make their way through the pueblo structures. The tight corridors and alleyways made it difficult for mages to engage any villagers more side by side. They were just going to have to utilize their magic, single-handed.

Suddenly, out of a side entrance, three village protectors emerged with crude-looking spears. Khrounzorn knew not to take the weapons lightly. They could shoot beams of energy from the tips, and despite the mages healing capabilities, it would leave a scar. Khrounzorn stepped forward and cast the front two village protectors encased in large bubble-like structures. The protectors began to drift upwards and away from the other disciples.

Sulyd and two other disciples engaged the other two protectors. It didn't take the disciples long to dispatch the villagers, despite wielding energy weapons. Khrounzorn didn't take time out to observe the slaughter; all he could concentrate on was holding the first two protectors in midair. One slip of his concentration would send the villagers crashing down, and that would most defiantly more protectors to their location.

Khrounzorn heard screams of pain in other buildings, with some directly above them. The sound sent a smile on the mage's face. The villagers wouldn't defy the long reach of their master ever again. The Darkness had too many spies, and Khrounzorn felt like he was finally contributing to the cause, finally.

Sulyd nods to Khrounzorn. Their job is complete; the mage releases the two village security men from their temporary prison, and the men fall to their deaths. Their group's job was nearly done. Now, it was up to the others to place fear in the villagers into cooperating. The only thing left for their detail prevented any more village security from bearing down on them and trapping them from escape.

That's when a strong force began to pull on Khrounzorn, one that announced the presence of a much superior force. One that only lived in blackmour drowmauder legend. The presence was ancient and substantial like an invisible foe was chocking the mage. Khrounzorn stumbled backward a few steps. It was undeniable at this point, he knew what was living among the villagers, why they had been so defiant. Only a Dark Oracle or a High Mage could reach out like it that, but if the legend was true, the being was neither; it was something so monumental the dark disciple didn't dare to think of such a monstrosity.

The legend of the drowmauders told their young was of the first dark magic user the Darkness had anointed; the Dark Sorcerer Ghalror Knozif. An unknown process chose the sorcerer, whisked away to the Darkness' home, and slowly the master of shadows taught Knozif the ways of dark magic. He was supposed to have been the only drawmauder ever to learn every little spell, every technique the Darkness possessed. In the Merciless Reach, Ghalror Knozif became warped both physically and mentally by the poisonous air.

What's left of Ghalror's sanity was stripped away by the dark magic he was subjected to, much like the celestial being that became the Darkness. By the time the dark magic user fled the Darkness' service, the blackmour drowmauder had become so powerful that legend said Knozif rivaled the master of shadows power. If it was true, but legends could rarely be believed, Knozif had been insane, and it was difficult to decipher what made the dark sorcerer do the things he did.

"The Obelisk of Knozif." Mumbled Khrounzorn.

"What?" Questioned Yaimaemdra. The mage had a confused look like he was about to commit Khrounzorn into an insane asylum. But drowmauders didn't do such an act. If you were insane, they just killed you.

Khrounzorn recovered in time to respond. "The legend of Knozif. Isnt that the place he was supposed to live?"

"A giant tower?" Sulyd's worrisome face had deepened. The mage was worried about his comrade. "Is that what you're talking about? Some Sorcerer's tower that stretched to the heavens is that what your mumbling about?"

"I know it sounds crazy, but I have never felt anything as powerful or malevolent as the substance that was trying to kill me a moment ago."

Sulyd Yaimaemdra shook his head. By this time, the other mages in their unit had noticed their argument. It was making Khrounzorn uncomfortable, and that's when he knew he wasn't going to able to rely on his fellow mages. This was something he would have to do on his own. The young mage disciple clenched his fists, hold back his anxiety, and cleared his throat. "Sulyd, you and the other mages finish up here. I have something I must do." Khrounzorn spun around on his heels and ran off with Sulyd, calling out from behind.

~

Khrounzorn Chirelroth made his way through the pueblo building make, with adrenaline pumping and his heart racing. The mage finally made it out of the mud buildings and to the plains behind the village, where they grew their crops. The air smacked his drowmauder face and made his long dark hair whip in the wind. The sky was grey as if it was about to rain, but then on Doksalfur, the sky was always grey.

The young mage couldn't see much further than fifteen or twenty feet in front of him, because of the thick, low cloud cover. It acted as a blanket, concealing the field of grain stocks. But not even that was going to stop Khrounzorn from going to the source of his torment. The powerful magic draw was guiding his body, or better yet dragging him along the dirt-filled path. It was like swimming in a murky sea with no direction of where to go only that the dark magic was guiding him, despite the inability to see.

Khrounzorn began to whistle a tune he had never heard before, but his whistling never missed a beat. It seemed that the immense dark magic that was guiding him soothed his nerves as well. What would he discover at the end of his journey? That was the question the mage was about to uncover, whether good or bad.

"I can't see a damn thing. Is it always like this?" Wondered Khrounzorn.

A cold breeze seemed to come out of the west, followed by a salty smell, as if an ocean was close. But the dark disciple knew what saltwater smelled. That musky scent was unmistakable. But that is ludicrous, wasn't it? There was no ocean close to the rolling plains. It was like Khrounzorn

Chirelroth had stepped from Doksalfur and into another world, another dimension altogether.

"Where in the hell am I? Where is this dark power drawing me to?" Then something dawned on Khrounzorn, but he had to shake it off. "There is no way I'm in the Merciless Reach. If this power is from Ghalror Knozif, then there is no way he has brought me into the home of the darkness. Legend said he fled the Darkness. Anyhow, the Merciless Reach has unbreathable, poisonous air."

Then the dark mage emerged from the thick fog cover, and the sky became more transparent. The sky was still grey, and the air dense and cold. Stone and rocky terrain filled the rolling tundra, with no grain fields insight. The hillside where pronounced, appearing more like a mountain range than rolling hills bordering a plain. Khrounzorn moved onwards, as the powerful magic towed him along. A sense came to the mage, telling him he was close to his destination.

The mage disciple knew he was close, possibly within walking distance, the dark magic dragging his along was whispering to him. Off in the distance, about three-quarters of a mile to his right, a distortion appeared. The only way to tell something was off was by using his mage senses. Normal eyesight wouldn't even register the distortion at all. Even his mage-enhanced senses struggled to pick it out of thin air.

The grey air was still, and nothing moved. The only thing that was remotely alive was the howling wind. Then it happened, like someone throwing a pebble out into a calm lake, the atmosphere rippled, and the distortion started to tear at the illusion that concealed the Obelisk of Knozif. For one solitary moment, Khrounzorn saw the fabled home of the notorious dark magic user clear as a summer day. Despite being too far away to concentrate on details, the mage saw the ancient tower as if it was too real to contemplate. It was aged, with a pitted exterior and the Magnetite shade, the weather-beaten structure still seemed to stand tall. The obelisk towered towards the grey sky as if it was an extension of it.

Then before his own eyes, the Obelisk of Knozif slowly disappeared behind the curtain of tears that slowly sealed the mythical tower back into it cloaked hideaway. Khrounzorn is dissatisfied. He has found the tower and knows he is close, knows it's up to the mage to go to it and confront its dark master.

Khrounzorn cautiously approaches the tower of doom, with it still under its invisible cloak. The mage disciple reached out and felt the cold stone structure before him. The magical cloak rippled, as it had done earlier. The corner of the obelisk was grimy as if the cold stone hadn't been cleaned in over a millennium. Khrounzorn ran his hand back across the surface of the tower until reaching an arch doorway than was locked. Placing both hands on the warped wood door forced the cloaked spell to recede and show the obelisk.

Being this close to the tower, now made it seem like it was an extension of the sky. The dark mage cranked his head to see the tower's pinnacle, but it was useless. Khrounzorn knocked on the door, and an echo bounced around in the spacious interior; still no one came to the door. The mage looked skywards and called out, "Hello, is anyone at home?" His voice echoed up the outside of the tower structure and disappeared into the grey atmosphere.

"Well, they can't say I didn't ask them if I could come in. But if the butler's not answering, I will have to help myself, won't I."

The dark mage placed palms of both hands flat on the warped surface and imagined he was opening the door. The mage's hands began to glow a cherry orange, and the door began to vibrate rapidly. The waves of energy forced the door to pound hard against the arched doorframe. Suddenly, the door burst into fragmented pieces, and the entranceway was clear. Khrounzorn tilted his head back and shielding his face with his arms, keeping splinters from striking him.

The atmosphere was cold and stale inside the obelisk. It was dark, and with the permanent grey sky overhead, very little light shone through the one large window. Khrounzorn forced to feel his way around with his mage senses since he couldn't see any more than a few inches in front of him. There was a lone source of illumination coming from what appeared to be the top of the dark tower. It was faint, but strong enough Khrounzorn could see to negotiate up the steep, spiraling stairway.

The mage attempted to reach out and expose the source of the illumination, but something was blocking his attempts with superior to his own. Khrounzorn could hear his boots scrape the stone staircase, but nothing else, and that was bone-chilling. The close he drew to the top of the stairs, the more luminous the light was becoming, but he still hadn't figured out what it was. It didn't seem to be coming from a lit candle or torch; he didn't feel any heat, and the air around him was quite cold still.

The one thing that had become prominent was the dark magic strength. If Khrounzorn thought it was daunting before, it had become a tsunami of energy traversing up the obelisk's spiral stairs. The mage kept his mind clear and ready, along with his dark magic for anything that might happen. But concentrating with the pressure of the opposing magical force was challenging to deal with. It was like a mounting pressure opposing his ascent, ready to burst at any moment.

Finally, Khrounzorn reached his destination, and the room at the top of the tower was as bright as day. He could see everything in exquisite details, including the minuscule cracks in the interior walls. There wasn't much furniture in the spacious room, just a long ancient wooden table that seemed to come from a different time and place. The table stretched across the width of the room, only leaving a spot at the end for a single body to get passed. The table trim had an exotic design that stretched down the legs of the table. A single flower wrapped around a snake-like creature with a forked tongue protruding from its mouth. A vine is full of thorns wrapped around the body of the serpent as if it was integral to the serpent's own body.

Two high-back chairs made similarly positioned oddly. The chair positioned on the other side of the table, facing Khrounzorn at the other end, facing the room's entrance, as if someone had been awaiting his arrival. A half-empty plate sat the far end where the chair facing the mage was. A lone torch was positioned directly behind the elongated table, casting a looming shadow over it and the lone figure in the room.

The figure stood there dressed in a sorcerer's robe. The robe was grey, matching the dark sorcerer's skin. Unlike many blackmour drowmauders, who had purple-tinted skin, the dark sorcerer has ash-grey skin.

Khrounzorn wasn't sure if it was from Ghalror Knozif's obsessive usage of dark magic, if the Merciless Reach had done this to the sorcerer or if he was a distant relative of the drowmauders and didn't share their skin pigmentation. The cuffs, trim of the sorcerer's hood and across the figure's chest, was a thick line of drowmauder purple, which made Khrounzorn curious of Knozif's origins.

"Ghalror Knozif," echoed the dark mage.

The tall and bulk figure gave the mage disciple a malcontent grin. The dark sorcerer licked his lips, exposing a set of canine fangs that appeared to be able to puncture skin. Blackmour drowmauders weren't born with fangs at all. *What are you?* Wondered Khrounzorn.

The dark sorcerer looked at his visitor with his emerald eyes. "You will address me, my young friend, as your liege or High Dark Sorcerer Knozif. And I am the evolution of our kind, Khrounzorn Chirelroth."

Evolution, what the fuck does that mean? The mage took a few steps backwards. A fear had emerged in Chirelroth's stomach.

"It means have become something greater than any drowmauder had ever dreamed of. The blackmour drowmauder condition no longer pertains to me, I have transcended into something greater, something that one day you might become, if you follow me."

"Wait, you can read my mind?"

The dark sorcerer nodded. "I can. And so, will you, in time." Knozif reached out with his hand.

"What, follow you?"

Another nod from the dark sorcerer.

"But weren't you corrupted by the Merciless Reach, by your possessive behavior towards dark magic? Are you even Ghalror Knozif any longer?"

"Watch your tongue, my young mage."

Suddenly a sharp pain began to matriculate inside Khrounzorn's shoulder. The burning sensation was small first, but the it grew as if his muscles were consumed from the inside. The mage began to suffer from the pain, and he knew that Ghalror Knozif was causing his discomfort. There was a sense of pleasure coming from the dark sorcerer's eyes as if he was enjoying watching his victim suffer.

"Is this what you do to your followers?"

"Only the ones that resist, but to be honest, there haven't been many that have come. You're the first in a long time, a millennium. I sensed your potential and knew you could survive the rigorous training involved in reaching the pinnacle of our profession. How do you think you found this place or even discovered my presence, young mage? It was an invitation, by my own making. I wish for you to join my cause."

"You betrayed the Darkness, abandoned the master for your own self-ish needs, and you want me to join your crusade?"

The mage disciple understood he had gone too far. He sensed the seeming madness and anger resonating within Ghalror Knozif. Khroun-zorn didn't have enough time to react. He was barely able to form a protective shield when a bolt of lightning struck him and knocked him backward. Luckily, he deflected the attack with a partial shield bubble, sending the bolt of electricity into the ceiling, forcing the ancient structure to rain stone debris down on them both.

The dark sorcerer stepped forward. Knozif's fingertips still had smoke resonating from them. The mage shook off the dizziness and attempted to get to his feet before another outburst came. "Your tongue, my young friend, will have to be suppressed. It will defiantly find you in neither land if you don't control it. I will only offer you a spot at my side, one last time. Then I will have to consider you a hostel and deal with you accordingly."

Khrounzorn understood he only had one chance at surviving this ordeal. He reached out to sense what the dark sorcerer was thinking, but everything was blank. Either the mages weren't good at probing minds, or Ghalror Knozif had closed himself off to Khrounzorn. The young mage would have to work fast, and he didn't believe arcane magic like haste would work, so he reached back and created a cyclone that would act as a diversion. The storm of dust and stone debris, picked up from the tower floor, began to emerge and rage in front of Knozif. At the least, it would disrupt the sorcerous hell fury.

Khrounzorn took this opportunity while his opponent was distracted with the cyclone to propel arcane missiles of frozen icicles, fire, and other solid objects. But since he was only a disciple of magic, some of the magical missiles didn't quite form as he imagined them. The dark sorcerer deflected them all with ease.

"Is that all you have, boy?" Screamed the dark sorcerer. "Is this what the drowmauders been teaching you. I could teach a pet that much. If you joined me, your magic ability and power would increase substantially."

With both hands clutched as if the sorcerer was grabbing ahold of the ceiling above, Ghalror Knozif. Then he made a throwing action like he was forcing the structure above Khrounzorn. Suddenly stone fragments began to rain down on the mage. He couldn't put up his shield bubble in time, and several large portions of the ceiling fell on him. The mage lost his breath and bearings temporarily, not knowing what was occurring.

The young mage didn't see the shadow materialize through the entrance doorway. Then a familiar voice spoke. "I see you have been up to your old tricks again, Knozif."

The dark sorcerer didn't respond but made a huffing sound of disbelief.

It was Bihirara Walviesh, Khrounzorn's mentor. Suddenly the stones covering the mage disciple lifted off Khrounzorn, and a protective bubble wrapped itself around him. Swiftly the protective bubble began to lift out the half-demolished window. Suddenly a mighty explosion erupted, sending him tumbling to the ground. Khrounzorn looked around with his head still spinning. A few of his fellow mages were standing nearby. They had come to his rescue.

As the mage recovered, he stood up just in time to wittiness, Ghalror Knozif leap from the tower window-seal towards the newly arrived mages. The dark sorcerer's robe flapped in the wind, like a cape on a masked hero, but Knozif was no hero, he was more like a vengeful god. Their nemesis landed with his hands flat on the ground to break his decent. The ground shook like a quake had just struck the rocky plains.

Ghalror looked up at the flock of mages, which now was at two-dozen. The dark sorcerer stood up and whipped his hands clean, deliberately making loud, slapping noises. The sorcerer looked at the mages and gave them a sly smile, one that seemed quite maleficent. "So, this is the cavalry? A cadre of students that think they can do dark magic. I hate to burst your bubble, but I'm about to school you in the dark arts."

One-by-one, the mage disciples thrashed the dark sorcerer with everything they had. Firebombs, ice missiles, lightning strikes, everything they had been taught. But nothing could penetrate Knozif's energy shield. It shone like a halo around the dark sorcerer. Then after it seemed the attacks on their nemesis had subsided, the dark sorcerer unleashed hell on the mages. Out of the terrain came razor-sharp monoliths of stone and rock. These starship-sized structures ripped out of the ground and impelling a few mages. Those that hadn't been killed by the bombardment of earth and stone scattered about to save their lives.

Khrounzorn noticed Ghalror enjoying himself. He was entertained by the death and destruction he was causing. That only frustrated the mage. Khrounzorn let loose on the dark sorcerer with everything he had. With the sorcerer's attention, averted and his energy shield down the wave of magic struck the dark sorcerer like a freight train. The barrage of magic overwhelmed Knozif and ignited him into millions of pieces. He had done it! Despite his control and lack of magical knowledge, Khrounzorn had destroyed the second most potent dark magic wielder ever to live.

But just as suddenly the dark sorcerer had been destroyed, Knozif began to regenerate himself. "Shit!" Khrounzorn understood they were outmatched, no matter their numbers. None of them had ever been taught, let alone accomplished regeneration. That was Knozif's vast knowledge and a lifetime of using dark magic.

The mage disciple saw it in the sorcerer's eyes. Despite his grip on dark magic, there were too many of them; he was outnumbered, and neither side would win the day. Knozif was like a rat trapped in a cage with nowhere to go. But Khrounzorn felt something vastly approaching. Nothing of a physical nature, mind you; this was something other-worldly. The dark sorcerer waved a hand, and a swirling, empty void appeared directly behind Knozif. Now the young mage understood what Ghalror Knozif attended to do. He wouldn't detonate himself to devastate the mage ranks; no, the dark sorcerer was too craven to do that. He would flee into another dimension.

"You may have won this round, but I will not forget any of you, not your ugly faces nor the mages I know you will become."

The dark sorcerer took a few steps backward and disappeared into the black portal. The Obelisk of Knozif also vanished along with him. Then the portal vanished as swiftly as it had appeared. None of the mages could chase the sorcerer, no matter how much they desired. None of them could make a traveling portal appeared out of thin air, and even if that was remotely possible, where had Knozif gone? His real home, some alternative realm they were aware?

The Dark High Mage snaps out of his dream.

Khrounzorn lifts the beaker from its holding cradle. The high dark mage stared at the substance and smiled. "Ghalror Knozif, I have done it. You may have beaten me by substantial years, but now I have created the ability to follow you. But unfortunately, I'm now to friable to chase you. This is the last trick I have to equal your mastery of dark magic."

The Dark High Mage begins to pour the greyish-purple liquid into four equal metal canisters. He watches the martial merge before he sealed each one carefully. Then placed the canisters into a backpack with blackmour drowmauders writing on each. The ancient language named each cocktail pack as the property of the dark starship would deliver to the elemental fleet.

A dark and substantial shadow consumed the work table, and the High Dark Mage looked up to see his second in command, Caresce Zaistrol. The master mage was an excellent soldier and expert assassin, but she never could finish her studies, and Khrounzorn forced to promote her before she had been ready. His last master mage had been killed in battle by elementals. His head chopped off at the neck base. But what she lacked in dark magic skill, she made up for it with her assassin skills.

Zaistrol bowed in respect. "High Mage, my men are ready for the mission."

The assassin's long grey hair blended well with her purple skin. For a dark elf, she was breath-taking and had many suitors, but she was celebrant. Caresce was loyal to her duties and the drowmauder servitude towards the Darkness. She also had a husband back on the drowmauder homeworld, but she doubted she would ever reunite with him again. Her husband was a major in the Darkness ranks, and she a Derun Dehugezrur; death would surely claim them both.

Zaistrol was slender, with elongated limbs, including her fingers, making her perfect for a derun dehugezrur. Her swift movements and ability to disappear in a heartbeat didn't make her the ideal assassin, and it made her legendary. When she had come to their clan, Khrounzorn wasn't sure if he had believed half of the hype surrounding her legendary status, but her exemplary record was flawless, and the dark high mage discovered first hand why.

"So, you say, Caresce." The high mage straitened his kimono and held his stern, non-wavering expression. It was either he doubted what she was saying or not satisfied with her answer.

The master mage bowed to remain in the dark high mages' good graces and not disrespect her superior.

"If I have done something to dishonor you, master, tell me what to do, I will do it." Zaistrol lifted her eyes to a not so level of the dark high mage. "I will maim my useless vessel of a body to satisfy you."

Khrounzorn's dissatisfaction disappeared from his hardened face. "That won't be necessary. Your body is far from useless. I have never had a reason to doubt your performance until this latest episode. You failed to destroy even one of the elemental fleet escorts."

Caresce sucked in her breath and not releasing it until the high mage thought she might pass out.

"Our performance may not have been at the expected level, Master Chirelroth. But we have been more than accurate with our precision strikes in the past."

"Yes, I will concur your record had been flawless until this last failure. I haven't lost my confidence in you or your team. The mission I have for you might bring down the elemental fleet for good." The dark high mage gave the younger drowmauder a sly smile. "It might eradicate them, leaving the elemental resistance wounded, or at least in space."

High Dark Mage Chirelroth slowly strolled to his private chambers, followed by Caresce Zaistrol.

Khrounzorn sighed. *I still don't understand precisely why you hid your tower in the middle of that town, Knozif, but I have learned to create illusions greater than your dark sorcery did. The blackmour drowmauders still don't understand many things you did, but I am about to surpass all your dark abilities.*

The high dark mage waved his crinkled hand, and the chamber door opened. Chirelroth and Zaistrol walked in. The high dark mage's bed chambers were elaborate for an underground chamber room. The room was dark since it had any windows, and only a handful of candles lit the room with a purple illumination. Zaistrol stopped directly after entering. Khrounzorn slowly turned towards the commander, fluffed his mage robe, and gave Caresce Zaistrol a roguish smile.

"It is our time to let our presence be known to our enemy."

The dark high mage reached for something on the lone bookcase and a hologram of several elemental fleet ships. Cmd. Zaistrol looked at the purple hologram, then returned her attention to the high mage. "What do you mean, dark high mage Chirelroth? We have conflicted with the elementals and their mortal allies for a long time."

"The Darkness and its allies have been at war with the elementals. We have been working behind the scenes, doing the dirty work, ask the Shadow Lord."

"I will the next time I get an invite to the Merciless Reach." But Zaistrol regretted it right after she said it. She began to shrink from the high mage.

Khrounzorn ignored the slight comment. There were more pressing issues that needed to be dealt with. He twisted his wrist at the top of the hologram, and the purple image magnified. The high mage began without turning his head back to Cmd. Zaistrol. "The elemental fleet has been reining havoc on the dark fleet."

"We have been isolating individual ships, taking them, and leaving the rest of their fleet in chaos."

"Childish games. I have something greater in mind."

Khrounzorn turned back to his display.

"The fleet is great in numbers. They have even destroyed many sectors of the dark fleet."

"Is this a history lesson, high mage?"

Khrounzorn gave the commander a dark stare, one that has made many derun dehugezrur agents shrivel in shame. But Cmd. Zaistrol wasn't nearly as intimated, and the high dark mage hadn't come to shred the commander's confidence. He needed her and her team to complete his plan.

"No, commander. I haven't told you all of this to insult your intelligence. I'm explaining the elements of my plan."

Zaistrol lowered her head, resenting her reactions. "Sorry, master."

"The dark cocktails I created will demoralize the elemental fleet. What will be left of them won't be enough of the dark fleet even to break a sweat." He points to the hologram, and four points on the purple image begin to contrast the rest of the hologram. "Your drowmauder assassins will sneak onto our enemies ships, place the cocktails on them, and a group of dark voids will emerge."

Four dark voids began to swallow the images up like a hungry anteater. Before Cmd. Zaistrol's eyes, the elemental ships disappear into the dark voids. Even though it took only seconds on the hologram, it seemed to Zaistrol that the disappearance of the ships took an eternity. It nearly took her breath away. Once the image vanished and the high dark mage had turned off the hologram image, she stood there speechless, not sure how to respond to it all. That was the reaction Khrounzorn was looking for. He was hoping the elemental ship crews will be just as shell-shocked.

"Impressive, is it not?"

The dehugezrur commander had just recovered at had to take a moment to respond.

"How do you know that your dark magic potion will work like that? I must assume it is a one-way ticket. I should know that if I'm going to sacrifice invaluable assassins to this plan."

Khrounzorn nodded. "Your absolutely right; it is a one-way trip. And the plan will work as I have displayed because the dark magic that will produce the dark voids is the same that swallowed the Obelisk of Knozif. I experienced it first-hand."

Khrounzorn saw through her dilated eyes that the commander still wasn't sure, but it wasn't her decision to make. She had only to see his orders through to the end, and the rest was on a high dark mage.

~

The *Nightstorm* positioned in front of the escort convoy. Commander Kimberly Swansen observed the three other star cruisers drift through the sector. The commander ordered an all stop. Something had wakened the ship sensors less than twenty-five thousand kilometers behind them, but as quickly as the isolated incident had appeared, it vanished. The commander sensed something moving among them, like a cloaked predator.

"Whatever and wherever you are, you're like a parasite searching for a host." Cmd. Swansen whispered.

A beep on her emergency com, allowing only her to access the call. "Yes?"

The scanning supervisor reported, "Mam. We have finished scanning the sector, and there is nothing left of whatever had set off the sensors."

"A ghost, then? Something is out there; I can feel it in my bones."

"Paranoia is a dangerous thing, mam. But if you're crazy, then we all are."

"Maybe we just are on edge from the last incident. Let's keep an eye open, just in case our friends come back."

"Yes, mam." Responded the sensor supervisor.

Suddenly an explosion shook the entire ship, setting off alarms all over. The noise is unbearable and made listening for anything that would give away what had shaken the vessel or what was happening beyond the commander's location. Then a sound of fleeing boot falls, either from the incident or in action towards it, came from the furthest hallway. Swansen couldn't tell, even when she left the place next to the observatory window and the junction hallway.

Have we been invaded, or has a threatening stowaway been discovered? The commander opened a comms line to the bridge. "Bridge, do you copy?" Nothing but static returned. No one on the bridge was responding. She was cut off from the rest of her crew, but she still was in command of the ship and responsible for her crew. Cmd. Swansen moved out into the hall. She looked to her rear, nothing. Then Cmd. Swansen looked forward, in the direction of the bridge. What direction would she take?

The commander should have headed for the bridge and her crew, that's what a good commander would have done and what the first admiral would expect. But, Cmd. Swansen was an unconventional commander, not saying she wasn't good at leading her men, but the commander had an unorthodox way of command. She made her way towards the rear of the *Nightstorm*.

Kimberly Swansen didn't pass any of the ship's crew on her way, which was odd. But despite the emptiness of the aft of the ship, she sensed something or someone moving around. The *Nightstorm* commander wasn't sure whether the presence had a physical form or if it was doppelganger cloaked in shade's skin. At a junction, she turned towards the interior of the ship. Something was drawing the commander towards their unwanted guest; she felt herself getting close. But what would she discover, who would she find once the commander caught up with their stowaway.

Then a flash shot by as if something ran at the speed of light. Swansen wasn't sure what it was, maybe the doppelganger she had feared it was, but perhaps it was something else; that's what she feared. Kimberly Swansen picked up the pace and began following the residue the flash-in-the-pan had made. It was like following a scented trail, or a set of distinguishable footprints in the mud.

"I've got you know, you little sneaky thing." Mumbled Cmd. Swansen.

Then a swift movement, one not much different the lighting quick flash she was following. Either she was following the same stowaway, which had slowed down or there were more than one stowaways on the *Nightstorm*. The commander continued her pursuit, turning down a shortened hall, that led to the maintenance catwalk and access panel for the ion drive. *What is this doppelganger trying to do, sabotage our propulsion systems? For what reason?*

Once the commander reached the next intersection, there it was, the figure she had been chasing. But why had it stopped? Had it sensed her approach, her pursuit of it. The character refused to turn around as it was taunting her, begging the commander to come after it. The figure wore shabby clothes, from what Cmd. Swansen could tell. The intruder had a faded, grayish-purple tinted cloak that hid the figures, authentic form. The only other thing the commander could see were black leather gloves and a set of what appeared like patrol boots. *Military issued?* Wondered Cmd. Swansen.

Suddenly a flashing sensation caught the commander's sight. When she looked over in between two support girders sat a metal canister with a detonation switch. The switch was what was flashing, like a countdown. The commander gasped and began to draw her fleet issued sidearm. But she froze halfway retrieving the weapon when the figure spoke.

"It's not nice to stare, commander." Said Caresce Zaistrol. The assassin slowly turned around.

The leader of the dehugezrur assassins slowly turned around to face her opponent. She tossed back her cloak hood and began to remove her weapon, a short serrated sword. The sword was only used to engage victims in combat; her killing weapon was a dehugezrur assassination dagger. The dagger was longer than most and had a nasty looking serrated blade on both ends, perfect for killing at any angle. It was a Derun Dehugezrur traditional weapon that dated back hundreds of thousands of years of usage by the dark elf assassins.

Zaistrol's dark eyes were giving the commander the shakes. She had never come face-to-face with a dehugezrur assassin. Her hand was shaking just as much as the rest of her body, making the grip on her Infused Meta Thermal blaster, unstable, and she nearly lost the grip on the gun as it cleared her sidearm holster strapped around her shoulder strap. That drew her attention away from the assassin, just a little too long.

Once the commander was able to control the weapon, Caresce Zaistrol had moved into striking distance, like a viper ready to deliver a deadly blow to its prey. The assassin slapped the blaster out of Cmd. Swansen's grasp, leaving the commander of the *Nightstorm* defenseless. The assassin was patting the short sword in the palm of her hand.

"Hadn't your elder ever tell you it's not polite to stare, commander?" The dehugezrur assassin leader began to chuckle that sounded more devious than anything.

Cmd. Swansen was rubbing her wrists. "Yours's must have abandoned you as an infant because your manners are the worst."

The comment set the assassin back on her heels.

"Ouch! That was rude, something I didn't expect coming from one of the first admiral's trusted leaders."

"What are you doing on my ship, planted explosive detonators?"

Caresce Zaistrol's attack position had slackened. The two women faced each other like next-door neighbors causally speaking.

"No, commander, I'm not attempting to sabotage or destroy this beautiful starship. We have something else in mind."

Cmd. Swansen had regained her composer, and her stall tactic was working. Suddenly the *Nightstorm's* deck shook, temporally throwing both women off-balanced. That was the commander's best shot. She removed a small pocket knife the first admiral for her last birthday, cupped it in her hand, and flung it at the assassin. But Caresce Zaistrol's instincts and training were far superior, and the assassin slapped the small weapon aside with one flip of the wrist and her short sword deflecting the pocket knife.

That was the commander's last-ditch effort, and now she had no way to defend herself. No sidearm, no knife, this wasn't what Kimberly Swansen had trained. She was a better tactics officer than a field combatant. She wasn't a marine. The commander took a step backward, and that's when the assassin struck. The sword blade sliced the air, as it was aimed for the commander's throat. Luckily Swansen had good reflexes even for a woman in her late forties, let alone a twenty-something.

The commander went into a barrel roll, and the blade missed her throat, only to slice the side of her shoulder. Swansen's evasive maneuver transformed into a tumble, and she struck the side of the metal bulkhead. The commander groaned and held her head. The shadow of the dehugezrur assassin covered her dazed body. Even with Kimberley's back to her deadly opponent, she could tell how far away the assassin was, by the size of the assassin's silhouette.

Cmd. Swansen awaited until the assassin had committed to her killing stroke, then rolled out of the path of the blade's path. Clink went the short sword. Kimberly heard the highly skilled assassin curse under her breath but didn't have time to listen to what was said. The commander rolled to where her blaster laid. Without thinking, she gripped the weapon with determination and a steady hand.

Caresce Zaistrol stood up, and even the sight of the blaster pointed at her didn't make the assassin shrink. The dehugezrur assassin's eyes concentrated on the commander's grip, and Kimberly Swansen knew she would only get one shot at this. If she missed, the assassin surely wouldn't, and she would be a dead woman. A lump formed in her throat, but her resolve didn't shrink. His hand was steady this time, as her courage had returned. She wouldn't die in a state of panic.

The assassin removed one of her dehugezrur assassin's daggers. Zaistrol held it in front of her victim with a death grip, allowing the commander to see the serrated blade. A demented smile protruded through the assassin's cold stare. *She's taunting me,* Cmd. Swansen admitted. But that alone wouldn't force the *Nightstorm's* commander to shed her confidence.

"I must admit, I am impressed by your perseverance. Too bad you about to bite the dust."

"Thanks for the vote of confidence."

Before she had time to finish, the assassin launched her killing weapon. The dagger soared through the air like a merry-go-round at a child's playground. Swansen sidesteps, aimed and prepared to fire her Infused Meta Thermal blaster. But something happened she didn't expect, Caresce Zaistrol raised her hand, and the dagger's blade changed course and sliced the commander's right trapezoid muscle, throwing off her aim.

The laser shot missed its target, but still grazed the assassin's top chest, leaving a singed hole in the assassin's blouse. The assassin fell back against the bulkhead but was still conscious. Caresce Zaistrol looked up at Cmd. Swansen and gave the commander a sinister smile. Before anything could happen, three-ship security guards show up and grab the assassin and placed her in shackles.

"Wait!" Ordered Cmd. Swansen. "What is that thing with the detonator? What will it do if it's not a bomb?"

"What the hell, I don't normally tell my victims of my plans, but what does it matter. It's not like you can stop it now. This ship won't blow up and take your precious crew with it. My master has greater plans for you all, the entire unit of elemental ships. Four holes will rip out of space-time, and your ships will disappear in these dark voids. You and your comrades will be gone, and the elementals will finally feel my master's wrath."

Cmd. Swansen gasps. "You mean the Darkness."

Caresce Zaistrol begins to laugh. "No, I mean my master, the High Dark Mage Khrounzorn Chirelroth."

The commander seemed lost, she didn't recognize the name, but she had more significant issues at hand. "Take her to the brig." Then she turns and snags her communication device. "Bridge, full reverse. Get us the hell out of here. Pass the message along to the other ships. Do it know, I command you."

Four empty voids appeared and began to drag the elemental ships into their terrible emptiness. The *Nightstorm's* ion engines roared to life, as the ship started to fight against an ever-increasing gravitational pull. Panels rip from the outer hull. Propulsion engines strain as the *Nightstorm* struggled to escape the void's immense power. "More power!" Barked Cmd. Swansen. "We need more power."

The starship began to fall back towards the empty void. One-by-one, each ship fell into each cyclonic void. Swansen's entourage was being swallowed alive, into a dark and unknown place. The commander looked back at the metal device with determination. Suddenly the *Nightstorm* shuddered and nearly knocked the commander out. Pain filled Kimberly Swansen's shoulder, but she knew she had to fight it off.

The *Nightstorm* jerked violently, and then the starship fell rapidly backward. There was only one thing for Cmd. Swansen to do. She crawled towards her blaster, held it tight in her hands, steadied herself. She wasn't sure what would happen once she shot the metal canister, but she had to try something before they also fell into the void.

"Her goes nothing."

The commander's aim was real, despite the obstacles laid before her and fired. The canister exploded, sending shockwaves throughout the ship. A portion of the *Nightstorm* incinerated, leaving a hole too large to patch. It could have fit a gaggle of escape pods in the hole, but that wasn't going to stop the starship. Without the void's device holding hem gravitationally in place, the *Nightstorm* shot away from its potential doom and into hyperspace.

CHAPTER 13

The site was an abandon cave in a secret location:

The secluded cave was full of shadows, with only limited lighting. Jetsuenete, along with Dirdanth, Gaitharrul, and the two shape-shifters; Erreodan, the powerful, and Nightzeneth stand before several other elementals. They all had been called to the meeting to discuss their next plan-of-action. Jetsuenete, the elemental leader, scanned the crowd. He recognized so many faces, many that he had fought side-by-side several times before. But for every recognizable face, there were at least two that weren't there. The elementals had lost way too many of their own over the years. Too many brave and courageous brothers had gone to the grave too early and Jetsuenete, and the other elementals planned to stop that.

The one thing that you had to understand about elementals; with their celestial heritage, they didn't necessarily die, their energy form merely left their bodies and found new forms to fill like the rising phoenix blazing a path for itself.

Despite possessing celestial genes, the elementals were heavily targeted by the agents of darkness, and their numbers had dwindled over time. How they were to defeat the Darkness and its allies if their numbers were way too few and the armies of darkness continued to swell? This issue was a dilemma the elemental leader had been battling with since he could remember.

Jetsuenete nodded to his second in command, and Dirdanth raised his colossal arms high in the air and called for silence. The whispers echoing throughout the crowd quickly vanished, and all eyes were on the four elementals standing before their brothers. The elemental leader took a deep breath and addressed the crowd.

"My loyal brothers, thank you for coming out on such short notice." Jetsuenete scanned the elementals in attendance. Many still had their battle armor on, and several were bloodstained. They hadn't had time to remove their battle gear. They were summoned directly from the battle-field. "I understand it might be an inconvenience for many of you, leaving the battlefield and pulling your troops out. But we have received some disturbing intel that we couldn't relay over normal com channels."

Jetsuenete looked at Dirdanth once again and his second in command to control of the meeting. Dirdanth switched on a holo map, and an orange sphere-like image appeared before the crowd. The elementals in attendance all had their attention glued to the image before them all. The illumination from the holo map reflects off Dirdanth's black colored gambeson that fits loosely on the elemental.

The gambeson with a silver and red wolves skull on his chest plate embedded on the right breast.

"As of the last intel report." Boomed Dirdanth. "Many of the agents of darkness, including the Darkness' bulk army, have invaded several mining moons, asteroids, and refining stations in sector Charlie-1156.78D." Jet-suenete's second in command pointed to many points on the holo map. "At first, this seemed random and nonessential to the war against the Darkness. But the more these isolated attacks continue to happen, the less random they appear to be and more strategic they become."

A murmur emerges and begins dancing among those present.

Erreodan, the powerful, broke the whispering by barking his resentful protest. "Why should any of that affect our war efforts? The elementals don't have time protecting individual resources. We are already too thin as it is."

Jetsuenete takes over the presentation to ease the elementals in attendance fears.

"I will not deny our numbers are dwindling more rapidly than I would like, brothers. But we can't ignore a pattern by our adversaries. One that might suggest that something else is at work. If we don't seize their efforts now, when do we stop this deplorable tactic? Will it be far too late, when we decide to act?"

"Why would the armies of darkness need these mined substances in the first place?" Questioned Nightzeneth, one of the shape-shifting elementals. "The Darkness has no use in the economic value it provides the mining colonies, and the armies of darkness have no use of such materials."

"It's unclear what they would be doing with these mined minerals and ore deposits, but it has to be something significant or the Darkness wouldn't be wasting valuable resources on these dead worlds. It's highly unlikely any of the stolen materials were utilized in their armor. Have you seen the rusted weapons and poorest quality of the reptilian armor? No, there has to be something else at work."

"If we are unsure of this, then why waste time or resources defending these colonies? Why are we worried about any of this until we have more intel? When we are sure about the purpose of these unorthodox raids?" Barked Erreodan, "I say let the Darkness waste time with these miners, and let us get back to demolishing their massive ranks."

Whispers return and move through the crowd.

"Hold a minute, my brothers." Called Jetsuenete. "We can't abandon anyone to the forces of darkness. Not even those we might find with lesser morals than our own. If that were the case, if that were our creed, then we would allow many species to perish under the might of the Darkness. But we don't, do we?"

A mass of whispers emerged, and the elementals in attendance began to agree with their leader. He had struck home his momentous point as if hitting a hot iron with a massive hammer. The elemental leader let it all sink in, giving his comrades something to ponder. Then Jetsuenete motioned for silence, and the crowd of elementals slowly simmered down.

"I say," called their leader. "That we assign a task force, either by choosing those most qualified to begin the search, and assigning a platoon of marines to aid in the hunt for these stolen mined ores."

Jetsuenete understood he wouldn't have time to handle this personally. The massive hunt would take a lot of their resources and many elementals in its oversight. Leading the elemental army, along with coordinating efforts with their mortal marine allies, took most of his time. He would have to trust this to another. Unfortunately, Jetsuenete understood they couldn't strip down the regular fighting force. He would have to assign a skeleton crew to handle this assignment.

Dirdanth leaned in and whispered something that Jetsuenete agreed.

"Dirdanth will be your point of contact. And anything you might need in this assignment will come from him. He will also be the one choosing those attached to this urgent assignment, and a chain of command will organize effective immediately."

As the five elementals walked away from the now dispersing crowd, Jetsuenete confronted by Erreodan. "I still don't see how we can deplete our military ranks to search out this mythical storage place. It's a wide-spread cosmos, and we have no clue where to begin."

Jetsuenete nodded in response. "You are so correct Erreodan." The elemental leader looked at each of the other elementals, now standing in a circle. "We can't afford to deplete our fighting ranks. But what else can we do? If we don't respond to this threat now, it could cost us down the road."

Nightzeneth lashed out, exposing his mouth of razor-sharp teeth. "Then why even attempt this? It seems so far-fetched. Our efforts could concentrate on defeating the armies of shadow and end this war for good. This may be what the Darkness had in mind all along. To deplete our ranks and weaken our resolve."

It was clear to Jetsuenete that the two shape-shifters, the leaders of their aerial arsenal, were dead against this deviation. He wasn't going to win their favor. But since he was their leader, Jetsuenete understood they both would comply with orders, if they were chosen for this detail. But the elemental leader knew he couldn't afford to lose either one on the battle-field. They were too valuable, and Jetsuenete felt that both shape-shifters knew it as well.

Dirdanth responded, "That's why I will be handpicking the elementals and marines that are best suited for this assignment. Trust me; the frontline militia won't even notice they are missing."

~

Deep within the Merciless Reach, inside the Darkness' residence, the Shadow Lord, one of the oldest of the master of shadow's agents, moved through the sinister halls. The shadows ran deep down both sides of the decrypted bastion hallway. The lighting produced a dark purple hue, and the demonic saturation ran deep throughout the sinister fortress. Lonely, perturbed eyes hid within the elongated shadows, giving off uncertainty on an unassuming visitor.

The Shadow Lord glided just above the putrefied bastion floor. His black cloak train barely dragged over the bastion floor. The air was stale and dense, less than desirable to breathe, but the Shadow Lord didn't have to worry about that, he was a creation of the dark power residing within its master. The Shadow Lord's translucent physical form passed by a section of wall, where blood seemed to seep down from cracks in the walls that flowed like a roaring river.

Screams of pain and agony could always be heard, like tortured souls were being ripped apart repeatedly. None of this seemed to disrupt the Shadow Lord's march towards its master's chamber. After spending an eternity in servitude within these doomed walls, nothing phased the agent of darkness. The agent had news to bring to its master. News that wouldn't sway the Shadow Lord one way or another.

As the dark phantom-like being approached the Darkness' chambers, the Shadow Lord could feel the immense power radiating from behind the looming walls and large double doors. They had as much decay on them as the rest of the bastion structure possessed. Caked-on blood loomed on the door's outer skin, and the iron-clad ring handles rusted to the verge of falling apart. They had the appearance of having been left out in the rain for all of the time.

The Shadow Lord suddenly stopped at his master's door, waiting for its invitation to enter. Despite the dark energy residing within the agent, it still didn't have the desire to enrage its master and endure the Darkness' wrath. There had been way too many victims that had been carried from its master's chamber cell to warrant the Darkness sinister rage. Despite not knowing what might happen if the Shadow Lord did cross that line, the agent of shadows wasn't going to tempt fate.

The Shadow Lord shoved on the massive chamber doors, and a loud creak filled the area just inside the chamber entrance. The intense radiating energy that had seeped through the decrypted chamber walls struck the agent of darkness like a stone wall. The chamber was dark and foreboding, but that wasn't going to hinder the Shadow Lord. The agent knew its master's chamber like the back of its translucent hand.

The Shadow Lord shoved on the massive chamber doors and a loud creek filled the area just inside the chamber entrance. The intense radiating energy that had seeped through the decrypted chamber walls, struck the agent of darkness like a stone wall. The chamber was dark and foreboding, but that wasn't going to hinder the Shadow Lord. The agent knew its master's chamber like the back of its translucent hand.

The being slowly drifted into the chamber's depths. The immense energy field acting as the Darkness' cell became more robust, the further into the humungous chamber The Shadow Lord got. The agent knew from all the times it had been beckoned to its master's quarters what point it could go to and where the energy field began. There was little atmosphere in the chamber, and what air was present was stale and foul. But the Darkness and its agents didn't need air to breathe, so this wasn't an issue.

A deep breathing sound emerged from deep within the darkness, like the very void was alive. The Shadow Lord stopped suddenly, sensing the cell walls of its master, directly before it. Despite the ability to see its master, the agent of darkness knew the Darkness was staring down on it's subject with a set of fiery eyes.

A deep growl, followed by a malcontent voice penetrated the void of darkness. "Speak," echoed the voice of the master of darkness.

The Shadow Lord bowed. "You called for me, my master?"

Another deep and baleful growl echoed from the darkness.

"I did. Speak to me, my tool of despair. What news from the industrialist have you brought me? How is the production of my new army coming along?"

The Shadow Lord tensed up. It knew it would come to this. Giving its master news of the substandard performance from the factory wasn't something the agent relished. The Shadow Lord glanced up at the

Darkness' star sized, demon-like eyes; it began the report. "My lord. The industrialist claims a production glitch and reports there was a substandard amount of units produced this period. The industrialist also promised, once the glitch hadn't been rectified, production would ramp up, and twice as many units would be produced before the next cycle period."

The Darkness let out an earth-shattering roar that seemed to shake the entire bastion. Luckily enough, the Shadow Lord wasn't standing, or the earthquake that followed the Darkness' tirade would have had the agent of darkness lying down on the floor, right underneath its master's glare.

Still, the Darkness' outrage did rattle the agent. And the Shadow Lord wasn't prepared for its master's accusations. "Lackluster production performance?" Boomed the master of shadows. "What does that mean!"

The Darkness reached out and with an invisible force grabbed on to the Shadow Lord and pulled the agent towards the energy cell. The Shadow Lord could feel the immense power radiating on its translucent skin. If the darkness drew the agent of darkness any closer, the celestial cell would begin to singe the Shadow Lord until all its dark energy buried deep with the agent and became nothing. The agent attempted to pull back, but its master's grip was too superior to do any good. The Shadow Lord was at the mercy of its master.

"I sense reluctance in you, my pet. What aren't you telling me?" Growled the Darkness.

The Shadow Lord knew it couldn't keep the secret very long from it master. Since the very dark energy that made up the master of shadows, also made up the agent, the Darkness could sense everything that the Shadow Lord knew. It would be better to let it out and deal with the consequences. But what the Darkness might inflict on the agent was far from the Shadow Lord's own knowledge.

"My lord." Began the Shadow Lord. The agent struggled with its master's grip. "The reason for the lack of production is a result of low raw materials at the plant. The industrialist..."

"What was that?" growled the Darkness. The fiery red orbs that were the master of shadow's eyes grew tight as if it was concentrating intensely on the shadow agent. "What do you mean by that?" Suddenly the Darkness' grip tightened.

"One of our container shipments was hijacked, your most diabolical one. Our escorts attempted to chase down the thieves and recover the shipment, but they failed." The Darkness released the shadow agent from its indestructible grasp. "We even brought out some of your dark magic wielders to track the thieves, but it seemed like the thieves, along with the shipment vanished into thin air."

The Darkness growled a low noise as if it was pondering the choices it had. "I know who to use to track down the missing shipments. Order Darkcloak to rendezvous with my Derun Dehugezrur at these coordinates." Suddenly a set of coordinates appeared in the Shadow Lord's very mind.

If the agent of darkness had facial muscles, it would have a scowl on it. *Darkcloak, of all agents, shouldn't be given this assignment.* The Shadow Lord thought, trying to keep the thought from its master. But the Darkness didn't need to read the agent's mind to know how deplorable the orders were to the Shadow Lord. Both agents of darkness had a running feud that has lasted since Darkcloak first came to the service of their master. Darkcloak had been given free rein, for the agent's ability to turn assets to their cause. The Shadow Lord always felt it was manipulation, not Darkcloak's techniques that drew these assets to the agent.

But what was worse than that, their master allowed Darkcloak to keep those assets for the agent's use. Most agents of darkness would have to turn the assets over once they had been obtained. That was what made the Shadow Lord and Darkcloak's feud grow. The Shadow Lord shook off its agony.

"Master, Darkcloak is nothing but a manipulator, and the Derun Dehugezrur are nothing but cutthroat assassins that run wild through realm after realm without any regard to the assignments you attach them to."

"That's what makes them both perfect for this assignment. Darkcloak's connections will allow the agent to sniff out the thieves' trail, and the Dehugezrur will eliminate and retrieve the stolen ore."

The Shadow Lord could only shake its luminous head. "Master. Shouldn't we be more concerned with the elementals searching for the storage of our raw materials? That could hamper the production process far more than a missing shipment."

The Darkness let out a sinister laughter.

"Those fools will never discover the stores of ore. I have them running in circles too much and besides the place where the storage of ore and the production faculty itself is too well hidden for them to stumble onto it. Dark magic has been cast on its dimension's gateway. Our spies in the elemental ranks will inform us if they get too close to it. They are the ones sending the defenders on their wild goose chase."

"Very well, my master."

The Shadow agent began to back away from the Darkness' prison not wanting to enrage its master further. The agent felt the Darkness' focus waning and that was a sign their conference was ending.

"I will do what you require of me."

Underneath, somewhere the Shadow Lord felt was safe, doubt about those orders manifested. Neither Darkcloak or Derun Dehugezrur would accomplish what their master desired. That the Shadow Lord was sure.

CHAPTER 14

Eighteen months ago, on an isolated planet known as
Rankour Twelve

The air is dry and stale as the wind swiveled heavily on Rankour Twelve. Dust and sand-filled the sky and visibility was at a very minimum. It was a desolate desert body in the Horrace system, which was inhospitable itself. It is just another dismal day on the horrific planet. The planetary body had been transformed a long time ago from a ravishing world full of life to its current dead state, by an asteroid collision. Rankour Twelve was a prime target for space debris colliding with its atmosphere.

Fine grains of sand and immense amounts of dust covered the surface of the planet. Gale force winds came out of the east and blew everywhere, making visibility difficult. Surface dwellers forced to wear protective garb to keep the sand particles from getting into their lungs. High amounts of radiation struck the surface of the planet, making it critical that those who ventured on the planet's surface protect themselves. Extreme and dangerous species moved just beneath sandy dunes, making it very dangerous to travel on the surface.

Rankour Twelve was a safe-haven for galactic outlaws, thieves, space pirates, and other undesirables that wanted to disappear without a trace. Most galactic authorities avoid the planet like the twelfth plague. There wasn't any planetary government, residing or patrolling the arid crust. It was a place where you watched your back, and the inhabitants used their own brand of justice.

One day, before the surface became a wasteland, a chunk of space rock came calling. The wave of radiation, from the collision of space rock and planet, incinerated ninety-nine percent of the surface population, leaving the surface of the planet in its devastated barren state. It took generations before the surface could be inhabited once again, with radiation levels spiking and laying waste to any vegetation that had grown on the surface and vaporizing any surface water. The isolation made it perfect for the galaxies' most diabolical and least desirables.

The undesirables that fled in haste to Rankour Twelve usually fled from some galactic police state or crime syndicate that they owed an extreme debt. These undesirables either housed themselves in make-shift shacks, ready to collapse on itself or utilized local transports that doubled as living courters. But then some made Rankour Twelve a temporary stopping point.

In the most secluded settlement on the dreary planet, two undesirables approach a busy spaceport bar known as Deadman's Reckoning. The dull illuminated sign had every third letter burned out. The place's exterior was ragged and worn. The rusty, aluminum siding barley hung to the building. The windows were covered with aluminum louvers, keeping the elements from getting inside. The bar's roof had major holes and had the appearance that it could collapse at any moment.

Both men wore ragged clothes, appearing as if they had been lost at sea for months. Their faces filled with dirt and sweat, and Tank believed that would only add to their ability to blend in with the local folks. Despite his namesake, Tank was a thin and frail-looking character. He had the appearance of not eating for a while, but he always had that appearance, and before his brutish partner came along, he had been a constant target both physically and sexually, in his line of work. Tank was the brains of their merry little band, which had included three others, but Tank feared retribution for one or two of their cohorts, and he had them eliminated. While the thieves hadn't ditched their last mate until they had secured the freighter, they had crashed. The man was left for dead from mortal wounds during the capture of the vessel.

Tank scanned the outside of the bar. No galactic authorities or hitmen for the crime syndicate they had been fleeing was present, but it was more out of habit than in need. He doubted that they would discover what they needed, but their options were severely limited.

Tool, on the other hand, was a mountain of a man and too Herculean to be a thief. The man was more than two-and-a-half meters tall and built like a hover tank. Tool had tree trunk sized forearms, an immense waistline, and was muscular all over. If Tank was the brains of their posy, Tool definitely was the brawns. Tool's one true deficiency was his ability to work himself out of trouble. He wasn't exceedingly intelligent and needed Tank to do most of the thinking for them both.

Little did the two thieves realize they were in deeper trouble than even either one could imagine. They weren't just fleeing from any one of the two dozen crime syndicates that they usually stole from. No, they had stolen a freighter of precious ore from the Shadow Empire, and now the two were on the run. They had outrun the empire's agents sent to kill them, which eventually led to the freighter's crash landing on Rankour Twelve. Little did either of them understand the trouble they were in. The Darkness would never give up pursuing them and recapturing the stolen materials.

Tool watched Tank's back, while his friend was preoccupied, but that was always his job anyways.

The bar had a reputation for attracting the lowest scum of the galaxy and that's how our two thieves found themselves here. The bar's reputation had preceded itself. What few authorities that did travel to the planet would avoid the establishment like the plague. They didn't have to worry about being arrested in this place. "So, this is the place?" Whispered Tank. "Not quite what I thought it might be."

Tool elbowed his partner. "Some shady looking individuals are hanging around the outside of the bar, boss." The big guy had a nervous expression like he was ready to ditch this place. But Tank understood the two thieves had run out of supplies and need a place to lay low. If they were going to find anyone who might assist them, they would find it at this low-rank bar.

Tank nodded in response. "Our type of place. Cum on, let's introduce ourselves."

It wasn't the Ritz Carlton hotel, but it would be a place for them to find a place to hide and possibly a way off the rock. The two galactic outlaws had snuck aboard one of the rare cargo ships they could find visiting the desolate rocky planet.

The two human males approached the bar's rusted and twisted doors. Rust lined the outer brass trim that once shined brilliantly, now had an abundance of dents on it, as its now deformed shape wrapped around the twin doorway. A figure seated in a dark corner of the overcrowded bar stares at the men talks to several patrons of the bar, searching for a place to lay low until they stowed away on a transport. The figure overheard a few of their conversations.

The figure turns away and smiles a sinister smile. "There is a sucker born every day." He looked down at the dense, brown liquid sitting in the cup in front of him. "This day won't be a loss after all." The figure pulled out a hand-held device, one that seemed to fit nicely in the stranger's palm. He switched the device on, and it began beeping a constant blue light; it was transmitting. The figure replaced the device where he had hidden it and prepared to receive the two outlaws.

The bar was as run-down as its exterior. The aluminum bar had an rustic appearance that ran down the entire length of the cramped building. A pug-nosed bartender paced up and down the bar serving a multitude of customers. The cliental of the Deadman's Reckoning ranged from every type of species and all types of professions. The one thing all the patrons of the Deadman's Reckoning shared was their desire to do business in private.

The two thieves had visited several places as the Deadman's Reckoning before, but Tank never got used to filthy places as the one they currently found themselves in.

After receiving their invitation, Tank and Tool approach a secluded booth in the back of the bar. Jankus LaGuettra was awaiting them there in an eerie silence, only occasionally lifting his metal mug. He was dressed in dark abnormal attire for an individual from the planet surface. The seated man wore dark shades over his eyes, which made it difficult to identify him and conceals his identity. He had lizard shaped eyes and olive skin tone with Gills on his neckline, that Tank and Tool couldn't see, making him unique, a true outsider, even for occupants of this planet. That might explains the reason why he sat in a secluded part of the bar.

The two men slide into the other side of the booth. Jankus LaGuettra was sipping on his steel cup and looked up at the men through his dark shades. For just a moment, he swore he could see LaGuettra's reptilian eyes through the concealing shades. Tool was getting a nasty vibe about this guy. His entire body was feeling numb, and that never happened to Tool. He had nerves of stone and rarely would seem jittery or nervous.

Tool whispers into Tank's ear, "Are you sure about this boss? I'm getting an eerie feeling from this dude."

Tank gave Tool a look that read Tool's mentor, and the leader was frustrated with him.

Tank let out a sigh, and his exasperation disappeared from Tank's face.

"According to our lack-luster resources, he's the only one that knows the terrain well enough to escape undetected." Tank whispered in return. He placed a hand on Tool's shoulder to calm the larger man down. "Just watch out for any bounty hunters and leave the negotiations to me."

Once the two men had sat down across from the mysterious figure, Tank began to speak to Jankus LaGuettra while Tool looked out for any of those bounty hunters.

"We need someone to get us out of here and get somewhere secluded, while the heat dies down. We have been told you're the best man for the job."

The mysterious figure just sat there, sipping on his aged drinking mug, staring at the two men.

"See partner; we are trying to avoid running into the authorities. We need a quick and clean get-away," Tool says abruptly after the individual didn't respond right away.

Then LaGuettra lightly pushed his steaming hot cup of whatever away from him and folded his elongated fingers together. The mysterious figure gave both men an eerie smile that sent chills down both men's spines. The smile was far from a human expression at all. Tank had never seen the likes of it ever, despite having traveled all over many different star systems.

"You see my friend. Everyone on this planet is running from something. That's why they come here," bellowed Jankus LaGuettra.

The individual tilted his reptilian head just slightly exposing his saurian neckline. It was like he was waiting for their response now. But LaGuettra still held his stern, calm posture.

"You still haven't answered our question. Are you the person we are looking for or not," asked Tank? He was starting to become impatient.

Jankus LaGuettra unfolded his fingers and laid them flat on the metal table, exposing his olive, rubbery skin with a purplish tent on his fingertips under his garb. He leaned back into the shadows of the booth.

"If you're asking me whether I can assist you in concealing yourselves, I have a place where no one will discover you. Is that what you and your companion seeking?"

Tank gave the lizard man a look mistrust and disbelief. The smaller humanoid wasn't about to take his eye off the unusual characterization of LaGuettra. This contact resonated with an uneasy feeling in Tool. He reminded the thief as a used car salesman, and what LaGuettra was attempting to sale them seemed just too good to be true. "What's it going to cost us?"

Jankus LaGuettra tapping his metal cup with a sharp fingernail and gave both outlaws a sinister smile, "Hum. I think we can discuss payment when we arrive at our destination." The lizard man looked around to make sure no one was observing their discussion. "Who knows. If you play your cards right, you might get off this rock with your head still attached."

LaGuettra began to chuckle in a low tone.

With all the head hunters on Rankour Twelve, someone fleeing galactic authorities may never see freedom. If the extreme environment didn't kill you, contract killers might. Either way, Tank and Tool's options were limited, and without allies, they were doomed to die on the wasteland rock.

"Our chances are that slim, are they? And you're the only one that can save us from potential doom, is it?" Tool's tone still is on the suspicious side.

Jankus LaGuettra stood up abruptly.

"Meet me outside in thirty minutes. I will leave with or without you. Either way, it's time for me to be going."

The two men left the corner booth quickly after Jankus LaGuettra had existed. They didn't want to be caught there alone. "Your tone changed quickly," observed Tank.

"You heard him, riches!" exclaims Tool.

"Ok, calm down." Responded Tank in a more calming way. "We have to reach the destination first. This place is crawling with hired authority personnel and bounty hunters alike. We will be lucky if we don't get spotted before we reach our guide."

The two make sure they weren't being observed, then headed for the exist as discreetly as possible, throwing hoods over their heads to conceal themselves.

LaGuettra removed a small device that contacted the Derun Dehugezrur. It began flashing in a coded rhythm as if to alert whoever was on the other side of the communication device of his departure.

～

Somewhere deep in the Merciless Reach

Darkcloak emerges from the shadows of the dark cavern. The agent of darkness cloak kept Darkcloak concealed except his demonic, red eyes. The rouge agent moved swiftly across the contaminated ground of the cavern, towards one of his assets. The asset was frail with a long neck and limbs. The drowmauder wore purple tattered cloths of his house and his skin was littered with scars. The asset bowed at Darkcloak's appearance.

"Master, it's an honor just to be in your presence."

Darkcloak stopped less than ten paces from the drowmauder. "You said you had something that would peak my interest."

The drowmauder nodded. "Indeed master. I think you will find this stimulating."

"I'm waiting," said Darkcloak, with the agent's arms crossed.

The drowmauder motioned towards a flickering portal mirror. The drowmauder and Darkcloak watched as the scene came alive on Rankour Twelve.

In the distance, three speeder bikes float on the planet's surface, going at a rapid pace to identify the riders. Dust clouds build a wall behind the riders as they scampered across the deserted plains. The bike's light construction made for a rough ride. The wind current shook each bike violently as their vast acceleration fought against the gale winds.

"Interesting company you keep, my friend?" Mummbled Darkcloak.

The drone transmitted what it was seeing to its master. No one would spot the drone, all anyone would see was the hot sun beating down on them, and sand dunes with no trace would be found, and the agent could come and go as it pleased without a hint left behind.

"Everything is going as planned Darkcloak. The asset is now heading towards the rendezvous point." The shadow agent hesitated. "Soon, Sharradomina's plan will be realized, and the last remnants of the elementals will be wiped out, permanently." *All you need is a fool to be the vehicle of destruction, but who could service such a powerful entity as the one the asset possesses?*

Dark Cloak turned towards the drowmauder. "Tell the Derun Dehugezrur's that the plan is in motion, and their package will be delivered on time." The shadow agent replaced the recording device in its stored location.

~

Then, in a feeling of fool-hardness, Tool, the trailing rider, peered back, trying to see through the wall of dust and sand they were making in their hasty escape. Tool's anxiety wasn't elevated by the roughness of their flight across the arid plain. The muscle was more worried about getting arrested by authorities more than anything. The large human held on for his life, with a white-knuckled grip, not wanting to think of what might happen if he did fall off.

The outlaws had been in some desolate places, but this planet seemed to take the cake. After hopping from planet to planet, causing chaos and mayhem as they went, their escape ship had crashed on the planet's surface, fleeing from a multitude of agents of the gangster organizations that wanted their very heads. Once their merry band of raiders had many more members, but with the many numbers of skirmishes they have had over the years, their numbers dwindled to just the two of them. They still had warrants in quite a few systems. If they ever were caught, most likely, neither one of them would see a cell.

What didn't seem to bother the muscle-bound outlaw, did linger on the mind of his partner. Tank had begun wondering where their guide was leading them, ever since they had left the ragged bar. Neither men knew the area and that's what worried Tank. Could their guide be leading them into a trap? Was this mysterious figure looking to cash in on the bounty the crime lords had placed on their heads?

Tank had to shake off this notion, or it would get the better of him, leaving both outlaws exposed to anything. Tank was better off when his head was clear and focused on the task at hand. Not on the what if sceneries racing through his head. The three figures rode on for a while longer until clearing of sand dunes appear, and their guide started to deaccelerate. Slowly they come across a structure that is barely visible to the human eye. It appeared to be old, beat up and abandoned.

"How in the hell did he know this structure was way out here in the middle of nowhere"? Questioned Tool.

Their guide dismounted his speeder and slowly approached the minuscule building. Both men look at each other in wondering what he would do next. The man walked several feet from them then halted suddenly like something was impeding his progress. Tank and Tool looked at one another confounded, not knowing what was going on. They seemed lost without a clue where they were, nor where they were heading.

Sand and wind protruded onto the man's face, as he reached out to touch an invisible object in the dusty air. Suddenly, as if their guide had called upon some magic device, a keypad appeared. Without any hesitation, Jankus LaGuettra then placed his bare elongated hand onto the scanning pad. A scanner scanned his reptilian handprint, making a beeping noise as a blue laser light scanned the hand, and then the entire access pad completely disappeared. Electrical surges shot all around the perimeter of the building as the invisible gate exposed itself to the newcomers as it shutdown.

Once the electrified fence perimeter completely disarmed, LaGuettra looked back and motioned to the two men that it was safe to proceed. Hesitantly, the two men followed him towards what appeared to be the building's only entrance. But Tank refused to be caught off-guard. He knew looks could be deceiving. He looked too and fro, making sure no trap would spring on them. If he had learned anything fleeing the crime syndicate, it was never to take anything for granted.

It appeared, from the exterior of the shack or building or whatever they wanted to classify it, that it hadn't seen visitors in it in a long while. That made Tank quite nervous, but he didn't let Tool know it nor their guide. He wasn't sure how LaGuettra would react to his unease.

Then they reached the worn-down entrance, and it had even a more run-down look than the rest of the building. LaGuettra reached in his pocket, and the two men watched as he retrieved a dingy scanning card. Tool got a good look at the card, and he could see scuff marks all over the device like it had been over used. LaGuettra slid it into the slot and the metal door. At first, nothing happened.

"Is it broken?" Questioned Tool.

LaGuettra ignored the dense behemoth and waited a little longer. A loud vibrated behind the large steel door, like metal sliding across metal girders and rust sprockets, moved along with the locking mechanism. Then suddenly, a loud 'thump' echoed behind the door, stopping the orchestra of rust sounds. The door mechanism released itself, and the door slowly hissed open, exposing the interior of the inner-most room still somewhat encased in shadow.

The three men stepped inside, and the other men removed their shield helmets, revealing worn and beaten faces. Their guide removed his helmet, but still wore his pair of shades.

"So, this is the big surprise hu?" He glanced over at his leader, and then returns his gaze to their guide, "This is the place you promised us that had riches beyond our imagination?"

Jankus LaGuettra turned towards Tools, "My friend, haste makes the soul spoiled. Just remember that the riches here will reveal themselves in due time. The riches in this place are beyond your wildest imagination here; you just have to know where to look, my friend."

That's when the leader, Tank stepped in, "Ok Tool, check over there and see what you can find. There's bound to be something we can use."

Tool moved over to the south wall out of the main room into a much smaller space. It was tiny and full of dust, and what little light that bled through the cracks in the wall of the place didn't lead back in this clos-est-sized room. Tool flashed his illumination stick in the middle of the room, and it exposed what stored in the room.

Tank surveyed the main room. The front room is filled with dust with a few covered tables that appeared to haven't been used for a long time. The paint on the walls where weather-beaten, very little light pro-truded into the room since the windows were all bordered uptight. The bar looked old a decrypted, "I doubt that it has been used anytime sooner than these tables."

Then an image appeared right in front of Tank's eyes. The image was difficult to see in the darkroom, but he swore it was looking right up at him. It held a hug of ale in one hand, and when it looked up at him, it had glowing eyes. He shook his head to clear it and the image.

"Hey captain, look at this." Tool called out. "I think there is some ale left in these canisters" The large man moved the canisters on the floor around and looked at his friend. "They might not be stale after all."

Tool took a deep sniff into one of the canisters. "Want me to crack one open?"

Tank nodded his head.

Tool started to go through the ale canisters to find one suitable for them to consume. While Tank moved over towards a huge object in the adjacent corner. It also was covered with a tarp, and he thought, *This item is large enough to be a small piano. Wouldn't that be ironic, it would be like going back to the old west days. But what in the hell is a piano doing in a desolate place as this anyways?*

He threw back the dusty tarp, and to his surprise, he discovered it was an old fashion jukebox with a digital library installed. Its digital face was flashing back at him as if speaking directly to him. The florescent digits flashing, temporarily hypnotized Tank as the ancient machine requested him to 'make a selection'.

Tank looked around the gloomy, silent room. This place, despite its alienation, seemed eerily familiar to him. "It's like I've been here before, but I know I haven't ever set foot in this place."

Tank looked up and Tool asked him, "Boss, got any wrenches on you? The copper pipes need to be assembled before we can drink our miseries away."

"No, I think we left that stuff in the last town. By the way, have you seen Jankus LaGuettra?"

Tool looked around the room, "I haven't seen him since we discovered the ale."

Just then, a noise came from the darkness, in the direction of the storage room in the rear. Jankus LaGuettra emerged in his usual manner and startled Tool. Tool's surprise almost knocks him over the canisters of ale, "Fuck man, you have to stop doing that. You almost scared me enough to shit my pants."

Their guide looked at his guests through the dusty, old shades he refused to remove.

"I must put that on my to-do list," responded Jankus LaGuettra in a sarcastic manner.

"Where have you been Jankus LaGuettra," probed Tank?

With a crooked smile, "I have been preparing the surprise I promised you. I know you will absolutely enjoy it."

Tank looked over at the dust-covered top of the old jukebox, hesitated inside a thought, then a smile appeared in the corner of his dust-covered lips. "What if we found something worth the trip already?" Tool looks at his leader in astonishment. "Maybe we have something that intrigues us, and we don't need any of your surprises LaGuettra."

Jankus LaGuettra stepped into the light and, with his dusty shades firmly on his face, "My dear Tank, I have absolutely no idea what you have discovered in this place. The reason we traveled out to the middle of nowhere to discover the most wonderful thing you will ever experience in your life. All you have to do is give me your attention and trust, you haven't seen anything yet."

Tank and Tool look at each other with a look of disbelief. "Gentlemen, if you, please follow me this way," he motions to the back of the building. "We can proceed with the afternoon's events."

The two men move towards the direction their guide had directed. Down the three men went, deep underground they descended. Each man forced to light an illumination stick since their trip void of any type of light. The stairwell was slippery, and the men could smell mildew that seemed to be embedded into the stone wall. A strange stench outside of the dampness could be detected.

"Why in the fuck are we coming down into this abyss? Why is it so damn dark down here?" Cried Tool.

"Someone must have forgotten to pay the electric bill this month," responded Tank. Then the two men broke out in laughter.

"Good, you both still have your sense of humor. Just remember my friend nocturnal creatures do their hunting in the darkness."

"What the fuck does that mean LaGuettra?"

The two men reach the basin of the staircase and walk a few steps before Tank turns in the general direction of LaGuettra, "How much further are these treasures you have promised us Jankus LaGuettra."

"Patience is a virtue. Just remember that marvelous things happen when you are virtuous."

Suddenly a sound of a massive stone wall opening and grinding on the invisible pavement below them shredded the silence of their decent. Then Tool screamed out a murderous scream and falls to the cold, wet ground. "Captain, help me, I've been shot."

That was followed by a humming sound, that's when Tank realized he was unable to move away from the wall. He had been handcuffed to the structured stone wall with a pair of energy handcuffs. They had been placed on him to prevent him from retrieving his friend. Then from the darkness, Jankus approached Tank and stopped just in front of him, still wearing his shades.

"Jankus LaGuettra, what the hell have you done? You shot Tool." The sounds of Tool's screams echoed in the distance. "Hang on Tool, I'm coming to help you." Tank tries to free himself of his restraints. But the energy cuffs don't budge. The heat from the cuffs singe Tank's human skin, and he lets out a scream of his own. The tingling from his cuff wound is temporally, but his hand becomes numb until the sensation returns to his hand. The energy cuffs are restrictive and don't allow for movement. Tank is helpless to save his friend. He is at the mercy of Jankus LaGuettra.

"There's no use trying my friend, I set the dial on the cuffs to high and broke the energy setting. You in this for the long haul."

"What is this all for? Why are we down here for, and why did you shoot my friend"?

With a deceptive chuckle, "Its all for the surprise I promised you my friend."

Just then, a sound of the wall closest to Tool was lifted in an upwards motion, and very heavy breathing came through a crack in the interior wall. "Oh, speaking of the devil, here he is now." LaGuettra started a burst of twisted laughter.

In the darkness, a roar emerged in full force, then, Tool gave out a loud scream of fear. Then from the darkness a crunching sound as if a vicious jaw forcing its way into flesh filled the stench and damp air and then the wet sound as if a bloody body was being dragged back through the wall.

"Damn you, Fuckin Bustard!" Tank attempted to reach out for their guide and failed. Then LaGuettra's laughter was close to his ear. "What the fuck are you?"

The lizard man knelt next to Tank and removed his shades, exposing a set of reptilian eyes glaring back at the human. Tank could now see Jankus' eyes, which were now glowing bright blue. I told you nocturnal creatures hunt at night, my friend. I guess you should have listened more carefully to me, and you might not be in this situation."

"What are you, where do you come from, and what's behind that wall?"

"We are the force that keeps the universe in balance, and we are the seekers of societies that outgrow their surroundings and bring those societies back to a reasonable existence. We are what you would call, the Grimm Reapers of the galaxy. And that my friend is a pet of my dear friend, that I promised to keep shielded from making a social wreck of everything."

"You're a bloody killer, you know that. That's all you are, a killer!"

"Call us what you will, it is your prerogative." Jankus LaGuettra stood up, "Now I must leave you. I have other pressing issues, and I know you're all tied up for the moment. I'll leave you with no hard feelings, good-day, my good man."

He walked up the stairway and exited the dungeon. As Jankus LaGuettra walks towards the building's exit, screams come from the beneath his feet, and he leaves with a smile upon his face.

LaGuettra reached into his suit and retrieves a communicator devise. The Derun Dehugezrur agent pressed the call designator and awaited the arrival of his contact. The shadow agent doesn't have to wait very long. Soon after he switches on the communicator, a familiar voice echoes from behind.

"Why Jankus LaGuettra, I thought we would never speak to one another again. It's been such a long time."

An illuminated figure emerged before the spy.

The shadow agent spun around, but the surprise doesn't illuminate LaGuettra's face, it's more like a familiar jester, one that suggests the agent was expecting the owner of the voice. LaGuettra adjusts his attire.

"It's done, the package is ready for delivery. All you have to do is send someone to pick it up."

"Is everything completed?"

"Yes." Responded Jankus LaGuettra. "The thieves have been taken care of, and the asset is ready for delivery. It has been taken care of in the manner as we discussed."

Darkcloak removed the hood of his concealment. "Killing two birds with one stone?"

LaGuettra nodded. "Indeed."

In a grumpy Darkcloak responded, "Very well, I'll send someone out to retrieve the package. Meanwhile, I want you to stay with it until they arrive. At least the master will be happy."

"Wait! What about my payment?"

"Isn't serving the master and doing the Derun Dehugezrur's work enough for you Jankus?" Silence from the shadow agent. With a growl, Darkcloak continues. "Well, in that case. I can deliver it after we receive our prize possession." Echoed Darkcloak.

"No, no, that won't do. I want you to bring it out personally, before they take it away. That's my final decision. I can sell the specimen to other interested buyers."

A menacing expression, one that might suggest Jankus LaGuettra's life would come to an end by the hands of the dark agent. Then Darkcloak relaxes its tense muscles. "Very well. You defiantly drive a hard bargain, but you have delivered what you have promised."

Darkcloak slowly turns away and disappears into the sandy abyss.

LaGuettra whispers. "Good luck with this, my friend. Fuckin elemental beings. They are nothing but a pain in the ass."

CHAPTER 15

A heavy frigate slowly makes its way across the Canus Fifteen sector, better known as the Black Eye of the galaxy. Its slow movements made the cargo ship easy prey, so it had a small entourage of escort ships as a ring of protection. The cargo ship would be an excellent target for any space pirate, with its vast variety of cargo as it approached the interstellar junction, were any pirate ship could flee to several hiding sectors in space.

The cargo ship's manifest provided many different types of cargo, everything from thermal protective suits, to food supplies intended for refugees on far-out colonel post and weapon supplies for the marines on Brohine. The BZ2-12 launch cannons could rupture even attack freighter hulls. The problem with hi-jacking the weapons as they were far too traceable and the manufacturer had designed a homing beacon into the casing of the weapons the marines could easily trace.

The darkness of space led to many places that ambushes could lurk, and that kept the escorts always on alert. A dark and menacing cloud loomed, making scanning impossible or sending out emergency alerts and calls for help. Travelers had to worry about the continuous vortex manifestations that could appear right before a navigator's viewport and swallow a ship the size of the cargo ship whole.

The Black Eye possessed many dense spots where the escort ship's sensors couldn't penetrate. Shadows ran across the backside of the frigate as it traveled away from a dense cloud of particle matter, providing many spaces to hide. A light flickered inside the dark cloud as if the ship's passing awoke a horrific cosmic beast. But as swiftly as the flash of light appeared, it vanished as quickly, keeping whatever was there shrouded in the cloud's darkness.

Suddenly an energy source began to power up inside the dark cloud, but the cargo ship's sensors still had no notion of what was about to happen. Before the escort ships realized, a linear accelerator weapon fired, and a beam of concentrated energy surged towards one of the escort ships. The escort ship incinerated instantaneously.

The attack alerted the three other escorts to the pending invasion. Alarms were set off all over the remaining ships, and they form a protective barrier from behind the cargo ship. All the escort ships could do was await the onslaught. It would be like bringing lambs to the wolf's den.

The frigate the escort ships were protecting, was way too bulky to outrun any type of warship, including heavy-line battleships and strike cruisers. The enormous cargo ship was made for shipping and didn't have the maneuverability as a strike cruiser or the heavy armor of a Hercules Class Battleship. The cargo ship only had rudimentary defenses that wouldn't stop any warship, that's why the cargo company hired escorts.

Out of the dark cloud, a strike cruiser uncloaks and presents its massive bulk to the escorts. All three escort ships became dwarfed within the cruiser's humongous shadow. For an attack vessel, it was sleek, fast, and quite agile. But to the escort ships, the strike cruiser, the *Necromancer Leviathan* is like a colossal beast emerging from the depths of the sea. The strike cruiser possesses a substantial nose that houses the cruiser's bridge, half a dozen small laser torrents, with two linear accelerator weapons under its belly.

The star cruiser's massive wingspan placed the defenders in one collective shadow. Its wingspan began at the rear of the ship, fans out like a bird of prey pointing its wings at its victim and collimates to a pair of dagger-like points. This type of design gave the strike cruiser optimal maneuverability.

The Necromancer Leviathan doesn't avoid the defender's laser fire. It lets its immensely powerful energy shield deflect the bombardment of pin-prick shaped projectiles of energy to bounce off harmlessly. The defenders didn't have the power to overcome the cruiser's substantial girth. They are outsized, outgunned, and have no support coming to their aid. The escort group captain orders the security detail to move in on their attacker, hoping to make the cruiser crew confused.

The Necromancer Leviathan advanced on the frigate's location, like a predator creeping up behind its prey. The ship's shield continued to swat the oncoming defender's attacks like unwanted flies. None of the escort's laser attacks made it through. All three defender ships collision alarms began to go off simultaneously, as they draw in too close to the *Necromancer Leviathan.*

The defenders didn't realize the black, cylinder floating just beyond the strike cruiser's position. What the defender ships didn't realize was this device was launched by their attacker, to prevent the defenders from escaping. It was a proximity generator that created an artificial gravity well and drew in the defenders and anchored them to the device. Rats, caught in a trap.

From the bridge of *the Necromancer Leviathan,* the bridge officer asked, "Sir, shall we deploy countermeasures and take the defender ships out."

Soft breathing keeps the bridge from being deep silent. "No. Let the device do its job. Let the defenders rip themselves apart, in an attempt to escape."

And that's precisely what happened. The more the defending ships tried to break the artificial gravity well, the proximity generator had produced, the more, the smaller ships began to tear apart. That didn't stop the defenders from attempting to flee their potential doom. The *Necromancer Leviathan's* commanding officer observed all of this from behind the dark eyewear he wore. A smirk consumed the commander's face as if watching a stand-up comedy show. He was enjoying the trap the pirates had sprung.

Theo Ninnies, better known as 'The Rattlesnake of the Delta Galileo sector', didn't even budge as the scene unfolds before him. He was as still as a statue. "Have you seen anything more wondrous than this?"

"No, sir." Responded the pirate bridge officer. "It is a marvelous sight."

One-by-one, the three defender ships ripped themselves apart. Debris filled the perimeter field of *the Necromancer Leviathan.* Theo Ninnies took off his concealing eye wear, exposing his one golden eye and his one glossed-over dead eye. The one glossed over with the deep scare that ran through it from his upper right brow, down to the brim of his lip.

"Commander." Called the Rattlesnake. "Recall the proximity generator once the debris field has cleared. Then you may proceed towards the *Calamity* and begin docking procedures." Theo Ninnies clicked on the ship's com system. "Crew of the Necromancer Leviathan, this is your captain. We will begin siege procedures. Squad commanders make sure all your units are armed. If any of the cargo ship's crew resists, you have my permission to use deadly force. But I do not want any unnecessary murder. We may be pirates, but we are also civilized men. Over and out." The Rattlesnake turned towards his bridge commander. "I will be in my chambers until we are ready to board. Contact me once that begins."

The bridge commander nods his understanding, and Ninnies exists the ship's bridge.

～

The Necromancer Leviathan docked, and the space pirates began to clear the way, eliminating any resistance that might impede their plunder of the freighter *Calamity*. Bodies of the ship's crew littered the hallways. It was like the pirates took each crew member of the freighter as hostels. There were even a few of the *Calamity's* crew were cuffed and forced to their knees. The rear quarters had already been sacked, and the pirates were making their way towards the cargo hold sections when Theo Ninnies entered the sieged cargo ship.

The Rattlesnake wore all black leather, with a purple stripe on each inner half of his well-armored top, with skull and crossbones etched into the leather. The pirate captain's leather breaches were all tied into a one-piece outfit, with the same design, all the way through. The pirate captain wore cavalier boots that appeared to be designed for combat, with the rugged, thick leather supporting his thin and frail body. A flowing leather cloak that matched the rest of the captain's attire with a high collar was attached to the captain's outfit.

The pirate captain possessed a B-16 Fusion Meson Blaster strapped to his hip. The captain always carried the sidearm. He claimed, "Being an outlaw of the galaxy placed a prime target on my head." Theo Ninnies' cloak tossed behind the pirate, like he was a superman, flying through the hallway. The pirate captain sidestepped scattered debris and dead bodies as he made his way towards the center of the cargo ship.

Pirates leap out of hidden corridors and locked staterooms with a handful of goods, clothing, and stashed food supplies that the crew must have owned. The closer the pirate captain came to the middle part of the ship the more of his crew began to appear shouldering crates of cargo. Pirates emerge from several different passageways with their hands full. Many times, the Rattlesnake resorted to doge and weaved around his crew. It was so chaotic, like maneuvering through an asteroid field.

Suddenly two pirates emerge from a cooler storage bay carrying a hefty sized create. They weren't paying much attention and nearly ran down their captain. Theo Ninnies threw his hands up in defense and slapped them against the metal storage container his crew was moving. The icebox was cold to the touch and made the captain throw his hands back. It was merely a reaction to the temperature difference.

"Wow, that container is quite cool boys, what do we have inside?" The pirate captain made the men place the cooler on the floor and broke open the containers lock. To their amazement, the container was full of deep-fried Povlova with almond caked icing. The captain turned his nose at the smell of the cooler contents. Both crewmen weren't reaching in to swipe at the food either.

"What is this, something they feed to their pets?"

Both crewmen nodded in agreement with captain Ninnies.

The pirate captain tossed the slimy food from his grasp and looked for something to wipe his hand clean. That's when the voice of the security detail commander boomed from around the next corner. "Some species eat such things as a delicatessen, my captain."

Lt. Commander Coleridge Zayne's shadow first appeared like a phantom moving through the night. Then the security details officer appeared. The man looked as if he had more than his share of meals, with a bulge beginning to show around his midsection. His security uniform, all the pirate officers, were supposed to wear identifying uniforms while none of the crew forced. Commander Zayne wore a similar dress that his captain wore except his was solid black with no purple lining and no cloak to trail behind him. The security officer also possessed a battle helmet and firearms on his shoulder arm bar, instead of the skull and crossbones the captain had on his chest.

Commander Zayne wore a smirk that said he was acting coy towards their captain, something he was quite known for. Usually, the pirate crew knew Captain Ninnies wouldn't deal with such insubordination behavior, especially in front of his men. A similar smile emerged on Ninnies's face as if the two pirates were brothers.

"Zayne, you are a sight for sore eyes." Barked the pirate captain.

"That I am, captain."

A sob and crying sensation broke up the pirate's brief battery of words. All four pirates look down at one of the *Calamity's* nearby hallways and saw the freighter's crewmember squirming around on the floor, trying to break his energy binders. A false sense of compassion came over captain Ninnies's and the pirate knelt to get face-to-face with the captive.

"Why do you seem so distressed, my friend?"

The captive quivered and tried to pull away.

"Please don't hurt me." Quivered the cargo crewmember.

"Oh, I am shocked that you would insinuate that I could be so cruel."

The three other pirates chuckled.

"Boys. Have you ever heard of anyone from my crew mistreating captives?"

"No, sir." Called the pirates in unison.

Captain Ninnies turned back to his captive.

"See now; you have nothing to fear from me. Unless you resist, and then my boys will treat you like hostels, and that is another situation altogether. I would highly recommend you be a good boy and cooperate, and you have don't have anything to fear."

The captain stood up and began to turn away when the quivering cargo ship crewmember asked, "Will you let us go?"

The captain looked back with an insolent expression.

"So, you give away our position? Huh, do we look that stupid." Laughed one of the pirates.

Then a thin woman wearing a cotton trim business outfit, not the leather attire the pirate officers wore. His long flowing red hair made her look like a Greek goddess riding upon walked up to captain Ninnies and handed him a datapad. She wasn't one of the pirates, or in the way the rest of the crew was. She was the captain's assistant and bonafide accountant for the outlaws. The captain didn't bother looking at her. Instead, he began to skim through the inventory list on the device.

The young woman had her petite hands cupped behind her back, and she was rocking on her heels. It was apparent she was a little on edge. But what wasn't apparent was why she wasn't new to the plundering of seized goods. Was there something aboard the ship that was making her this way? Or was there something else? The pirate captain thumbed through pages and pages of the ship's manifest, humming as he did.

"Interesting. The cargo ship has enough food stores to feed a small colony for eighteen months."

"Indeed sir." Responded Alverta Brink.

She continued to show a good deal of unease that finally drew the attention of her boss. The Rattlesnake tore his attention away from the manifest. "Ok, what's eating at you, Ms. Brink?"

The pirate assistant gave Capt. Ninnies a look of shock. Her light skin began to turn a reddish tone and she began to look away. "Is it that obvious?" The assistant looked back at the captain with a more concentrated look. "I didn't want to bother you, but you have a communications call coming from an unknown source."

The Rattlesnake let his arm drop, still holding onto the data pad. She had his undivided attention. The captain no longer possessed a lighthearted expression. His facial muscles had tightened and there was a stern, almost numb persona. "Was there a call ID code attached?"

She handed the captain the call pod. Ninnies switched on the pod, and a coded ID number reflected in his hand. The captain became even paler than before. "Well, I think I better take this call. Please transfer it to my chambers."

"Yes, captain." Responded Alverta Brink.

"Your returning to the ship?" Questioned Commander Zayne.

Captain Ninnies almost acted as if he hadn't heard the commander's question. "Commander, continue collecting the things you think we will need, I want to be ready to push off in three hours."

"Three hours?"

The captain began to walk towards the rear of the cargo ship.

"Sir, yes sir." Responded Zayne.

Theo Ninnies had just changed out of his captain uniform into a silk robe and slippers. There was nothing like being comfortable; the captain had always proclaimed. That's when the communications device began to flash. The captain sighed and thought, *nothing like the comfort of home.* Ninnies took a deep breath and switched on the device, and a grainy holographic figure appeared.

The captain sucked in his breath. The tension made his body tight all over- the opposite of what he wanted. The image flicked on, and a holographic image appeared on the captain's desk. The orange-tinted three-dimensional figure wore a cloak that seemed to cover the figure's body completely. Every time Ninnies received the call from the private call ID, he knew it was never a positive experience. It placed the pirate captain on edge. His nerves were leaping from his very skin.

The figure seemed to be waiting for the pirate to acknowledge its appearance.

Theo Ninnies bowed. "Shadow Lord. What may I ask gives me the honor of this call?"

The three-D image didn't move. It was stoic and still, unwavering.

"Captain. I came to ask a favor. I hope you're not too busy plundering cargo ships to aid us in our time in need."

The pirate snickered, hoping the servant of darkness hadn't noticed. "It's always a pleasure serving the Shadow Empire."

Capt. Ninnies performed a half-mocking bow.

"Are you sure? I sense the irony in your tone, captain." The sinister voice boomed.

"The Shadow Empire's credits spend as easily as any other. And you always pay your debts, unlike some others." The pirate captain gave the half flicking hologram a slight smile.

The Shadow Lord growled. "Watch you condescending tone captain. The master doesn't have a sense of humor."

"It's not like you have one anyways", mumbled Theo Ninnies. "I guess it's good that my space pirates and I are contractors to the Shadow Empire and not full-fledged employees."

The Shadow Lord leaned towards the device, exposing what would have been a frown if the agent had a face. That didn't keep captain Ninnies from receiving chills down his back. Mocking the Shadow Lord wasn't the smartest thing to do. Although there was a great distance between them and the agent was in another realm, it didn't mean the Shadow Lord's reach couldn't snag the pirate by his throat and threaten his life.

"That doesn't give you the leeway to mock the master or the shadow agents. I doubt if even your arrogance makes you blind to the fact you're not beyond our reach, Rattlesnake."

The smile disappeared from Theo Ninnies. "I didn't mean to disrespect you or the dark master."

The Shadow Lord's image had returned to a full-body copy. The halo-image flickered once again. Silence became quite uncomfortable for Ninnies. "Speaking of disrespect, what is the nature of sudden communications?"

The Shadow Lord unfolds its elongated arms.

"We would like you to lure the elemental leader into an ambush." The Shadow Lord became silent once again.

"Jetsuenete! Are you insane? The elemental leader would see right through any farce we would put on. No, absolutely not." Pouted the captain.

"Relax, captain. You have put on illusions before. Your crew is the best there is, and I have extreme confidence in them and you."

"We are information dealers, mostly. Stealing intel is a different game than fooling a creature of the abilities Jetsuenete possess."

The Shadow Lord growls again. This time it unsettles Theo Ninnies. He isn't sure he wants to deal with the shadow agent any longer. But the pirate isn't sure if the phantom-like being could feel his reservations or not. The pirate's palms were sweating profusely. His throat had become dry, like it was wearing a winter sweater. Ninnies felt like the agent of darkness had pushed him down a dark alley with any way of escape. He swore that the phantom figure was going to force his pirates to entrap the elemental leader.

Ninnies sighs. *There goes any trust we have with the elementals. I will be a marked man if I do this job.* The captain begins to crack his knuckles, one at a time. "You're placing my boys and me in a precarious position."

"I understand the difficulty of the position you're in with this. We will be willing to compensate your crew for the job."

"What about a way to ensnare the elemental leader. We don't have anything in our arsenal to detain an elemental, especially one as powerful as Jetsuenete."

The Shadow Lord didn't waver. It was like the agent was waiting for this line of questions. But most of the shadow agents he had met, which the Shadow Lord was the only one Ninnies had ever met, he assumed could read mortal minds.

"We can provide you with restraints that will keep the elemental's unique abilities at bay. We will also send a khuuvoid beast to neutralize and distract the elemental."

A khuuvoid beast was a beast that could resist elemental abilities, with its super thick cranium, and had colonial arms that could wrap around most species it encounters. It was stronger than anything that it would encounter and nearly blind. It would be a much fairer battle than any of the pirates attempting to take on the elemental.

CHAPTER 16

An isolated fortress hidden in plain sight, on the planet Aucarro, based in the Regules Eight sector, stood as a symbol like a leviathan protector and home base of the Elementals. The location was perfect for the elementals and their mortal allies. It was near the gateway of the cosmos, where they could take one of the millions of interstellar pathways, making space travel quick.

The moon's surface was rocky and with little to no atmosphere, and didn't provide enough breathable air, but the elementals didn't need a lot of air to breath, despite their enormous size. These omniscient-like beings were created to live off minimum air, unlike any living species, and their massive quad lungs acted as filters for the recycled air, where the enormous pair of lungs served as the respirators for the defenders and the smaller pair, located behind the more massive pair and linked by a tough cavity that allowed transference from the larger and smaller pair, as the filtering devices. Their mortal allies weren't so lucky, because the marines wore physical respirators over their faces to breath. This made maneuvering on the surface cumbersome for them. The bulky breathing tanks usually collided with the mortal's weapons slung over their backs.

Since the elemental stronghold was in a secret location, no battles had ever occurred on Aucarro. The discovery of the fortress, by the first generation of elementals thought the fortress was there on purpose and Jetsuenete and his comrades, had no attention breaking that tradition.

The celestial descendants had built a landing port below the surface that surrounded the entire fortress, like a vast moat. The lower landing bays and docking wasn't just for landing and launching allied spacecraft. It was also a place where the marine's and their elemental counterparts could have tactical assemblies and pre-launch briefings. There also was a large arms locker, training faculty, along with two mess halls and even living barracks.

The barracks were arranged in a fashion to make accessing each section of the underground base easy. Each living chamber could house up to three marines, with retractable beds. The barrack chamber was small and cramped, not providing much for comfort. The only thing marines were allowed in his barrack chamber was the captain's tiny supply of uniforms and tactical gear that included battle armor, canteen, and medical supplies. No weapons were allowed into the barracks. The marines had to check-in and out their weapons at the armory. That is where marine repairs were completed to their weapons. But supplies were always running low and always in demand. The war had taxed the elemental allies' resources and too often the marines were low of urgent supplies.

All of that was boxed in by two humongous cargo holds, which kept all the allies' equipment. Only non-lethal equipment was housed in the cargo holds. Spare parts for siege equipment, dropships, and many other supplies that didn't belong in the armory ended up in the holds.

The landing surface was smooth, but it still contained the sediment from the rocky substance that made up the entire moon. When ships took off or landed, the exhaust ducts from the ship would throw the filament everywhere, creating a cloud of residue all over the landing bay. Hanger bays could also be an issue, with the rock ceilings sagged and even collapsed in on themselves on occasion. The hanger bays were braced with support frames, to prevent further canopy drooping. This wasn't an issue in the rest of the subterranean environment. The consensus was the heat from ships were causing the rock settlements to become unsettled and forcing the underground hideout canopy to sag.

The launch bay had a doorway that acted as camouflage for the subterranean base. Once cleared to land or take off, two massive hangar bay doors would swing outwards, splitting the moon surface, giving ships access to the landing bay. The automated hangar doors would slowly close, making a loud 'bang' as the twin hanger doors closed shut, grinding the metal against the stone surface.

The Citadel itself was a thing of marvel. It had stood for millenniums, or at least as far the elementals understood the ancient scrolls when they discovered the fortress's location. The granite composition foundation was sturdy and could take on a three-hundred mile-an-hour head-wind. It had a robust and durable exterior, and it could support nearly any type of weight the occupiers could force onto its structure. Without a way to heat the fortress, the halls of the Citadel were freezing, but since the elementals were much closer to supernatural beings, they needed very little warmth.

The shape-shifting elementals endured long journeys through interstellar space with nothing but their thick and scaly draconian skin. It might be the reason they're called Intergalactic Tarragons or their more common designation, space dragons. This thick, scaly outer layer provided enough insolation for the shape-shifters to stay warm.

Jetsuenete could only stare at the cold stone wall of the Citadel. A tainted and caliginous voice boomed at the elemental leader. It was like the defender was caught in an unbreakable trance. Inside a dark and sinister void, his mind was in limbo, chained to a nightmarish existence which used derision as its menacing anvil. Jetsuenete's eyes are glossed over, like a pair of silver orbs dangling in their sockets.

A forbidding sensation loomed all around the elemental leader like something was attempting to penetrate Jetsuenete's mental armor. The elemental fought back at the invading entity trying to take over, as the Darkness surrounded the elemental and tightened its grip. Deeper and deeper Jetsuenete fell into darkness like he had stepped over a cliff's edge and tumbling through the endless darkness.

That's when the decrypted voice of the Darkness rang in the elemental's ear. "I have you now." The shadow deity growled. "There is no escaping my grasp. You will be my puppet and, I will act as the puppet master."

Jetsuenete strained to pull away from the Darkness stranglehold. The strain began to drain the elemental of his enormous energy. It was like his adversary had him leashed up by his throat. Jetsuenete felt the tightening noose becoming even tighter, like a dog chained to a stake. A bead of sweat began to trickle down the elemental's colossal forehead. Veins began to appear on the surface of his neck as he battled to regain control of his extremities. The invisible restraint seemed only to grow tighter.

"Get out of my head, you barbaric thing," Jetsuenete responded.

The elemental began to soften his physical battle with the Darkness and began combating his nemesis within his elemental mind. That's when Jetsuenete recollected the conversation with the celestials and the results of the near possession in the cavern. The lead celestial voice began to fill his head, blocking out the Darkness' wicked words.

Calm down. Echoed the celestial voice. *You need to be calm inside your head. Then when your mind is at rest, dig deep for your celestial abilities. Stretch your mind, and then you will be able to extract the Darkness from your mind and body.* Those words seemed to echo in the elemental's head like an empty cavern, magnifying the celestial being's words of wisdom.

Jetsuenete knew those words ran true. It was the voice of reason, one that would fill his head if he was thinking clearly. But with the Darkness inside attempting to betray the elemental's very existence. The elemental leader needed wisdom and guidance from ancestors that had long ago vanished the very embodiment of the elemental's existence. Those words energized him and gave him the strength that was draining from his body.

Jetsuenete took in a few deep breaths to center his mind and his body. The calming effects seemed to be working. The Darkness' malevolent voice began to fade as if the elemental had shoved the master of darkness down an elongated hallway, far away. The elemental leader began to sync his body and mind together, like that were one. Powerful energy ran through Jetsuenete. He ultimately regained all the elemental strength that had been drawn from him, as a vampirism leech removed.

"You will be gone harbinger of insanity. I command you to leave my body. Leave my mind to be at rest. You shall not possess me, derelict. I will not act as your vessel of destruction. I command you to release me!"

Jetsuenete violently raised his arm as if to push away his invisible tormenter.

The rancorous rage faded even further.

The Darkness let out an ear bursting scream of distress like the deity was being dragged away with an immortal chain of doom. The Darkness let out one last threat, before disappearing. With a growl, the master of shadows retorted. "You will not vanquish me in such a manner. We are destined to be one. We will be of one mind, and you will see the enlightenment I have, myself discovered. You shall not break the chains I have forged for us both, elemental!"

Suddenly a desecrated face flashed decrypted fangs and snarled at Jetsuenete. Then the image vanished from sight. The Darkness was gone! He was free from the demonic bonds of his nemesis and could finally relax. Jetsuenete was breathing heavily as if the elemental had fought a tremendous battle with a thousand foes and barely escaped with his life.

The elemental's twin hearts began pounding deeply, one after another. Jetsuenete had never experienced such an emotional withdraw before. Recover would take a moment before the elemental was back to his old self, allowing the extreme adrenaline of his encounter to wear off. But for the first time since the false talisman incident, he felt he was whole again.

A beeping noise drew his attention away from his excited state. The blue illumination was reflecting off the genetic chamber standing right before the elemental, supported by a rail system that would allow easy transport of the cocoon chamber. The blue color was a reflective property of the saline solution within the genetic pod. The readout panel still flashed a red light on the chamber door. It told Jetsuenete that the DNA convergence was still processing.

The thickness of the solution made it impossible for even the elemental to see the submerged body through. All that was visible was the silhouette of the body inside. He would just have to wait and let the process take its course and trust in the machine to avoid making any critical mistakes. The last thing Jetsuenete wanted was to destroy the figure. The elemental couldn't take his eyes off the chamber or the figure living inside it.

I believe the chamber reminds me of elemental eggs. Its surface is smooth like the eggshells, even though the eggs are organic, and this chamber is steel. They both are elongated and broad as an escape pod. The elemental moved over and placed a hand on the tempered glass. The solution sloshed around with his touch, and the glass mirrored the inside of the chamber. It was warm to the touch. It had to be, because it was an incubation chamber, just as much as it was a genetic generating chamber.

Jetsuenete took in a deep breath and closed his eyes. With all the war-faring they had done. Lately, he hadn't had time to concentrate on his biggest project. This created subject would be the elemental's future like they were their ancestors. *If this is a birthing chamber, does this make me its immortal father?* He asked. That's when it came to him. Jetsuenete snapped open his eyes. *I will name them the Immortals.*

But the elemental leader had high hopes on his current assignment. If it succeeded, the immortals might have the best chance at defeating the Darkness once and for all. Jetsuenete looked back to the control board at the data pad lying across the dark touch screen. This would be their best chance at ending the war.

There was another item glowing yellow next to the pad. If Jetsuenete's current assignment was the end game that he hoped, then the second item on the touch screen was the appendix to that plan. Supplanting both would set their descendants up without any worries, but as well as Jetsuenete knew, nothing ever went as planned. He looked back to the incubation chamber. Would the new generation get a chance to fight? Would they get the opportunity to prove their worth and skills to the cosmos?

Jetsuenete hoped it wouldn't be necessary. Hopefully, they were in a position for the endgame with no more death, no more killing. Slaughtering those that are in the service of their foe took a toll on their psyche. Even a genetically enhanced species, bred for one purpose, war, could get burned out. *It's better to save them from their destiny than to force them into service altogether.* Jetsuenete responded to his question.

A shadow emerged from the granite hallway, then the footsteps of a colleague came into the room. The elemental leader smiled as his closest officer and friend Dirdanth appeared in the doorway. Jetsuenete had requested the elemental officer's presence. A secluded meeting, just the two of them. They had many of these types of meetings, usually Jetsuenete asking for Dirdanth to dissect his leadership skills and decision making right after a battle. The elemental leader liked to get his second in command input as soon as he could. No interference from taxing Gaitharrul, which never let anyone else have two-cents in. Or the shape-shifting brothers who'd rather dive into a battle and improvise as they went.

The two friends clasped each other's right arm to the other. The two elementals grip were like vise grips latching onto the other's flesh. It was a solemn greeting, one that showed respect and comradery. Jetsuenete peered deep into Dirdanth's red tented eyes with their silver-filled pupils, and Dirdanth did the same in return. To anyone that wasn't an elemental, those pair of golden orbs would intimidate both friend and foe. But Dirdanth was nearly Jetsuenete equal in both intelligence and fighting skill. The difference was the elemental leader's compassion for victims of all kinds.

"Brother." Claimed Jetsuenete.

Dirdanth nodded in return. "Brother Jetsuenete."

"I'm glad you have accepted my invitation. Please make yourself at home."

The two elementals entered the center portion of the room.

Dirdanth moved with elegance but with a definite purpose, showing why he was more than a formidable opponent on the battlefield. The blue illumination coming from the incubation chamber caught the elemental's eye. His eyes tightened as if to express disdain for the egg-shaped device. Jetsuenete notices his brother's reaction. It wasn't the first time Dirdanth has physically expressed his displeasure with his leader's pet project. No matter how much the elemental leader tried to convince the other of its importance, Dirdanth always seemed less egger each time he witnessed the chamber. Jetsuenete could see it in Dirdanth's eyes.

"Isn't it a beautiful thing, Dirdanth?"

Dirdanth snickered disdainfully. "You mean your little freak show?"

No, my brother." Jetsuenete motioned for Dirdanth to approach the incubation chamber. "They are a wondrous thing and they will be our descendants. Those that will pick up the sword and battle-ax and continue our efforts against the Shadow Empire."

Dirdanth snapped his head in towards his leader. "Are we so old that you have to make our replacements? Or is it the distaste you have with our inability to defeat the Darkness?"

The elemental leader gave his brother a soft, uneasy look only a mother would dare.

"Dirdanth, we been fighting this war for nearly a millennium, and four generations of our kind have fought for thousands of years each."

"Over ten-thousand years," barked Dirdanth. "In fact, it's been half a million years since the dark days of the cosmos and we are still fighting this wasteful engagement."

The elemental leader shook his head. "Don't you believe it's time for us to fade away and allow a new set of descendants to take up the battle?"

Dirdanth's facial muscles tightened up, and a fearful melancholy that made the elemental's face look like a prune appeared. The elemental looked at the incubation chamber, then back to his longtime friend with a stoic and steadfast expression, like Dirdanth was a machine. The two warriors had known each other for a long time, and Jetsuenete had trouble picking up on any emotional cues. The elemental leader was afraid to lose Dirdanth's respect, but worse, he was worried his close friend might refuse what task he had to offer.

"You are trying to put us out in the pastor! I sense it in your tone. I can see it in your eyes, you want us to transcend and leave the fight for your experiments." Barked Dirdanth.

The elemental leader raised his hands as if surrendering.

"No Dirdanth, you misunderstand my intent. You are right when I say we should move aside, and even the celestials transcended for the first elementals. They could no longer gain anything in the war against the Darkness. In that respect, I see the same thing for us. But we are mistaken in our beliefs that the celestials merely vanished into non-existence."

Dirdanth crossed his large arms across his mountainous chest. The elemental leader could tell his friend was going to put up a momentous resistance to his idea for their kind and the immortals.

"Then where did they go? What did they become if not into cosmic dust?"

"It's difficult to comprehend what these beings became, even for an intelligent species like us. The best way I can explain it is they became one collective voice, always lingering and always watching us."

Dirdanth began to chuckle. "You want me to believe the celestials became a cosmic phantom, and their obsession is voyeurism?" The elemental dropped his arms to his side and gave his leader a look of sadness.

"It's nothing like that. They are there to aid us in our most time of need. Sometimes they come to me when I am unsure about a decision I need to make, after a hard battle." Jetsuenete touches the fragmented jewel, and Dirdanth looks at the golden gem. The jewel fits in the palm of his hand, but to an ordinary mortal, the jewel would have to be cradled in a human's arms. The elemental leader picked it up and gazes at it.

"What's that, another one of your science projects?" Questioned Dirdanth.

"This, my friend, is how we ascend to a greater existence."

Dirdanth huffs and a scowl forms on the elemental's face. "You want us all to become a piece of jewelry?"

Jetsuenete shakes his head.

"No. When the celestials became one collective being, they merged their existence into a temple structure that became their living home."

"And where is this so-called temple?"

"It's hidden. No one knows where. Like our ancestors, however, I want the elementals to transcend, merge our elemental essence into jewels like this, for safekeeping. We still live on, just inside gems scattered throughout the cosmos. That allows our descendants to take over, and our enemy believes we have died off."

"Then what?" Questions Dirdanth.

"When the immortals need us, they call upon us individually, and we return to aid them in the war if it's still raging."

Dirdanth gently took the golden jewel into his hand. The crystal sliver fits perfectly in the palm of his demi-god hand. The elemental admired its shine, and that's when he sees a small being, an elemental dragon inside. Consciousness comes to the elemental. His silver pupils widen as if something beautiful had just come to him. Jetsuenete could sense the bewildering wonder flowing through his long-time friend. Dirdanth rotated the golden jewel around a quarter of a turn. The little thing inside the jewel has the elemental mesmerized. His massive nostrils flare, and Dirdanth several deep breaths.

The elemental peered at his brother with a renewed sense. "You want us to hibernate like the twins?"

The shape-shifting elementals normally hibernated inside large translucent eggs, like the jewel. It regenerated its energy levels and its elemental abilities. This is what the twins, Erreodan and Nightzeneth would be doing if they weren't entrenched in the war efforts. Not allowing them to hibernate took away years off their lifespan and diminished their ion fire.

"You want us to be in hibernation, like this creature, like the shape-shifters do." Boomed Dirdanth.

Jetsuenete smiled. "Something like that. Just remember once we are called back, we are stronger than ever."

"Who would oversee the hibernation eggs?"

"It could only be one individual, someone we trust unconditionally. But who could this individual be?"

"Yes, who is the question?" Barked Dirdanth. A flash of determination appeared in the elemental leader's eyes. "You have someone already in mind, don't you?"

Jetsuenete nods. "High Priest Tefbei Nakht."

Dirdanth eyes widen, and it appears if the red in the elemental's eyes are flames. It is clear to Jetsuenete that the elemental doesn't approve. "Are you insane? He's a traitor to his people and a servant of the Darkness!"

"Former servant, and yes, he has done disposable things, but that's all in the past. He has redeemed himself, and his mind wiped clean. The high priest now serves us. Our purpose is his own. He is the only one we can trust with this information. And I want you to carry out the plans."

Dirdanth spun around, and the two elementals face one another. There is a genuine shock in the elemental's eyes. "Why me?"

Jetsuenete picked up the data pad in his large hand. "I have other matters to attend to, and I trust you to carry out this assignment until the end. You can do that for me, can't you?"

"What are you up to, Jetsuenete? What unorthodox plan are you working on now?"

"I have a lead on the ore the Darkness stole and where the excess is being held. It could give us insight into what they are planning. I must oversee this operation."

"Why do you need to do this personally? Send some of the marines to extract this intel. We need your leadership on the frontline."

Then there is a pause. Neither elemental said a word, and the elemental leader didn't need to say a word, his face told all that needed to be said.

"There is something else isn't there? Something you're not telling me."

"Captain Ninnies may have a lead to the where-abbots of the Sword of Eternity."

"The pirate? Why would you trust anything that comes from his mouth? All he cares about is getting paid. He will sell you out at the first chance you give him."

"His intel has always been accurate. He has never led us astray." Returned the elemental leader.

Eye of the galaxy. This wasn't something Dirdanth or Jetsuenete would ever agree. "Another expedition to a false talisman? This feels like a set-up, possibly an ambush. Don't go, Jetsuenete. I implore you."

"I must. It might be the intel we have been searching. The talisman could be the thing we need to end this war. To save our kind."

"Then let me go along with you. I can watch your back in case it is an ambush."

Jetsuenete only shakes his head. "I can do this on my own. I am taking a squad of marines with me. Nothing will happen to me. I need you to fulfill the assignment I have given you. If all fails, at least our species will be protected. Our future supplanted."

Dirdanth took a step backwards. As if surrendering the fight. "Your dead set on going, alone aren't you? Is this some type of quest to test your abilities as a leader?"

"I need you to complete both ends of the task I have assigned. If I don't return, the elementals will survive, and our descendants will rise in our place."

The elemental leader looked over at the incubation chamber. But despite all his reservations, Dirdanth has never failed to do what his friend has asked of him. But the elemental leader understood his friend wouldn't just stand by if something happened to him. "I don't like it, and you know that. I can see it in your eyes. Even though I do it under great protest, I will take the elemental eggs, once they have all been converted from our brothers to the High Priest Tefbei Nakht. But you must agree to return to us once your fool-hearted mission is complete."

"My friend." Proclaims Jetsuenete. "I hope we see one another again. But this is our last meeting, may wisdom and success be with you always."

The two elementals grasp arms like they had at the beginning of their meeting.

~

A few Days Later

The place was dark and cold. Dirdanth utilized his elemental senses to make his way through the maze of tunnels and passageways. There were torches at every intersection, which provide a sense of direction. All the passageways and the tunnels the connected them appeared, all the same, it was still difficult to tell where in the temple the elemental was heading.

Dirdanth recognized the elemental icon branded on the rocky wall. Two enlarged circles, one was bordering the other. A triangular shape intersected the top and both left and right bottom corners of the two circular borders. At each end of the triangle, crescent moons were facing away from the three-sided shape at its top and two sides. There were three elemental symbols, the dragon for the shape-shifters, the wolf for the hunter clan, and rattlesnake for the support units. On the innermost circle was branded the individual legions of each elemental. The branding on the temple walls matched the high priest's smock, given to him once announced as the keeper of their secrets.

A light breeze blew through cracks in the ceiling, making the torch lights flicker on occasion. Dampness aided the cool breeze, making the elemental believe there was a waterfall or body of water nearby. The deeper Dirdanth moved into the underground temple, the warmer it became.

Dirdanth carried a black unlabeled case under his arm.

A shadow began to follow the elemental through the winding passageways. He knew that no matter what happened, his cargo would be safe with the high priest. *No one would ever be able to find their way in and out again.* That's when Dirdanth felt a presence in the room with him. The elemental turned towards a shadowy portion of the passageway.

"High Priest Tefbei Nakht."

The high priest moved out of the shadows, where a dark robe. The old man's appearance took Dirdanth by surprise. The former agent of darkness, now the high priest, had transformed into a frail and aged looking being, one that made the humanoid appear a lot less human and a lot more phantom-like. The high priest bowed.

"Master Dirdanth. It is a pleasure to have you as a guest." The High Priest Tefbei Nakht had his hands folded into the sleeves of his dark priest's robe.

Dirdanth reaches the case out to the priest. "A gift from the elementals."

The high priest opened the case and then looked back at his elemental visitor. "Only three eggs?"

Dirdanth nodded. "More will come once we transcend the rest of our elemental brothers. During our elongated sleep, you will hide these eggs and our secrets within these walls. You will be the sole proprietor of all the elemental secrets. Guard them with your life."

The high priest nods and bows again. "I will do so, as you command master Dirdanth. I am here to serve you and the elementals."

"Remember. If anything happens to the hibernation eggs, I will hold you responsible. And my wrath will be great upon your bold head. Furthermore, a religion will be created, and you, high priest, will oversee relaying the history of the elementals, the story of our origins, and he will convey our message of peace and prosperity. He will also be charged to protect the eggs spread across the galaxy, and he alone will know the locations of every egg."

"Your secrets will be hidden inside of my heart and I will preach your lessons as if they were my own."

CHAPTER 17

*T*he *Necromancer Leviathan's* hallways were a little cramped for the entourage of marine escorts Jetsuenete had brought. All twelve mortal soldiers surrounded the elemental, three in front, the on both sides, and three in the rear. They all acted as a fortress surrounding the elemental leader, but even with their numbers, the pirates still outnumbered them, twenty-two pirates to every marine. Jetsuenete still had no worries, the elementals had been getting intel from Captain Ninnies for a while, and the elemental leader felt safe on the pirate ship. The elemental also possessed an ability to sense when things were out of balance in the cosmos, though without the ability to change things

Overconfidence wasn't usually something Jetsuenete would allow himself to be blinded by. The elemental had typically been vigilant about the potential downfalls that overconfidence brought. That wasn't saying there weren't elementals that allowed their pride to consume them. Dealing with the pirates was a common thing for the elementals. Dealing with the pirates was a common thing for the elementals. Jetsuenete felt comfortable on their ship, even with the disparity of the numbers.

The main hallway of the pirate ship seemed to be less lit than the elemental leader had remembered. The hallway light had a yellowish tint against what usually would be a bright white illumination. Shadows seemed to fill their passageway, giving the impression that shadows were the real occupants of the ship, not the humans that occupied the *Necromancer Leviathan.*

With his elemental senses, Jetsuenete could see down the walkways, but it seemed irregular that the pirates would keep the hallway in such shadows, or had they done that just for his arrival? Something gave off the aura of shielding the elemental's high-tuned senses, making everything that generally Jetsuenete was in tune to, like looking through a fog baseline.

Their arrival at the docking platform gave no impression anything was amiss or had Jetsuenete missed something among all the commotion upon exiting his escort vessel? No welcoming committee including the captain himself, which was abnormal. Captain Ninnies always made it a habit to greet the elemental leader personally, every time Jetsuenete had visited. But that was fine with Jetsuenete. He had preferred to exchange pleasantries, get on with their business, and get back to his men.

Jetsuenete's entourage had been swiftly escorted down one of the many hallways leading away from the docking area and told they would meet with captain Ninnies shortly. That was something else that seemed to be off to Jetsuenete, but his mind, like his heightened senses, was too foggy to make any sense of it all.

The elemental leader hadn't visited captain Ninnies and his band of renegades more than a few times in person. Most of the meetings were with messengers and vidcom transmissions. They always had received the intel through digital channels and paid for it similarly. But once Jetsuenete had discovered what possible information the snake had for him, the elemental leader instantly decided this needed his undivided attention and personal visitation.

But this feeling seemed unorthodox, the sensation was a contrast to the celebratory emotion felt upon their arrival. Jetsuenete, now treading down the shadowy hallway, just felt something was off. His elemental senses were screaming at him, but he didn't know what he should be paying attention to, the disturbing physical elementals that leaped out at him, or the distortion of his senses. Had Captain Ninnies sold them out? Were there traitors among his entourage? Or spies among the pirate crew? All questions were more challenging to answer than he had time to uncover.

They were being guided down a side walkway and not down the main corridor of the ship. Was that bizarre? Maybe. Or the main hallway might have some maintenance going on, forcing a course change. *No matter,* thought the elemental. *We will convene with the captain, retrieve the data he has for us, and then depart.* To Jetsuenete, this visit would end as swiftly as their arrival.

Jetsuenete overheard the marine's radio coms echoing from behind, but didn't pay attention to what his entourage was discussing. Something like they weren't crazy being escorted down the snug passageway. The elemental was sure the marines weren't overly happy with the dark shadows creeping upon them. He could just imagine the conversation. Something like: "Bleep this! How are we supposed to keep this immortal fool safe with all these shadows concealing who knows what?"

The woman introduced herself as Alverta Brink. She led them further down the corridor, replacing their pirate escorts. Jetsuenete watched her diligently through the corner of his eye while reaching out with his elemental senses, staying alert. What was the elemental searching, he still wasn't sure, nor what to expect from their pirate hosts? He had to remind himself they were thieves, and thieves weren't all that trustworthy. But to Captain Ninnies' defense, they were information pirates that acted more like spies than thieves that occasionally, to the elementals chagrin, would siege cargo ships.

Jetsuenete watched the young woman walk. Her long legs were moving in a synchronized rhythm that seemed to hypnotize the elemental, slightly. Not that a human would ever distract the elemental leader from his duties. She was humanoid, he was the descendent of celestial beings. Jetsuenete began to think, *in a perfect world, where they weren't at war with the forces of darkness, the elementals, and the space pirate's would-be adversaries, and the intergalactic outlaws would be fleeing, not selling them information,* to Jetsuenete and the elementals. Thinking about all of this just kept Jetsuenete from worrying about the alarms still ringing all through his body.

"Ms. Brink, how long have you worked for the good captain, and how do you like serving pirates?" Quizzed Jetsuenete. It was more distractive than one that was probing for information even though he was genuinely curious.

At first, the young woman didn't answer. Either she was hiding the truth or she was pondering the elemental's question and wanted to give a wholehearted answer. Still the silence seemed to last for eternity. "It's been three years now since serving captain Ninnies. And yes, I do like working for him." She responded confidently without ever breaking her walking stride.

She hadn't answered her guest's line of questions. But did Jetsuenete expect a detailed, drawn-out answer? He had, though, expected a little more than what he had received. Was the woman acting coy with him, or was she hiding something? Jetsuenete broke his concentration towards those alarms going off inside his head and decided to prod a little deeper.

"I noticed that it wasn't much of an answer. Do you care to elaborate working for the captain, or is there something within that answer you are trying to avoid?" The elemental attempted to prod the woman without seeming too nosey or sound as if he was interrogating her.

"Of course, I have neglected to answer the question with a detailed answer. What do I call you, your grace?" The young woman didn't turn around. "Of course, you wouldn't take such a tittle. Captain Ninnies told me that your kind isn't too prideful or desired such titles. What should I call you then?"

"Captain Ninnies was correct. Our kind, being a warrior class, titles don't inspire us or drive us in any sense. But I have to admit, and pride seems a little too abundant. Overzealous in our abilities, or at least in certain elementals, seems way too common these days."

"But that still doesn't tell me what to call you?"

The woman turned around swiftly as if she wasn't sure if the elemental would provoke an attack her way. Her long flowing red hear tossed into the air and slowly made its way back onto Alverta Brink's think shoulders, spread out as if she had just gotten out of the shower. Her cotton trim outfit was a contrast to the other pirates. Some wore leather attire in a more relaxed environment that told Jetsuenete they were officers, while the other ship's crew wore cotton fatigues, but not in the style of the young woman.

Ms. Brink's clover colored eyes darted back with venom as she wanted to strike her guest with fright from her gaze. Like assistant could turn the elemental to stone through her venomous look. She held that look for a moment, but the look dissolved, and the captain's assistant's face softened. The anger had only lasted only a moment, and the elemental decided that she must have realized his comment had hit the wrong nerve.

The calm face returned, and the wrinkles that had suddenly formed above and below her emerald green eyes vanished. "Sorry, I normally don't lose control like that." Jetsuenete decided that she was covering up something, but it was honestly none of his business. "Jetsuenete is perfectly fine."

"Let's just say that Captain Ninnies saved me from a destructive lifestyle, and he was the only one that gave me aid when others turned their back. The things I do for the captain keep him out of interstellar prison, even though it's not the sort of legal." She sighs. "I don't know why I'm telling you all of this, but if someone with galactic authority decided to audit the pirate's paperwork, I would be the one to go to jail."

The elemental had a shocked look about him. He couldn't believe what he was hearing. Now the alarms going off in his head began to make sense. The pirate captain wasn't quite what he was portraying himself as, especially to this human female. She was in just as much danger as the rest of them. Jetsuenete set his immortal senses on high alert.

"Come." Said Alverta Brink. "I have talked for too long, and Captain Ninnies must be wondering what has happened to his distinguished guest." She spun on her heels, and the entourage began towards the far end of the narrow hallway.

The escort posse reached the end of the hallway and led out into the main hall. It was a lot more lit up and wide enough to let their entire entourage stand side-by-side as they walked down the hallway. The central passageway now littered with space pirates, unlike the back walkway they had been traversing. The main corridor was well lit, and many durasteel doorways with their automatic doors shut lined both sides of the passage.

Possibly crew's living quarters or storage rooms that the good captain doesn't want us to have access. The elemental shrugs it off, he has more concentrating on the meeting before them and the possible discovery of the talisman he had been searching for most of his life. The chatter from Jetsuenete's entourage started up again. This time they seemed less agitated but still on edge. But that was marines for you, always geared for a fight, even if none was required.

They weaved their way through the many passing crew members of the *Necromancer Leviathan,* like a small skiff maneuvering a rough sea. Then Captain Ninnies' party appeared near the end of the hallway. The captain was dressed out in his captain leathers, making him look like a costumed pirate, instead of a leader of men of all ages. A smirk appeared on the captain's face making Jetsuenete think the pirate looked superficial, but still, all the elemental wanted to do was receive to data and leave.

At this point, it all seemed like a stage performance, where you knew each actor was too dramatic. The rest of the captain's entourage all dressed like they were all decked out for a masquerade ball. Part of Captain Ninnies' entourage was the imperturbable Commander Zayne. Jetsuenete had never personally met the commander, but the elemental had heard rumors and knew the pirate was full of pride, to the point of loving the sound of Zayne's voice.

As the crew of *the Necromancer Leviathan* drew closer, Jetsuenete thought the pirate entourage outnumbered their entourage. Now Jetsuenete was becoming ever so agitated, and paranoia was setting in. *What have I gotten myself into? I should have listened to Dirdanth and allow an elemental or two escort him on this trip. But then why did I make this trip in the first place?* Jetsuenete took a deep breath.

The elemental leader delivered a forced smile, despite being on edge. Jetsuenete towered over his human hosts, but Captain Ninnies didn't show any nervousness that most of his crew was displaying, no matter how much they tried to fake it. Jetsuenete understood most mortal's apprehension. Humans never liked to appear inferior, at least in his opinion, to others. That's the vibe the pirates were expressing. The marines were different. The mortal soldiers that aided the elementals had become accustomed to fighting with the giant beings. It was now commonplace for them.

The captain was first to greet them.

"Jetsuenete, my good compadre. It's been a long time. My you look stronger than ever." Perspiration began to fall from the captain's brow. That's was about all Jetsuenete needed to know something was making the pirate nervous. The elemental began to scan the hallway and physically searching for anything out of the ordinary.

It took a minute for the elemental leader in responding, and when he did, the calmness had left his voice. Now only caution and aggression were there. "Captain Ninnies. What's up with all the secrecy? Why have you led me on a detour through your ship? I sense much apprehension from your crew."

Captain Ninnies brushes off the accusations. "Nonsense, my friend. You must be imagining things."

"Let's get this over with, do you have the data you promised?"

Captain Ninnies nodded to Commander Zayne, and the pirate handed over a rounded device. It fits into the middle of Jetsuenete's palm. The device was small for the elemental, and he had to be cautious not to crush it. Then something caught his attention, a noise he had never heard of before. It sounded like a wild beast crying out, and it shook the walls. That's when Captain Ninnies motioned towards a crew member, and the pirate left in a hurry. That was all the confirmation he needed. They had indeed walked into the trap. His senses hadn't misled him.

"Dirdanth was right. We walked right into their trap, and I ignored all the signs." Mumbled Jetsuenete.

Before the elemental could respond, his marine entourage began shouting, and laser fire riddled the spacious hallway that had been littered a moment ago with the pirate crew. Now only the elemental, his entourage, and the pirates that were challenging them occupied the space. Suddenly something burst into the back of the pirate line, making the mortals all flee in fear, Jetsuenete just couldn't make out what had just arrived, without his enhanced senses. Whatever the creature was, it was swift, massive in bulk, and had a mountainous cry.

The only pirates left standing in between Jetsuenete and the enormous creature are ones engaged the marines, but the elemental leader didn't have time to see if any of his entourage had fallen. Jetsuenete was concentrating on the mammoth four-legged creature snarling back at him. Less than twenty-five feet from him was a creature of legend, one he had never seen personally before: a night stalker, one of the Darkness' infamous doppelgangers that could morph into nearly anything.

The night stalkers were a race of shadowy furriers that mimic living things. They can't copy inanimate objects such as starships, weapons of destructive nature, nothing that doesn't have a living origin. They come out of the shadows, twirling like a serpent of smoke, black and decrypted. They must have touched the living thing it is going to mimic, at some point. The pitch-black serpents twist together like silly putty, intertwining with one another until they form the mass of its imitated form.

It usually comes out of the darkness as four black serpent-like clouds twisting through the air, end over end. These doppelgangers often hovered over ground (they weren't a ground-based entity) about a foot or two. Once the four doppelganger serpents engage one another, their black bodies weave together like yarn being stitched by a seasoned sewer until they form the physical shape they desire. In this case, it will be a vicious, werecat with protruding lower fangs that nearly ran along with its massive head. The beast possessed paws that could engulf a mortal human's torso, a long and razor-sharp tail it can whip its victims with powerful jaws to rip trap its prey as its razor-sharp teeth shred flesh.

The difference from a normal werecat typically lived on jungle planets such as Vicious Prime. In the Nemesis Orion sector, this doppelganger predator carried their black coat of fur and an even darker set of eyes. Its roar was so fierce it shook the hull of the pirate ship. The elemental knew it was here for him. He could sense the doppelganger cat sniffing for his sent, and once it picked it up, it tossed aside the dead pirate it was in the middle of devouring.

The beast stared right at Jetsuenete with its pitch-black voids of eyes. The two adversaries would go head-to-head, and the elemental leader wasn't sure who would win the day. He had never had even seen a doppelganger, let alone did battle with one. Nerves shot through the elemental leader's entire body and real fear, not of death or defeat, but the unknown. He couldn't sense the outcome of this battle like he had so many others he had engaged. The creature took a few prowling steps towards its new prey, and Jetsuenete reached for his battle sword, but it wasn't there. *They must have stolen it when my back was turned.*

The only way the elemental could fight this creature was with his omniscient abilities, which he had little command over at this moment. Unlike his celestial ancestors, he had possessed only a few of their omniscient abilities. He was sure that was to prevent any elemental from turning the Omni powers the celestials possessed against any living species and acting like a god. The good news was he still possessed some of the celestial's god-like abilities.

Jetsuenete possessed Omni kinesis, but he could only manipulate physical entities, and even in physical form, the doppelganger had a supernatural origin. It had a dark magic property, which made his Omni ability next to useless. The one talent that the elemental had been using during combat situations against lager and faster foes was omniscient combat. It enhanced his already superior reflexes and mental abilities. Using the omniscience in battle only amplified his abilities.

Without his elemental battle sword, quickness would be Jetsuenete's greatest asset. So, the elemental leader dug deep and retrieved a little extra strength, as the omniscient combat power began to resonate throughout the elemental's body. A rush of energy filled Jetsuenete and seemed to rejuvenate the elemental. It almost felt as if two of them were going into battle, the elemental leader with his gifted abilities and the omniscient enhanced version, the one that would take down the doppelganger.

Both adversaries began to move towards one another. Without glancing back to see if his marine escorts needed him, Jetsuenete launched towards the clash with the dark entity. The doppelganger let out a ferocious roar, as it launched towards the elemental leader. The clash was epic, as the two colossal beings crashed into each other. A tremendous shockwave rocked the ship's hallway. Ship lights blew, sending sparks of electricity everywhere as if someone had shot fireworks all down the hall.

The sound of the steel bulkhead flexing under the immense back-pressure the two adversaries were creating, echoed down the main hallway. Wielded seems to creak their protest and gave the impression they were about to break. The ship became dark, as the shockwave temporarily knocked out the ship's power before the emergency lights kicked. Blue flashing strobes filled the main hallway, and the colossal beings could barely see each other. But neither needed sight to battle the other; they had other senses that could contribute to the fight.

Jetsuenete could sense the doppelganger's huge maul with its flesh shredding teeth attempting to grab onto his skin. Fortune, the elemental was wearing his battle armor, preventing the dark entity from sinking its teeth in him. The elemental was struggling to keep the powerful beast from overpowering him and pouncing onto his body. Jetsuenete was holding back some of his omniscient combat power, fearful the doppelganger's dark origins would sense the extra power and begin to drain it like a bloodthirsty vampire.

Jetsuenete felt the might of the doppelganger's hind legs, as the entity pushed against him. The front paws begin to push down on his shoulders, while the doppelganger's maul keeps the elemental's hands busy. The elemental begins to slide on the metal flooring of the ship, and his adversary begins to take control of the struggle. He was losing the confrontation, and the elemental wants to survive, he must dig deep for everything he has.

Jetsuenete reached back for the remaining omniscient combat power, and instantly he feels his muscles grow, and his grip on the doppelganger strengthens. He began to feel the other Jetsuenete take control. The rush of omniscient energy power through the elemental's blood and throws a rainmaker punch to the beast's throat. The Doppelganger cried out in pain, and Jetsuenete's counterattack stunned the creature where it stood.

That gave Jetsuenete a chance to regain his footing and repositioned the doppelganger in his grasp. No longer was the dark titan powering down on the elemental's shoulders. The doppelganger had been forced into a submissive position where Jetsuenete could rain down powerful strikes onto his opponent's head.

That wasn't going to last long, as Jetsuenete landed one omniscient punch, then a second, then he prepared a third strike. Each strike to the doppelganger's maul seemed less like hitting flesh and bone and more like attempting to battle an apparition. The first strike was solid, resisting Jetsuenete's fist, and the elemental could hear the crunching of jawbones, but with each subsequent punch, the resistance of the flesh lessened and the third strike seemed to be like punching through the air.

The doppelganger is morphing into its original form. *I have to find a better way to attack it. I need to find another omniscient power to use.* Omniscient combat power is only good against opponents with physical form. The werecat was staring at it, not attempting to wiggle out of the semi headlock Jetsuenete had it in. The doppelganger merely looked at the elemental as if it was mocking its adversary. *What do you think you have won?* Thought Jetsuenete. *Well, you have never battled an elemental before. We are resilient and non-conforming. We have wills of steel.*

The doppelganger in werecat skin still didn't budge. That's when Jetsuenete thought the werecat was giving him a smug grin. The doppelganger seemed to fade back into its viper state, and for a moment, the elemental thought the doppelganger was going to fall completely apart. But the celestial descendant didn't realize that was part of the being's ploy. Suddenly the werecat snapped at the elemental and nearly swallowed Jetsuenete's arm fully.

The only thing preventing the doppelganger from devouring the elemental arm was cosmic manipulation. The elemental had reached down, at the last moment to draw out the omniscient power from his arsenal of abilities. Even though omniscient gifts didn't work on beings such as the doppelganger, it did prevent the shadow creature from taking his arm. The elemental grinds his teeth in frustration, *how could this have happened, how did he become this lazy?*

Jetsuenete stood there with an aura of foreboding like the elemental had enough of the doppelganger's game. A flash resonated from the elemental's free hand and blinded the doppelganger. Jetsuenete was free! Saliva or a slimy residue filled the elemental's armored forearm that appeared to be saliva but could have been the doppelganger's venom, trying to whittle down the armor and get to his arm. The elemental wiped off his arm while still eyeing the creature. The dead stare Jetsuenete had on his stone-cold face, was so sharp it could have sliced right through the doppelganger's dark apparitional essence.

To this point, their battle had been a stalemate. If the elemental leader had his battle sword, it could slowly absorb omniscient beings. The elemental's battle sword forged in the depths of the Orsoreich, a deep pit of fire that was bottomless, was his favorite weapon. No one knew how deep it went, the only that had ever confirmed as it had a great drawing power that only drew in omniscient power and beings. It was like a black hole for celestials. Legend told of how a few celestials got too close to this bottomless pit and, despite their omniscient ability, was lost forever.

But you know legends and how they tended to stray from the truth.

But Jetsuenete didn't need to worry about that, because he didn't have the elegant broadsword. The doppelganger lifted its chin as if daring the elemental to come for it. The dark holes that were the creature's eyes still were empty. *You are a smug SOB, aren't you?* The doppelganger mumbled a language the elemental wasn't accustomed to, so he wasn't sure if the entity was toying with him or cursing him up and down.

Simultaneously both combatants launched at the other. Once again, the collision was epic, and the ship's floor shook and began to buckle. The two combatants did a choreographed dance; wherever one combatant went, the other was his shadow. Back and forth, the two adversaries battled without any progress for either. But something inside of Jetsuenete told him that wasn't the doppelganger's goal if it had ever been; to win the battle. He wasn't sure how or why he knew this, but it just seemed that this entire conflict was a ruse.

Jetsuenete slapped the werecat, and the creature, no matter the shape it chose, hit the elemental leader in return. The sting from the strike was painful, but Jetsuenete was able to resist the pain. In the werecat form, the doppelganger snapped its deadly tail at the elemental once; it missed. Twice, a near miss, but Jetsuenete could feel a breeze wisp by his shoulder. Both swipes of the entities' tail forced the elemental backward, and the second tail whip nearly forced the elemental over. Jetsuenete looked behind him, as his giant hand braced the elemental from his fall. There was a body rubbing against his forearm. The elemental looked back and gasped at the sight.

All his marine entourage was dead. Their bodies littered the floor, and it was the reason the elemental leader nearly tumbled down. That's when he knew the evidence matched the crime. He had an inclination that they had walked into a trap, the elemental leader's senses warning him at every corner. But why had he been lead into a trap in the first place? What was the end game, and who was profiting by it all?

Jetsuenete brushed himself off, but the doppelganger hadn't approached while he was recovering. Why hadn't it attacked him? He wondered. What was it waiting for? The elemental grunted his frustration and clenched his fists. He was ready to pounce, but still, the doppelganger was waiting, for who? For what?

That's when a clapping noise came to the elemental. It was coming from behind, forcing Jetsuenete to turn around. Captain Ninnies and his entourage, including Ms. Brink were standing before him. The pirates all had a glee look on their faces as if their esteemed guest had played his part. *This must be part of the ruse*, thought Jetsuenete.

"Terrific battle, my friend." Boasted the pirate captain.

Jetsuenete grunted.

"Why such dramatic production? What is your end game? I assume there isn't the information on the data disk you gave me, is there?"

The pirate entourage all laughed.

"Very clever, my friend. How long did that take you to figure out?"

Captain Ninnies stuck out his hand as if expecting the elemental to give up the prize. Jetsuenete hesitated but finally tossed the disk to Ninnies. The pirate handed the disk to his Ms. Brink slid it into a vid projection, and what came out was an empty white video. The captain smiled his crooked smile.

The elemental shook his head. By that time, the elemental was wiping the blood off one of the marine's face. "What you expected, I assume?"

Jetsuenete nodded his dejected face.

Before the elemental knew it, a group of pirates snuck up behind him and, after a struggle, clapped a restraining collar and cuffs onto the elemental leader. Jetsuenete struggled, but he didn't have the strength to resist. It was like his omniscient power had been extracted from his body. The captain pointed at his prisoner, "These restraints neutralize your elemental abilities. Making it easier for your transport without the fear of killing my men."

"Just tell me one thing, why?"

"Well. I guess you will discover that soon enough. It's out of my hands now. All I care is being paid."

CHAPTER 18

The elemental leader lay on the cold stone bedding, staring up at the decrypted cell wall, through the pitch darkness. Jetsuenete was still feeling the immobilized effects of the restraint collar they had placed on him, even after its removal. He felt numb all over and the extra energy, the other elemental leader; the one he called his battle essence, had long disappeared. The elemental no longer felt the Omni-combat power; in fact, he even felt dilapidated and worn out, without much energy. The elemental thought he felt as decrypted as his cell walls looked.

The place was cold and uninviting. The only heat came from the energy field that kept Jetsuenete imprisoned. The elemental thought he was held in a dungeon or an underground faculty, with the stone wall directly in front being the only thing the elemental could see. The energy field illuminated the stained and aged stone wall, making the pitch blackness a rosy orange color. Nothing else was visible from his cell, and something was restricting his other enhanced senses. *Is it the after-effects of those restraints?* Jetsuenete wondered. *Or could it be something more sinister?*

The elemental attempted to sit up, but his head began to spin like a toy top. He couldn't keep control of his balance and felt like his body was in a constant free-fall. The dark cell seemed to spin around and around, making Jetsuenete flop back down onto the stone bedding. He touched his head, but it refused to stop spinning. The elemental took in deep breaths. His lungs were now on fire like he had breathed in something toxic. Jetsuenete was forced to breathe in the air around him, like his elemental abilities, his ability to create his atmosphere was being blocked somehow. That's when he felt the sensation. An evil eye was watching him with malcontent.

The elemental attempted to sit up a second time, but this time Jetsuenete chose to lift only his upper torso, not his entire body. A force seemed to push on his colossal chest, making even that little jester impossible. The elemental leader swore it felt like an invisible, gargantuan hand was forcing down on him. Jetsuenete felt like a child's toy, being toyed with, not one of the most powerful beings in the cosmos.

Suddenly a sinister voice, one that seemed too familiar to Jetsuenete, echoed in his mind. He couldn't tell if it was only in the elemental's mind or a residual effect of his imprisonment. *The Darkness,* Mouthed the elemental leader. He felt the sinister master of shadows toying with him. The words were indecipherable. All the words whispering in his mind seemed to be from an unknown language. Despite that, the elemental could sense the Darkness near him, no not near, but very close, but not close enough for either being to drive the other insane. Though Jetsuenete thought the Darkness couldn't be driven any more insane.

The elemental felt the Darkness prodding his mind, but for what was unclear. A stabbing sensation began to form at the top of the elemental's head. Then the sinister voice began to speak in an ancient tongue he had never heard before. This one was different than when his adversary came to him in his chambers. The malevolent voice seemed to mumble a chant.

"Get out of my head." Jetsuenete cried in a low tone. It came out more like a yelling-cry than a forceful demand—something the elemental had never done before.

Suddenly a shadowy figure appeared before his cell entrance. At first, the elemental couldn't see the translucent figure draped in black. His visitor camouflaged by the darkness surrounding the elemental's keeper provided the Darkness a veil of confinement. But Jetsuenete didn't need to see the agent of darkness; the elemental felt the Shadow Lord's essence. He squinted his eyes, that's when the agent of darkness stepped forward to where the energy field keeping him in his cell reflected off the apparition-like figure. Jetsuenete had never seen anything such as the Shadow Lord, but he felt right at that moment, it seemed to fit the place.

"I hope you are comfortable. The master would have me skinned if I had any skin if you felt any discomfort at all." The Shadow Lord said, in a slightly less contemptible voice than the Darkness had come to the elemental.

Jetsuenete shook off the wooziness and sat up to see the translucent figure clearer. The figure reflected the orangish tent of the cell energy field. It made the translucent figure appear part of its existence, almost like the shadow agent had a red halo surrounding his visitor. By leaning forward, Jetsuenete relieved the Shadow Lord had no face, it was more like a black mirror that someone had shined to polish, but still possessed an essence of secrecy.

"What's wrong, elemental? Cat got your tongue?" The figure began to chuckle a deep tone that sent chills up the elemental's spine. He had never been so full of anxiety before. With all the battles, he had fought and the multitude of species he had fought, Jetsuenete had never felt such a strong foreboding as he now was experiencing.

"Why have you brought me here, fiend?"

Jetsuenete had the impression that if the Shadow Lord could smile, it would be doing so, right about now. At this point, the elemental noticed his visitor floating inches above the stone floor.

"Come now; you're an intelligent being. I'm sure you can figure that one out for yourself. I'm not allowed to divulge anything the master doesn't want you to know, not that the master would care either way. But I like watching prisoners squirm. I can't wait to begin your torture sessions."

Jetsuenete grunted. "By your master, you mean the Darkness, correct?"

"You are as astute as my master had predicted. Very good. Yes, my master is the Darkness, among the many names others use."

"So, he has brought me to this hell hole to torture me? What's the end game fiend? Probing me about elemental information. Secret codes that the Darkness thinks I have or just effecting those that follow my lead?"

The Shadow Lord began to cackle. "Oh, you will discover that in due time. The master will do whatever it desires."

Jetsuenete possessed an inquisitive expression. His eyes had widened. The jaw muscles tightened as if the elemental had been filled up with unwanted air that still lingered inside his mouth. His cheekbones seemed to protrude out like a volcano ready to erupt. His body was erect, and the elemental sat at attention as if the elemental was a schoolchild prepared for his teacher to begin instructing.

"You're in the Merciless Reach. The home of the Darkness, the place itself is imprisoned in, thanks to your ancestors!" A grinding noise began, but Jetsuenete didn't know where it was coming from. If the elemental didn't know it, he would swear the Shadow was making the sound but did the shadow agent have teeth? "As you have realized, your abilities are subdued, and you're at the mercy of the Darkness."

"The Darkness' dark magic and power are magnified in this place?" Jetsuenete looked around as if looking for something.

"You can feel the master's intensity, can't you? Its dark, menacing power. It's the lost essence that lives in this place. Isn't it magnificent?"

The elemental leader grunted his disapproval.

"Sit tight, and your time will come soon. Then the fun will commence, and then you will wish it had was delayed."

The Shadow Lord began its sinister laughter, as its dark translucent form began to fade away from Jetsuenete's cell, like a phantom dissolving into the nighttime air. The conversation had left the elemental even more lost in his cell than before the Shadow Lord appeared. The info he had been able to extract was he had been neutralized and brought to the Darkness' lair, the reason is still undefined, but he was sure it couldn't be anything good.

Something else that was clear was the Darkness' power was increased immensely. The elemental nemesis must draw power from the dark energy from the decrypted citadel and even the Merciless Reach itself. The elemental heard about the Darkness infamous home realm and of the stigmatism that came with those myths. But now Jetsuenete was beginning to believe some of those legendary tales. His restraints and the inability to sense his elemental abilities, while the dark sensation that lingered about seemed to be his nemesis displaying its strength, thousands of times more potent than Jetsuenete had imagined.

"The question I must ask is, how will I break my bonds and escape this sinister place." The elemental mumbled.

Jetsuenete brought his arms closer and tried to warm himself with his body heat. The elemental had a lot of thinking, and he doubted that anyone would come to aid his escape. *How in the cosmos will I escape this fiasco?* The elemental stared intently at the cold black stone of the adjacent cell wall.

The air was thick and foggy. There was a stench about that the elemental couldn't explain. Jetsuenete roamed the countryside, wading through the darkness without any clue where he was going to or coming from. It was like the elemental was blind, alone, and without any of his enhanced senses. There seemed to be lingering wickedness radiating from a distance that could explain the congestion in the air.

Jetsuenete moved further into the thick cloud. He couldn't see the cloud itself, so the elemental had no clue how thick it was or the composition. There was a toxic element in the cloud, as the defender of the cosmos walked through its bulk. The elemental could taste it on his tongue, in the pores of his skin, the toxicity through his very nose. But where had the cloud, the one he couldn't see, extracted the toxic chemical or whatever that was burning his nose. In fact, where had the cloud itself come from? A burning building? Some evil monstrosity? Maybe an unknown source.

Then out of the darkness, a howl emerged, one that sent chills up a person's spine. The owner of the cry sounded both enormous and nefarious, even to the elemental. It seemed like whatever had made the insidious noise was a reasonable distance away, but something was vastly approaching, whether it was the creature that had howled or another one. Dried branches are heard breaking at a rapid pace. Jetsuenete swore the sound bouncing from the far right of his current position, then to his far left.

Could there be more than one species out there? And were they sprinting towards me? Jetsuenete wondered. Suddenly the elemental realized his throat was parched, and his palms were sweating. He hadn't realized a high level of anxiety had crept upon him. *Were had that emotion come from?* Jetsuenete wondered. *Could that be a direct result of the alien environment I am currently in?* Maybe it had to do with his lack of visibility or that he didn't have his heightened senses to rely upon. *You never realize how much you miss something until its gone.*

The crunching noise had come extremely close, at this point and Jetsuenete froze. The elemental couldn't move, couldn't even breathe. All he could do was wait for the creature to draw closer. Then without warning, the noise stopped, like whatever had made the nose just vanished. The silence was suddenly followed by an extremely high pitched yelp as if whatever was approaching had suddenly intercepted. But what could have seized the approaching creature? Was it maleficent, or was it friendly to Jetsuenete?

After the yelp, silence returned and seemed to dominate the night. It seemed like forever, and the elemental wasn't sure what to do or how to respond? Was something much more significant and more aggressive coming for him? What had intercepted the approaching night stalker? Too many unanswered questions for the elemental. None of this was helping Jetsuenete's anxiety.

He was going to have act and fast. The elemental couldn't just stand there and do nothing. Jetsuenete finally sucked up his fleeing courage and set aside his anxiety and took a few hazardous steps further into the darkness. A dried branch broke underfoot, here and there. But nothing like whatever had been approaching. An eerie sensation began to take hold as if the elemental's anxiety had returned with a stranglehold on him.

The toxic air began to thicken, and Jetsuenete's breathing became more labored. It felt as if some type of toxic poison was filling his elemental lungs, preventing clean oxygen from fueling his body. As the elemental was concentrating on his breathing, a deep growl suddenly came from behind. With a slight hesitation, Jetsuenete turned around. But all he faced was a dark empty void. He listened for anything moving, but nothing but silence surrounded him. "Who's out there?" Jetsuenete whispered.

There was no answer to the elemental's call, not even a growl in response.

The elemental spun around slowly, but he was alone in the darkness.

The elemental called more boldly. "I said who is out there?"

Jetsuenete's voice echoed out into the void this time. He listened as his raptured voice repeated through the darkness, through the dense cloud cover and out over the land, as it stretched beyond his position. That's when heavy breathing began. It sounded menacing and close and vastly more significant than the elemental. One that was supposed to scare him to death, but he was Jetsuenete. The elemental had faced many tribulations and threats on the battlefield, so the hell if he was going to let a little deep breathing scare him off.

At first, the menacing breathing was behind the elemental, but then the sound began to surround Jetsuenete from every direction as if the source of the ominous breathing and the growl was everywhere. Like it was in the air itself. The elemental called out, "Who are you?" He paused before continuing. "What do you want with me?"

His voice raced towards the dark horizon.

Then a sinister chuckle bellowed from the beyond.

"What do I want with you is indeed the question."

That voice thought Jetsuenete. *I know it well. The Darkness! But it can't be, the master of shadows can't follow me here. This is my safe zone. My head should be safe from any intrusion.* Then the sinister growl, followed by laughter, penetrated the darkness. "I can be anywhere, foolish being. I can be inside of your mind, your dreams, if I so desire. Who's going to stop me, you?"

Jetsuenete shook his head. "No, you don't have control of me! I am an elemental, and you can't cast your imperial indignation onto me."

Something seemed to squeeze the elemental, like a giant crushing a soda can. Jetsuenete began to have shortness of breath, and his dual hearts started to beat irregularly, while his vision began to blur, not that he could see anything in the first place. The Darkness stayed in his head, because Jetsuenete felt the master of shadows inside him, not that he could hear his adversaries demonic voice. He was too worried about being turned into a kabob.

The elemental reached out as if he was attempting to grab something in the dark, something that might save his own life. But there was nothing out in the darkness, at least nothing Jetsuenete could utilize. The Darkness chuckled again as if mocking his opponent, the master of shadows was enjoying this. A ringing began in the elemental's ear that wouldn't subside. It seemed to replace the Darkness' malcontent voice.

Jetsuenete grabbed for his throat. His breathing issues only seemed to increase, and now he has issues breathing, but his windpipe had shut off. *This is it,* the elemental thought. *This is how I will die, in tormenting agony.* That's when the elemental thought about it. He had to admit that the Darkness' power was amplified, here in the Merciless Reach. *That's it! I'm not out in the darkness, unable to see or use my elemental abilities. The Darkness has entered my mind and is twisting in on this canvas of doom. Its merely a dream and he isn't killing me!*

Jetsuenete let go of his throat and relaxed his mind. If the elemental refused to allow his nemesis to enthrall his mind and manipulate and subdue him, he had a chance to survive. At least in his theory. Jetsuenete relaxed his entire body, not just his mind, in hopes that the Darkness would release him as if a child bored with a play toy. Things began to slow down. The elemental's anxiety suddenly vanished, and he slowly drifted into peaceful serenity. It no longer felt as if he was being bombarded by a twisted, manipulative being, hell bend on warping his mind. Now it seemed as if nothing mattered, and his torture was over.

A thick mist past by the elemental and Jetsuenete drifted off into a deep and hazy unconsciousness. The torture wasn't twisting his mind. It seemed as if he was free of the Darkness' grasp.

The elemental leader was no longer in agony. He sat there, imagining himself floating on the smooth surface of the lake. There was a serenity floating on the surface without any worries, soldiers dying at your feet or adversaries attempting to kill you. Jetsuenete realized the darkness he had been in before, were all a nightmare. He hadn't experienced any of it. It was a place the Darkness had used to break him. It was how the Darkness drove his victims insane—a canvas of despair.

Jetsuenete felt like he was driftwood floating on top of a smooth body of water. The elemental's arms were spread like they were paddles in a canoe, just waiting to begin their trek towards the far side of the lake. He even felt small bits of splashing water striking his face. The tactic worked, the Darkness had left Jetsuenete alone, as soon as the elemental let go. The elemental was floating in a small lake with small waves splashing on top of his humongous forehead. A blanket of thick, gray fog was drifting inwards from the far bank. The east bank was visible, just left of the incoming fog. Slight noises filled the air. Insects calling out for their mates, lake dwellers singing in the fog covered air. A sent that blended from all the lake resources filled the air.

The elemental looked around, not seeing the stone walls of his prison cell, but the lake's image, the surrounding vegetation, the inhabitants of the lake, and the sounds that accompanied the calm atmosphere. Jetsuenete understood that it was all in his mind. He had never visited such a place, nor had he ever heard of a place so calm and lack of death. All he remembered was the killing, the mass slaughter of the battlefield, and watching colleagues perish. This place just popped into the elemental's mind, maybe from all the horridness he had experienced his mind needed something serene.

Jetsuenete closed his eyes and soaked it all in. *I refuse to let my present condition strip my confidence down. I know I'm still imprisoned, lying on a stone bed, in that dingy, creepy dungeon. I may not understand why I am incarcerated or what my adversary wants with me, but I will soak in the peacefulness, gain strength from it and persevere.*

Suddenly, the peaceful scene snapped back, and Jetsuenete returned to his cold, dreary cell. His jailer was once again sieging the elemental. The nemesis voice whispered in his head. Jetsuenete's headache had returned ten-fold. Had the Darkness' torture ever subsided or, like the nightmare in the dark and the lakeside vision, had it all been an illusion?'

Unlike the darkness illusion, where his torturer had struck Jetsuenete's anxiety and filled with paranoia, this time, the elemental leader had control of his emotions. Jetsuenete would not allow the Darkness to rattle his normally calm nature. He couldn't do anything about the physical discomfort, but he could block the Darkness from controlling his mind. The elemental mumbled something, most likely an insult, but it only came out bland and inaudible.

Then the front stone wall of his cell, the one that possessed the doorway to his cell, became blazed. But no heat was coming from the fiery stone, which shot alarms off in Jetsuenete's head. *Another illusion.* The elemental tried to shake off the image, but his movements were restricted, and he was only capable of chafing the skin of his neck.

Out of the fiery illusion, a pair of damnable eyes appeared through the inflamed stone wall. That's when Jetsuenete understood he was witnessing the imagery of his adversary. The set of eyes belonged to the Darkness. The perilous eyes were inspecting its prey. The elemental could feel the egregious aura emanating from those sets of eyes- a familiar growl game from the inflamed stone wall.

"Don't think you can escape me that easy, elemental."

"I wouldn't think of it," Jetsuenete responded in a muffled tone.

The diabolical set of eyes moved in closer as if its owner wanted to intimidate the elemental. The black orbs narrowed as the Darkness scrutinized its captive. "All your immersed power, all your omniscient heritage won't save you know, will it?"

"Keep talking nonsense, you large oaf. You can't intimidate me."

The Darkness squeezed the elemental even tighter, making it difficult to breathe. *If this diabolical being chooses to press any more, I won't have any organs left.* Jetsuenete felt the heat of the Darkness' breath, but something confused him. Had the master of darkness disembodied itself and was now in the room with him, or could its reach extend from its forced prison? Jetsuenete understood the limitless power the shadow entity possessed and how it could do many things in the Merciless Reach

"You're a foolish being." Growled the Darkness. Jetsuenete felt an invading, contemptable sensation suddenly flow throughout his body. "Don't you realize it by now? I can take whatever I want from you. I can ransack your mind, steal any vital information you possess, and leave you a bumbling fool."

The elemental spit at his nemesis. "Go back to your slumber, beast. You have nothing to threaten me with."

"Grrrrr!" Growled the Darkness.

The dark entity shook the elemental like a rag doll.

"You're too foolish to be a celestial descendant. You have no clue what I have planned for you. You will be my gateway into defeating your pathetic army of freaks and mortals. I will unlock your mind, torture you until your mind nearly slips, then bring you back for more pain."

"Do your best! I can physically take anything you can dish out."

"Maybe you are careless with your body, but what about your mind?"

The fiery illusion started to dim, but the Darkness' eye's intense gaze grew. Jetsuenete felt the invading sensation increase as if the Darkness was squeezing just a little tighter. The elemental tried again to slither out of the Darkness' grip, but with similar results as before. He was becoming fatigued from the episode, feeling his grip on reality slipping, which wasn't all that difficult to do in the Merciless Reach.

"You don't realize how much a key you are to the Shadow Empire's future."

With what remained of his breath Jetsuenete dispised the Darkness. "My…friends…will…res..ue me."

"Ha!" Bellowed master of shadows. "No one is coming for you. You are truly alone."

Jetsuenete used what power was left in his mind to stab the invisible hand, drawing a sudden reaction. "Ewwwww." Cried the Darkness. The dark entity tossed the elemental across the cell and slammed into the far wall, knowing the elemental unconscious.

The torture sessions had continued. The Darkness had made each one even more diabolical than the last. There had been half a dozen torture sessions to this point, but no matter what the master of shadows had done, Jetsuenete was becoming a nuisance. A tough nut to crack. His labored breathing had become worsened with each torture session. Even though the elemental had crumbled, yet, there were signs of his body giving out and the Darkness sensed it.

The headaches had increased as well, not aiding his ailing body at all. The one thing that Jetsuenete seemed to improve was his ability to see in the dark chamber cell. Slowly his eyes had been able to adjust to the darkness, and now he could see silhouettes of things that were further down the hall.

The hallway and the stairwell that led to his cell floor could be deciphered with a little assistance from his cell's energy field. The fluorescent beams illuminated just enough of the underground level to provide shadows of the stairwell. Where they led to was anyone's guess, at least to Jetsuenete anyways. He was sure they led somewhere, most likely to the tower level of the bastion, where a multitude of shadow guards and other agents of darkness must dwell.

Jetsuenete still didn't know where the Darkness' chambers were, but he wasn't sure he wanted to know. Coming face-to-face with the deity, in its dwelling, wasn't something he would cherish. It was bad enough to encounter its strength down in the dungeon. He preferred just to lay there, but if his memory was correct, another torture session couldn't be too far off.

The elemental looked back from his stone bed to the cell's back wall. Even though he couldn't see it, Jetsuenete envisioned the cracks from the multitude of times the Darkness had tossed his body against the stone wall. He had bruises from each incident. The elemental didn't need to see the injuries, every time he turned the wrong way, and he could feel the bruises protesting.

He had the bruises on his mountainous upper back, on his pain-stricken lower back, his thighs and his padded, monstrous chest. The stone bed didn't help the soreness either, giving him a restful sleep. Jetsuenete wasn't sure if the torture or the lack of sleep was worse. He guessed it probably didn't matter either way. The elemental moved a little, leaning on one elbow, but he wasn't sure why.

A sound echoed down the hallway, like chains being moved and a heavy door opening. *The Shadow Lord.* Jetsuenete thought. If the agent of shadow was coming to visit, the Darkness most likely wasn't coming to torture him. *What does that fool want?* Jetsuenete listened as the agent approached. The Shadow Lord didn't walk on the stone floor; that's not how the elemental was tracking the agent's movement. It was the sound of chains clanging together.

Chains? Now there is a new twist. Chains hadn't been used in any of his torture sessions to this point. This would be something new to deal. Surely, they wouldn't whip him with something as crude as chains, or would they? Jetsuenete, at this point, wouldn't put it past his adversaries. There had to something else that they intended to do with the chains. Finally, the Shadow Lord appeared, the chains were draped over both arms. The rusty ends hung over each thin arm, and Jetsuenete thought that's what he heard clanging.

As soon as The Shadow Lord got close enough, the agent of darkness stopped. It floated about ten feet from Jetsuenete's cell. The illumination made the figure, and the chain it held appear as a translucent apparition. Something inside told the elemental that the Shadow Lord was grinning like the agent was mocking the prisoner.

"Have you come to play?" Questioned the elemental.

"Hardly. I have come to escort you to the master's chambers. That's where the fun will commence."

Jetsuenete huffed. "Has your master gotten bored with torturing me from afar?"

"You may ask the master of darkness when you bow at the feet of the Darkness."

Inside the Darkness' chamber, it was just as dark as it had been inside his cell. But Jetsuenete knew he wasn't alone. His breathing was slow and steady. His duel hearts beat in unison, displaying complete control over the elemental's emotions. Jetsuenete had learned, since the six other torture sessions, which all took place in his cell's confinements. This would be the first time the torture would commence within the Darkness' chamber.

A distortion was present, directly in front of the elemental. *That must be the celestial prison perimeter, keeping the Darkness from roaming anywhere it desired.* The imprisonment hummed as if it was a highly powerful energy field, one that could contain an entity such as the Darkness. Jetsuenete was cuffed and tied to the chamber floor. He had to assume his captors were confident with the elemental's abilities subdued, the chains would be enough, and being in the presence of the master of shadows would be enough to keep him from escaping.

The heat was nearly unbearable. It was like the elemental had been tossed into a fire pit, but Jetsuenete didn't have a choice. He was tied to the decrypted floor with no way to break the chains that bound him. The Shadow Lord was nowhere in sight; it was just the elemental and the Darkness. Sweat rolled off his forehead, and his palms were dripping perspiration. He flexed his hands to keep circulation flowing; it also kept Jetsuenete's mind occupied.

The Darkness suddenly appeared through the gray matter that concealed the master of darkness and its throne of deception. The Darkness' predatorily eyes narrowed and focused on its prey. The elemental felt his adversaries gaze long before he saw it. A force grabbed him with an intensity so great that it could have burned out his existence instantly. Jetsuenete understood it was the Darkness' invisible grasp, and the torture was about to begin.

In its sinister and decrypted voice, the Darkness bellowed, "I am exhausted from our little game, elemental. You will give me what I want, or I will destroy you right where you kneel. I want the codes to the elemental mainframe server."

Jetsuenete mumbled something inaudible; it was more like reciting a childhood rhythm than answering the Darkness' question. The Darkness sensed the elemental's defiance and cried out. "You fool! Are you seriously going to defy me, down to your last breath? Are the other elementals so loyal to you, or can I find someone else to turn?"

A silvery liquid oozed from the Darkness invisible grasp and ran down Jetsuenete's face. The liquid substance burned like acid and left scarring on the skin. Once the acid substance found their insertion points, the more than a dozen lines of liquid penetrated Jetsuenete's elemental skin. The elemental let out a momentous cry, and his eyes opened wide. The silver liquid had struck home and was working on the nerve endings of the elemental leader. Jetsuenete sensed his nemesis watching in anticipation. But what type of reaction was the master of darkness looking for?

"Give me what I want!" Barked his adversary.

Jetsuenete refused to give anything up. Was it out of resilience, inner strength, or was it from the inability to think or respond to the Darkness. He had been through so much, and even an elemental's body could only take so much. Jetsuenete's mind was beginning to wander like he was losing control. Was it from the silver liquid? Were they meant to break his mind or his body down?

The elemental felt the acid-based liquid's ill effects.

CHAPTER 19

Captain Theo Ninnies looked out onto the pitch-black space. The scene was serene and quiet, something he knew wouldn't last long. The pirate's betrayal of the elemental leader had placed a target on their backs, and now they were on the run. *The Necromancer Leviathan* crept along at a slow pace, but the captain knew his ship was nibble and could keep up with most star cruisers. Both classes of starships had the same propulsion systems and which are made by the same shipbuilders.

Alverta Brink, the captain's assistant, approached the captain's position cautiously. "Are you all right, captain?" She was hesitant to bring up his deal with the Shadow Lord and the betrayal of the elemental leader.

Without turning around, captain Ninnies responded, "I'm fine Ms. Brink. I was only contemplating my past."

The young woman looked down as if she was ashamed to remember her own. "The past can haunt us."

The captain smiled his standard, crooked smile as if he was the only one privy to an inside joke.

"Yes, it can. But I fear my choices will haunt the crew, making us all wanted men and women. The elementals, if nothing else, are tenacious hunters. I am afraid my actions have placed a bull's eye on all our backs."

"Sir, if I may interject. Everyone on this vessel has a checkered past, myself included. You have been more than fair to your entire crew, judging us on our merits and not on our past digressions. You have acted like the father none of us have ever had."

Theo Ninnies understood his assistant was referring to her issues as a child and the role he had played getting out of the situation she had found herself. From the captain's understanding, Ms. Brink's family were riddled by mounds of debt and sold their young daughter to a brothel house on Viunus B, a place that catered towards outlaws and scum of the galaxy.

By the time captain Ninnies got to her and extracted her from the situation, the young girl was emotionally damaged by her time at the brothel, and he understood she would need time to heal. He treated her like a daughter, nursing her with healing foods, with the best physiological doctors and other soothing methods. He saw something in her, something that told him the girl had more to offer than being a sexual cushion for lonely space travelers and crude outlaws.

His patience and training unleashed her brilliant mind. Captain Ninnies, for all his efforts towards Ms. Brink, treating her like family, became the captain's biggest asset. An extension of his mind. He understood that, in her mind, she owed him. But like any loving father, he was worried about her safety and her future. He was concerned for all their futures, and his recent actions placed them in peril.

"Sometimes, we all need assistance, Ms. Brink. Your situation, even though it may be unique, was in no way a reflection of your character. That was on your parents, not on the young girl you were. I am proud to have done what I had and have no regrets." The captain paused for a moment as if caught in the moment. "Have I told you I had a twin brother?"

It was his assistant's turn to pause. "No captain, I don't believe you have."

Without looking back, Theo Ninnies began to reflect on the time he was a young adolescent.

~

Flashback to Theo Ninnies' youth Vinore

I grew up on the small planet of *Vinore*. It was a quiet place to live with a two-percent nitrous oxide atmosphere, much like many humanoid planets. Vinore was the ninth satellite of the rogue star Ijanaif. It resided in the tail of the Scorpion star sector, isolated from much space-faring traffic and kept us safe from invasion or piracy. Crops were grown on farms outside of our village and commerce with surrounding villages that made it our little paradise. The planet had a bluish-green atmosphere and rolling plains that created the lush valley we resided. None of us we well-off, but noone starved and each helped one another.

I was an adolescent on the verge of manhood. I had a twin brother. We had the same crooked nose, the same uneven jawline, boy, was an odd-looking boy, the same frizzed hair. I could never keep it from looking like a desert bush. He had blond hair, and mine was a dark color. We both were tall and lean. I loved to go off on one of my adventures I'm so known for, while sometimes neglecting my chores. He would lecture me about the unfinished duties I hadn't completed.

Gabriel was a disciplined youth, but he had no tolerance for simple-minded individuals. I saw the uniqueness of their simplemindedness. Maybe that was the start of our declining relationship. My twin saw us as leaders of men and others as followers, no matter the means. We had constant arguments about over dinner. There was no check and balance in most of our heated discussions since his father rarely was around; he was a pirate himself.

"Did I ever tell you that?" Questioned Captain Ninnies.

"No." Responded Ms. Brinks.

Well, he was. Not that it mattered. He was a good man and an excellent provider, but he never was around to lend his fatherly advice. So, my twin and I kept up the charade until one day, he gathered several boys from town and convinced them, with some forceful persuasion, to beat some smaller children into submission. The children weren't doing anything wrong, except when my twin forced his own will onto them, they rejected it openly.

"What did your brother and his followers do to them?"

The captain sighed.

"That's an excellent question. We never found out. These children just disappeared and were never found again."

Ms. Brink gasped in shock. "You didn't find any of them? No trace at all?"

"Oh, there were pieces of ripped clothing here and there. I even found a blood-soaked stuffed doll, but I never knew what a child had owned it. And my twin and his followers weren't talking."

Then, after all that happened, Gabriel and I had a final confrontation. At the dinner table, my brother was criticizing me for neglecting more chores, while I was hunting down clues for the missing children. That didn't please Gabriel one bit. He pointed his dinner fork at me and called me lazy, and I had no future with my attributes. He even went as far as to say I wouldn't be welcomed in the family if that happened.

That's when both of us got-face-to-face. My brother threatened me with the dinner fork, like some crime detective trying to be menacing towards a suspect. My twin's face had scowl about it, and he was spitting on me as he criticized my actions. "None of this is your concern, Theo." He proclaimed. A few times, he even pocked me in the chest with his dinner fork.

I returned his threatening remarks, in a calmer tone, by saying, "At least I don't go around threatening those I believe are less intelligent than I and murdering innocent children. You act like a tyrant, and if I have a choice between following your lead and leaving this household, I'd chose the latter."

Oh, that sparked a chain reaction.

Gabriel took a swing at me, but with his rage boiling, he missed and nearly stumbled over into my arms. I might be a non-violent person, but I wasn't about to take a physical beating, even by the hands of my brother. I struck Gabriel in the neck, making him bounce off my fist like some pongo ball, and he began to stumble backward. That's when I knew there was no turning back.

My twin stumbled and crawled on his hands, with his front-facing me. I believe he was afraid to turn his back. I ran after him, with venomous rage buried deep within me. I moved to strike, and like a viper, Gabriel kicked at me and hit my midsection, forcing me to stumble back. That gave my twin a chance to recover.

We were back where we had started, except he had a bruised neck and ego; I had a sore sternum. Neither one of us was about to give ground, and it was the question who wanted to hurt the other worse than the other did. We were brothers, and no matter what, there was still love for one another. Or at least from my end.

It pained me to see him in pain, whether that was physically or emotionally. I took a deep breath, knowing one of us was going to lose this confrontation. I clenched my fingers and prepared for the worse. Gabriel broke the monotonous standoff and leaped to strike. He had done it so swiftly I could only watch as his closed fist missies towards the bridge of my nose. The attack struck my nose dead on, and the cartilage snapped, sending a river of blood down my nose. I think I was more stunned than anything, even though a sharp pain surged through my nose, leaving me defenseless to a barrage of wayward punches. Some of them landed, while others were too wild to come close to their intended target.

With my nose still bleeding, I ducked to protect my face from further damage, which opened the rest of my body to Gabriel's punches. At one point, the pain stopped hurting. I think my body just went numb. Later I felt the bruises up and down my legs and arms, but at that moment, all I could feel was my broken nose. I could also hear Gabriel's punches landing. The 'smack' of fists on flesh rang in my ears for days after our conflict.

Out of the blue, and I still can't figure out why to this day, I pushed my twin off me and punched his shoulder blade. Both of us let out an excruciating howl of pain that echoed through the small family home. I think his shoulder came out of its socket, and my hand now broken. That did end the fight because neither of us could physically continue or had the will. The damage had been done, and I was through with my vindictive twin as well.

"What did you do after that?" Questioned Alverta Brink.

"I packed up my belongings and headed out west, not knowing where I might end up. The funny thing was I heard that my twin had done some jobs indirectly for the Shadow Empire and ended up at one of those penial asteroid colonies, but it was only a rumor, and you know when pirates drink how they like to talk B.S."

Captain Ninnies seemed to be in a trance, but snapped out of it. But that didn't mean he still didn't have a glossy-eyed look.

The captain's assistant looked at him sideways. "You ended up in your father's profession?"

Captain Ninnies could only shrug his shoulders. "I guess. I never heard from any of my family. I worked my way up, did enough bad things to get a man arrested, which I came more than close to doing, and saved enough to purchase my own ship. I guess I proved my twin wrong."

Ms. Brink nodded. "I'd say you did. And ended up helping several lost souls in the process like myself."

A smile penetrated the captain's stern exterior.

"Now I'm afraid we will be on the run for my decision. I haven't the foggiest where we could hide."

"I'm sure you'll come up with something. You always do." She offered him a flirtatious smile.

Captain Ninnies never thought of his assistant in that way. Even though she was cute, he had always seen her as the daughter he had never had. He returned the smile. The captain returned his attention to the void of space, slowly flying by the bridge viewpoint. *If I only had the chance, I would have taken it all back. I would have refused the Shadow Lord's offer.*

"You know, I haven't been the schoolboy I portray. I have done some despicable things, but betraying the elemental as I did take the cake. I swore I would never get into the middle of this stupid war, and look what happened."

"The Shadow Lord wasn't leaving you with many options. He would have sent a legion of his followers after us if you had refused. Don't be too hard on yourself, captain."

Captain Ninnies looked out towards the passing stars with an intense stare. "We might be able to head down to the Trojia VII system. There are a few penial colonies we might be able to hide out in."

"What about the asteroid colony you said Gabriel was rumored to have ended up at?"

The captain shook his head.

"Too risky. I never like places that I can't escape from easily. Besides, if my memory hasn't failed me, those asteroid colonies are mining faculties, and there is nowhere to set the *Necromancer Leviathan* down. At least a planet based penial colony could supply a quick lift-off, and we could hide the ship. But that's all as a last resort and haven't gotten to that point yet."

"Well we will defer to your decision-making captain. You are the boss."

~

The star cruiser, the *Nightstorm,* flew past a nebula cloud. Commander Kimberly Swansen, observes the passing stars. She was scoping for something when the elemental Gaitharrul approached. The commander and her crew had recovered from the attack on their security patrol, where the *Nightstorm* was the only fleet ship to survive. The elemental possessed cobalt blue skin and translucent gray eyes. He had an eagle with its wings spread wide on his breastplate. The elemental was quiet in his approach and wanted nothing more than to allow the commander's crew to do their job.

The elemental had orders to hunt down the pirate captain and drag out the location their leader had been abducted. Gaitharrul possessed none of his leader's patience and was excited to rescue his leader. The commander wasn't sure she wants to see the elemental agitated. The elemental gripped the sidebar that surrounded the observation balcony that overlooked the entire bridge area. Only the commander and her executive officer used the platform, but an exception was granted to the elemental.

"You called me to the bridge, commander?"

Cmd. Swansen nodded. "I did. We have been scanning the nebula's outskirts and have noticed a constant change in readings that don't appear to be a natural phenomenon. It seems more mechanical."

"And?" Questioned Gaitharrul.

"We are about to do a more detailed scan, but to do it, we must get closer. I wanted to get your input since you oversee this expedition."

"Expedition, commander? This is a manhunt for a traitor, not a casual stroll through the galaxy."

Gaitharrul's toned changed to one that possessed contempt for the commander's nonchalant attitude towards their search. But the commander wouldn't notice it in the elemental's physical appearance. Only another elemental would notice the outrage in Gaitharrul's silver eyes.

"I understand." Cmd. Swansen returned. She turned to her crew and barked orders. "Helm, three-quarter speed and keep the ship steady. Start laser scans and search for life forms of any type within the nebula."

"Mam," called one of the scanning officers. "We will have to get extremely close to the nebula itself to do a detailed ioscan."

"Duly noted, helm confirm those orders."

"Confirm commander. I will bring the *Nightstorm* as close to the cloud as possible."

Gaitharrul didn't even bother looks at the commander. "Won't that spook the pirate captain if he's inside the cloud?"

"You wanted me to do a thorough job in our search. You want the pirate as bad as anyone, am I correct?"

Gaitharrul huffed. "Very well commander. Continue the sweep of the nebula."

The Nightstorm swung to a parallel position to the nebula cloud and began its bio scan. Just as soon as the scan started, something moved within the cloud, like a fish in muddy water evading a fishing line. The scanning panel began to loudly beep as it tracked the moving object. The commander ordered the scan onscreen, and the entire bridge crew watched the silhouette trying to make its escape.

"Keep up with it, Lt. Buckner. I don't want whatever it is to escape," barked the commander.

"It moves a lot like a ship. See its swift movements and the sudden acceleration." Whispered Gaitharrul.

Cmd. Swansen turned to her entire crew. "If this object makes a run for it I want us prepared to pursue it. See anything on the scanners yet?"

The scanning officer shook his head. "No, Mam. The object is moving too fast for the scan to give us proper readings."

The commander, in a professional manner, snapped her head back towards the scanning station. "Begin orbital scan. If we are lucky, maybe we might pick up a hull signature, if it is the pirate ship."

∼

The Rattlesnake ordered his ship to make maneuvers away from their uninvited guests.

"Sir, the cruiser is scanning us with orbital and bio scans. What are your orders?" Asked the officer-in-charge.

Necromancer Leviathan started to pick-up speed and was now moving at its cruising velocity. The bridge shook as the pirate ship hit a small batch of solid rock. The sound of the debris bouncing off the *Necromancer Leviathan's* steel hull echoed throughout the ship. The sound made the captain grimaced in pain, like a father watching his child tortured.

Theo Ninnies turned to his crew and barked orders. "Once propulsion reports we are ready, I want to break our cover and make a jump. I can't promise that we will make it. The ship that pursues us is an elite cruiser and will be able to match our velocity. I trust everyone to do their jobs. We are all family."

Once the Rattlesnake finished his pep talk. The sound of the ion engines warming up, as the Necromancer Leviathan began to gain speed. No one on the bridge said a word. It was like a morgue. The captain had become a statue, watching the nebula gas pass by and their exit becoming more apparent. Theo Ninnies braced himself against the balcony railing. His grip on the command railing was ironclad, and if the Necromancer Leviathan decided to tear itself apart, scavengers would find his own body frozen.

Closer, the slit within the nebula approached. Anxiety began to build within Ninnies. They would outrun their pursuers and flee to the penial colonies in the Trojia VII system, or their entire crew would parish fleeing from the elemental fleet. Captain Ninnies wasn't about to let his crew just to rot in a prison cell.

By this time, the Necromancer Leviathan was breaking through the dense cloud of the nursery of stars. It was too thick for them to see the other side, and the ship's sensors weren't helping their cause much either. They were flying blind, and the space pirates were going to have to trust their captain's instincts the most. The ship began to rattle a little from the force of their velocity.

"All I hope is that once we break through this cloud, our trip isn't cut off by colliding into the elemental cruiser. That would make for one bad day for everyone." Mumbled Captain Ninnies.

Suddenly the dense cloud dissipated as the *Necromancer Leviathan* broke through the nebula's impenetrable outer wall. They were free, and all that lay in front of them was the blackness of space and maybe a few dense stars in the distance. That's when the pirate's adversary appeared right behind the pirate ship.

"Captain, the Nightstorm is directly behind us and gaining rapidly."

Ninnies nodded to the helmsman. "Punch it. Let's see how well they can fly."

∾

The Necromancer Leviathan broke through the nebula, appearing directly in front of the elemental star cruiser. The pirate ship's ion vapor trail was seeding the space in front of the elemental cruiser. The entire crew of the *Nightstorm* braced themselves. Tension filled the forward compartment.

Gaitharrul barked out at the *Nightstorm's* commander. "Cmd. Swansen, it's the Necromancer Leviathan!"

The commander nodded and motioned for them to pursue their target. "Helm, I need full power, don't let the pirate's escape."

The Nightstorm lurched out and began the chase.

Suddenly a small asteroid filed emerged, providing an obstacle course for the two ships. Large asteroids could provide cover and small bits that were attracted to the larger ones, giving the larger elemental cruiser more problems than the pirate ship. The two ships entered the asteroid field, *the Necromancer Leviathan*, at full speed. The pirates were flying with nothing to lose and *the Nightstorm*, with a little more caution, even though the elementals wanted captain Ninnies for interrogation. The elemental cruiser was way too bulky to weave in and out of the rocky debris at full speed.

Neither ship could do a jump, because of the asteroid field stood in their path. One wrong turn at the speed of light and the Necromancer Leviathan could end up as debris itself. The Necromancer Leviathan weaved in and out of the way of the asteroids, like a professional slalom skier. *The Nightstorm* had to dodge the massive asteroids, while the small chunks of rock shattered on the cruiser's enormous hull.

Gaitharrul was becoming ever-so-frustrated, with the cruiser's inability to keep up with the pirate ship. The elemental clenched his large fists, in a display of controlled anger. "Commander Swansen, fire your ship's weapons. Disable the Necromancer Leviathan's engines.

The commander looked at her weapons officer, as he looked back with a worried expression, much like the weapons officer couldn't believe the order he had just given. It told her that firing at the pirate ship could cause more debris for them to dodge. The commander nodded to the weapons officer in approval. *The Nightstorm* fired a controlled energy blast at their target, but the beam just missed the tailfin of the ship and incinerated a small piece of rock trailing an asteroid they had just maneuvered around.

"Contact incinerated, commander. No apparent damage to our target." Called the weapons officer.

"Fire again!" Barked Gaitharrul.

The weapons officer looked at his commander, and she nodded in return.

The Nightstorm fired a second time. This time the concentrated energy beam struck the lower half of the left propulsion tank, stationed right below the left engine. It began leaking plasma and leaving a trail. The entire bridge of *the Nightstorm* erupted in cheers.

"Calm it down." Ordered Cmd. Swansen. "They're not finished yet."

The Necromancer Leviathan dodged into a larger asteroid group, making their flight pattern more difficult to track. Only the slowly dissipating plasma trail showed the path the pirates had taken. The elemental cruiser wouldn't be so lucky in following its prey. The commander ordered an all stop. *The Nightstorm* could only float in front of the dense debris field.

"Why aren't we pursuing them, commander?" Bellowed Gaitharrul.

"The debris field is too dense, and our ship is far too substantial to follow." Responded Cmd. Swansen in a calm manner.

"They kidnapped our leader, and you're going to let them get away?" Shouted the elemental.

"I have learned patience in my profession, master Gaitharrul. We can flush them out, to aid in the extraction." The commander turned to her weapons officer. "Prepare to deploy shockwave charges on my mark."

Shockwave charges were used by mining crews to clear debris field, such as the asteroid field. A shockwave would emerge from the canister device to obliterate the debris, giving the miners access to whatever they were attempting to mine. The drawback was, it was impossible to control the energy wave once the canister ignited. Mining ships were known to receive damage during charge usage.

The Nightstorm released one, two, then a third charge, and the crew could only watch as the first one reached the debris field. The first shockwave charge ignited, obliterating a humongous asteroid and several small debris around it. The scene was breath-taking. It was like watching a firework's display of rock. The explosion left a gaping hole in the condensed field. The second charge took a while to reach its targeted point because of how close the elemental cruiser was and the intensity of the first charge.

The second charge ignited, doing significantly less damage, but also opened the previously dense filed of rocks. The shockwave of the second explosion rocked *the Nightstorm* a little and pushed smaller debris of rocks out of their field of vision as if a cue ball struck and the billiards balls ricocheting off the table. But that wasn't the only thing the second charge disturbed. It also uncovered *the Necromancer Leviathan's* location, exposing the pirate ship's hiding spot.

Once the pirates were exposed, the ship attempted to flee into open space, but before that could happen, the final charge drifted towards the pirate ship. It wasn't clear what had attracted the final charge to the freighter, possibly the ship's antigravity well. The explosion ripped a hole into *the Necromancer Leviathan*, the size of a decent-sized comet. The pirate ship was at the mercy of their pursuers.

The pirate ship could only drift along without any propulsion to guide them. No escape pods jettisoned. The crew of the *Nightstorm* assumed the *Necromancer Leviathan's* crew had become temporally incapacitated. Plasma leaked out of both engines and filled the immediate viewport in front of the elemental cruiser. "Prepare a boarding party." Called the captain.

The bridge had become a mass of voices, as crew members ran from the bridge and to it, carrying out. Suddenly *the Necromancer Leviathan* exploded right before their eyes. The shockwave of the explosion set off alarms all over the elemental cruiser. Crew members ran around like wild chickens at a chicken farm, trying to comprehend what had just happened.

Gaitharrul spun around in anger. The elemental's eyes were raging with anger. "Why did you destroy the pirate ship, commander?" He was mortified. He wanted answers.

But the commander had none for him. "I didn't order another attack. Our ship didn't destroy the Necromancer Leviathan." All she could do was shake her head. "There must have been a horrendous reactor breach after the third charge exploded." Commander Swansen turned to her security manager. "Any signs of survivors?"

She knew instantly what the answer was going to be. "No, mam. No escape pods have jettisoned. No floating debris capable of supporting life. They seemed to have all perished."

The commander held her head low, dejection flowing through her. A sizeable elemental hand rested on the commander's shoulder. Gaitharrul had recovered from his initial shock. "It wasn't your Cmd. Swansen. Accidents do happen. We will have to find another way to rescue our leader."

The Nightstorm began its return flight to the elemental fleet.

In the shadow of the elemental cruiser, a lone escape pod rushed westwards towards the Trojia VII star system. No signs of life are evident. Nothing seemed to stir in the solitary surviving remains of the once sleek and powerful pirate ship.

CHAPTER 20

Deep within The Immortal Nexus:

The celestial realm was quiet and still. The silence is a direct result of something that has affected every domain connected to the Immortal Nexus. Something has happened that has made everything living within it on high alert. The place had a gray tint about it, not pure darkness but very little light shining down its inhabitants. The drab grayness wasn't anything new; it was the dead silence that created the eeriness.

The blacksmith's scaled-down shack possessed only one source of light. It bit through the grayness of the atmosphere surrounding it. Like the atmosphere surrounding the minuscule workshop, it also had no sounds coming from it. No meshing of the blacksmith hammer onto an unwavering surface that had echoed these rolling lands for eternity. No rhythm of pinging night and day. Nothing that would tell you the immortal realm was alive, just the singular light bleeding from a think crack in the workman's shop.

The seemly deserted workshop mirrored the entire realm, quiet and on alert, but from what was the ultimate question?

A small figure broke through the dense gloominess and approached the front of the minuscule dwelling. A pair of scaly hands tossed back the figure's cloak hood to revel reptilian-shaped eyes with lime green irises. Chaos blinked once, then twice to clear them. The blacksmith's lone carrier was quite familiar with the blacksmith's workshop. The dwarf-like creature had been inside the workshop so many times; he had lost count. It had been eternity running from one side of the realm to the other, chasing items for the blacksmith, and that had been a long time.

The eternal flame burned its array of colors inside the workshop's forge. Purples, reds, blues, and silver illuminated from the celestial forge. Still no blacksmith. The messenger was used to the hammering noise of the blacksmith hard at work. He had never known Kurzol never to be working on anything. The celestial forger of weapons was always busy, but this was a first for Chaos and the blacksmith, as far as the little creature could tell.

The small figure looked around the shop. Shop tools were scattered on several workbenches as if their owner had suddenly fled. Just another sign that told Chaos something was a miss. It wasn't like the celestial weapon's master to leave the workshop in such disarray. Kurzol was always known to place his craft tools back in there place once he was through with them.

The heat from the forge kept the place warm. Maybe a little too warm for Chaos's taste. There were two small workspace tables sat at each end of the forge, which centered the crowed workspace. An array of hammers, files, and other blacksmith tools usually hung on the back wall. The aged, stone floor was rough and uneven, the messenger had never known how the blacksmith could work on the floor, but Kurzol had never complained openly about it.

There was an opening that Chaos understood lead to tiny living quarters, but he had never seen the celestial weapon's master sleeping. He doubted the celestial needed to since his omniscient abilities could include the ability to heal the weapons master. *Maybe*, thought Chaos. *The blacksmith used his other-worldly powers to fuel his workman-like personality and kept him fed and never sleep-deprived.*

The little messenger snapped his head at a sudden movement. Something seemed to consume the entire workshop space like a heinous entity that has swooped down from the sky. Kurzol's looming shadow appeared before the lone celestial blacksmith appeared. The shadow crept along the stone walls like an unknown phantom was approaching. The colossal being wore a black leathery blacksmith apron. The weapons master had gray shaded skin that made the celestial being appear he was from another time and place. Kurzol had a creased forehead that split into three sections by the deep protruding creases. His workman's hands told the blacksmith's tale. He had spent an eternity forging weapons for the celestial beings, and his hands were rough and callused.

The weapons master approached the messenger assiduously. Kurzol head was hung low, and a mournful aura seemed to fill the space. It wasn't like the blacksmith to be so gloomy; typically, the weapons master was full of confidence and sarcastic towards Chaos. Not so on this occasion.

Kurzol looked at Chaos with gloom-filled eyes. It nearly killed the little messenger, the sorrow he felt. Chaos blinked, not needing to clear his reptilian shaped eyes, but in an act, ask the colossal blacksmith what was wrong. "You summoned me, Kurzol?"

The blacksmith nodded. "I did. We have a grave situation on our hands. One that I need your assistance with."

Chaos could only blink in astonishment. The messenger was as still as a statue. He was afraid to move, even breathe. The anticipation was so intense in the little creature. He wasn't sure whether the task he was about to perform, and yes, he would perform it because it was Kurzol, and Chaos never wanted to make the celestial blacksmith angry with him.

"The elemental leader, Jetsuenete has been kidnapped by agents of the Darkness."

Chaos was now really frozen in place. Had he heard the weapon's master correctly? The little messenger wanted to clean out his ears, but he couldn't move. A numbing sensation flowed through his body that made him temporarily incapacitated. All Chaos could do was listen, but even that was difficult with the ringing in his ear.

The little creature began to stutter, once his incapacitation passed.

"Kid … nnnapppeeeddd?" Chaos chattered.

His teeth seemed to mimic his voice's shaking tone.

Kurzol nodded as if the response was significant enough.

Chaos shook his head, and all his senses returned to him. "Thatsss, impossible. No one in their right mind could trap, let alone kidnap an elemental. They are direct descendants of the celestials. They can sense when danger is near. They can control things in the cosmos…"

"That omniscient ability is only in innate in a chosen few and is severely limited by the Merciless Reach." Barked Kurzol.

"Even so, why would anyone want to. The servants of darkness must know the elementals will come after them. They are like bloodhounds and won't stop until their leader rescued."

Kurzol nodded his agreement.

"Those responsible have perished. We know where Jetsuenete is imprisoned, I just need someone small enough and can move through different dimensions. I am bound to the Immortal Nexus and can't leave."

Chaos swallowed, and his palms began to perspire. He couldn't believe what the blacksmith was about to suggest. He could feel it in his bones. Just like when he retrieved the celestial cube of power to make the Sword of Eternity, now he would be asked to retrieve something even more precious to the celestials. The dwarf-sized being wiped the sweat from his forehead.

"What are you suggesting, Kurzol?"

Chaos was now shaking immensely.

The celestial weapon maker placed a humongous hand on the little creature's shoulder. Despite the strength of the blacksmith's hand, the touch was gentle. The weapons master was attempting to calm the little messenger down, but Chaos's anxiety was too large to contain. The dwarf-sized creature understood what Kurzol was asking of him, and it was none too settling.

"You are the only one, Chaos, that can move between dimensions. You can access doorways that are blind to others. You are small enough to sneak around the Merciless Reach undetected. You're the only chance the elemental has of escape."

"The Merciless Reach? It's the home of the Darkness, where its power is stronger than anywhere else. I wouldn't stand a chance. Even if I could access the doorway, not that I have any inclination to do so, the things that rumored to roam that decrypted landscape would devour me in an instant, not to mention the poisonous air."

"I have faith in you, my friend. You have always been someone I could count on, even if you might try my patience from time-to-time." The gargantuan blacksmith gave the little creature his best smile, but it still wasn't all that comforting.

The little messenger gave the blacksmith a scowling look, one that shed the weapons master's confidence in him. Chaos fought between the fear that was raging inside and the sense of duty. Kurzol had always placed forward to the little creature. That's when Chaos remembered back to when they had first met. The little creature had stumbled through the doorway of the Immortal Nexus.

The realm wasn't one that many beings wanted to stumble into, let alone live there. But that's what happened to Chaos. When Kurzol had discovered the reptilian creature, Chaos had fought through a hive of Venomous Wraiths that killed their prey with eitra poison. It's said that one bite and the figure turned slowly into a wraith. The process was slow, painful, and soul binding. Kurzol had discovered a drop on the dwarf-sized creature's torn clothing.

All the weapons master could figure, from what evidence left on Chaos was after evading the wraiths, even though he didn't see how, Chaos had stumbled onto a pack of Ice Banes, frozen abominable beasts that represented cyclops. The weapons master found ice stuck on the little creature's footwear, and Kurzol knew the only place to walk through the ice was the Ice Bane's lair.

If that wasn't unbelievable enough to the blacksmith, Kurzol discovered evidence that the little creature had evaded, despite the claw marks and rips all over Chaos's clothing, from a pack of Riccedin Wolves. Those creatures were the nastiest predators in the entire realm. It was a wonder the little creature had even survived.

The stench of the Infernal Glades lingered on the poor creature. It was the home of the riccedin wolves. The swamp water was a dark grey stain that never left the person's skin. The aroma of the glades and its hued pig scent loomed around the figure like it was entrenched in the uninvited figure's pores. The blacksmith had lived in The Immortal Nexus too long not to pick up on the stench instantly.

Ever since Chaos had felt indebted to the smith, even though Chaos ran with each errand, he was well compensated. Now the weapon's maker was asking him to enter the home of the Darkness. He shook his head.

"Even if I could enter the Merciless Reach, the solders that roam around and guard its Bastian, the horrors that reside around the Darkness' home would pick up on my scent instantly. I wouldn't come within a polar star of that place. I'm not a celestial being."

Kurzol removed a small device that fits inside Chaos's palm. It had an octagonal shape that made the device look pregnant, but possessed two rectangle points that were layered over three times, giving the top and bottom its thickness and able to stand upright without support. The device had a black tint with a blue outline. It was quite a unique looking thing that kept the messenger's attention.

"That is a Drake Emitter, and as long as you have it in your possession, everything within its invisible shielding will be undetectable by any creature that roams the Merciless Reach. Nothing will be able to sense your presence, and nothing will be able to see you."

"Like a ship's cloaking device?"

"If you want to put it in those terms, yes."

Chaos palmed the device. It danced in the palm of his hand. It amused the messenger until the blacksmith brought his attention back to their discussion. Kurzol was giving him a stern look, and Chaos knew no matter how he felt, he wasn't going to be able to refuse the weapons master.

"Well?" Asked Kurzol.

Chaos's shoulders sagged and felt deflated.

"What do I have to do?"

"The device will lead you to the elemental. It has the leader's DNA imprint in its memory. It will also lead you out of the Merciless Reach. Just don't lose it. If you do, both of you will become trapped in the realm with no way to escape. Oh, and don't forget to bring a respirator along. As you have mentioned, the decrypted air is toxic."

Chaos looked down at the chaotic device. He had an eerie feeling of dread lingering about him. *Ironic, isn't it? I chaotic device for a creature known as Chaos. What have I gotten myself into this time?*

∽

The air was stale and toxic. A constant humid heat seemed to pummel Chaos's entire body, like a blanket smothering the little creature. The messenger's arrival to the Merciless Reach had been one that felt his body was tumbling down a bottomless pit, through a nasty tunnel. Despite wearing the respirator that provided the messenger with clean oxygen, Chaos could feel the decrypted air against his cloths against his naked skin. It felt as if thousands of parasites were trying to eat through his flesh. The reptilian messenger had to shake off the after-effects of his tumble. His head was spinning, and his arms scuffed from the shortfall. The messenger had nearly threw-up in his respirator. His stomach turned upside down, and his head was spinning out of control.

But none of this was new to Chaos. He had ventured into several dimensions over his lifespan, and each time the same effects had riddled his body. But he knew the effects of the Merciless Reach would subside over time. But the one thing he had never experienced was the toxic atmosphere of the Merciless Reach. Even if he wore the respirator, he could see the dense, purple-black fog-like cloud looming in the air. It was a grey thing set against the darkness of the realm. Only a small outline of light illuminated the distance. That would be the only thing he could guide his progress.

Chaos checked his pocket, and the small device was still there. The drake emitter would be his bloodline while in the home of the Darkness, guiding him to the elemental imprisoned inside the dark Bastian and their key to escaping. The messenger replaced the device, took one last deep breath, and fought against his spinning head. He had no time to dwell on his ailment and allow his body to recuperate. The faster Chaos got to the elemental, the sooner they could flee.

Chaos looked out over the horizon, but outside the low receding illumination the one that had a reddish tint to it, the entire realm was filled with darkness. *Does this place ever get any light? Is it night time, or is it permanently dark outside?* He began to follow the device>s guidance and started heading east, or at least what Chaos thought was east.

He had walked for some time, and his legs were becoming sore with a slight ache beginning to develop. The rough terrain had made his back hurt as well and made the messenger believe none of the landscape was smooth. No farming had ever developed in such a horrible place. Well, no, duh! Just imagine what crops could sprout from the decrypted ground? From this toxic environment.

Chaos could hear his breathing through the respirator. In and out, the breathing apparatus worked. Soon the brave creature began to listen to noises in the distance. Booming voices that spoke alien languages that he had never encountered before. His curious nature forced the messenger to investigate, hoping the drake emitter would do its job. He dove into a small cavity, concealing himself from the approaching voices.

Chaos's anxiety was growing. Would he be caught or not? Suddenly the dwarf messenger felt two massive bodies pass by. He saw their silhouettes as the guards slowly passed. To the dwarf messenger, they seemed like momentous giants, both in bulk and overall size. Even though Chaos couldn't see their shadows, he could sense the creature's phantom essence. The giant's silhouettes were enough to scare anything to death, but luckily the perimeter security guards hadn't noticed Chaos one bit.

As they passed, he could hear their wicked tongues, still unsure what the two were discussing. Most likely, something foul that didn't concern him. It sounded like two garbage mulchers grinding waste in their metal jaws. He had to shake off the chills the image was sending him. Still, Chaos always was curious about everything in a new realm.

Then it dawned on the messenger. He could follow the guards, and eventually, it would lead him to the Bastion base. Even with the drake emitter, it would be a risk, but it was better than risking running into anything more dangerous. Suddenly, Chaos heard a menacing growl. The awful sound shook his insides. The little messenger had no desire to see what had made such deplorable sounds. It convinced him that his original plan was the right one.

Chaos waited until the two roaming guards were just out beyond his hiding spot and leaped out of the hole and cautiously made his way towards his new guides. Their patrol must have cut a pathway during their patrol since the walkway he used was much flatter and less full rocky terrain. Chaos had problems keeping up with the two guards, with their long strides, forcing his short legs to move in rapid secession to keep up.

Chaos was forced to stop several times to catch his breath. His heavy breathing was sucking too much air out of his respirator. But he never let his guides get too far out of view. Their booming voices always gave the uninvited visitor something to follow. Periodically Chaos made sure the emitter was still in his pocket, and each time to his relief, it was still there.

They must be taking me towards the back part of the fortress? They had made an oval patrol pattern that made the silhouette of the Darkness' home seem so far away. The one thing that told the little creature they were making their approach towards the decrypted bastion was the immense pressure pounding at his head. It was like stepping off into the cosmos and coming too close to a massive star. The pressure was so intense that it would draw you in, no matter if you wanted it to.

The closer in they got, the more pull the bastian seemed to have on Chaos. It was like a tug-of-war-game between the Darkness decrypted power, emitting from maleficent dwelling and the messenger. It was like the bastian was drawing him in. Suddenly more bone-chilling noises emerged through the darkness, but these seemed a lot closer. The sounds told Chaos that their owners were traveling swiftly and in the opposite direction. He was relieved by that, but something inside told the messenger that he didn't want to encounter whatever it was.

Chaos hadn't been paying attention to his guides and too much to the debilitating stress the dark fortress was placing on him to notice the guides had stopped moving. Chaos nearly ran into one of their tree-trunk legs. The messenger stumbled and almost fell into a dark pit. While dusting himself off, he heard their foul language. The guard's voices were deep and menacing. He even thought saliva was dripping from the monstrosity's maul. The sight made Chaos's stomach turn.

By now, the messenger's heart was beating rapidly. His anxiety increased, and soon he understood he would have to break from the mountainous creatures and pick up Jetsuenete's scent. He had made his way through the decrypted landscape of the Merciless Reach. Chaos sucked in his courage and peered over his hiding place. His guides were beginning to move away from him; it was now or never.

Chaos glanced to the left and then to the right. After not seeing any-thing, not that he was going to, the little messenger moved out into the open. He ran as fast as his tiny legs would run. His respirator was perspir-ing, and he could feel his breath heat up inside the mask. If his heart hadn't been beating rapidly from anxiety, he would have realized its increased beat. The messenger was too afraid to look behind him or up in the air, afraid to see a silhouette of some predator swooping down on his head.

Slowly the dark bastin's base came into view. The decrypted fortress bounced side-to-side as Chaos ran for his life. *Make it to the bastion, make it to the bastion*, he kept telling himself. Nothing had seen or picked up his scent. The emitter was working better than he could have imagined. Then a screech from above scarred the messenger, and he dove for the base of the decrypted fortress.

Something had flown overhead and out towards the distance. Maybe a watchdog patrolling the air or perhaps a wild species of the Merciless Reach. It didn't matter to him; all that mattered was getting inside without the intense pressure killing him. Chaos found a crack in the bastion's foun-dation and snuck inside since he was too small to pry open any secret door that might be underground.

The inside of the fortress was just as dark as the outside had been. The only difference would be the lingering smell and the reason Chaos knew this was he was running low on air and forced to remove his respirator. At least he could breathe the stale air inside the fortress. It was hard to tell, with wearing the respirator if he could survive outside without the mask.

Chaos moved deeper into the decrypted fortress, still trying to stay hidden from the Darkness forces. His vision didn't improve, but luckily, he held the drake emitter in his palm. The small device didn't make a sound but still seemed to lead the messenger down dark hallways that possessed no light what-so-ever, down steep stairways, through a waste ward dun-geon that appeared to contain some swampy liquid that was waste high. Chaos had to clean himself off, that's when a shiny object hung on the stairway leading up. The messenger moved towards the item and touched the pommel.

Suddenly, a montage of battles with elementals and marines fighting came to Chaos in a dream-like vision. The messenger leaped back. He nearly fell back down the stairway and landed against the decrypted wall. The little figure jumped off the wall, not wanting to let the fortress's skin filled wall rub off on him.

"I found it." Whispered Chaos. "Jetsuenete's broadsword. They must have stolen it while his back was turned."

The messenger pulled out something from his pack to wrap the elemental sword. He took the sword from its mooring, wrapped the elemental weapon tight and slid it over his small back. The weapon slapped his side as he attempted to walk down the stairs. Chaos followed the drake emitter to a corner of the lower level of the dungeon. A strong essence was coming from the last cell, according to the device in his hand.

Through the energy field lay a figure all crumpled up. It was difficult to see who's imprisoned in the cell, and Chaos was afraid to ask openly. According to the drake emitter, this was his charge. But at first glance, the figure didn't look like an elemental. Through the illumination bars, bloodstains filled the figure's clothing, like he had been beaten to death, but Chaos knew the figure was still alive. He could see its irregular breathing, but outside of that, the form laid there without moving.

"Hey, buddy." Chaos whispered.

The figure moaned but didn't turn to face the uninvited guest. It was making Chaos frustrated. With all he had been through, he wasn't about to have wasted his efforts. The messenger picked up a rock chip from the floor and tossed it at the energy field. 'zap'! It was loud enough to make Chaos jump back. He scratched the bare spot on his head. That's when he unstrapped the broadsword from his back.

After unsheathing the elemental weapon, he stared at the perfectly straight blade. "Let's see what you can do to it."

Chaos leaned in with the sword blade, with half-closed eyes. The luminescent field reflected off the blade surface. Blue sparking began to arch from the energy field of the prison and the elemental sword. Inch-by-inch, the blade forced its way through. Finally, the elemental blade touched the energy field, and before Chaos could blink, a cracking noise would accompany the sparking, and then the energy field's disappearance. Jetsuenete was free!

The power generated knocked the messenger on his backside, and Chaos had to shake his head clear, as the energy field had zapped him.

Once the messenger recovered, he slowly got to his feet, with the aid of the sword blade, and looked back into the cell. By that time, the figure had gotten up and was now staring at the new visitor. Chaos approached, and that's when he noticed how badly the elemental had been beaten. Bruises littered Jetsuenete's body. Cuts and abrasions made the elemental's face seemed puffy and round. The elemental's front was as littered with cuts as his back. Chaos noticed how hesitant the elemental was, and realized he must appear like the elemental's jailers.

"Jetsuenete." Whispered Chaos. "I'm here to rescue you."

The elemental didn't move. Was he dead?

The messenger reached out with his four-clawed handshaking. The elemental flinched, and that's when the messenger realized he might look more like the servants of darkness. He was going to have to do this bit-by-bit. The messenger inched his way towards his charge. Chaos exposed his palm towards the elemental, in a friendly jester. Slow and cautious.

"It's ok; I'm here to help you. You have nothing to be afraid of."

Jetsuenete allowed Chaos to draw close to him. That's when the messenger realized he might pull this off. Suddenly something scurried down the steps and stopped halfway to their location. It was a black rat. It twitched its nose at Chaos. *Great, now my rescue attempt will be intercepted when this rat warns the occupants of the dark fortress.*

"Get out of here, you rascal." He whispered.

The black rat scurries off.

When Chaos turned around to face Jetsuenete, the elemental was now standing. Now the elemental didn't have a scared expression on his face, but a stern warrior-like expression. The elemental's forehead was sloped down, and his cheekbones and jaw had become tightened. The elemental's face almost appeared to look like a mast. The figure's arms lay at his side and the elementals with his posture at attention like a good soldier.

"Who are you?" Whispered Jetsuenete.

Chaos swallowed hard. "I am here to aid you in your escape."

The elemental gave the little messenger a look of disbelief. The aggressive expression had been wiped from Jetsuenete's face and seemed to Chaos that the elemental would at least open to listening to what he had to say.

"You help me escape?"

Chaos nodded. "I even found your broadsword."

The messenger showed elemental's favorite weapon.

"I see that." The elemental took a few steps forward like he still didn't believe he was free. Jetsuenete looked down the hall, but there was no one there. He stepped out of the cell and looked down at Chaos. "Now what."

"We find our way out of this hell hole." Chaos pulled the drake emitter out of his pocket. "Before we go any further, you might want to hang onto this."

Chaos handed Jetsuenete the emitter, and the elemental looked at the small device with curiosity. The elemental palmed it like a child would a toy. "What is it?"

"It's a drake emitter. It allowed me to sneak across the wasteland landscape and enter the black fortress. I think it shields us from the Darkness and its agent's ability to sense our presence."

"Very well, lead the way. I will follow."

Chaos handed Jetsuenete his broadsword. "You might want to hold onto this."

Jetsuenete took the broadsword from the messenger, lifted the sword to his eye level, and admired its sleek design as if the elemental had never seen it before. As if he wanted to make sweet love to it. "You don't know how much I've missed you."

The two of them moved down the hallway and towards their freedom.

∼

Outside the black fortress, Chaos nearly fell to the ground, without his respirator. Jetsuenete helped the dwarf-sized messenger, put it on, and slowly his breathing returned to normal. The two of them took off towards the opposite direction of the bastion, hoping their presence would be missed.

Jetsuenete and his rescuer made their way through the decrypted landscape. The terrain is rough, and the elemental had to assist the messenger several times. The dwarf-sized being had short legs, and his breathing was labored. The respirator was beeping, warning of low oxygen, on top of the fact the messenger had traversed the rugged landscape just to get to them. They had just escaped from the bastion's influence, no longer being affected by the intense gravity. But the continuous pounding they had taken while under the dark fortress's shadow had taken a lot out of them, more so of Chaos.

Jetsuenete could hear the little creature's intense breathing, as the messenger took deep breaths. The elemental wasn't sure the little creature was going to make it. Their little escape group had to stop to let Chaos to catch his breath. In the distance, they have heard screeching that seemed to get closer with each instant. *They are tracking us,* the elemental thought. Jetsuenete had been regaining his strength steadily as they went. The sword itself was rejuvenating him. The short messenger gave looked up at the elemental with his hands on his knees.

"The Darkness will send a search party for us." Barked Chaos.

"No doubt. That's why we need to keep moving."

Chaos shook his head. "I'm not immortal. I need to rest; my strength is zapped."

That's when a barking noise echoed in the distance.

"Flesh hounds!" Echoed Chaos. "Those things are relentless."

"How do you know so much about the Merciless Reach?"

The messenger motioned to the drake emitter. "I have heard rumors of this place, from all my traveling. But most of what I do know has come from that thing."

Jetsuenete gripped the device snuggly in his elemental grasp.

"Come on, we need to get on the move before more things emerge, and we become overrun."

As the escapees started to move again, more disturbing noises began to surround them. It sounded like a million hellish things had surfaced and were pursuing them. It didn't help either that the elemental still couldn't utilize his elemental abilities in the realm or that there was no light to navigate. With each step they took, it was a challenge. Chaos nearly tripped over the jagged, uneven terrain more times than the elemental would have liked.

Suddenly a menacing growl came to them from a short distance away. That made both escapees look behind them. Then without any notice, a dark, hairless beast busted through the surface and knocked both over—chaos tumbling head of heels while Jetsuenete wasn't as affected. The elemental landed on his backside, but he was prepared to leap to his feet.

Even though it was too dark to see, the creature's silhouette was standing only inches from the elemental. The beast was a quadruped and was two-third the size of the elemental on all fours. It had a broad snout, most likely how the creature tracked them, and a massive maul. It was hairless like the beast had all its fur burned off. The creature was breathing heavily as if it had run a great distance.

The two adversaries were staring at one another, like their essence was locked on the other. Jetsuenete retrieved his battle sword and gripped it tightly. The elemental's adrielene was pumping, and his arms were beginning to burn. While being in the Merciless Reach, the elemental had his energy taken from him, not including all the torcher he had endured. Gripping his broadsword brought all his power back. He felt as good as he ever had like the venom had extracted.

The beast was scrapping the decrypted ground, like a bull in a bullfight. The creature was issuing a challenge; one Jetsuenete was more than up for the challenge. *Ok, you bruit. Let's see what you have.* The elemental heard the beast flare its nostrils and huff in his direction- a call for Jetsuenete to engage in warfare with the creature. The battle was on. The elemental gripped his sword pommel and held it in attack position.

The four-legged creature roared a ground-shaking bellow, then charged. The elemental waited to figure out what side his adversary was choosing. He could feel the beast's approach by the shaking of the ground.

Then at the last moment, Jetsuenete side-stepped the attack and swung his humongous sword at best as it passed. The blade struck the creature square on the top of its head and bounced off like the creature was made of stone. Sparks arched from the strike.

Jetsuenete repositions himself after the attack. *My sword blade didn't do any damage at all. It only skimmed over the creature's surface, like it possesses a protective shell.* He could hear the beast huffing again. Jetsuenete needed a new plan of attack, but what could he do without knowing for sure how to penetrate the creature's tough exterior. The creature charged again, but this time the beast tried the opposite side. Jetsuenete swung his blade, but this time it was at a different angle. This time, instead of leveling the broadsword straight across, skimming the beast's tough exterior, he swung in a downwards motion, trying to discover a soft underneath.

The results were the same. The elemental's attack scrapped the creature's tough lower belly without any more success. Jetsuenete felt the sword being deflected off the underside and left the elemental vulnerable. Neither combatant was in the position to take advantage of the other since the elemental was off-balanced from the previous attack. The shelled creature had slid to a stop and wasn't facing the elemental. This gave the elemental time to reconfigure his battle tactics.

What did the elemental Jetsuenete know of its adversary? He couldn't merely side-step his attacker, as he had learned. The creature had a hard casing like a giant turtle. It seemed more like stone than a shell was, but he hadn't found a soft spot in its armor. The most excellent celestial blacksmith crafted the elemental blade in the cosmos. It was well balanced, its blade was indestructible, and the broadsword was quite easy to wield, making Jetsuenete an efficient solder.

But that didn't matter if the elemental couldn't penetrate the beast's hard shell. How was he doing to defeat this foe, if the elemental didn't know where its weakness lies. While Jetsuenete's attention was drawn from the creature, the beast attacked. The elemental didn't realize until it was too late that this attack was going to be straight. Jetsuenete wasn't going to be able to side-step the beast. The beast lowered its stone-like head and rammed into the elemental with a debilitating force.

The elemental did a half summersault, as he had been caught in the middle of a leaping attempt to avoid the creature's massive forehead. Jetsuenete landed had on his side, sending pain down his back. Usually, the elemental's omniscient abilities would have warned him of the attack, while his back had been turned. But since the effects of the Merciless Reach subdued his senses. This match would most likely have ended shortly after it began if he had all his abilities at his disposal.

The elemental shook off the dazed effect. How can I possibly defeat this creature? I have nothing at my disposal to penetrate this thing. Then the elemental looked over at Chaos, and that's when it dawned on him. His broadsword possessed the ability to open unknown portals. The only question would be, could he get the weapon to work inside the doomed realm? Well, Jetsuenete wouldn't know unless he tried.

The elemental slowly got to his feet, still having shots of pain run down his spine. He felt like an old man with very little control over an aging body. Once the elemental stood upright, he glared at his opponent, who now seemed to have no interest in him. The creature seemed to be pulling something out of the decrypted ground, but it was unclear what. Jetsuenete glanced back at the weapon, and there seemed to be no change in its physical exterior.

The elemental warrior took a deep breath and said, "Well, here goes nothing."

Jetsuenete raised the weapon and began to concentrate on having the creature vanish. A high-pitched noise came from the weapon itself. It sounded like the broadsword was singing, a high-pitched tone. He had never attempted this before and wondered if this was supposed to act in such a manner. The weapon began to vibrate to the point of not being able to hang onto it. Soundwaves shot out in every direction. It seemed to Jetsuenete that the weapon was pulsating. *Well, if the realm doesn't know we are here, this should surely do it.*

The commotion attracted the attention of the beast. It snarled at Jetsuenete, and the shadow of its teeth reached the elemental's location. He couldn't see inside the creature's mouth, and he wasn't sure he wanted to.

The beast began to step slowly towards his position as if approaching a challenger. The beast's huffing became louder, as the creature approached. Jetsuenete could imagine the creature's nostrils flaring, just as they had previously.

The beast's silhouette came into view as if it had crawled out of a dark cave. By that point, Jetsuenete's weapon was humming at the motion was nearly too much. The beast growled at the weapon as if it knew what was coming, and that's when a tiny black void opened right between the two adversaries. A sudden wind picked up from the portal opening, and both the elemental and the stone creature struggled to stay upright.

The wind current picked up, and the creature began to slide towards the portal. Jetsuenete looked for something to grab onto, but all there was crusty black turf. The elemental was struggling to stay upright and still hold the broadsword, but there was no need at this point. The black void was now an independent entity, no longer need the assistance of the elemental weapon. The creature tried its best to keep from being sucked in. It clawed at the charred surface, but much like the elemental, it was losing that battle.

Jetsuenete fell to a knee, but still managed to control the weapon. His adversary wasn't having luck; its momentum had dragged the beast too close to the portal to save itself. The creature was leaving claw marks as it moved closer to its impending doom. Finally, the creature was sucked into the black void, letting out one last growl. The elemental was next.

Jetsuenete's body slid closer to the void, but he saw the portal was starting to shut down. Could he possibly hold on long enough to survive? Jetsuenete slammed the broadsword into the crusted earth, trying to act like an anchor, but that didn't seem to work. The elemental's grip on the sword pommel was slipping. It didn't seem like that tactic was going to work. Jetsuenete took in a deep breath. It was all up to nature now. Could he hold on?

Suddenly an invisible bubble-shield wrapped itself around the elemental. It was translucent and next in invisible on the backdrop of the pitch darkness. But something was indeed stopping his descent. As the elemental looked back, he saw Chaos gripping the Drake Emitter. Somehow, he must have dropped the device, and the messenger must have picked it up. Now it was the only thing keeping him from his death.

Slowly the mouth of the black portal closed, and it seemed to blend into the already dark environment. They were in no more danger. Chaos dropped the emitter, and the invisible bubble disappeared. Jetsuenete dropped to the crusted ground, sending crusted ground everywhere. Chaos and Jetsuenete looked at one another without saying a word.

Then a leathery sound swooped down on them. They both ducked as a whisk of wind passed over. Neither one knew what was attacking them. Neither could see in the sky, and it was apparent that's where this new threat was coming from. The leathery sound swooped down in their direction a few more times. Neither one knew what to do. Jetsuenete couldn't see the messenger's face, but he thought he could feel Chaos's fear.

Then a scream came from the little messenger's direction, and before the elemental could react, his rescuer had been picked up by a winged demon and swift away. Jetsuenete could see the silhouette of Chaos waving his arms about as the little messenger disappeared into the darkness.

CHAPTER 21

After the elemental leader escaped from the Merciless Reach, Commander Kimberly Swansen and the crew of the *Nightstorm* rescued Jetsuenete. The elemental was drifting in deep space for some time, but since oxygen wasn't an issue, he was never in danger. Jetsuenete was brought back to the fortress on Aucarro. After rejuvenation, the elemental leader is found strapping his battle armor on, like the rest of them were doing, preparing to do battle. They all understood an imminent attack was forthcoming.

Everyone from the elementals in residence, their mortal marine allies, and even a few of the newly created immortals were in preparation in the main training foyer, connected to the arms storage, on the other side of the lower level of the fortress were preparing for an all-out siege of the fortress. Nothing was said, but a feeling sunk deep in the fortress that the return of Jetsuenete would spark a full-fledged invasion.

Jetsuenete was finishing up dressing when Dirdanth walked in. The black-cladded elemental had not-so-pleased look on his face. "I see you have recovered. You look well, maybe better than the last time we saw one another."

The elemental leader looked up, and at first, his stern exterior was exposing how he felt on the inside. Then a huge smile broke the surface of his strict demeanor. "Thanks to the salient tank, yes, I believe I have fully recovered." The elemental winced from a sharp pain like someone was stabbing his side with a sharp object. He attempted to conceal it from his friend. Then without warning Jetsuenete's mind began to drift away for a moment, and a grim expression, like he had lost someone close to him, replaced the stoic smile.

"Jetsuenete, are you ok?" Questioned Dirdanth. Jetsuenete's second in command took a few steps towards his friend. "Are you sure you should be gearing up so soon after your ordeal?"

The elemental leader gave his stoical expressions, one he tried to hold firm, but failed. Then Jetsuenete's commandeering face transformed into a genuine smile. One that only a few, including Dirdanth had seen. Usually, the iconic leader walked around with a series demeanor refusing to smile, even at stupid jokes.

"Yes, my friend. I can understand your worrisome nature, but trust me, I am fine. I can't let you all go into battle, while I watch from the sidelines. I have a funny feeling that we will need all hands on deck for our next confrontation."

Dirdanth nodded. "Of course, we will. Especially since your escape from the Merciless Reach. I'm sure that didn't please the Darkness one bit."

Jetsuenete looked over at the first generation of immortals and smiled.

"I have to admit, Jetsuenete. They do look good."

The elemental leader tore his stare away from the newest members of the family. "Makes you feel like a proud papa, doesn't it?"

"In a way." Responded Dirdanth. "They have been training in the training wing since the incubating chamber opened up. They look like excellent additions to the family with superior fighting skills that I wasn't expecting."

"What? Did you think I would design them with less than superior fighting skills?"

Dirdanth only shrugged his shoulders.

Jetsuenete glanced back at the first immortals and saw the shape-shifting twins; Erreodan and Nightzeneth becoming friendly with the three newcomers. It made him warm inside like it was their first day of school.

The two elemental both stared at Balduwulf. The immortal was a mountain of a warrior, just as tall, muscle-bound, and well armored as the elementals themselves. Jetsuenete understood that over time, the immortal would carry the torch for the elementals and become the greatest of them all ever to live. Generations of mortals and their kind would tell epic stories to children and inform descendants of this larger than life immortal.

He used an array of weapons, but none were as violent or nasty as his ego. The immortal didn't just kill opponents; he annihilated them. He wore a wolf skin cloak that never left his side. Some even in his squad said he was part wolf, and the god-king made him in the likelihood of ancient wolfing warriors.

The other two immortals were much smaller and less threatening. One was thin and lanky but would use his lack of girth to his advantage with swift movements and intellect. The other was designed to analyze his opponent's weakness and was good at adapting his fighting technique on the fly. Jetsuenete was attempting to explain.

"I guess we will find out how good of warriors you have made." A voice said from behind. Jetsuenete and Dirdanth both turned to see Gaitharrul, who's cobalt blue skin and gray eyes were giving both elementals an intense stare. Jetsuenete understood in his absence Dirdanth had decided to tell the rest of the elemental about the immortal project. He was sure it was all a shock to them all and were just adjusting to their bioengineered descendants.

"Why is that?" Questioned Dirdanth.

"Look for yourself." Gaitharrul handed the pad he had been watching, on his approach of the elemental leader and second in command.

A raging storm had developed on the horizon. A mass of Dragalyite solders and an entire brigade of Blackmour Drowmauders made their way over the desert of gray dust and moon rock towards the fortress. The whole tablet screen was full of the invasion. There were no bare spots of any sort.

"An invasion party!" Barked Dirdanth.

"Indeed," returned Gaitharrul, in his typical calm and sadistic manner.

"How did they amass an invasion battalion so quickly? You just escaped the Merciless Reach." Barked Dirdanth.

"Most likely, they had an invasion battalion on standby, and the Darkness used Jetsuenete's escape as an excuse." Returned Gaitharrul. "We spotted their drop ships immediately, then three colossal Scythe-Doom scepters came out of nowhere, and an entire invasion force emerged from within."

Scythe-Doom Scepters appeared on the tiny screen; were Draught-Naught type fleet ships of the Shadow fleet had appeared out of the sky. These gargantuan fleet ships shadows could engulf dwarf stars and could be seen from light-years away. It is told their energy vapor was so massive it once was described as a giant space dragon devouring stars as it went.

"They must have used a portal gate to appear right inside the star system before launching." Answered Gaitharrul.

"To hide their appearance most likely and shield their true numbers." Responded Jetsuenete.

Both Gaitharrul and Dirdanth nodded in agreement.

"Unfortunate, there are too many of them for us to defeat, even if there were only dragalyite solders. We need reinforcements, or this will be our last stand."

Dirdanth shook his head. "We are elementals. They have nothing that would kill us."

"No, but our mortal allies would die." Returned Jetsuenete. "I want a until of marines escorting each immortal. I don't want them exposed alone."

"What, are you afraid your creations won't live up to the high standards?" Questioned Gaitharrul. The elemental had a mocking tone in his voice and a sly smile.

"No, Gaitharrul. They just haven't been in a battle yet, and I don't want them to be overwhelmed."

"Hu." Sniffed Gaitharrul. "Instincts will take over and then watch them cut through the army like butter."

The fortress rocked, with rock dust falling from the ceiling.

"Must have siege machines." Dirdanth returned.

The elemental leader turned to his second in command.

"Remember what we discussed before my capture."

Dirdanth nodded.

"I want you personally responsible for delivering the elemental eggs."

Gaitharrul gave both elementals a questionable glance, but Dirdanth motioned the confrontational elemental off.

"I will do my best."

~

On the battlefield, which separated the invasion army and the elemental fortress:

The elemental lined up directly across from the fortress perimeter, awaiting the invading army. Jetsuenete looked at his elemental brothers. There had been more of their kind before, but now their numbers had dwindled to under two-hundred. They didn't even have their full complement, as many others had been sent throughout the cosmos to defend other systems. *I wish we had time to recall our entire complement, then maybe we would stand a chance in this conflict.*

The elemental leader looked over where Dirdanth was commanding his battalion and then towards Gaitharrul with his. The shape-shifting twins were on either side of the small brigade. The elemental leader let out a puff of air. *Fifteen-hundred solders in all are too little to combat the majority of the Darkness' army.* Jetsuenete returned his gaze at Dirdanth and then to Gaitharrul. Both gave him the ready signal.

"When they come over the prominence, concentrate your firepower on each wing. If we bottleneck them, we might stand a better chance. Once we accomplish that, bring the rain down on them, kill as many as you can then fall back. Let the second wave of defender have at them." Barked Jetsuenete.

The elemental leader knew that their numbers would reduce when the marines are cut down, but it wasn't anything Jetsuenete could prevent. All the defenders could hope to do was deflect the attack long enough for a cadre of allies, both mortal and elemental could flee. They were too outnumbered to claim victory this day.

The enormous invasion army busted through the landscape. The Darkness' army stretched across the landscape, making the invasion army seem limitless. Flyers, appeared above the invading horde, while the Scythe-Doom scepters loomed over the battle like overbearing mothers.

Someone called out. "There are android fighters among the army ranks. A mass of them!"

"That's what they were using the stolen ore for. The stash we could track down." Bellowed Gaitharrul.

Once the Shadow Empire's army broke through, the elemental braced for impact. Jetsuenete ordered the twins to take to the air and begin bottle-necking the invaders. "Beware of those flyers! Bring in some anti-aircraft battery cannons."

The battery cannons utilized ion energy that could rip through space-craft hulls. They had two portable cannons that could maneuver over the rough terrain with trolleys. They were smaller versions of the cannons, but just as effective. The issue with these weapons was that they tended to overheat and wasn't all that reliable. But they didn't have much choice, and they needed all the assistance they could get.

The first wave of the Shadow Empire soldiers emerged. Dragalyite, Drowmauder, and even androids charged the waiting defenders. The site was overwhelming. It was like the entire plains were run over by a plague of solders. A disease that couldn't be curtailed or cut off at the source.

The shape-shifting twin elementals launched first, getting ahead of the defender line. Their enormous leathery wings flapping in the wind. Erre-odan on one side of the battlefield with Nightzeneth on the other. Both flying shape-shifters swooped down on the invaders and began raining down ion fire onto their enemies. At first, the plan seemed to be working, as the attacking horde began to fold onto themselves, forcing their mass numbers to work against the invaders.

Dragalyite solders, Blackmour Drowmauders, and metal soldiers began falling over one another. The shape-shifters flew over the top of the invaders destroying everything in their path. Some of the unfortunate Shadow Empire soldiers perishing, while many other scattered for cover. That's the alien-looking ships, ones that look like were crescent shapes in design, with rounded wingspans and had large flaps that gave them their ultra-aerodynamic abilities.

The bomber's unique shapes gave them the ability to traverse through numerous altitudes and climates without wavering on their mission objectives. These bombers used plasma cannons mounted on the under. One of the pursuing flyers chasing Erreodan, fired its lasers, and the shape-shifter was forced into evasive man, flying away from his ground targets. The flyer was right behind the elemental in pursuit.

Nightzeneth wasn't going to be chased by a mindless attacker. He spun around from his killing spree and faced off against his attacker; the pilotless flyer wasn't programmed for retaliation. So, it flew right into Nightzeneth's counter-attack. The shape-shifting space dragon propelled its ion fire into the flyer, and it ignited into a ball of flame. Then the emerald-green shape-shifter stared back at a squadron of droid flyers with his pitch-black eyes. The drone fighters flew through the remains of their destroyed comrade without slowing.

Nightzeneth snarled at the invaders and shot them with his was deadly silver ion gas. Three more drones ignited in the air, while the others separated in every direction, making the shape-shifter chase them down one at a time. The drone he was chasing was swift in the air, but not as maneuverable as Nightzeneth, with all his battle experience and his thunderous wingspan. The elemental shot at the drone. But apparently, it had learned from its comrades how to evade the silver fire.

The drone dodged Nightzeneth's fire first to the left, then to the right. Each time the ion fire just missing its intended target. Becoming frustrated with the machines aerial tactics, the shape-shifter nose-dived closer to the drone. Unfortunately, the elemental was too occupied with his target to sense the other drones sneaking up behind him.

The drones shot at the shape-shifting dragon with one of the laser shots singeing a portion of a leathery wing. Nightzeneth screamed out in pain, but that didn't stop his descent towards the drone. The shape-shifter flipped around, souring on his back, with his razor-sharp talons facing the new threat. Nightzeneth let out a war cry and released a rein of ion fire and the perusing drones. The attack scattered the drones, but the ion cloud left behind shielded the elemental's ability to sense them.

Before Nightzeneth could turn back around, the drones, hidden from the cloud, shot at him. One laser fire shot missed to the left, but a second struck the lower right talon of the space dragon. A third shot grazed the neck of the behemoth elemental. Nightzeneth folded his wings in for protection. The substantial thickness of his wings would deflect the laser fire. But that's when the attacks stopped.

Only one drone fighter emerged from the dissipating ion cloud. There was something different about the drone, but Nightzeneth couldn't figure it out. He was too busy concentrating on the new threat. Suddenly a rocket was launched from the drone, and the elemental tried to shoot it down. The missile dodged the ion fire once to the left, then again to the right, but it didn't stop its approach. By this time, the projectile was near to its target, and all Nightzeneth could do was wait.

The missile exploded right where Nightzeneth's chest was, sending an intense amount of pain through the shape-shifter. He no longer had bodily control. His entire scaly body had gone limp. Instead of soaring, Nightzeneth's body was in a freefall. His senses were slipping, and the elemental blacked out.

∾

Explosions lit up the battlefield as Jetsuenete led his battalion through the build-up of bodies. Marines, Dragalyite solders, Blackmour Drowmauders, and metal solders lie in piles. The body count was multiplying rapidly. There was a mixture of all types of blood filling up the rough terrain. Cries of mercy and the sound of death as crude weapons of all types cut through armor and flesh. The elemental leader raised his broadsword and sliced through another venomous body. Was it dragalyite or drowmauder blood that filled his blade, he was unsure and didn't care.

Some of his last victim's blood splashed on his face. Instead of wiping his face clean, he let it be war paint on his grey skin, to mark the occasion of this mass slaughter. Jetsuenete moved through the wade of bodies, sidestepping those that wouldn't move out of his way. He looked skyward, not having heard the shape-shifters for a while. The sky a silver-gray color and was full of ion clouds. The haze seemed to act as one giant blanket, mixed in with spots of burning drones falling from the sky. *Do the twins still provide us with cover in the sky, or do we have to worry about bombardments from the heavens?* Wondered the elemental leader.

For every elemental ally, there seemed ten adversaries. They appeared too overwhelmed for victory, but the elementals would press on. They had to because they were made for this, fighting on the battlefield and not fleeing to the hills. Jetsuenete and his elemental brothern had one duty, defeat the armies of the Shadow Empire, the Darkness' right hand.

The elemental leader hadn't seen Balduwulf or any of the other immortals since the invasion had begun. Were they dead? Had they been slicing through the opposition by now? The elemental leader didn't have a clue. Another dragalyite solder came at him and then disposed of the reptilian without much effort. His elemental senses were working at a heightened level.

Jetsuenete's disorientation made him wonder if they should retreat if he should call for them to gather their forces and head for one of the elemental safe zones scattered throughout the cosmos. This battle was a lost cause, a one-way ticket with no return. It was evident to him that this invasion was meant to do one thing, reduce their numbers, frustrate the elementals, and scatter them. Could their mural handle a retreat? Could they not afford to flee the fight or perish right here, ending any shot the rest of all living species had?

Jetsuenete pushed on and laid waste to five more Shadow Empire soldiers. That's when the elemental leader saw Dirdanth with a few of his marine escorts. The elemental had blood on his armor but didn't appear to be wounded much at all. One of the marines was assisting a fellow marine, who seemed to have little use of his legs. The mortal was like a rag doll. *That is what separates us from the Shadow Empire,* Jetsuenete thought.

Jetsuenete utilized his superior reflexes and elemental senses without even looking at the new threat, caught the reptile in midair, slammed the dragalyite to the ground, and as Jetsuenete ended the cold-blooded creature's life Jetsuenete whispered. "This is my effort to keep my promise in rescuing your species from their bondage. You haven't left me with much of choice, but understand I have no ill will to you or your brothers. I do want to release the dragalyites from slavery."

Jetsuenete shoved his larger-than-life blade through the reptile's rusty armor and ended the dragalyite's life. The scaly hand that was gripping at the elemental's grip on its throat stopped moving and dropped to the ground. Jetsuenete let the dead reptilian go and spun towards Dirdanth. The two elementals acknowledged each other, as their filthy backs touched, both warriors lowered their weapons from a fighting position.

"Have you seen Balduwulf or any of the other immortals?" Questioned Jetsuenete.

"No, I haven't." Returned Dirdanth. "Any site of the twins?" The elemental second in command looked skywards.

"I was wondering the same thing. I haven't heard screaming from falling drones or the blood-curling cries from either twin," returned the elemental leader. Jetsuenete scanner the area surrounding them. "Any assessment of how we are doing?"

Dirdanth crunched his nose inwards, making the elemental look piggish and nose-less.

"Are you kidding. It's a bloody mess out here. I'm lucky to be able to track our losses and who's still with us."

Jetsuenete huffed. "That's what I was afraid of."

"Are you thinking of a retreat, is that why you're asking me?"

"Just wondering how overwhelmed we are. It had crossed my mind. We are outnumbered ten-to-one by my last count."

Dirdanth shook his head. "Don't look at me." Suddenly a Drowmauder solder emerged from the array of bodies, wielding a dark elven blade. The elemental swatted the much smaller creature back with a strike from his fist. "I'm not the one in charge. If you think it's time to gather our losses and flee, I will support your decision."

Jetsuenete scanned the area, still unsure what to do. Anxiety began to fill him, and a sense of dread. Had he waited too long? Had the elementals and their allies should have engaged this invasion force in the first place.

Had all Jetsuenete's past success made him overconfident that he had been duped into facing off against the Shadow Empire's might.

The elemental leader growled. "Make your way through our ranks. Collect those still alive, marines, elemental and immortals and order a retreat. Have them make their way to one of our safe havens."

Dirdanth nodded his understanding.

The two friends embraced each other.

"If this is the last time we…" Dirdanth began.

His friend cut him off. "Not now. Don't think that way." Jetsuenete looked his friend square into his red tented eyes with their silver- filled pupils. "Just remember what you promised me."

"Yes, yes. Delivering the elemental eggs to the high priest, I've got it."

Jetsuenete watched his friend with the elemental escorts disappear into the mob of fighters. Then the elemental leader turned and took the two remaining marines left from his escort unit and began to back out of the battlefield. He blocked out any noise and began to concentrate on a singular voice.

~

Foes surrounded Balduwulf and his fellow immortals. Their marine chaperones had all perished, leaving the newly created immortals alone to fend for themselves. But if you asked Balduwulf, that's how the immortals liked it—left to their device, dependent on only themselves. The immortal puffed out his barrel chest and gripped the power ax in one hand and a short sword in the other.

The metal warrior reflected the sunlight, with its amour plating, and perfectly aligned without any visible seams. It was like the metal solder had been manufactured with a precision unknown to the immortal. He had never seen such artistry. He had to assume it was manufactured, what omniscient creature would make such a thing in its likeness? "Some sort of Machine God must have built this thing." Mumbled Balduwulf.

The machine moved with skill and grace that made it difficult to decipher that it was an android warrior of some great, omniscient design. The machine is proficient in its movement like no mortal biped could ever have and with such speed. If Balduwulf hadn't been amerced in the conflict, he might have been at aww.

"Only an immortal could match this machine warrior's skill. This can't be a machine at all. Maybe it has a soul of one of our kind." Mumbled Balduwulf once again.

The machine had no visible eye socket, and Balduwulf wondered how it saw anything, let alone keep up with the defending warrior's graceful movements. Only one red central eye looked out at the immortal, as they dueled. Balduwulf had never seen anything like it at all. But Balduwulf had to admit; he was a newborn. Its cyclops, cyborg appearance was eerie, but that didn't seem to faze him. Then it dawned on him. "It's a drone solder!"

If it's a drone solder, there must be a control ship nearby. Balduwulf once again looked around by like before finding nothing in his immortal eyesight range. These machines had a controller that operated them, explaining the lack of a sensor array of the visible bionic eye. The immortal stared right into the digital eye.

"Where are you?" Balduwulf screamed.

The immortals didn't possess the same attributes as their elemental makers, but they did possess the unwavering ability to fight and never would back down from a battle. The immortals were super-human and possessed extreme fighting skill-sets, stamina, and lightning-fast reflexes that mortals didn't have. The one thing that wasn't handed down to them was the ability to sense their opponent's movements, thoughts, and emotions, but that would only slow them down anyways. Battle confrontations were about reactionary reflexes, not overtly complicated thought processes.

Balduwulf's armor was similar to Jetsuenete's and the other elementals. His armor had a wolf's head imprinted on the chest plate, with nothing else. The chest plate armor was coal- black strong and made of nearly indestructible material. The immortal wielded a power ax that could give his opponent an electrical charge when the double-sided blade struck its target. The immortal also carried a short sword that could penetrate seams in armor and used to separate the armored plates.

The immortal scanned the horizon within proximity of his location for the central droid controller. He had heard of combat officers who used floating platforms in a protected environment to usher these lifeless soldiers into combat. It was a disgrace to the real soldiers who had given their very lives in battle. But as skillful as this machine solder was, and considered it a very skilled combatant. The machine couldn't react to its opponent as a living one could. It was solely dependent on its operator.

Then there was the reptilian warrior in the rusted armor, Balduwulf was also battling. The immortal couldn't see the gargantuan's face. His adversary wore a battle helmet that only allowed its stunted snout to be exposed. The creature's reptilian eyes penetrated the shadows of the helm, giving the beast a sorrowful glare. The armor seemed burnt in some spots that its rust, thick amour didn't hide. In places, it appeared the immortal's adversary had its very muscles embedded on the outside of its body. It wasn't a pleasant sight to behold. Luckily enough for Balduwulf, most of its body was shielded by its rust, blood-stained armor plating. Even the creature's double-bladed weapon seemed foreign in design.

But as the scene played out and he could tell the alien fighter seemed to have skill beyond any standard solder. Balduwulf's weapon was advanced to the dragalyite's crude bladed weapon. The dragalyite met Balduwulf's strikes, blow for blow while utilizing the second of the weapon's blades to cut into the protective armor of its target. The twisted, malformed head of the creature seemed to be seeping some type of cream-colored foam. It was like it was the way it sweated because it appeared to be coming to the exposed surface of all its flesh.

Their weapons clashed, as the sound of metal weapon colliding with metal echoed. Balduwulf and the dragalyite solder struggled against each other. The reptilian challenges the immortal strength, and it surprised Balduwulf because the droid matched the immortal in speed; the flesh warrior was matching his strength. But despite all that, the Balduwulf was still confident he would win.

Balduwulf's grace and agility were like no other. He moved with light-ning-fast quickness as if the warrior was choreographed the fight like a dance. His bulk strength would allow the immortal to overpower most opponents while keeping the girth ones at arm's length. Each time the warrior's blades struck his opponent's weapon, sparks flew and created damage to his adversaries.

Balduwulf's fighting prowess and ability were unmatched, even by the android solder. Each opponent's offensive blow was returned with an equal elegant defensive strike of his own. The abominable solder with the blood-stained armor slashed at the warrior, and their weapons clashed, sending sparks flying. But just as fast as the immortal had faced the first attack, he spun swiftly around and met the drone warrior's strike with just as much agility. Before the drone could fire its energy weapon, Balduwulf sliced right through the drone's weapon, sending the tip of the rifle flying. The result of the strike ignited sparks from the energy weapon and exploded in the drone's hand, sparking a fire that would short circuit it and scorch its shiny untainted armor.

Balduwulf retracted his blade and met a second strike from the horrid reptilian fighter. Simultaneously, the warrior stabbed the drone through its metal, eyeless head, and severing it from its body. The drone's head and body went their separate ways, as mechanical parts ran from the gape in its body, sparking tiny fires within an electrical spark discharges. The drone's body fell to its knees, but still with fight left in it, refused to topple over. The drone just stood there, kneeling to the swift warrior. Finally, the agile warrior kicked over the defeated drone's body, as if it was an empty trash bin.

With both short swords, the faceless warrior struggled against the beast warrior, now trying to sever his head clean-off. With one short sword in hand, the warrior sliced the beast's hand off, making the unruly creature cry out in agony. Green blood dripped from its wound, and now it was weaponless against the faceless warrior. Green blood splattered against the spectacle that was the immortals near spotless armor. Then in one fluid motion, the faceless warrior, that moved swiftly.

Balduwulf looked around at the carnage, and that's when he realized one of the immortal's lay dead. He and the other immortal ran to their brother's side. The immortal's body was savagely cut and maimed like a gigantic beast had gnawed on the immortal's body to the point of not recognizing the warrior. The immortal's armor had massive claw marks embedded in it. The site made Balduwulf sick to his stomach.

The other immortal looked up at Balduwulf with a baneful expression. "It's a shame, isn't it?"

"What is?" Questioned Balduwulf in a scornful tone.

The other immortal gave Balduwulf a mistrusting glance. "The desecration of our brother's body. By the way, they call me Espen." The immortal reached out with his right hand.

Balduwulf only looked at Espen's hand as if it was an alien species.

"It was his fault. If he had been a better combatant, we wouldn't be staring down on this body as we are. I have no sympathy for a failed immortal."

That left Espen speechless. Balduwulf turned and walked away.

EPILOGUE

The secrete temple was quiet, cold, and less than inviting. A howling wind whipped through the maze of temple passageways, forcing the torchlights to flicker. The elemental could tell not many visited the hidden temple, but the high priest did not need for that many visitors these days. The high priest had planted the elemental seeds with vigor and loving touch, but his real work was yet to come.

The echo from Dirdanth's footfalls bounced off the stone walls. The leather case positioned under the elemental's left arm. He wasn't about to let it fall from his grasp, which would break Dirdanth's promise to his close friend Jetsuenete.

Since the temple was built inside a mountain, the ceiling and walls had a rough, rocky texture, and small granite particles seemed to fill the air. The maze of passageways that made up the elemental temple had the illusion that the high priest had been busy excavating the mass number of tunnels like a worm burrowing its way underground.

The elemental used his innate elemental senses to make his way through the chaotic weave of empty hallways. For anyone that didn't possess the elemental's sensing ability, those individuals would be lost for eternity, trying to make their way through the secret temple. Finally, the visitor emerged into a spacious room. Dirdanth had to assume this was the main worshipping room. A few rows of aged meditation pillows were aligned at the front of the dimly lit room. A wooden podium positioned at the rear of the space, facing in the direction of the rows of pillows.

A lone torch was the only source of light in the room, and it only sheds light on the rear portion of the spacious chamber. The room possessed an aged and eerie feeling. The limited illumination filled Dirdanth's, silver eyes as if they were inflamed and illuminated even the red wolves' skull on his chest plate. But the elemental could see the heavy shadows that clung at every corner, giving anything hiding among them easy cover.

"Must be how the high priest summoned to the followers of the sect." Mumbled Dirdanth.

The High Priest had been gaining followers over the last few decades since he was to pass on the elemental's tale. The religion was a brilliant idea of Jetsuenete's. Dirdanth wished he had thought of it, but the elemental had to admit he was doubtful that turning the shadow agent was the smartest thing they could do. But he had been wrong before.

Dirdanth knew he wasn't alone in the room and that's when he spotted the high priest's silhouette, High Priest Tefbei Nakht relieved the elemental staring at him through the waning shadows. He stepped out of the dark corner and into the light. The tiny mortal was wearing the same, plain smock that the elementals had dressed him in before sending the mortal here. His priest's smock had become dingy and tattered, most likely from the temple's cave-like dwellings.

The mortal had also seemed to become frail, and his skin wrinkled. He hadn't been in the place for more than a few decades, so Dirdanth felt it was the elemental eggs he housed that he was doing it to him. *Where are they feeding off his essence, making his body seem aged and frail?* The high priest smiled at the elemental, and Dirdanth nodded back.

"It's so good of you to drop by, master Dirdanth. I receive so few visitors these days."

The elemental caught a glimpse of a mural in the process of being carved into the rock wall behind him. It began with part of two dragon bodies, with their wings only partially done. Then there was a partial circle that appeared to be some sort of linage linking the dragons constructed as well. There seemed to be a sense of déjà vu. Dirdanth shook his head to clear it. High Priest Tefbei Nakht noticed the elemental staring at his work and smiled. "Do you like it?"

"What is it?" Responded the elemental.

"It's a representation of the elemental linage. To help the followers of the religion to understand where your kind comes. I take great pride in it, and I hope it will represent your kind."

Dirdanth grunted under his breath. "I'm sure it will." He had never liked the mortal, especially when he was an agent of darkness. The emotional mistrust had never evaporated from Dirdanth's mind. All the death and destruction the former agent of darkness had created left a bad aura around the priest.

The elemental couldn't say the feeling had improved at all, since Jetsuenete had nominated the mortal to be the chronicler of the elementals and the keeper of their most ancestral secrets. *Once a betrayer, always one,* considered Dirdanth. Nothing would change his mind, even after he had transcended, like the others.

The high priest pointed towards the case under his guest's arm. "I see you have brought me a gift."

Dirdanth removed the case and handed it over. The high priest nearly dropped it, and Dirdanth almost rushed the frail mortal. The elemental had no issues carrying the case, but he had forgotten the mortal didn't possess his superior strength or stamina. High priest Nakht placed the case on top of the podium.

"Heavy, isn't it." Proclaimed the priest.

Dirdanth didn't respond. He just observed the mortal with contempt.

The high priest struggled with the case's latch; it seemed to stick for the curator of the elemental heritage. Finally, after what seemed a while, the high priest opened the case. A shocked expression that told Dirdanth it wasn't exactly what he was expecting came over the priest. The mortal looked up at his guest with confusion.

"Just three eggs, this time?"

The contents of the case possessed one, golden elemental egg, one green, and one silver egg. All three were translucent and carefully placed in its slot inside the case. Even if the case was dropped from I high elevation, the case or its contents wouldn't be damaged. The design was made to be the elemental egg's protector's, their incubation chamber, their resting spot until they were needed once more.

Dirdanth nodded. "Until the last stage is complete. Then you will receive the rest of the elemental eggs for safekeeping. In fact, there is only a few more elementals left that haven't been transcended, including myself."

"And will that be, master Dirdanth?"

"All in due time, High Priest Tefbei Nakht. It's a matter of waiting."

"For what, may I ask? How will I know the time is right to awaken the defenders from their slumber?"

"That, I have no way of telling you, because even the elemental's do not know. Jetsuenete trusted you with our secret. I think he meant to trust your judgment as well."

"And you, master Dirdanth?"

The elemental grunted. "Do I what, High Priest Tefbei Nakht?"

"Do you trust me?" There was no sly glean in the priest's eye.

Dirdanth could feel any distrust or malcontent in the mortal' tone. He was just going to have to defer to Jetsuenete's trust in the priest.

"The celestial council will aid you, that I am sure."

Custretera was less than a hospital planet. It was a backwater satellite that had minimal resources. The planet was positioned inside the Trojia VII system. That provided protection from pirate invasion. Help was only a transmission call away. The planet wasn't the only penial colony in the system, but it was the only one that was underground. Custretera was the fourth most inner planet in the star system. It was connected to the other penial colonies by way of holographic communications that were, at times, less reliable.

Occasionally comet storms would disrupt communications and temporally create isolation. That would open the door for space pirates to sneak in. The Custretera penial colony set up a defense system that set the operators back a few tokens. Supplies runs ran on a twice a month cycle, providing the colony with food, raw materials and weapons for the acting guards.

The planet's surface water supplies had been poisoned by a multitude of industrial accidents, which made perfect for a penial colony. Over time all living species had died off from the lack of water and a toxic environment. The surface landscape had terraformed from green rolling hills to a vegetation less place, blacken and uninviting.

Even the landing pad and cargo holds were built under the toxic surface. The colony could only receive one shipment at a time because of its minuscule size. Processing took a while receiving, unload and release of a cargo ship before receiving another. It was the sole reason shipments were staggered, providing less wait time for vessels on the surface. The underground receiving section consistently stayed busy; it would be easy to sneak in.

The escape pod had fought for landing clearance, and only after hours of waiting did the ship get approval. After passing customs, Captain Theo Ninnies and his associate Alverta Brink walked out of the customs office. The captain looked confident and had little worries. He had a plan formulating in his twisted mind, but it wasn't a complete one, and he had been winging it, to this point. Now he had defined goals to start working. While his assistant was worried about their current situation and well, she should be. They were in the presence of gang members, thieves, and murderers, but how that differed from the pirates, she had served before their ship exploded.

Ms. Brink hugged her leather satchel to her breast. "Are you sure this is a safe place?

The captain gave her a trusting smile and nod.

Alverta looked around at the make-shift buildings, and it made the penial colony look like a rundown place that had been slapped together with rusty bolts and sweat from slave labor. It reminded her of the places she had lived before meeting Capt. Ninnies, especially the brothel she had been forced to clean floors.

"This place is deplorable; I don't see how people live in these conditions. Why are we here?"

Alverta looked around in a worried state of mind.

"Centuries ago, the planet had a vibrant life on the surface. The multitude of raw resources made Custretera a hotbed of activity for those searching for untapped, raw materials. Manufactures came from every direction. These manufacturing tycoons didn't take mind that what they were about to do was rape the planet of its resources and leave the citizens of Custretera no way to support themselves. Slowly the people that lived here were forced to move.

These corporate tycoons didn't bother setting up safeguards to protect the surface from chemical spills, surface contamination, and the poison that was to follow. It took less than three standard years to demolish the surface, leaving the resources left tainted. The only thing left to use this planet was a penial colony, as you can see."

"That doesn't explain what we are doing here?"

Theo Ninnies looked up to the rafters. Metal layers acted like the protective skin of their circumscribed. They were inside of a giant metal box. The irony was strong these days, especially for thieves and outlaws.

"When they built this underground colony, they cut more corners than management would have ever admitted. Looking at this place, you can develop sympathy towards these poor souls, no matter what they have done." The captain took in a deep breath. "If you want to know why we are here, just look around. There is a lot of heat on us, and we need a place to lay low. I paid the administration a lot of tokens to keep our presence here a secret. I have a plan trust me, and I can get us through the pain we are both feelings here."

"But why here? Why can't we hide somewhere else?"

"Because this is the last place they will think of looking for us. Right under the authorizes noses. Soon as I acquire a ship, we will chart a place to make our new home."

www.ingramcontent.com/pod-product-compliance
Lightning Source LLC
Chambersburg PA
CBHW020123310726
48970CB00006B/1704